# KAYEL WYLIE

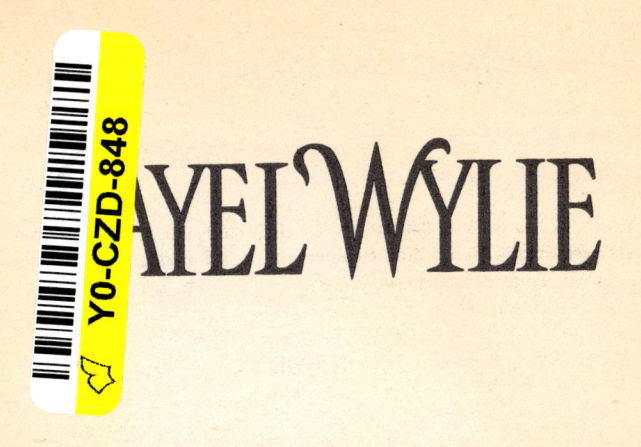

Wicked Charms

POCKET BOOKS
New York   London   Toronto   Sydney   Singapore

This book is a work of fiction. Names, characters, places and incidents are products of the author's imagination or are used fictitiously. Any resemblance to actual events or locales or persons, living or dead, is entirely coincidental.

An *Original* Publication of POCKET BOOKS

POCKET BOOKS, a division of Simon & Schuster, Inc.
1230 Avenue of the Americas, New York, NY 10020

Copyright © 2003 by Jayel Wylie

All rights reserved, including the right to reproduce
this book or portions thereof in any form whatsoever.
For information address Pocket Books, 1230 Avenue
of the Americas, New York, NY 10020

ISBN: 0-7434-6447-8

First Pocket Books printing September 2003

10 9 8 7 6 5 4 3 2 1

POCKET and colophon are registered trademarks of
Simon & Schuster, Inc.

Front cover illustration by Frank Accornero

Manufactured in the United States of America

For information regarding special discounts for bulk purchases,
please contact Simon & Schuster Special Sales at 1-800-456-6798
or business@simonandschuster.com

Acknowledgments

Many thanks as always to my editor, Lauren McKenna, for her patience and guidance, and my agent, Timothy Seldes, for his excellent advice and unwavering support. Thanks also to Marcia Addison, M.L.I.S., for her always-excellent assistance in matters of historical research (if it's right, praise her; if it's wrong, blame me). Extra penitent and effusive thanks to John R. Justice, Solicitor, for being without question the most patient and understanding boss a writer with a day job ever had and to everyone else in my office.

*for my sisters, birth and otherwise: Sarah Kathryn,
Rachel Anne, Marcia, and Isabel
all of whom I would have chosen*

Historical Note

Henry II and Eleanor of Aquitaine were real people, as were Richard I and Prince John. Everyone else in this book is a fictitious creation, including Princess Katherine.

Prologue

*Falconskeep Castle
1180*

William Aiden Brinlaw knelt at the edge of the cavern's crystal pool, bathed in silver light. The icy water lapped over his hands as he reached out to it, and hot tears slid down his face. "I have to go away," he spoke to the light shining up from the bottomless depths. "I have to be a knight."

"And what is a knight?" The spirit's voice was like a whisper in his ear, a murmur from inside his own mind. The first time he had found this cave, he had been afraid—the spirit had always hated men. But now he loved her, the same as he loved magic. He believed she loved him, too, the same as she had his grandmother, mother, and sister and all the women of Falconskeep before them.

"A knight is a man, a warrior," he tried to explain. "My father is a knight."

"Your father . . ." Her voice was cold, contemptuous, almost laughing, and the light gathered in a knot far

below the water's surface, shrinking back from him. His mother said the spirit saw in all men the first who had come to these cliffs and driven the ancients into darkness. *"Your father is a dragon,"* she said now.

"I don't know what that means," he answered. "And I don't have time to learn." His father was Lord Brinlaw, another William. His castle was far from here, to the north and east, a pleasant place near a river. He had rebuilt Falconskeep for his wife, Alista—it was her ancient keep, burned twice in her lifetime—and for his daughter, Malinda, who was her heir. Brinlaw Castle was new by comparison, built during the reign of King Henry's grandfather. But the name Brinlaw was old, traced back to a Saxon chief. "My brother, Mark, is waiting to take me to London. I'm going to live with the king."

"And be a knight," she answered, the light expanding outward again, illuminating his face and glittering on the shining, mottled walls. Spells and stories were carved into the stone from floor to ceiling in the faery tongue, and he had read them all, or as many as he could reach. He could read and speak the faery language as well as his sister, better than his mother, as well as French or English. He could work the spells. But some of the words were strange even to him—the creatures they described seemed more like mountains and waters than people, and their actions made no sense. He read them, and the spirit tried to explain, but her words were as strange as her carvings.

"I have to," he said. "I can't stay with Mama and Papa forever; I have to find my place in the world." He was the second son; he would never be Lord Brinlaw unless Mark died, an unimaginable horror. As a squire at the royal court and a companion to the king's youngest son, he would have a chance to distinguish himself, to carve out his own greatness the way his father had. "My brother will be a lord; I can't just be nobody."

"Nobody?" He had never heard her laugh before, and chills danced down his spine. It was not an altogether pleasant sound. *"The first wizard in a thousand generations is not nobody."*

"Magic is for girls," he answered, blushing hot. He wasn't supposed to be able to read faery language; he wasn't supposed to be able to work spells. Falconskeep belonged to the women of his family, its castle and its magic. When his mother had first seen what he could do, making snowflakes fall in a design by simple force of will, she had been so frightened she could barely speak. And his father was ashamed. He never said it, but Willie could tell—every time the subject of his magic came up, his father stopped talking altogether, would leave the room if he could. Brinlaw didn't like that Malinda, Willie's older sister, was a sorceress, or that their mother was, either, but he knew there was nothing he could do about it; it was their heritage, their curse. But he had never expected one of his sons to be so afflicted. "I have to go," Willie said, starting to get up.

"*Little wizard.*" The light began to coalesce again, gathering brighter just below the surface. "*Give me your hand again.*" The shape of a woman formed, a beautiful woman with hair the color of flames billowing over her shoulders. Her eyes were blue, as blue as Willie's own, and her pale skin glowed with light. She seemed to be swimming upward, as solid as he was himself, reaching up to him, her fingertips almost breaking the surface of the water. "*Aiden,*" she murmured, her voice changing, a strange, almost-singing lilt. "*Come and take my hand.*"

He knew he shouldn't do it. This spirit had tried to drown his father once, and his sister's husband, Tarquin. For years his parents had tried to forbid him to come here at all for fear she meant him harm. But he couldn't resist her. "I am my mother's son," he spoke in the faery language as he put a hand into the freezing water. "I am not afraid."

Her hand closed over his wrist, drawing him closer, but she didn't drag him into the water, and her smile was soft and kind. "*Dragon,*" she said, the word echoing around them, the old voice he remembered echoing with the new. "*You will be the dragon.*" A sudden, searing pain seemed to burn from her icy palm, a shackle of fire around his wrist. He opened his mouth to cry out, then stopped with barely a gasp. He was not afraid. "*You will be greater than all of them.*"

"Yes," he answered, his eyes falling closed, and his voice was different, too, deeper and calm, a man's voice from his twelve-year-old lips.

Suddenly she let him go, the pain stopping as quickly as it had begun, the force of her hold dissolving so quickly, he slipped and almost fell face first into the water. He opened his eyes just in time to see the woman-shape dissolve as well, melt into pure white light. *"Little dragon,"* she called as the light sank away, the same, strange voice he had come to know and love. *"Remember what you learned."*

"I promise." He looked down at his wrist, his heart beating faster. The shape of a dragon was burned into the flesh, a drawing like the ones Malinda made to conjure, the tail twisted around his arm, the head reared and snarling on the back of his hand. "I will always remember."

1

*London
1196*

A letter from Sir Aiden of Brinlaw to his parents, Lord William and Lady Alista

My dearest lord and lady—

You will no doubt be surprised to learn that Prince John has chosen to bestow on me the honor of marriage to his youngest sister, Katherine. That he does so purely to annoy his kingly brother, Richard, in his absence on holy Crusade in no way diminishes my joy. While I have only been acquainted with the princess twice in our lives, both times while she was in nappies and could barely speak, I remember her with great fondness and have no doubt our union will be an unqualified success. She has expressed a resolve to never leave the side of her queenly mother, Eleanor, while she lives, and as the presence of that royal personage tends to afflict me with a strange malaise leading often to vomiting and hives, I suspect we will be living quite frequently apart. But I am resolved to give her new estates in Scotland my most loving husbandly attention.

Our betrothal will be finalized in writing in three weeks' time, on July the twenty-fifth. You should not by any means feel bound by duty to attend—I know how little this marriage will please you and how little you love the royal court. In any case, I will be leaving immediately thereafter for the Scottish highlands to secure a castle there, Glencairn, which Richard has presented to his sister and John has made the chief portion of her dowry. I do not know what I will find there, as the former lord has died with Richard in the Holy Land after an extended absence from his home estates. Therefore, I cannot say when I will return or when I will actually be married.

Try not to despair of me completely, and remember me in your prayers.

*Your loving son,
Aiden*

Aiden studied his reflection. "Not bad," he congratulated his squire, rubbing his freshly shaved chin.

Robin looked back from laying out his master's best black tunic for the betrothal rite. "Not bad?" He laughed. "After four days drunken in the stews, I call it a miracle."

"I meant your shaving, Master Spite-Tongue," Aiden retorted, smiling himself. "Not my face." He braced his hands on the mirror frame, the eyes of the dragon he had carved there level with his own. The mirror was a magic spell, the first grand conjure he had worked after he left Falconskeep. He had carved the dragon frame from a single trunk of oak and rubbed his own faery blood into the grain to give the wood a dark red sheen, then ground the glass from sand in fire, breaking it and starting over time and time again until the surface was smooth and the magic was complete. "But my head is killing me."

"I shouldn't wonder," Robin agreed. He brushed a thick layer of dust from Aiden's best mantle with an expression of disgust—somehow it had found its way under a tavern's table to a very dirty floor at some point the night before. "You should ask Lady Alista to brew you up a cure."

"I would, if she were here," Aiden answered, getting dressed.

"She is," Robin said. "She has been for the past two days, and Lord Brinlaw, too." Aiden tore his way through the collar of his linen shirt to stare at him, aghast. "And Sir Mark, your brother, arrived from Brinlaw Castle last night," the boy finished, a look of angelic innocence barely masking a grin.

Aiden put his arms through his sleeves, the better to strangle his squire. "And why did you not tell me?" he asked, forcing his voice to sound calm as he advanced.

"I did," Robin insisted, backing away but laughing all the same. "The very day they arrived." He ducked behind a chair as Aiden lunged for him. "You were in Cheapside, tupping that Sadie creature, and I came in, remember?" Aiden froze, confused. "I told you that your lady mother would be horrified to see what you were doing," Robin pointed out, as if this justified him for all time. "You threw your boot at me and told me if you saw my face again before you came home on your own—"

"I would slit your throat and drop you in the Thames," Aiden finished grimly. "You don't really mean to say you thought I would have done it."

"I've seen you do worse," the boy retorted, but the twinkle in his eyes gave him away. "So I came home and told them you were indisposed."

"Knave," Aiden muttered, grabbing up his tunic as he turned away. "I ought to whip you for a wretch and send you packing to your mama."

"She would only send me back," Robin answered. "And if you whip me, your mama will never forgive you."

"No doubt," Aiden muttered. He pulled the tunic over his head and turned back to the mirror to tie the laces. "So what did they say? Was my father angry?"

"No, my lord," Robin said, sobering as he fetched his master's boots. "In truth, they didn't seem surprised."

Aiden smiled at his reflection in the mirror, the darkly humorous grin that made maidens' hearts go a-flutter. "No," he admitted. "I suppose they wouldn't be." After thirteen years in London, tearing up the town, even his parents had to know what he had become, at least to the world at large. His mirror was perfect; with a single word in ancient faery-speak, he could make it show him his dreams. But standing before it now, he could only see the shell the world could see, the handsome trickster, the seducer, the prince's favorite rogue. He could not see himself.

He heard the door open behind him, then a woman's voice. *"For now we see as through a glass, darkly,"* his mother said, making him smile. Of all the noble ladies in London this morning, only Alista of Falconskeep would tease her son in Latin—with holy writ, no less. "Careful, Willie. Vanity is still a sin."

"So is blasphemy," he answered, turning to her. "And I am Aiden now, remember?"

"Oh, yes," his mother sighed. "I do remember." She accepted his kiss with a hug of her own. "Your father still hasn't forgiven you completely for giving up his name."

"I didn't give it up," he joked. "I'm saving it for later." In truth, he had dropped his first name, William, after his father, the very day he arrived at court, and King Henry had heartily approved. *I've been plagued with one Will Brinlaw all my life,* he had laughed. *I have no need for another.* The king had taken the young squire from Falconskeep completely to his heart, including him for good and ill in the wellspring of jealous love he felt for his flawed youngest son. By the time Aiden was knighted and Henry was dead, leaving John's older brother Richard on his throne, every trace of young Willie Brinlaw had long since disappeared, at least in his outward appearance. "I'm glad you've come," he told his mother now, hugging her again before he let her go. "But we have to go to the Tower—John will be waiting."

"Let him wait," she smiled, a twinkle of her own brand of mischief shining in her eyes. As a child, he had been utterly dazzled by her, and in truth, she was still just as beautiful as ever. Dark brown curls still peeked from the edges of her veil, refusing to be tamed, and her dark brown eyes were still as bright. No one who didn't know her well could have believed she was nearly sixty years old. *Faery magic*, Aiden thought. But he saw sadness in her eyes behind the teasing, sadness for him. "You look very like my father," she said, reaching up to barely touch his cheek. "He was probably vain as well."

"I doubt it," Aiden answered. "He was too busy to be vain." His grandfather, Lord Mark, had fought for King Stephen in the dark days of civil war. His wife, the sorceress Blanche, had conjured her own death trying to bring him home. Her ghost had told the child Aiden of their love, telling him he favored Mark much as his mother did now.

"She loved him more than life," Lady Alista said, following his thoughts as easily now as she had in the days when he had dogged her every step. "That's one of the few things I can still remember about her, how deeply she was in love. Even when her mortal body died, she stayed with him as a falcon because she couldn't give him up."

"I know," he answered, surprised to hear her speak of such things. His mother had never loved her faery magic, would have denied it if she could have. The memory of her mother's pain had always haunted her, and she avoided it like the wages of sin.

"That same love lives inside you," she went on, her tone turning urgent. "You are a child of Falconskeep as much as of Brinlaw—"

"More," he promised, taking her hands in his. "I am your son, Mama; Mark belongs to our father."

"You both belong to both of us, and to yourselves most of all," she answered. "All of you were born of love, a love that never fades."

"I know that, too," he smiled. No one who had seen his parents together could doubt their passion even now.

"Then how can you want this betrothal?" A tiny line appeared between her brows, as always the first warning of her anger. "You do not love this woman; you said yourself you barely even know her."

"Katherine is a princess," he said, pulling free of her grasp. "Prince John honors me greatly by offering me her hand." Robin brought a stool, and he sat down to let the squire lace his boots.

"John's gifts are very like his father's," she said bitterly. "More to the good of the giver than the man who receives them. You said it yourself in your letter—he means to annoy his brother, Richard, by giving his favorite sister to . . ." She let her voice trail off.

"You can say it, Mama," Aiden grinned. "John is giving Richard's pet to a scoundrel, a godless drunkard and seducer who cares nothing for chivalry and for morals even less." He had managed over the years to keep most of his more scandalous sins secret from his parents, first with the help of King Henry and later as a co-conspirator with Prince John. He had learned the ways and charms of women from the king's own cast-off mistresses, soft, pretty creatures with laughing eyes and a talent for discretion. But a recent dustup involving his seduction of another knight's promised virgin bride had been too heinous to keep hidden. The silly girl had decided she loved him and had spilled her secret to the world (and, more important, her intended) in hopes of forcing Aiden to marry her himself. It hadn't worked, but the subsequent uproar had been loud enough to reach the ears of Brinlaw.

"You are hardly godless," his mother scolded now, "whatever you may pretend."

"It doesn't matter why John is giving me Katherine." He stood up again, and Robin buckled on his sword. "If I make this marriage, I get Glencairn, a castle of my own—"

"In Scotland, where you will not be wanted," she cut him off. "If what you want is a castle, your father has three with lands for more besides—"

"All of which belong to my father." He should have known they would never trust him to know what was best for himself. If he were to be crowned Holy Roman Emperor, they would question the wisdom of the Pope. "Brinlaw will be Mark's, and Falconskeep must go to Malinda whether she wants it or not. Mary must have a dowry." He stopped for a moment, softening his tone. "I am making my own way in the world, making my own fortune," he finished. "Isn't that what you want? I know it's what Papa has always wanted; that's why he sent me to London." *He's ashamed of me, Mama,* he suddenly wanted to say. *He's ashamed, and I can't stand it.* But he couldn't say it; he couldn't even think of it for longer than a moment. He never could.

"Your father does not want you promised soul and body to a woman you can never love any more than I do," she said. "Do you truly believe you could come to love this princess?"

"Better you should ask can Katherine love me," he retorted, turning away. His reflection stared back at him again, now angry and impatient. The image was handsome, no question—many a maid had sworn as much, melting in his arms. He had his mother's glossy curls, but his eyes were piercing blue, and in body, at least, he was the perfect shape of a knight, a head taller than the tallest of his friends with the broad, strong shoulders to match. And his mother was right; he had inherited her heart, tender and quick to love, as hard as he struggled to hide it. He wanted the kind of love she spoke of more than almost anything, burned for it with a near-religious fervor. But his years at the royal court had taught him well that a prayer was not a truth and that appearances could lie. There was something else inside him, a truth more secret than his heart and more vital than his blood. A truth he could never reveal to anyone outside his own blood kin. "How could she love me?" he asked softly, still facing his face in the magical mirror conjured with fire and the blood they shared. "Can a woman love what she can never understand?"

"Every woman does." His mother smiled, teasing him.

"You ask me why I marry without love." He turned back to her, his heart plain in his eyes. "I'm a wizard, Mama. I don't have a choice." *I'm a man,* he wanted to say, *I won't have a husband to hide behind.* But of course he could not. He thought again of all the lovers he had known, noble and peasant and bawd. Who among them could have seen his magic and not denounced him for a demon? What woman could know his heart in all its darkness and not turn away in fear? *You will be greater than all of them,* a voice whispered in his memory. *You will be the dragon.* "It doesn't matter if I love Katherine or if Katherine loves me," he finished. "I can't have what you and Papa have, so I may as well have a princess."

She wanted to argue with him; he could see it in her eyes. But as little as they saw each other now, she still knew when to give up. "My darling stranger, Aiden," she sighed, surrender in her tone.

He hugged her close for a moment, enveloping her in

his arms. "Not a stranger, Mama," he promised, pressing a kiss to her forehead and wishing it were true. "Or a fool." He let her go with a smile. "Will you come with us to the Tower?"

"Thank you, no," she answered with a shudder that was only half in jest. She had always had a horror of the royal court. "Your father and Mark will go."

"Oh, joy," he muttered. "And the miller's daughter? Must I present her as well?"

"Mark's wife stayed home at Brinlaw with the children," his mother frowned. "Don't be a snob, Sir Aiden. It isn't becoming." Robin draped his freshly brushed mantle over his shoulders, and Lady Alista smiled. "And you're such a pretty thing."

"Mama, really," he scolded, offering her his arm.

Brinlaw and Mark were waiting downstairs, cloaked and ready to depart. "Finally," Mark grumbled, coming to meet them. "What were you doing so long?"

"Hello, Brother," Aiden said, embracing him. As a child, he had climbed Mark like a tree; now he could look him in the eye. He turned to his father. "Hello, Papa." Like his wife, Brinlaw looked barely more than half his age, his dark hair just starting to go gray. And Mark looked just like him, a second casting of the same fine statue. "Thank you for coming."

"Don't thank me yet," Brinlaw joked, embracing him as well.

"You mustn't blame Aiden," his mother said. "I kept him hostage, trying to make him see reason."

"I suspect you had no luck," Brinlaw said, letting him go. "So who is this woman you say you mean to marry?"

"Katherine, princess of England," Aiden said, masking his annoyance with a grin. "Daughter of Henry the Second; sister to Richard the First—perhaps you've heard of them?"

"Pawn of Prince John the Usurper," Mark pointed out with a scowl.

"Mark," Lady Alista warned gently, putting a hand on his arm.

"Careful, Mark," Aiden said easily. "John is beginning to take that sort of thing to heart." Robin opened the door as the grooms were bringing up the horses. "And he hates to be kept waiting."

"So I've heard," Brinlaw muttered with a sigh as he gave his wife a kiss. "Very well, then. Let's go."

The betrothal documents were signed in Prince John's audience chamber in the Tower rather than a church. "For privacy," the prince explained as his clerk spread the scroll on the table. Aiden looked up at his father and brother, standing like sentries on either side of him, wearing identical expressions of distrust that made them look even more alike. "But the good bishop will bear witness for us here as well as in the cathedral," John finished with a smile.

"I don't doubt it," Brinlaw said before Aiden could speak for himself. "But where is Princess Katherine?"

"In a convent in Aquitaine with our lady mother,"

John said easily. "I will sign for her—I would in any case."

"It doesn't matter, Papa," Aiden said, shooting his royal friend an apology with his eyes. "We can't be married until I secure Glencairn—"

"Which raises my next question," Brinlaw said, the steel-blue of his eyes more telling than his diplomatic smile. "What is this Glencairn, and why must it be secured? I thought the king sold Scotland back her freedom before he left England on Crusade."

"Scotland is its own country, yes," John said, an edge coming into his tone. "But Glencairn is an English castle, built after my brothers' rebellion. You'll recall the Scottish king tried a bit of treason of his own while my father was distracted and got himself imprisoned for his trouble."

"I was one of those who captured him," Mark answered. "But if this castle is English, why must Willie secure it? Why can you not give it to him outright?"

"Charles of Glencairn has died on Crusade," Aiden explained, his voice calm only with an effort. Willie, indeed. He wasn't a child, or an imbecile, for that matter. In fact, he suspected his wits were rather sharper than Mark's own. "He was a young man and an only son—there is no heir. But the castle is in Scotland, and it has been without a master for some time."

"The Scots may well have overrun the place by now," John agreed. "But Aiden can soon put it back in English hands, I think. It's worth having, my lord, I can assure you. My father spared no expense in its original construction, and the builder who designed it drew the plans for my mother's own house in Aquitaine."

Brinlaw scowled, obviously unconvinced. "So this document makes the castle Aiden's?"

"This document makes my sister Aiden's," John answered with a scowl of his own. His throat was beginning to redden; he would soon fly into a rage, the spoiled brat who loathed to be questioned breaking through the fragile crust the years had barely constructed around him. "But until their actual marriage, Glencairn belongs to her."

"So if the marriage never happens, Glencairn is won for England, but my son gets nothing at all," Brinlaw finished, never one to hesitate to infuriate his king or even his king's usurper brother. "Very clever, John—your father would be proud."

"The marriage will happen," Aiden said, turning to face his father. "I will make it happen." Mark's face turned pale, but Brinlaw's didn't change—filial insolence scared him no more than royal rage. "I will sign this betrothal, and I will marry the princess, with or without your permission." He was bluffing, of course. If Brinlaw should disown him, he would lose what little status he had. Not even John would let him marry Katherine then, and they all knew it. But his pride wouldn't let him be silent. He couldn't allow his father to destroy his plans, even with all good intentions. He didn't trust John any more than his father did; he had already considered the possibility Brinlaw raised. But he had resources not even his father could guess.

He met Brinlaw's eyes with his own, his face a stony mask. "Glencairn Castle will be mine."

"You dare?" Mark said softly—even at thirty-eight, he would have died before he defied Brinlaw's judgment. "Our father means to protect you, idiot—"

"Aiden knows what I mean," their father cut him off, his scowl melting into a tiny smile. The sadness Aiden had seen in his mother's eyes now shone in Brinlaw's as well. "And I do understand him." He took the quill from the fascinated clerk and held it out to Aiden. "Sign it, then," he said. "And you will have my blessing."

"Thank God," John grumbled.

"Thank you, Papa." Aiden took the quill and signed the scroll, barely scanning its text. *I will have the castle*, he thought, remembering the spirit's promise. *I will be the dragon.*

2

Glencairn Castle

A letter of Charles, Lord Glencairn, to the damsel Evelyn, his betrothed bride

> *Greetings and all faith,*
> *I cannot think how this word will reach you from so far away, but since your own has found me in the desert of the infidel, I must trust in God's grace that it will. In regards to your letter, lady, I must chastise you for your childish lack of discretion. While the sentiments expressed by you were naturally most pleasing to my lover's heart, I must insist in future that you hold them in silence until my return for the sake of your own modesty. I can only imagine the embarrassment of the clerk who penned the missive on your behalf; indeed, I wonder much that you managed to prevail upon him to do it. But never mind—such beauty as yours can be forgiven all the world.*
> *In reference to the plainer matter of your letter, I must remind you that I am on Crusade, fighting for*

the liberation of Jerusalem from the heathen. My mind and sword are fixed as one upon Almighty God. I cannot be expected to fret upon the petty ills of housekeeping at home. If you find yourself in difficulty, I suggest you call upon your own kinsman and laird, Malcolm, for assistance. As to the other matter you mention, I am naturally pleased at the prospect, but I caution you most gravely against giving your hopes free rein. These matters very often do not come off, or so I have often been told, and I would not have you grieved by disappointment. If we are to be so blessed, I cannot think but God would wish to wait until we are married. In any case, when I return in sacred triumph from my labors here there will be time enough to think upon such things.

I shall commend you to my Lord in prayer and ask no more in return.

Charles, Lord Glencairn

Sir Alan, marshal of the garrison at Glencairn, handed the scroll back to Evelyn, his honest face red as a berry. "The parchment looks quite tattered, mistress," he ventured. "Perhaps I misread Lord Charles's meaning in some bits."

"No," she answered, forcing a smile. "In faith, it sounds just like him." Somehow she resisted the urge to crumple the parchment into a ball and fling it into the fire for the sake of her dignity. She and this noble knight were standing at the very center of Charles's great hall, and while Sir Alan had tried most chivalrously to keep his voice down as he read, the entire household was watching.

"Perhaps it was written in haste, in the very heat of battle," the marshal persisted. "In any case, it must have been written many months ago."

"No doubt," she laughed. "The 'matter' he didn't wish to speak of is now a full year old."

"And a fine little lad he is, too," the knight said staunchly, making her smile in earnest. These Sassenach nobles didn't respect her, for all her father had been a Highland laird for fifty years, but they could be kind, particularly Sir Alan. He had never once failed to acknowledge that the child she had borne beneath this English roof was half an English nobleman himself. "In truth, mistress, I think he writes with great affection, for all his fussing," the marshal said now. "When he returns and you are married, he will be most proud of his son."

"Of course he will," she nodded. "How could he not be?"

"Mistress Evelyn!" Molly, one of the youngest and lowliest of the English servants, came running in from the courtyard like the forces of the Hun were at her heels. "I'm so sorry," she wept, babbling before she'd even reached her. "I was only gone for a moment, I swear."

"Sorry for what?" Evelyn said, putting a hand on her shoulder.

"Ella," Molly answered tearfully. "She's gone. She's run away."

"Ella?" Sir Alan repeated, confused. "Who—?"

"My milk cow," Evelyn explained with a sinking heart.

"Ah," he nodded, relieved.

"I had taken her up into the hills, like always," Molly explained. "You're right, mistress; the grass is better there, and she likes it. But I . . ." She stopped, blushing scarlet and staring at Sir Alan.

"You left her for a moment," Evelyn finished for her, stifling a sigh. She feared she knew too well what must have happened—Molly was a very pretty girl.

"Only for a moment," Molly gratefully agreed. "But when I came back, she was gone. I've been searching and searching . . ." She melted into tears again.

And where is your fine swain now? Evelyn thought, though she supposed she was hardly one to criticize. "Hush now, lass, for pity," she said aloud. " 'Tis only a cow, after all." A cow she had to have to feed her son, but let that lie—the poor chit was already hysterical. "Have you looked on the mountain?"

Molly stared at her, wide-eyed. "No, mistress," she said slowly. "I couldn't . . . it's nearly dark."

"Bollocks," Sir Alan laughed. "It's high summer and not even dinnertime—the sun has barely started to set."

"Molly is afraid of the mountain because of the standing stones," Evelyn explained. "She thinks that if she walks among them in the gloaming, the faeries will carry her off."

"Ridiculous," the knight scoffed, making Molly shrink miserably behind Evelyn, all but clinging to her skirts.

"That well may be, but I can't make her go if she believes it," Evelyn replied. "And if the cow has strayed as far as the mountain, she could fall over the cliffs." She touched Sir Alan's arm. "I have to have that cow, sir knight. If you sent out a patrol—"

"Mistress, are you mad?" he said, aghast. "You can't really be suggesting I send noble knights in search of a cow."

"And why not?" she demanded, her redhead's temper getting the better of her ladylike discretion. In all their blasted stories, knights-at-arms were forever going on quests for noblewomen for stupid things like a feather from the phoenix. But when she asked them to go after something practical, something her child could not live without, something they could retrieve in no time and be back in their hall for dinner, he looked at her as if she'd lost her mind. "What great work are they doing that cannot be abandoned for an hour? Dicing? Polishing their swords? Chasing the housemaids?" At this, Molly let out a little gasp, and Sir Alan's expression turned sour, but she couldn't resist one more jab. "Or are English knights afraid of faeries, too?"

"No, mistress, they are not," he answered coldly, every trace of sympathy gone. "But neither are they cowherds. If your son needs milk, I suggest you send this silly creature down to the village to fetch some."

Her son. Her problem. "The villagers need their milk for themselves, or hadn't you noticed, Sir Knight?" Evelyn retorted, lowering her voice but sharpening her tone. "And what about tomorrow?"

He looked away, reddening under his beard as he muttered, "Be that as it may."

"Indeed," she said sarcastically, but in truth, she was giving up. He wasn't going to help her, and the longer they argued, the darker it would be and the harder her quest would become. She turned away from him, catching Molly by the arm as she went. "When we both break our necks in the dark, I hope your conscience hurts you." Glaring at another knight who had ventured close enough to eavesdrop, she stalked out of the hall and across the courtyard, dragging the poor girl behind her.

"I am sorry, mistress, truly," Molly said, stumbling as they crossed the drawbridge. "Are you very angry?"

"Furious," Evelyn answered. "If I were to beat you as soundly as I'd like to, I'd probably scar you for life." She stopped for a moment, dropping Molly's wrist and squeezing her hand instead. "But since I don't believe in beatings, I suppose I can't," she finished with a weary smile.

Molly smiled back, the panic leaving her eyes. "Thank you, mistress," she said, following meekly as Evie started off again.

The castle was built on a peninsula that stretched

into the loch with a narrow strip of rocky land as the only access. "So who is he?" Evelyn asked as they reached the end of this and started down the road. One way led southward, to Edinburgh and England beyond it; the other led up into the hills toward the village of Evelyn's clan. They turned this way, starting up the gentle slope that would grow steeper as they climbed. "Your suitor," Evelyn pressed. "Who is he?"

"A Scottish boy," Molly finally answered. "My mum would kill me if she knew."

"No doubt," Evelyn smiled. "Those Scots are a nasty lot."

"I didn't mean that," Molly hastened to assure her. "You're beautiful, mistress, as fine as any English lady, and much nicer, from what I hear. And Angus . . ." A blush rose in her cheeks. "Angus is lovely."

"Is he, in faith?" Evelyn teased. The only Angus she knew from home who would be of an age with Molly was skinny as a reed with a neck so long he looked like he carried his head on a pike. But each lass to her liking, she supposed.

"Yes," Molly giggled. "But he always seems to be getting me in trouble."

"Oh, aye," Evelyn agreed. "Lads are bad for that—you can take my word."

"Oh, no," Molly protested. "Nothing like that! I couldn't. I'm a good girl. . . ." She let her voice trail off, her blush burning brighter. "I'm sorry, mistress," she muttered.

"You are a good girl, Molly," Evelyn answered, giving her shoulder a pat to show she wasn't offended. "See you stay that way." The road ahead curved sharply back to the right, skirting the cliffs above the loch to reach the Scottish village. Below them, she could see Glencairn Castle, the grand English fortress that would someday belong to her son, and above them rose the mountain, a great, green crag crowned with spikes of gray—the faery stones. The sun was going down behind them, and a thick, white mist was already beginning to rise from the heights—dragon's breath, her father would have called it, only half in jest. But Evelyn wasn't afraid. "Come along, then," she said, leaving the road and starting up the slope. "I want to be home before it gets completely dark."

"Me, too," Molly answered, following more slowly. "You think I'm a perfect ninny, don't you?"

"For being afraid of the wee folk?" Evelyn said, turning back to give the girl a smile. "Nay, love, not a bit." The girl trudged a bit more bravely to catch up, and she offered her a hand—the little Sassenach was already panting, for all she was years younger. "They've stolen many a plainer lass than you," she teased.

"Truly?" the girl said, wide-eyed. "Then why aren't you afraid?"

Evelyn smiled. "My father's folk are descended from the faery," she explained. "My clan was born on the mountain." She could still remember her father's eyes as he told of the days of glory when the ancients ruled the Highlands and the English still lived in caves in France. Her mother had scoffed at his stories—*the devil's kirk*, she had called the standing stones, a place of evil. She had forbidden Evelyn and her older sister, Rebecca, ever to go there, and Rebecca had been happy to oblige. But Evelyn had slipped off to the mountain whenever she got the chance, thinking the beatings she received whenever she was caught well worth it for the escape. The stones had been her castle then, her own magical hall; among them, she was a queen. *Leave her be*, her father would laugh. *Just look at her—she's half a faery herself.* But he was dead now, and her mother, too, and Rebecca's husband, Malcolm, was the new laird of their clan. And Evelyn lived with the English.

"I didn't come this far before," Molly said, breaking into her thoughts. "Maybe we should call her."

"Aye," Evelyn said, stopping. "We should." She looked around the rolling green humps of the slope for a glimpse of the cow's red hide. "Ella!"

"Ella!" Molly echoed. "Ella, please come home!" They stopped and listened for the bell the cow wore around her neck. "Where can she be?"

"Miserable beast," Evelyn muttered. If the cow really had fallen over a cliff, what would she do? She had no money to buy another, even if one could be found. Ella had been a gift of charity from her sister, sent along with Max's ancient nursemaid, Margaret, when the child was born and Evelyn found she could make no milk of her own. The castle had a dairy, but it was very poorly managed, and the milk it produced went to feed the English garrison their cheese and butter. Max was a year old now; he needed more milk every day, pure, fresh milk from a cow well grazed on the wholesome grass of the Highlands, not some skinny beast fed on molded corn.

"Ella!" Molly shouted again, climbing onto a rock to get a better view. "Let us find you! We won't be cross, I promise!" They had reached the last curved shoulder of the mountain before the final slope, and the standing stones rose just above them, pale and forbidding in the failing light, cloaked in their mantle of mist. "Ella, please!" Suddenly they heard it, a bell ringing out from above. "Oh, no," Molly said in dismay.

"Wait here," Evelyn ordered. "Sit down right here on this rock and wait for me."

"Mistress, please," Molly begged, catching her by the arm. "Don't—"

"Lass, don't be daft," she cut her off. "I'll be right back, I promise." Shaking off the girl's hand, she headed up the final slope.

The fog closed in around her almost at once, soaking her through with its chill. "All right, Lady Ella, you'd better stop where you are," she called, her voice coming back to her as the cries of a stranger, twisted in the mist. The poor beast would be exhausted from her climb and probably frightened as well. "It's time we went home where it's warm." She tripped on a loose pebble and nearly went sprawling. "And safe." The sun that just a moment before had floated well above the horizon was suddenly almost gone, its last rays barely penetrating the fog, and the stones that had still seemed far away suddenly loomed before her like the gate to a hall of giants, and she stopped, confused. Had they ever seemed so big before? Could the dusk make such a difference?

She walked between the pillars, craning her neck to try to see their tops, and a sense of desolation closed around her, thicker than the fog. *Charles doesn't love me,* she thought, venturing deeper. *He doesn't want our son.* She had come here for a reason, but suddenly she couldn't remember what it was. Why should she be on the mountain in the middle of the night? But it wasn't the middle of the night, it was barely sundown, and she was looking for . . . something. She just couldn't remember what. "This is wrong," she whispered, fear tightening her heart into a fist. It was dark; she could barely see her hand before her face, and the stones were all around her, paler shadows against the black of night. She looked up at the sky, and a tiny slice of death-white moon appeared among the clouds, then disappeared—a midnight moon. A bell rang in the distance, and for a moment, lucidity returned—the bell was what she was seeking, the reason she had come. But why was she chasing a bell?

"I have to go home," she insisted, barely caring she was talking to herself. "My baby needs me home." Somehow she had lost her reason, talking to the mist.

WICKED CHARMS 33

The music of the bell was gone, replaced by something else, something more complex—a harp played on the wind. A melody emerged, plaintive and sweet. Perhaps a minstrel had lost himself as she had. But then the harp was joined by other sounds, a flute like birdsong, and voices singing through the mist. Madness . . . she was on the mountain; no one else would come here. Rebecca wouldn't come; it was forbidden. Her father was dead, and everyone else was afraid.

Just beyond the mist a glow began to rise, light behind a curtain. She smelled smoke, torches and a hearth fire, and someone was laughing—a merry hall, a haven in the dark. She was wanted there; she was invited. "Dreaming," she whispered, closing her eyes. Somehow she was sleeping. Somehow she had wandered into a dream.

My love . . . The voice was masculine, deep and resonantly tender, words in a language she should not have understood like a caress against her cheek. But she did understand him; an answer rose to her lips in the same language. She had to hold her hand over her mouth to keep the words from coming out, squeeze her eyelids more tightly shut to keep herself from seeing. The presence moved behind her, and hands caressed her shoulders, a man's hands, warm and hard, but gentle, almost reverent, like no touch she'd ever known. *I love you,* he insisted in his ancient tongue, and she shivered to her bones. She felt his kiss against her cheek, warm breath against her skin. *We are meant.* Even with her eyes still closed, she could see the light brighten around her, feel the air turn warm. Even the curtain had fallen; she was inside the dream. If she opened her eyes, she would be there. She would see his face.

"I cannot," she spoke in good, plain Gaelic that echoed in her ears. "You have to let me go." She pressed her fists against her eyes, willing the dream to fade. "My baby needs me. I have to stay with Max." A killing sadness rose inside her, and tears spilled down her cheeks. "You have to let me go."

Cold wind rushed suddenly around her, the warmth of a lover's arms swept away in an instant. A terrible clanging assaulted her ears, and something warm and heavy crashed into her, knocking her to the ground. She screamed, opening her eyes as she fell, certain she was falling into hell. . . .

Ella the cow was standing over her, gazing down with wide brown eyes as she chewed. The sun had barely slipped behind the mountain, its last rays glinting off her clanging bell. "There you are. . . ." Evelyn climbed to her feet, catching hold of the rope around the animal's neck. She was still shaking; she was still . . . but no. It must have been a dream. "Come along, you," she ordered, giving the cow a tug. "We're going back where we belong."

3

Aiden pulled his horse to a stop at the crest of a hill, his breath cut short by the beauty of the land before him. Dawn was breaking over the green of Glencairn. The hills rolled away before him like waves on an emerald sea, their crests foaming with mist. A tiny ribbon of silver glinted in the newborn light—the river that would flow to the very foot of his castle to make its moat a natural lake—or loch, as it was called here. He followed the river with his eyes as it twined along the muddy track that passed for a road until he found a spire of reddish brown peeping over the shoulder of a hill. "There," he said softly, barely louder than a whisper. "There is my Glencairn."

The rest of his party was still encamped some half a mile behind him, his squire and some five dozen men, knights and foot soldiers all totaled. He hoped to find his castle peaceably held for England when he got there, but if not, he wanted to be ready. His father had fought the Scots on numerous occasions and had warned him to be careful. "We called them berserkers," Brinlaw had told him. "Madmen—once they start a fight, they won't stop until every man is dead on your side or theirs. They don't hold lands as we do, but what they have, they will defend, and they have no love for outsiders, particularly the English. The farther north you venture, the less welcome you will be." This last had been intended to scare him into reason, make him give up his quest. Glencairn was farther north than Brinlaw himself had ever been. But Aiden couldn't give it up; seeing the valley now, he was even more certain. This wild land was meant to be his.

He wheeled his horse around, headed back to roust the camp, and suddenly a tiny figure sprang up from the road like a sprite leaping out of the earth. "Stop, brigand!" the boy shouted, if human child he was. He was dressed in a dirty shirt and a kilt of green and gold—a Scotsman's tartan. His hair was flaming red, braided into two tiny braids that stuck out from the back of his head and quivered with righteous fury. "Ye're not wanted here!"

Aiden tried not to smile. "Not wanted by whom?" he inquired, letting the reins go slack. If this infant decided to hop around some more, he wanted the horse free to step over him without trampling him to pulp.

"Step down from that horse, Sassenach, and I'll show you," the boy swore, drawing a sword barely longer than Aiden's own dagger.

"Will you, in faith?" His father had called the Highlanders fierce and unfriendly, but this was ridiculous. He had no wish to hurt this child, but he wouldn't be put off the road by him, either. "Very well, then." He got down slowly from his horse, one hand on his sword hilt as a warning. "Show me who you are."

Suddenly hoofbeats crashed through the brush on either sloping side of the road, and a pair of riders blocked his path to the boy. "His name is Hamish, son of Laird Malcolm of Glencairn," the tallest of these said, a boy of about sixteen with the same red hair and wearing the same tartan as little Hamish. The third boy was somewhere between the other two in age, the middle brother, no doubt. He said nothing, but he drew his sword and pointed it at Aiden's throat. "You're trespassing on our father's lands, Sassenach," the oldest boy finished. "You should have stayed in England."

"I have no quarrel with the laird, your father," Aiden answered evenly, his ear adjusting quickly to the boy's lilting accent. He was fairly certain he could put an end to this standoff in about a minute, but not without killing or maiming at least one of these pups. And that hardly seemed diplomatic. "But I am not trespassing." The boy holding him at sword point was sweating, and Hamish had climbed on to his oldest brother's horse as if he craved his protection. They were frightened—no doubt they had seen his troops. "My name is Aiden Brinlaw." He took his hand from his sword hilt. "I am lord of the English castle at Glencairn—"

"Liar!" Hamish shouted. "My auntie—"

"Hush yourself," his oldest brother stifled him, clamping a hand over his mouth. "Glencairn Castle has a lord already, Aiden Brinlaw; we have seen him."

"Not lately, you have not," Aiden shot back. "He has been on Crusade with King Richard. He has died there." All three of their faces showed shock in different ways and to a different purpose. Little Hamish's eyes were frankly dismayed, his mouth dropping open. The boy who held the sword let it drop, turning to his brother as if for direction. But in the oldest one's eyes, Aiden saw more speculation than surprise. One English lord was already dead; another was seemingly in his power. This boy was forming a plan. "Prince John has sent me to take his place," Aiden finished, reaching for his sword, diplomacy be damned.

"Not so fast, Sassenach." The oldest carried a grown man's sword, and he drew it with adult speed. "Why should we believe you, or your Prince John?" He got down from his horse, his sword point inches from Aiden's throat—a more threatening pose, but a tactical error, more proof of his inexperience as a fighter. "And if we do, why should we let you live?"

"Gerald, don't!" the middle boy said, his voice cracking with alarm.

"Scotland is free," Gerald went on, coming closer. "We've no more use for your castles."

"Da will be angry," Hamish warned, clinging to the horse's mane.

"You should listen to your brothers, Gerald," Aiden said, his manner easy and calm. He was in real danger now, he knew, and a cold tingle ran down his spine. "Glencairn Castle is an English manor, no matter how free your Scotland may be. Slay me, and your own king will see you hang for fear of retaliation."

"Make him stop it, Davey," Hamish said, sounding ready to cry.

"Gerald, please," Davey warned.

"Shut up, the both of you," Gerald ordered angrily. "You make me ashamed you're my brothers."

"They only mean to save you," Aiden said, turning slowly, making the boy circle him. This Gerald wasn't giving up; Aiden had apparently misjudged him. Not even the mention of hanging had made him flinch. Like Papa's berserkers, he meant to kill this English intruder or die in the attempt. But perhaps there was another way. "You're a very reckless boy, Gerald," he went on, meeting the boy's eyes steadily as if to gaze into his thoughts. "That is no plaything you carry."

"You're damned right it is not," Gerald answered. "This claymore belonged to my grandfather. My father gave it to me."

"Your father gave you that?" He turned his gaze to the sword itself, focusing on the blade, the lethal shape of the steel. "A perverse gift for a child . . ." He let his eyelids fall, seeing the shape in his mind, watching as it melted . . .

"No!" Davey shouted as Aiden opened his eyes. A thick serpent writhed in Gerald's fist where his sword hilt had been a moment before. "Set it loose!" The snake struck at the boy's face, venom dripping from its fangs, and he flung it away with an oath Aiden didn't understand. The serpent reared up from the ground, seeming to grow bigger, a snake into a dragon, and the boy sprang back with a yelp.

"I thought you meant to kill me," Aiden said, taking the creature by the tail and holding it before him. "Don't you want your sword?"

"Witch!" Gerald shouted, grabbing the reins of his horse. "Devil's spawn!" He sprang into the saddle, nearly unseating Hamish, who stared at Aiden with glassy, frightened eyes. Yanking the horse around, the young Scotsman galloped away with his brothers close behind him.

Aiden let out his breath in a sigh, letting the conjure fade. "Excellent," he muttered. "Well done, idiot." He'd wanted to make an impression on his Scottish neighbors, and he definitely had. "No doubt they will welcome me with open arms." He looked down at the sword in his hand—a claymore, the boy had called it. It was a pretty thing, finely wrought, with a crosspiece curved like a boat. Its shape reminded him of his own grandfather's Falconskeep sword, wrought in ancient times by the spirit who had taught him magic and given him his mark. He looked down at the dragon tattoo that curled around his wrist, and he smiled. His father now carried the Falconskeep sword, but Aiden had held it once. He had dipped it in the spirit's waters and renewed her blessing on its blade.

"Lord Aiden!" Robin came scrambling down the hill.

"There you are," he said, coming to a stop with a grin. "We had begun to be worried."

"No need," Aiden promised, clapping the boy on the shoulder. He put the claymore through a binding on his saddle, its blade nestled safe against the blanket. "We're almost home."

Evelyn sat cross-legged on the solar floor, her arms outstretched before her. "Come on, Max. You can do it." Her son had pulled himself up on his feet against the seat of a chair and was watching her warily, rocking back and forth as if warming up for a sprint. "Come on," she urged again, smiling, and he smiled back, showing his tiny front teeth. "Silly boy . . . come to Mama." Margaret had brought him to her an hour ago, already exhausted at mid-morning by his antics. But Evelyn could have played with him happily all day. He lifted one foot, considering. "That's right. Come on." He let go of the chair with one hand and almost took a step. Then he let out a piercing crow of either triumph or frustration before thumping back to his hands and knees and crawling quickly as a beetle to her arms.

"Never mind," she sighed, scooping him up to kiss his pudgy cheeks. "Walking isn't everything." She buried her face in his neck, inhaling his warm-milk and rose-petal smell. "My baby . . ." Closing her eyes, she could still feel her dream from the mountain the night before, feel a phantom kiss against her cheek. In truth she had barely slept all night, remembering how it felt.

Max squirmed impatiently, trying to get free. "Ma-mee . . . go!"

"All right, all right." She set him down, and he began to climb her like a tree, pulling himself back up to his feet. He had been playing this game for a week now, desperate to stand but unwilling to walk. "Watch yourself," she warned, extricating her braid from his fist. What *had* happened last night? Had she been dreaming? Was she going mad? "It felt real, Max," she said, still holding his hand to help him balance. "Do you believe in faeries?" He fixed her with a blue-eyed gaze as if he understood and was considering the question. "Do you think they came for your mammy?"

"Evelyn!" Boyish feet were clattering up the stairs and through the gallery. "Aunt Evie!" The solar door burst open, and her sister's sons came in, the two younger ones falling over one another to reach her first.

"You have to come with us now," Davey said as Max sat down with a thump, too excited by his cousins' sudden appearance to keep his balance. "You have to hurry."

"What are you talking about?" Little Hamish was pale as paint under his freckles, and she touched his dirty cheek. "Gerald, what happened?"

"Davey is right," Gerald answered. "Bring the bairn. We'll explain on the way home."

"Oh, I don't think so," she said, standing up. Young Gerald was the picture of his father and every bit as bossy. "What has frightened Hamish?"

"I ain't scared," Hamish said, bristling with indignation.

"I'm glad to hear it," she smiled. "But what—?"

"There's a Sassenach on his way here to lay claim to this castle," Gerald explained, glancing toward the door as if fearful of being overheard. "He says your Charles is dead, and Prince John has given it to him."

"Dead?" She stared at him stupidly with Max tugging himself up on her skirt. "How . . . ?"

"On Crusade, he says," Gerald answered. "His name is Aiden Brinlaw, and he has troops with him, English troops." He started to say more, then turned his eyes to Davey, the two of them exchanging a wary look. "You don't want to be here when he comes."

"He's a witch!" Hamish burst out.

"He is not!" Gerald retorted, turning red.

"He is so, Aunt Evie," the little one insisted. "He turned Gerald's sword into a snake—"

"He did not," Davey insisted.

"Oh, yes, he did," Hamish said, refusing to be put off. "That's why we ran away."

"We did not run away," Gerald said, his jaw clenched hard. "We came to warn Evelyn."

"Hush, all of you," Evelyn interrupted, sitting back down in a chair. "I have to think." Her mind was racing in circles. Charles was dead; he was never coming back. Max would never have a father. But she couldn't stop to grieve, not yet. She had to keep her wits about her, think of what to do next. Another Sassenach knight was coming to take Charles's place—but what about Max? The silliness about the man being a witch and turning swords to snakes didn't much concern her. Rebecca and Malcolm both brought up their children to believe the English were devils incarnate. But what was she going to do?

"You don't have time to think, Aunt Evie," Gerald said. For a moment he looked like the little boy she had spoiled unmercifully before she left home when her father had still been laird. "This Brinlaw was right behind us. He could be here any minute."

"Gerald, I can't leave." She looked down at Max, smiling up at her from the floor, oblivious to disaster. "This is Max's home." She smiled back at him, but it was a poor effort. "I have to fight for him."

"Are you mad?" Gerald demanded. "What will you—?"

"Go home, Gerald," she cut him off. "Go home, and take your brothers with you." She ruffled a hand through Hamish's fire-red hair, then gave him a push toward his brother. "You heard me. I said go."

"You *are* mad," Gerald answered. A shout rose from the hall below—a troop of riders had been spotted approaching from the south—and the boy's eyes widened with fear. "Aunt Evie, please . . ."

"Hurry, Gerald," she urged him. "I promise I'll be all right."

For another long moment he hesitated, obviously searching for the words that would convince her. Then he rushed forward and hugged her with all his might.

"I'll tell Da what has happened," he said, letting her go. "He'll know what's to be done."

"No doubt." The other two hugged her as well, and she kissed Davey's tear-stained cheek. "It's naught to cry over, sweeting," she promised. "Now go." With a final backward glance, they obeyed, running from the room as quickly as they had come in.

"Ma-mee?" Max said, frowning up at her. "Ma-mee doe?"

"No, lambie," she said absently. "Mammy's not going anywhere." But she couldn't stay; Charles was dead. She had been worried that he didn't love her, and all the time he was dead. News traveled so slowly, he might have been dead for months—he must have been. He could have been dead before Max was even born. She paced around the room, a terrible rage rising up inside her. Another knight was here to take his place—that's how she was meant to be told the father of her child was dead. He would put her out, this new Englishman, her and her bastard with her. She would have to go back to Rebecca, back to the clan with an English bastard. *Da will know what's to be done*, Gerald had said, as if this should comfort her. Laird Malcolm would know, all right. He would know what other landowner he wanted as an ally, what other poor wretch was pining in need of a wife. He would marry her off to the first man who would have her; Rebecca would make sure of it. And Max would have nothing, would be less than nothing at all.

"No!" she shouted, the rage boiling over. She snatched down the banner that hung over the mantel—Charles's coat of arms—and ripped at it with all her strength until she had torn it in two. "He will not! I will not!" She flung the pieces in the fire, and the silk caught flame at once.

"Oo," Max murmured, fascinated. "Burn . . ."

"You're damned right, lambie," she said bitterly, scooping him up in her arms. "Let it burn." She pressed his face close to her throat, fighting angry tears. She wouldn't cry; she couldn't. Her eyes could not be red and swollen; they had to be bright as the blue summer sky. She could not be weeping and unhappy; she must be charming. She would have to be perfect. "Mammy has got to be pretty," she crooned to the child in her arms. She had captured one Englishman already; she saw no reason why she shouldn't have another. "She's going to catch you a da."

4

Glencairn Castle was both more and less than Aiden had hoped. The structure itself was beautiful, its rough red towers rising stark and grand against the green hills behind it and reflected in the crystal loch below. But inside, the rooms were dark and bare, far more like a fortress than a home. The great hall was basically a bare stone cave with rough wooden tables and benches and a fire pit in the center of the floor with an iron grille set into the ceiling above it to let the smoke escape. A pair of women was turning the day's meats over the fire even now, filling the room with a thick, gray haze. His own belongings were set haphazardly all around, waiting to be carried upstairs, adding to the general effect of barely ordered squalor. "Oh, no," he said, laughing and shaking his head. "This will not do at all."

"Not exactly a London palace, is it, my lord?" the marshal of the garrison, Sir Alan, agreed. "The rooms upstairs are a little better, and there's a solar just beyond that gallery with a proper hearth, at least."

"No separate kitchens, I take it," Aiden said, nodding to the cooks.

"There used to be," Sir Alan answered. "Nothing fancy—Lord Charles had a wooden shed built out by the vegetable gardens after his father died. But the Scots kept sneaking over the walls at night to burn it down."

Aiden stared at him, aghast. "You can't be serious."

"I only wish I were not," the knight said with a grim little smile. "It's mostly boys doing it, we think—they've made it a kind of game or a dare, harassing the English. We have to keep a guard on the stables at night to keep them from stealing the horses."

"And when you catch them?" Aiden asked.

"We don't, often, but when we do, we give them a flogging and send them home again," Sir Alan answered. "This isn't England, my lord, and these people are not serfs. Since His Majesty sold the Scottish king his crown back, we have no real power over them, and they know it. The English village is near to being deserted because the people there don't feel safe from the Scots."

"I shouldn't wonder, when you don't protect them," Aiden said sharply. John had been right; this was the beginning of just the sort of thing they had feared. Apparently he had arrived just in time. "What have you been doing, Sir Alan?" The knight flushed red, and Aiden turned away before he could bluster a response. "Quarter the foot soldiers I brought with me from England in the village with two knights to command them, one new arrival and one from the old garrison.

Fly my banner over the houses they stay in, and keep the gates of the village under guard," he went on. "We'll build a barracks beside the wall after the new kitchen here is done—that construction starts today, in stone, with a breezeway to connect it to the castle proper." He looked around at the bare walls of the hall and frowned, but there was no point in hanging them with tapestries for the cooking fire to ruin. If his mother or one of his sisters were here, they would set things right soon enough, but what did he know about keeping house? Just enough to know this one was not being kept. "Put a guard on that as well," he finished.

"Why are you telling me all this?" Alan asked, still flustered and red.

Aiden grinned. "Because I'm putting you in charge, of course," he said. "You will be my steward as well as marshal of the guard."

The man's expression changed from anger to shock. "Why me, my lord?"

Because you're the only one here who knows what's going on and still had the courage to tell me, Aiden thought but didn't say. "Why not?" he shrugged instead as if it hardly mattered. "Gather the garrison in the courtyard, in armor, if you please," he went on. "This manor is English soil, the Scottish king be damned, and any mischief done here will be taken as an assault. The walls will be guarded day and night, and any Scotsman captured trying to breach them for whatever reason will be cut down in the act or hanged the morning after." He thought of the three who had accosted him on the road that morning, fierce little Hamish and his brothers, and he shuddered to imagine them hanging from a gallows. But apparently this was war. "No matter how young he might be."

"Forgive me, my lord, but are you quite certain that's wise?" Sir Alan asked. "The old lord thought it best to try to keep the peace, and Lord Charles believed he was right."

"The old lord is dead, and so is his son," Aiden answered. "I am lord here now, and I will not be harassed."

"Very good, my lord." The knight was plainly not convinced, but he had accepted Aiden's word as law, and that was an excellent start. "Will you see the solar?"

"Yes," Aiden nodded, "I will." He followed the knight up stone stairs to the gallery and through an oaken door. "Now this is better," he said with a smile of relief. The room wasn't pretty, but it was clean, and the carved black table and benches were more to a nobleman's taste. "Have my chairs set here, and the iron trunks." Sir Alan nodded, and the footman who had followed them from the hall hurried back out to obey. *They all act as if they're frightened half to death,* Aiden thought. "So tell me honestly, Sir Knight," he said aloud. "Will Lord Charles be missed?"

"Of course," the marshal answered, shocked. "He was a very pious young man."

"Pious is good," Aiden nodded. An iron bracket

hung above the fireplace as if to hold a nobleman's banner, but it was bare but for a single, tattered scrap of golden silk hanging at one end. A low fire burned on the hearth to chase away the Highland chill that apparently persisted even into August, and bending down, Aiden found another silken scrap lying just outside the reach of the flames, one end of it charred black. "Interesting," he remarked, picking it up. "Someone has burned a banner."

"It must have fallen," Sir Alan said, an unconvincing liar.

"Indeed," Aiden smiled, standing up. "So Charles was a good master?"

The man was obviously torn between plain speaking and loyalty. "The old lord died too soon," he finally decided. "Lord Charles was not ready to take on such a task as Glencairn, and he felt the loss of his father very deeply. They had quarreled just before the old lord took ill, and the young lord blamed himself."

"And so he took the Cross," Aiden finished, shaking his head. How many idiots had blundered into holy war out of remorse, only to stain their souls far more sorely in the desert? Even his own father had fallen into this trap in his youth. Luckily, remorse was not one of Aiden's more prominent emotions.

"In a manner of speaking," Sir Alan agreed. "But there was something else, a matter you should be told about. The reason Lord Charles quarreled with his father . . ." He broke off, obviously searching for the proper words. "After Scotland was released from English rule, the old lord thought it prudent to make an official alliance with the local clan," he began again. "Charles was already set on Crusade when his father insisted he must marry the sister-in-law of the local chieftain."

"Marry?" Aiden echoed, snapping to attention. Charles's quarrels with his conscience were none of Aiden's concern, but if the dead man had a wife and heirs, that could be a disaster. "I was told Lord Charles had no family."

"And so he did not," Sir Alan hastened to assure him. "He and the young lady were never actually married, but they were betrothed, and she came to live at the castle." He paused again, clearing his throat. "She is still here," he finished. "And she has a son."

Aiden couldn't help but laugh as much with real amusement as relief. "The pious young Crusader has a Scottish bastard?"

"Mistress Evelyn is a lady of good character, my lord," Sir Alan insisted. "Her late father was laird of their clan for many years, and while we do not recognize that title as such, I believe her blood to be as noble as my own."

"A fine, chivalrous speech, Sir Knight," Aiden smiled. "She must be very pretty."

"She is that, too," Sir Alan agreed with a disapproving frown. "And her son is as fine a little lad as you could ever hope to see."

"So may God bless him," Aiden said, sobering with an effort. In truth, the man's loyalty impressed him, sentimental as it was. He found he rather liked Sir Alan. "But I fear there isn't much that I can do for him or his pretty mama, either. They certainly can't stay here."

"No," Sir Alan sighed. "They will have to be returned to Laird Malcolm. But I must confess we will all be sad to see them go. The servants are all quite fond of Mistress Evelyn. Just yesterday, a servant girl lost her cow . . ." He stopped, embarrassed. "But of course you are quite right."

Aiden had to admit he was intrigued. From what he had heard, the English living in the Highlands held their neighbors in a barely tolerant contempt. Yet Sir Alan spoke of this Scottish doxy like she might be the tragic heroine of a poet's romance. "Where is this Evelyn now?" he asked.

"Upstairs," Sir Alan answered. "She is having her belongings packed to make way for your own."

Leave it be, warned the sensible cynic who lived inside his head. *Let her go—don't even look at her.* He was here to secure the castle, to bring the Scots to heel and make the manor turn a profit. The last thing he should be thinking of was a pretty girl with problems he couldn't solve. But he was hopeless; he couldn't resist. "I should express my condolence," he said aloud. "Take me to her at once."

* * *

Margaret and Molly were frantically packing with Max crawling to and fro between them and generally getting in the way. But Evelyn was calm. As the women scrambled and footmen tromped in and out with the new lord's trunks, she sat in the wide window seat, studiously twining ribbons into her long, auburn hair.

" 'Tis glad I am to be going home for good," Margaret announced as she folded Max's shirts into a hamper. "These old bones have had quite enough of drafty castles."

"I just wish I were going with you," Molly complained. "They say this Aiden Brinlaw is a very devil, that Prince John only sends him to a place when he means to see everybody punished." Max was dragging a stack of bed linens off the table one fistful at a time, and the girl took them out of his reach. "I heard his squire telling one of the other boys that he once hanged a hundred Saxon bandits in a single day."

"I wouldn't be a bit surprised," Margaret answered. "His father was a terror in his day—back when my husband was alive, he used to spit against evil every time he heard the Brinlaw name." She made a quick sign of the Cross as if to be safe. "He was a Lowlander, you know, from the border lands." She stopped and looked over at Evelyn. "But listen to us, nattering on about nothing when your poor Lord Charles is dead," she said, going to her. "My poor, sweet lamb..."

"I'm all right," Evelyn answered, getting up. In truth, she wanted to hear all the gossip she could about this Aiden Brinlaw, and she didn't want to think about Charles. "Molly, you said you saw his squire." Two more footmen carried in the biggest mirror she had ever seen and set it near the window. Its massive frame was carved like the body of a dragon with its head rearing over the top, and the glass was so clear, she had to touch it to be certain it was real. "What does he look like?" she said, gazing at her own reflection.

"Brinlaw's squire? He's just a sprout," Molly sniffed. "No more than twelve or thirteen, I would think." She came and stood beside Evelyn, as fascinated as her mistress by the mirror. "What sort of man would have a thing like this?" she mused softly, touching the frame.

Evelyn smiled. "A very vain one, I should think." She liked her gown—green had been the best choice—but her hair was wrong. "Hand me my comb." She untied the ribbons one by one until her curls fell back to her shoulders. So Brinlaw was a soldier, the prince's executioner, and he liked the look of his own face. He would be arrogant, but she could manage that. Given the proper incentive, she could manage anything. Max settled at her feet with a thump, and she smiled. Yes, she would manage.

Aiden stood in the doorway without speaking; his voice had run dry in his throat. The most exquisite woman he had ever seen was standing in front of his mirror, smiling at her own reflection. She was dressed like a noblewoman in a plain green gown, but instead of hiding her hair under a proper noblewoman's veil, she wore it loose like a harlot, her vibrant auburn curls falling in a tangle to her waist. Taking a step closer, he could see her eyes were blue, the same color as the Scottish sky, and her skin was creamy-pale, barely sprinkled with golden freckles across her little nose. But most luscious of all was her mouth, her full, pink lips turned up in a wicked smile that burned through him like a flame. This was what Charles had abandoned for Crusade? No wonder God had taken him. He wasn't just pious; he was too good for this earth.

"My lord," Sir Alan spoke beside him. "This is Mistress Evelyn."

Evelyn looked up, startled, to find a stranger reflected in the mirror behind her, the bonniest man she could ever hope to see. A head and shoulder taller than she was, he was certainly the biggest Englishman she had ever seen. "My lord?" she said, turning around. "Then you are Lord Aiden."

Her voice was as seductive as her smile, slightly husky—but perhaps she had been crying. "Yes," he agreed. "Are you surprised?" She offered her hand, and he kissed it, the perfect courtier.

"I thought you would be older," she said boldly, his kiss making her shiver. His hair was dark, brown but almost black, and his skin was as smooth as her own—astonishing! No man should have such skin. But there was nothing feminine about him, nothing that spoke of weakness. "Or crippled in some way."

"Did you, in faith?" He laughed, utterly charmed. He

had expected to find some frightened little creature, weeping and cursing her fate. After Sir Alan's speech, he had thought she would be a delicate blossom of a girl who would quiver with fear at the very sight of him. But this girl wouldn't shiver at the devil.

"Yes," she said, the corner of her mouth turned up in the beginning of that shockingly sensual smile. "I thought all the young, able-bodied knights of England had gone on Crusade with their king."

"Indeed?" His eyes were so dark, she had thought they were black, but as he came closer, she could see they were actually blue, the color of summer midnight. She found herself remembering the night before when she'd been lost among the stones, the sudden darkness that had fallen as she had slipped into a dream. "I fear you have been misinformed, my lady," he said with an impudent smile that showed his white, even teeth. "I am much too wicked to go on Crusade—I would ruin God's grace for everybody with my evil ways."

"I don't doubt that a bit, since you're so free to admit it," Evelyn retorted, returning his smile with her own. "I wonder that you don't seek absolution for your sins, being so quick to confess."

"Confession is no problem," he agreed. Her eyes as she teased him were mesmerizing, and that smile was driving him mad. An hour ago he had believed he knew firsthand every mood and emotion the female heart could muster, from ecstasy to contempt. But no woman had ever looked at him the way this Evelyn looked at him now. She must realize her situation was desperate, but she didn't seem to care. She must see him as her enemy, but she didn't seem afraid. She challenged him; she flirted. He had no idea what she was thinking; no clue what she really felt. She was a perfect mystery, an enigma wrapped in the most delectable of forms, and he wanted her more than he had ever wanted any woman in his life. "But to be truly absolved, I would have to feel contrition," he continued. "And I can never seem to make myself feel sorry."

"A most grievous flaw in your character, my lord," she chided. "You ought not to be so proud of it." He knew just exactly how handsome he was; she could see it in his eyes. The Scriptures said the devil was an angel once, driven out of heaven for his pride. Watching Aiden Brinlaw brag on his sins, she knew just how this angel must have looked.

"Ma-mee." Max tugged at her skirt, trying to stand, and she reached down and picked him up. He stared at Aiden with wide blue eyes. " 'Oo da?"

Aiden watched her cuddle her child with obvious affection. "This is Lord Aiden, lambie," she said, giving Aiden a sidelong glance as provocative as her smile. "He's here to steal your castle."

"Lord Aiden was just saying you must leave us, mistress," Sir Alan interrupted, coming closer to join them. "But he wanted to tell you himself."

"How very chivalrous," Evelyn said with the slightest sarcastic edge. Men were born to be managed; she'd known as much from the time she left the cradle. He wouldn't put her out. But she couldn't let him think she cared one way or the other; she couldn't seem desperate. "I do hope you'll let me finish packing."

"Of course," Aiden said, feeling as if he were riding a runaway horse. Somehow the situation had gotten away from him; her pretty blue eyes had distracted him from his original thought. Yes, he'd told Sir Alan that Charles's mistress would have to go, but that was before he had seen her. "Though I do resent being called a thief," he offered, giving the baby a pat. The last infant he had tried to make friends with was Mark's youngest—the little wretch had expressed his disapproval of his uncle's sinful ways by spitting up all over him. "What's his name?" he asked, watching for telltale signs of eruption as this one gave him a wary smile.

"Maximellian," Evelyn answered. "Charles's father had already thought of a name for his son's heir before he died. But I call him Max." The English knight was smiling, but his cocksure attitude was somewhat dampened, she noticed. "What else should I call you but a thief, Sir Knight?" she pressed on bravely. "You are taking his inheritance."

"Not me, my lady," Aiden answered. "The king." Max was a pretty baby, he had to admit, though he looked almost nothing like his mother. "Your intended died in the field without bothering to tell anyone you existed, you or Max, either one."

Evelyn felt her smile turn bitter, another wave of fury against Charles and his damned "discretion" swelling for a moment in her heart. "But I do exist," she pointed out. "And so does Max."

"Yes, but King Richard didn't know it," Aiden answered. *And wouldn't have cared if he had,* he added in his head but was tactful enough not to say. Richard's ideas of chivalry rarely extended past the masculine delights of battle to include the feelings of women, no matter how lovely they might be. "As a royal charter, Glencairn reverted to the crown on Charles's death, and the king sent word to his brother back in England to make certain it was properly secured. Prince John, in turn, sent me." He watched a half a dozen different emotions flicker over her face, an unmistakable rage behind her smile, and a womanly intelligence in her eyes he had previously only associated with his mother and sister, the witches of Falconskeep. But he couldn't give her what she wanted, even if he wanted to. Glencairn belonged to Katherine, not him. "He had no idea I would find you here, nor did I," he finished. It wouldn't have made the slightest difference if they had—a betrothed mistress was not a wife, and a bastard was not an heir. But she didn't have to know that. "I am sorry."

Evelyn smiled. "Then you are absolved." She handed Max to Margaret, who had crept closer to hover and watch the English stranger as if he might really have been the devil incarnate. "We will leave at once."

"No." The word escaped him before he thought, an

unheard-of phenomenon for him. "I will write to John on your behalf." A part of him was watching the rest in disbelief—had he lost his mind? His situation was delicate already; could he truly mean to add this woman's complicated problems to his own? But he couldn't seem to do anything else. He couldn't let her just leave; he had to solve the puzzle of that smile, to taste that wicked mouth. "I will explain that you were legally betrothed, that only Charles's taking the Cross with King Richard prevented your being married." *That should warm the prince's heart,* he thought. The whole thing was ridiculously foolish; he was playing with fire, gambling his future on a pretty face. But he was a wizard; surely he could bring it off.

Evelyn just stared at him for a moment, struck dumb by sudden hope. Her offer to leave had been no more than a bluff; she had been fairly well assured he wouldn't let her leave the castle. She had seen her hook go in, seen desire in his eyes behind the arrogant smile. But she had never expected anything like this, an honest offer of help. "You would do this?" she finally managed to say.

"Of course," he repeated with a grin that was so boyishly triumphant, she couldn't help but smile back. "As a knight of chivalry, I can hardly do anything else."

"A knight of chivalry, in faith?" she teased. Half an hour's conversation, and she already knew this was a joke, he thought. She was adorable. He could manage John, make him see it all as a big joke, and in the meantime, he would have her and the castle, too. Not the most honorable course of action, he would admit at the throne of judgment, but quite satisfying. "And what must I do in return?" she asked, as if she were reading his thoughts.

"Nothing, my lady. I promise." He took her hand and raised it to his lips, inhaling the smell of her skin. She would have to wait for John's answer; that would give him time enough to employ a few charms of his own. She would be satisfied, too, even if she didn't win her son a castle. "Only stay at Glencairn."

"Are you sure?" she asked, lowering her lashes, the trick of a practiced flirt. She might be a little rusty after two years among the English, but at home she had been so accomplished, her own sister had wanted her put out of the clan for fear she would start a riot. She could make him love her in the time he would have to wait to hear his prince's reply. She could make herself his bride.

"Positive," he promised. His hand closed more tightly around hers as she moved to withdraw it, and suddenly a shiver passed through her to the marrow of her bones, a feeling wholly unexpected that had nothing to do with her plans. She looked up at him, startled, and for a moment she thought he must have felt it, too—a flash of shock passed through his eyes as well. "Say you'll stay, Lady Evelyn," he said, his voice turning soft. "Stay in my protection."

"Of course." She looked down without thinking to

where their hands were joined. The mark of a dragon was painted on his flesh ... but no. The dragon wasn't painted; it was embedded in the skin like a brand, not ugly like a scar but beautiful and strange. What Englishman would carry such a mark? Still without thinking, she touched the very tips of her fingers to the dragon's forked tongue and traced the curve of its neck along the back of his hand, a queer sense of recognition tingling along her spine, as if she had seen it before. He wore the dragon on his flesh, on his banner, even on the mirror where he admired his own face. And this would be her husband. She looked up into his eyes again. "If you wish it, we will stay."

"I do," he promised, unable for a moment to say anything else. Something had passed between them, some spark—he knew she had felt it, too. She touched the spirit's mark as if she knew it—she certainly wasn't afraid. A hundred lovely creatures had seen this mark, teased him about it, demanded to know how he had come to wear it. But none had ever touched it so, as if she already knew. But that was madness; she was flirting with him. They were both of them playing a game. "I would have it no other way," he said, pushing his foolish thoughts away. He wouldn't give her his castle, nor would he give up the princess. But he would have her, and in the end he would somehow help her, too. And that would have to be enough. "Thank you, my lady," he finished, kissing her hand again before he let her go.

"No, Lord Aiden. Thank you." She felt him shiver as he let her go, and she smiled. He wasn't a brute; he could be tamed. That was what the tingle she had felt was all about, desire and anticipation. He thought she was already his. And so she would be. "But you need not address me as 'my lady'; I have no formal title."

"Evelyn, then." Sir Alan was giving him a glare to freeze the blood, and the old woman and the servant girl looked so horrified, he couldn't help but smile. No doubt he and Evelyn would shock the household into swooning as a congregation before they were done—a most amusing thought. "And you must call me Aiden."

5

A letter of Sir Aiden Brinlaw to John, Prince of England

Hail and honor, great and terrible sovereign—

At last we have arrived. Matters at Glencairn are much as we had feared. The castle is a barn with pretty turrets; the garrison is lazy. The peasants I have seen so far are pathetic—my father wouldn't have them in his jail. As for the Scots, let me just say this—even their children are monsters. Three nasty little buggers belonging to the local laird attacked me before I even reached the castle. I thought I was going to have to hack off their little heads to make them leave me in peace.

But even with all that, I can put things in order here within the year. The defenses are sound, and a bit of discipline should bring the troops in line. The present marshal of the garrison seems to be capable enough and ready to obey me. In a few months Glencairn should be a proper English manor, ready to welcome you in comfort when Richard finally does return to turn you out of England. Of course, I will have to nearly kill myself with work and marry your horrid little sister in the bargain. But now that I am here, I think I know how you can make it up to me.

Dead Charles the Virtuous has an illegitimate son, and his mother, Evelyn, is the prettiest, sauciest wench a man exiled to the wilderness could ever hope to find. Not to put too fine a point upon it, Johnny, I want her. She is the sister-in-law of the aforementioned Laird Malcolm (making her auntie to the bloodthirsty dwarfs who attacked me, come to think of it). She and Charles were betrothed—an arrangement between their houses, I believe—and while our English comrade was too set upon his holy quest to actually marry her, he did find the time to bed her, producing Max, who looks to be no more than two years old, maybe less. He babbles nonsense, but he doesn't seem to walk yet, so take that as his age.

The point is, I have promised Evelyn that I would write to you on her behalf, explaining her plight and asking if anything can be done to secure an inheritance for the little bastard. Before you think I have been taken ill with a sudden attack of chivalry, let me say again: This girl is adorable. I realize her claim has no merit at all; I simply wish to tup her before I send her home. Is that so much to ask? I may even find her a husband if the whim should strike me—the marshal is in love with her already, and he has no wife that I've seen. But in the meantime, she will make me a fine diversion, assuming you approve. Really, Johnny, I consider it the least that you can do.

Your grateful servant,
Aiden

Aiden had fallen into bed half-dressed sometime after midnight, abandoning the scrolls and accounting books of Glencairn Castle on a table near the bed. He awoke to the sound of these crashing to the floor, along with a flagon of wine.

"Holy Christ," he grumbled, sitting up. "Robin, what did you do?" But his squire was nowhere to be seen. To all appearances, he was alone.

"Dere!" The small voice chimed up from the floor at the foot of the bed. "Lo!" Aiden peered over to find Evelyn's Max sitting in the very center of the chaos, the edge of the tablecloth still clutched in his chubby little fist, grinning as Aiden appeared. "Lo dere."

"Hello there to you, too," Aiden guessed, amused in spite of himself. "How did you escape?" From what he had seen, the women who cared for this creature were loathe to let him out of their arms, much less their sight, Evelyn included. He looked over at the chamber door and found it standing ajar. "Where is your mama?"

"Mamee," Max agreed. He watched Aiden get up and start gathering up the fallen papers with an approving eye. The wine flagon had been half-empty, mercifully, but it had still managed to soak one of the books and a goodly portion of the rug.

"Lovely," Aiden muttered, wadding up the tablecloth and tossing it away, then dragging the sopping rug out of the little one's reach. "Thanks, maggot." He sat down at the table and pulled out his writing things—if he was up, he might as well begin his letter to John.

"Tanks," Max nodded, still watching. Now using Aiden's chair as a ladder, he struggled to his feet.

"Very clever," Aiden said, sharpening a quill. "Shouldn't someone be looking for you?" He split the point and opened a bottle of ink, staining his fingertips in the process.

"Mamee dere bay-bay doe bye," Max explained with an expression so earnest, Aiden couldn't help but smile. "Dere!" Max crowed, smiling back.

"No, thank you," Aiden retorted, pulling out a fresh page of parchment to begin his letter. "I have been revered for many talents, but not one of them makes me a nursemaid."

"Dere doe pease!" the little one insisted, bouncing against the chair and jostling Aiden's arm, making his script go awry. "Pease!"

"Will you be still?" Aiden gave him his sternest look, and for a moment he looked wary—he even stopped bouncing. Then he reached for Aiden again, wordlessly pleading with his mother's wide, blue eyes. "What is it?" He scooped up the little creature, making him crow with delight. "Haven't you caused enough trouble already?" Aiden demanded, holding him up. "You ought to be ashamed." Max giggled, utterly unrepentant. "Maggot," Aiden repeated, setting the child on his lap. "Here, play with this." He took the leather cover from one of the cleaner-looking scrolls and handed it over, and Max promptly put it in his mouth. "Careful," Aiden muttered, shaking his head before going back to writing.

While Max was making friends with the new liege lord, Evelyn was turning the castle upside down looking for him. She had been rearranging the furniture in her new quarters, trying to make it all fit, when Margaret had come in to confess she had lost the baby somewhere on the second floor. "I only looked away for a moment," the old woman had insisted.

"Aye," Evelyn had answered grimly—if it hadn't been so irritating, she would have found it funny. "That's been happening rather often lately." Fairly certain the child wouldn't attempt the stairs on his own, she had confined her quest to the sleeping quarters, searching the room of every noble knight—every knight but one. "He wouldn't," she said softly, stopping at Lord Aiden's door.

But apparently he would. The door swung open with barely a touch, and there was Max, perched happily on Aiden's lap. "Ma-mee!" he cried as she came in, waving some sort of leather pouch like it might have been a banner.

"There you are," Aiden said, looking up. "We thought you'd be along."

"Did you, in faith?" she said, laughing to cover her

astonishment. In truth, she was flustered by more than Max's appearance. Yesterday, the Sassenach knight had looked like a picture from a book on chivalry, he was so perfect, every stitch in his costume perfectly rendered and every hair in place, and she had found him handsome. But now his hair was falling in his eyes; he hadn't shaved; and he was naked from the waist up. And to her shock, she found him beautiful. "And just what are you two doing?" she demanded, going to join them.

"We are writing the prince," Aiden answered. She looked very pretty in her morning gown with her hair pulled back in a kerchief; he heartily approved. "Would you care to see?"

"Your letter?" Max laid his head back against the man's chest, utterly relaxed, and she felt a strange ache in her throat. Maybe that was why he seemed so handsome, the way he held her child. The only man who had ever touched Max for more than a moment was his cousin, Gerald, and that only rarely, yet the child seemed perfectly at ease. "What does it say?"

"Don't you want to read it?" In truth, he was bluffing—he had barely begun to write, or he would never have offered. Most of what he had to communicate was not for her eyes by any means.

"I would if I could," she answered lightly, smiling. "But I can't." The palest flush of pink rose in her cheeks. "I don't know how to read."

"Oh." Not his most witty reply, but he was rather

flummoxed. His mother and sisters all read English, French, Latin, and even a bit of Italian, not to mention faery script. But now that he thought about it, he supposed they were hardly the norm for noble ladies. Indeed, most of the women he had known had probably been illiterate. He had just never thought to ask.

He looked so taken aback, Evelyn didn't know whether she should be embarrassed or amused. "You could read it to me," she suggested.

"I could," he agreed. He held the letter up and pretended to peruse it. "You aren't interested in the state of the armory, I suppose."

"No more than I already know about it," she said, sitting down on the bed. "Skip to the part about Max." The baby's eyes had started to drift closed, but at the sound of his name, he opened them and giggled. "Read me what you've written the prince about him."

"I haven't, really," Aiden answered truthfully. "I've written more about you." He scanned the page, pretending to read. "She seems a noble lady in every sense of the word," he said, spinning the words as he said them. "And though she has said nothing to disparage the memory of her beloved, I fear great advantage has been taken of her tender heart." He glanced up, pausing to give her a chance to respond. She smiled, raising a single, delicate eyebrow. "In short, I want to help her," he went on, his eyes turned back to the page, his mind casting about for inspiration. "I would not be my father's son if I were not moved by her plight," he decided, satisfied. "The rest is mostly about crops and such," he finished, looking up again.

"I see," Evelyn said, looking down to hide a knowing smile. The truth wasn't in him, her mother would have said—when he had read the bit about being his father's son, she had thought he would laugh outright. Heaven only knew what was really written on that page, but she was almost certain it was not what she had heard. *Ah, well,* she thought, *at least he cared enough to lie.* In truth, she was probably happier not knowing exactly how he had described her to his prince; the important thing was his mentioning her at all. "I don't know what to say, my lord," she said, getting up. "I'm thinking I should blush."

"Not at all," Aiden said, confused. He hadn't really expected her to leap into his arms, but she didn't seem moved in the slightest by his chivalrous gesture. Indeed, she almost seemed to be amused. "I wrote nothing but the truth," he insisted, getting up as well. Max grumbled, kicking his feet, and he turned the child around without thinking to let him rest his head on his shoulder.

"Then I do thank you," she said with a smile. Watching him hold Max was far more telling to her than any letter, even if what he'd read had been the truth. A liar he might be and a devil besides, but any man who cradled her child in his arms without even thinking about it was more than worthy of praise, so far as she was concerned. "So what will he say, do you think?"

"Who?" Aiden asked, still trying to work out the meaning of her smile.

"Prince John," she answered, laughing now as well. "Will he be as sympathetic as you are, now that you've explained my situation?"

"We can only hope." Max had started to squirm again, so he set him on the floor. "But you can never tell with John," he said, watching the little creature crawl under the table with a giggle of impish intent. "He prides himself on being unpredictable."

"You know him well, then?" she said, leaning back against the bed.

"Too well," Aiden laughed. "I've known him since he was four years old and I was six. Our fathers went to war together, and they took us with them."

"Good heavens," she laughed, genuinely shocked. "Your poor mother—didn't she miss you?"

"Not at all," he answered. "She was with us, too. She always went with my father on campaign. I was actually born in a tent."

"Oh, now you lie," she scoffed.

"It's true, I swear it," he insisted, leaning closer, one hand braced on the bedpost. "You could ask her yourself."

"Maybe I will someday." It was strange, she thought; with Charles, she had always seemed to struggle to find something to say, assuming she bothered to talk to him at all, and he had been the same. But she and Aiden seemed to just fall into talking every time they met, and when they talked, she seemed to forget everything else. He was standing far too close for propriety, she noticed now for example, and good lord, she was leaning on the bed! "So are you fond of the prince?" she asked, taking a prudent step away.

"*Fond* is a very strong word," he said with a twisted smile. She was blushing suddenly, and she had retreated from him a bit, but she wasn't running away. "His father spoiled him horribly, I'm afraid," he said, watching her and thinking how adorable she was.

"They say the same thing about me," she laughed, touching a scroll on the table. "Is he wicked, then?"

"More selfish than wicked, I think." He stood up and followed her around the table in a slow sort of courting dance. "But perhaps I am no judge."

"No, you wouldn't be, would you?" she said with a teasing smile. "Being so wicked yourself." He was standing too close to her again, but she didn't really want to back away. He was so handsome, looming over her, his bare chest so close she could have touched him by raising her hand. And he smelled so nice, not like some sweaty brute of a knight but clean and warm. Even his breath was pleasant, for all he had just woke up. "Are you selfish, too?"

"Horribly," he promised. "And you?"

"No," she demurred, shaking her head. "Just . . . well, maybe a little." She smiled the tiniest bit as her eyes darted from his, and he felt his own smile broaden. "And I'm definitely vain."

"You have cause to be." She looked up as if to speak again, then stopped, her blue eyes wide. "You're very pretty, Evie."

"So are you," she retorted. In truth, she was feeling rather dizzy. Many men had told her she was pretty; many men had looked on her with lust. But no one had ever smiled at her like he did or looked at her like this, not even her almost-husband. "So now I'm to be Evie?"

"Yes," he said, touching her cheek. He wanted desperately to kiss her, but the waiting was almost as delicious; the thrill of anticipation was making him feel weak. "Unless you don't like it."

"No," she said. "It's fine. My father called me Evie." His voice had turned so soft, so different from his usual tone. He wanted her . . . but wanting wouldn't be enough. In the end Charles had wanted her, too.

"The one who spoiled you." He leaned closer, touching her mouth, the pad of his thumb barely brushing her lower lip.

"Yes." She needed to back away from him; she was making this too easy. She wanted him to marry her, not tumble her into bed in the middle of the morning with her baby playing underneath the table. But it seemed so natural to wait for him, so right to want his kiss . . .

"Dere!" Max suddenly shouted, banging his heel on the floor. Looking up, they found Robin coming through the half-open doorway with Margaret the nursemaid close behind.

"Excuse me, my lord," the squire said, hiding a grin

with a bow. "This ancient dam would like to know if you are molesting her lady." The boy gave Evie a grin that fell just short of a leer. "I told her you would have bolted the door if that was your intention, but she didn't seem to believe me."

"That will do," Aiden said sternly, giving him a warning frown. "Lady Evelyn, may I present my squire, Robin, son of Raynard?"

"The sprout," she teased. "Or so I have heard him called." Margaret was gaping at her like she might have sprouted horns, she noticed with an inward sigh, but she refused to let herself care.

"Sprout?" Robin echoed, indignant. "Who would dare to say it?"

"You might be surprised," she answered, smiling at Aiden. "Come, Margaret. I found Max."

"Aye," the nurse said sourly. "I see that."

"Thank you for your help, my lord," she went on, picking up her child. "And for your kind words in your letter."

"Not at all," Aiden answered, smiling back. As annoyed as he was to be so rudely interrupted, he was delighted by her reaction. She didn't seem embarrassed in the least. Of course, that didn't mean Robin wasn't in for the thrashing of his life. "Will you dine with me, Evie?"

"And where else should I dine?" she said with a laugh. Settling Max against her shoulder, she made a pretty curtsy. "Yes, Aiden, I will dine with you." She gave Margaret a pointed glance, and the nursemaid turned away. "I will be most pleased."

"Bye!" Max called with a happy grin, waving as they left.

"A very pretty lady," Robin said with a sigh when they were gone.

"Yea, truly," Aiden answered, swatting him in the head. "Now shut up and fetch me my bath."

Margaret followed Evie back to their quarters, her stiff old joints making her look like a crab as she hurried to catch up. "If your mother could see you, what would she say?" she scolded as she closed the door behind them. "Playing the strumpet for some Sassenach—'tis glad I am she didn't live to see it."

"How kind of you to say so," Evelyn retorted, setting Max on the floor. "She's probably gladder than you."

"When you were betrothed and waiting to be married, 'twas all very well to do a bit of bundling, I reckoned," the old woman continued undeterred. "I didn't care to see you made a fool of, but at least it wasn't your fault."

"No one made a fool of me," Evelyn said angrily. "No one ever made me anything." Sleeping with Charles had been her decision; indeed, she had seduced him, hoping to convince him to stay in Scotland and marry her instead of running off on Crusade.

"But this one will make you a whore," Margaret continued, barely pausing to listen. "I nursed ye at my bosom, lassie, and I love ye like my own. I cried right along with your mother to see your da ruin you with all his foolish talk. But I never thought to see ye fall to such a state as this."

"My father never ruined anyone—Laird Malcolm should be so foolish," Evelyn began. Then she stopped. Why should she defend the laird of Clan McCairn to such a one as this? "Keep your peace, old woman," she ordered, turning away. "And keep your talk of nursing—I know a cow that does the same."

"Aye, but you cannot," the crone shot back, scuttling around the bed to make Evie face her again. "So don't you take that tone with me, lassie. I'm no English peasant to be ordered about like a dog. And you, my bonnie lassie, are no English lady, whatever that Brinlaw might call you, and you'd do well not to forget it." She said "Brinlaw" the way a sane person might say "Satan," and Evie couldn't help but smile. "Aye, go on and laugh at me; go on and smile," Margaret said scornfully. "Brinlaw smiles at you; he laughs to think how easily he'll have you in his bed."

"Dear God, will you shut up?" Evie groaned, turning away again. It was like her mother come back from the grave to taunt her, her mother and sister in one. "You'll frighten Max, keening like a loon."

"Better frightened than dead for your sins," Margaret declared in a voice that trembled with righteous condemnation. "He sickens at the slightest chill; even you have seen it, and all because his mother got him in shame. Would you see him in an infant's grave—?"

"I would see him in this castle!" Evie shouted, whirling around, her patience exhausted at last. "I would see him lord of Glencairn—"

"And how will you see that?" the nursemaid scoffed. "Pretty little fool, what do you think you will do? Do you think that English devil will give you his castle for a kiss?"

Evelyn made herself smile, refusing to lose her temper any more. *She is only an old woman,* she thought, chanting the words inside her head like a prayer to calm her. *An ignorant old fool who thinks the world drops off at the Lowlands and falls into the void.* "Something like that," she said archly as she sat down on the bed and put Max in her lap. "It's all right, lambie," she soothed, stroking his brow, and he snuggled against her shoulder.

"Fool," Margaret repeated. "Your da should burn in hell for making you so proud."

"Now I am too proud?" Evie said lightly. "A moment ago, I was shameful."

"You need not be either," the nurse said, softening her tone. "You have it in you to be a good lass, as good a woman as your sister. Give up this madness; go home to Laird Malcolm—"

"Laird Malcolm is the one who sent me here." She didn't shout this time, but her voice turned cold as February rain. *Help me, Malcolm,* she had begged, running to her sister's husband as a last resort. *Rebecca wants to send me to the Lowlands—she will make me marry this horrible old man and never see my home again.* The old man had been a widower with half a dozen brats, each of them as ugly as their da. But at least he had been a Scot.

Never fear, Little Sister, the clan's new laird had promised. *I will put this right.* The next thing she had known, she was living in a castle full of foreigners with a dying old man and a boy who didn't want her.

"Laird Malcolm sent you to be married," Margaret said. She touched the kerchief that covered Evie's hair. "He thought you would be happy—"

"No, he did not," Evie cut her off. "He thought *he* would be happy—he would have an alliance with the English to protect the clan. He thought Rebecca would be happy—she would have me out of her house. He never thought of me at all." She looked up at the old woman she had known all her life with the cold eyes of a stranger. "But it doesn't matter, Margaret," she promised. "I don't need Laird Malcolm. I can take care of my own happiness, mine and Max's, too."

"By playing up to a Sassenach who thinks of you no better than he might a pretty doll," Margaret said with tears in her eyes. "At least your Charles was born here at Glencairn. This man is a stranger. . . ." She touched Evelyn's cheek with fingers gnarled and cold. "I cannot watch you make yourself his whore."

"Then go home," Evie retorted, jerking away from her touch. She turned her face away from the pain in the old woman's eyes. Margaret was the last tie that held her to the clan, the last link to her home. If she left the castle, Evie would be alone with the English indeed. *But they like me*, she thought, steeling her resolve. *Some of them even love me.* She had come here a frightened, foreign lass who barely spoke their language, but somehow she had won their hearts and made them think she belonged. They didn't respect her, but they wanted her there, more than her sister had ever wanted her or ever could. *The old lord loved me, even if Charles did not*, she thought, remembering the way Charles's father had smiled as she sat by his deathbed, holding his withered old hand. She looked down at Max, now dozing peacefully against her breast. *Aiden will love me, too.*

"I will do it, lassie," Margaret warned. "I will leave you here."

Evelyn looked up at her and smiled. "So do it, then," she answered. "I don't care."

6

Aiden's day did not progress quite so well as it had begun. First he ordered Sir Alan to assemble the knights to make their oaths of fealty only to be told that half of them were out hunting and not expected home before dark. Then he went out to inspect the construction on the new kitchen only to have it start raining, a heavy downpour that drove everyone inside, including the builders. Then when the weather finally broke, he rode out to have a look at the village, and that was worst of all.

The single lane was a mud trough fit more for pigs than people after the rain, and most of the buildings grouped around the village green looked to be falling to ruin. The villagers turned to stare at him as he passed, but very few so much as nodded, and he noticed that nearly all of them were men.

"Where are the women?" he asked Sir Alan, riding at his side.

"What women?" the marshal joked. "What few there are work in the castle during the day. King Henry sent soldiers here, not housewives."

"And what about the Scots?" Aiden asked, meeting the gaze of a greasy-haired fellow in a leather tunic until he dropped his eyes to the earth and shambled away.

"The Scots marry the Scots," Sir Alan explained. "Laird Malcolm takes to Englishmen sniffing around his women about as well as you take to Scots burning your kitchens."

"Lovely," Aiden muttered.

"The records say the original settlement had some five hundred men with a dozen of them married," the marshal said as they pulled to a stop near the outer gates. Construction on the new soldiers' barracks was continuing briskly, at least—most of these men were his. "Now there are fewer than a hundred cottagers and crofters living in the village and no English at all outside the gates."

"Because they're afraid of the Scots," Aiden finished for him with a scowl.

"Partly, yes." The marshal nodded. "But it's more than that, I think. The English care no more for the Scots than the Scots care for the English. The peace has been kept for the last twenty years, but only by each group keeping its distance." He looked up as the sky began to drizzle again. "And we're the ones who suffer for it."

"So Laird Malcolm has no such problems?" Aiden asked.

"Nay, nothing like," the other knight said, half bitter

and half in awe. "His clan has the prettiest little village you ever saw in your life, neat little lanes and sturdy little houses and pretty little children loitering about." He gave his new lord a grim little smile. "Quite the barbarians compared to our English, wouldn't you say?"

"Indeed," Aiden muttered, turning his horse around. Men without families had very little interest in building permanent, flourishing homes. But perhaps he could change that, too. "Come on," he ordered, headed back toward the castle. "I have seen enough."

He walked back into his own great hall just as the sun was setting, feeling as gloomy as the weather. The knights were back from hunting, apparently, but none of them seemed glad to see him. In truth, they barely looked up, and they all looked as depressed as he felt. Dinner was being served by the cooks from the spits over the fire, but the only creatures that seemed to care were the dogs that snuffled under the tables, waiting for scraps to be dropped.

The room itself was enough to put him in a foul temper. The shutters had been fastened back and the few narrow windows cleaned on his orders, but the failing light they let in just made the barren hall look that much uglier. His father had in his life so far brought three castles back from the brink of ruin: his own ancestral keep at Brinlaw, his niece's inherited home of Bruel in the southern marshes, and Falconskeep, the home of his wife's faery line. Each of the three was different in design; each had been allowed to fall into varying degrees of disrepair before his father acquired it. Yet Aiden remembered each as a place of gracious comfort, a home worthy of Brinlaw's pride. "How did you manage it, Papa?" he mumbled to himself, reaching down to scratch the head of the wolfhound nuzzling his knee.

"Talking to the dogs again, my lord?" Robin teased as he came up the steps to meet him. "Let me know if he should answer." Before Aiden could give this a proper retort, the squire shook his head and went on. "Never mind—I have come to fetch you for dinner."

"Fetch me?" He looked around at the men digging into their trenchers with energy if little joy. "Aren't I here?"

"Not here." Robin grinned. "Lady Evelyn has asked that you dine with her in the solar."

"The solar?" Aiden echoed, his spirits beginning to rise. His manor might be horrible; his peasants might be disgusting; his hall might be a cave. But Evelyn was lovely, and soon she would be with him. "Thank God," he muttered, following his squire up the stairs to the gallery and through the solar door. "But why are we dining up here?"

Then he stopped, stunned silent. His solar had been transformed. The rushes had been taken up completely and replaced by a thick carpet that covered most of the floor. The shutters had been fastened back here as in the hall, but here, tall white candles had been set on each windowsill so their light reflected back into the room from the thick, green, mullioned windows. The table, formerly shoved haphazardly toward the hearth, had been centered near the door and covered with a green muslin cloth with edges stitched in gold. The side benches were gone, and a second chair was set cozily close to his own at the head of the table. More candles stood on the table in polished brass holders, and another pair of chairs had been set before the hearth. Every speck of dust and cobweb had been swept from the walls and corners, and the beams and mantel had been polished to a dark, rich glow. Hanging over the mantelpiece was his own smaller banner, the dragon of Brinlaw.

"This is why," Robin answered, grinning from ear to ear. "Doesn't it look nice?"

He turned back to his squire, his eyes still wide with shock. "Did you do this?"

"No, my lord, not a bit. I was just as surprised as you," he answered. "Lady Evelyn did it. She cooked your dinner, too. So I'm hoping you're not very hungry, for I mean to have the scraps."

"Evelyn?" Aiden felt like an idiot, prattling questions, but he couldn't believe his eyes. The room had been barely inhabitable when he'd left it; now it was as cozy and inviting as any he'd ever seen. Yet all that had been added were a few bits of fabric and some candles. "How did she do it?"

"With great energy, my lord," Robin joked. "She's quite persuasive, by the way—she had three of your best knights in here moving the furniture around. I thought I ought to warn you." He lifted the lid from one of the pots on the hearth, and a savory aroma of meat and herbs filled the room, making Aiden's stomach growl as if he were suddenly starving.

Aiden couldn't seem to stop staring at everything around him. "Where is Evelyn now?"

"I am here, my lord." Turning, he found her standing in the doorway, wearing a velvet gown as stylish as any in London and the tempting smile that had charmed him the very first moment he saw her. Every inch of her was polished to perfection, from the gloss of her hair to the cut of her sleeves. Like the solar, she was everything he could have wished. "Will you forgive my being late?"

"Of course." He took her hand and raised it to his lips. "I will forgive you anything."

She smiled. "Let's hope it doesn't come to that." He leaned in to kiss her lips as well, but she took a sidestep back, slipping her hand from his. "But will you not sit down, my lord?" she urged. "Your dinner is prepared."

"I see that," he said with a smile. "Everything is lovely."

"I'm so glad you think so." In truth, she had worked herself ragged all afternoon, preparing the field for play, as it were, giving herself the advantage. She had been a natural flirt since infancy and was well accustomed to winning her own way with men with no better weapon than her own pretty self. But Aiden apparently knew the rules of the game every bit as well as she did and played it every bit as well. That morning's skirmish had not gone at all as she would have predicted—if Robin and Margaret had not come in when they had, he might well have won the prize in only the second round. Obviously, she would have to make a bit more of an effort. The stakes were far too high for her to lose. Aiden played only for a lover's tumble; she was playing for her life. "I heard your day didn't quite turn out as you had hoped," she said, joining him now at the table.

"No," Aiden agreed with a grimace as Robin served the roast. "But we were talking about you, a far more pleasant subject." He looked at her and smiled. "You look beautiful, Evie."

"Why, thank you, Aiden," she answered with a ladylike nod. "How kind of you to notice." In truth, putting the solar to rights had left her with very little time to spend on herself, but she thought she had used it well. She had brushed her hair with a fine-toothed comb until every strand was smooth and gleaming, then scrubbed her face until it glowed. Her hands were scrubbed as well, the nails rubbed with soap and lamb's wool to whiten them and the palms polished with clean, white sand to make them soft. After much consideration, she had put on her very best gown, velvet in so dark a shade of green it looked black until she moved into the light. The sleeves were lined in silk of palest gold that showed where they belled at the bottom, and the bodice was trimmed in lace with gold corded lacing down the front to cinch it tight across her breasts. It was not her most becoming gown, but it was definitely the richest. She had worn it only once before, on the day she was betrothed. But she wouldn't think about that. "I had meant to serve you myself, but your Robin says he must do it," she said, giving the squire a teasing smile as he filled her trencher. "What a ridiculous custom."

"Why, Evie, I am shocked," Aiden answered. "You question the sacred rites of chivalry?"

"I question any system that puts a healthy, able boy like this one to playing serving maid when there are crops to be harvested and larders to be filled," she retorted, and Robin snickered. "Did you do the same when you were his age?"

"I had it much, much worse." Aiden laughed. "I was squire to King Henry." The dinner was by far the best he had eaten since leaving the royal court, lamb roast steeped in milk with herbs and some sort of green salad cooked just until it wilted, and fresh, wheaten bread instead of the Scottish oatcake he had already come to dread. "Not only did I have to serve him at table, I had to bring him wine and wafers in the middle of the night whenever his mistresses got hungry."

"And Robin does not?" she teased. "Do your mistresses not like wafers?"

"Not a one of them," he retorted. "I make certain of it—it's the very first thing I ask." He took a sip of wine.

"So tell me, Evie," he said, mock-serious. "Do you care for wafers?"

"I love them," she said, feigning-solemn as well. "I eat them by the platterful. I never get enough."

"Oh, dear," Aiden said. "Alas for your sleeping, Robin."

"Have no worries, Robin," she amended. "I'm no one's idea of a mistress."

"Forgive me, lady, but you are most sorely mistaken," Aiden laughed. "You are every man's idea of a mistress."

"Am I, in faith?" she said lightly, but he detected a glint of steel behind her wide, blue eyes. "Very well, then, I'll say this. No man is my idea of ruin." She bit into a morsel of meat, catching the juice at the corner of her mouth with the tip of one delicate finger. All his life, he had heard the Scots were barbarians, but she had the manners of a princess . . . but he would not think of princesses tonight. "I hope you aren't disappointed."

"Devastated," he answered with his devil's grin. She found herself fascinated, watching him eat. He ate heartily of every dish, even the greens, like a man on the brink of starvation, but his hands never spilled so much as a drop on the tablecloth or let so much as a crumb fall into his lap. A royal squire, indeed . . . a king should have such manners. "But love does not always mean ruin, does it?" he said, refilling her cup.

"Does it not?" she retorted. "I must confess, this

whole men's business of love confuses me. Men speak of love, but they mean something else very different." She raised the cup to her lips, her eyes teasing over the rim. "You forget, Aiden, I am not some blushing maiden. I already have a son."

"So you have no love for love?" he asked, intrigued.

"I have no love for what you're calling love." She took a fig from the bowl Robin had set on the table. "Men think tupping is the grandest thing since Christ's salvation, so they come up with all manner of grand reasons why they should have it," she said, taking a bite. "That is what you call love." She wiped the juice from the corner of her mouth. "But believe me, Aiden, once a woman has been tumbled, she knows it isn't so much."

Aiden just stared at her, barely crediting his ears. She couldn't really be saying the words he had heard, nibbling a fig like Eve in the Garden of Eden. No woman so lovely could be so plainspoken, too; that would be too much to ask. "Evie, you are a perfect wonder," he said at last, taking a fig of his own. "And Charles, if I may say so, must have been a perfect fool." He took a bite, the sweetness a poor substitute for the kiss he wanted instead. "I pray you, don't judge all men by his model," he finished. "I promise you, tupping can be just as grand for a woman as it is for men."

"And you would know, I suppose," she retorted, blushing a bit. In truth, she had never intended to say so much. She had a sharp tongue, she would have to confess, but she usually maintained a certain level of decorum. But something about Aiden seemed to bring out the worst in her. "We should talk about something else."

"Nay, I want this settled," Aiden persisted with a grin. "I have a personal interest. Do you really mean to never 'be tumbled,' as you call it, ever again?"

He was teasing her now, the prideful swine. "Oh, I don't know," she said airily, wiping her fingers on her napkin. "If I should ever marry, I might find out you're right. Some fine, strapping Scotsman could sweep me off my feet and make me like it." She took a sip from her cup. "I've even seen a few who might be able to do it, now that I think about it," she mused. "I do like the look of a fine pair of knees under a well-pleated kilt." She looked up as Robin doubled over with a sudden hacking cough. "Poor boy, are you all right?" she said, feigning concern. "Here, have a sip of wine."

"Yes, Robin," Aiden said, his tone fairly dripping with venom. "Do get a hold of yourself."

"Sorry, my lord," the squire sputtered, trying not to snicker. "I must be catching a chill."

"Yes, you seem to be catching something," Aiden said. "Or you will."

"Thank you, my lady," the boy said soberly, handing back Evie's cup.

"Yes, Evie, thank you," Aiden said, pushing his chair back from the table. "Dinner was delicious." Robin hastened to clear away the trenchers. "Did you really cook it yourself?"

"Of course," she said with a smile. He seemed glad enough to change the subject now, she noticed. "My mother taught me how to cook when I was just a child. It's one of my greatest gifts."

"Then you are twice as selfish as I thought," Aiden said, standing and offering her his hand.

"I beg your pardon?" She laughed as she took it.

"How is it my knights are starving and my castle is a disgrace?" he said, leading her to a chair by the hearth as Robin tidied up. "Until tonight, I assumed you were too beautiful to trouble yourself with keeping house, but now I know the truth." He sat down at her feet, the perfect courtly lover. "So I think you must be lazy."

"I must protest, my lord," she laughed. In truth, she was rather embarrassed, but not because of her housekeeping. No man she had ever known would have sat at the feet of a woman for all the gold in Rome. Yet Aiden, the richest, most highborn nobleman she had ever met, seemed not to mind it a bit. "What have I to do with your knights or your castle, either?"

"You are their chatelaine, are you not?" He glanced over at Robin, who nodded, making his escape. "You are responsible for their comfort—"

"No, Aiden, I am not," she stopped him with a smile. "Your knights are English; your servants are English. I am a Scot. They do what I ask of them as a favor to me, not because I have any right or authority to ask it." He looked so shocked, she couldn't help but laugh. "It's true; I swear it," she said. "I've always thought Glencairn was a disgrace. When I first came here, I couldn't believe people really lived in such a place."

"But you weren't allowed to fix it." He turned toward her, rising to his knees. "But you could. If I were to give you the power, you could put it right."

"Of course," she said, smiling but confused. Suddenly he looked as young as Robin, his eyes avid with hope. "It could be beautiful."

"Yes," he nodded, clasping her hand in his. "We will make it beautiful." He felt as if a heavy stone had been lifted from his heart. He didn't know how to make Glencairn a home, but Evelyn obviously did—the solar was proof enough. While he rebuilt the structure and whipped the garrison into shape, she would put her womanly gifts to work on the household. She wasn't just beautiful; she could be useful as well. "Come here," he said, struck with a sudden inspiration. "I want to show you something."

"Come where?" she protested, even more confused. He seemed to be tugging her down to the floor. "Aiden, what are you doing?"

"You will have to read the accounts," he explained, drawing her down beside him with no regard whatever for her gown. "Or be able to sign your name, at least— Robin can be your clerk." He scraped a spadeful of cold ashes over the clean-swept hearth. "Watch this." With one finger, he traced the letters of her name in the ashes. "There."

"There what?" she laughed, half-certain he had lost

his mind. He was sitting so close beside her, she could feel his warmth through their clothes and his breath against her cheek. But he was concentrating on a scribble in a pile of ashes.

"That is you," he explained. "Evelyn." The quizzical look on her face was priceless—that darling little eyebrow was quirked up halfway to her temple. "Here," he said, brushing the ashes smooth. "Let me show you." He shaped her hand into a finger-quill and guided it over the ashes, forming the letters again.

"Aiden, really . . ." She felt herself relaxing in spite of herself as she found the rhythm of it, fascinated by the way the letters formed beneath her hand. He was crazy, a grown man playing in the dirt and expecting her to play with him, but it was sweet, too, and completely unexpected. Nothing she had seen in him before could have prepared her for his suddenly deciding she needed to know how to write. *A pretty doll*, Margaret had called her, a toy to him. But why should a toy write its name? "How is it?" she asked, turning to him as they stopped.

"It's good," he promised, turning to face her as well, but suddenly he could barely see the letters. Suddenly he noticed she was pressed against his side, and her mouth was so close to his, he could almost taste her.

"No, it's not," she snickered, looking down at what they had written. "Look, it's all crooked . . ." Suddenly he touched her chin, turned her face back up to his. Before she could react, he had kissed her, deep and full on the lips. She gasped, instinctively pulling away, and his arm came up around her waist, folding her closer. But his kiss turned softer, backing away, a half dozen little kisses feeding on her mouth, and she felt herself begin to melt, her body curving toward him as her lips began to part. His hand was on her face, his palm cradling her throat as he deepened the kiss again, his tongue invading her mouth. *Tupping can be grand for a woman, too, Evie,* he had promised. For the first time in her life, she could imagine how that could be true. The way he touched her, the tender way he held her close; he would make love to her slowly, savoring her the way he savored food and wine. But she was not a dinner; she was a woman, the mother of a child.

She turned her face away, freeing her mouth, trying to think clearly, and his kiss moved to her throat, warm and wet against her throbbing pulse. "Oh, no," she said huskily, making herself laugh as if she thought him very silly. "I don't think so, Aiden." She couldn't trust her body, no matter how many exciting new thrills he might teach it to feel. Only her mind could win the game.

"What?" She was pushing him away. "Evie, what are you doing?"

"Going to bed," she answered, climbing to her feet. In truth, her knees felt weak as water, but she wouldn't let him see her stumble. "No man's mistress, remember?"

"Oh, come, you must be joking," he protested, unable

WICKED CHARMS 97

to help himself. Women had refused him once or twice before in his life, but never at such a moment. He'd won her already; he had felt her melt into his arms. She couldn't really mean to just walk out. "Evelyn—"

"You see?" she interrupted. "This is exactly what I was talking about—and there you were, trying to make me think I was wrong." She wiped her face with a napkin, brushing off the soot as if she were horribly annoyed, but he noticed her hands were shaking, and her tone was more peevish than genuinely angry. "I just wish you could see how ridiculous you look."

"I am ridiculous," he agreed, rising to his knees in a mockery of desperate love. "I am dying for you, Evie—how can you be so cruel?"

"Good common sense," she retorted. He was back to teasing her, she noticed, turning his failed seduction into another arrogant jest. But there was no mistaking the shadow of desire she could still glimpse through his tunic. "Thank you for the lesson, my lord, but tell me this. Did your English mistresses like it when you rolled them around on the floor?"

"After they gave it a chance," he joked, laughing in spite of himself. She started out, and he went after her, still on his knees. "Evie, wait, I beg you!" he protested elaborately.

"You ought to beg," she scolded, but a smile was twisting her mouth. "Good night, my noble lord." She planted a motherly kiss on the top of his head. "I'll see you in the morning." Before he could protest further, she had swept out the door in a swirl of velvet skirts.

"Holy Christ," he muttered, falling back on the carpet as if he were in agony but smiling all the while. "Just you wait, my lady." He smiled more wickedly still, remembering the way her lips had parted for his. "Just you wait."

7

A letter from Malcolm, Laird of the Clan McCairn, to Aiden of Glencairn Castle

Best regards and welcome,

It was with deepest sadness that I heard tell of the passing of Charles of Glencairn. His father was ever a friend and an ally, and we looked forward to the day when Charles himself would have been our kinsman. But the Lord will take his own unto His bosom, and in His own good time. I have no doubt the English prince did well in sending you in his place, and I will be glad to welcome you as neighbor.

*All that remains to be settled between us is the matter of my wife's younger sister, Evelyn. As she has no doubt told you long ere this, she was meant to marry Charles upon his return, and she **has** borne him a son, a fact which, I must confess, has caused my wife much grief. While we all of us hold Evelyn most dear and grieve with her in the loss of her intended, the good of the clan must be considered before the interests of my own, though they may be much* *loved. To that end, I would ask that you convey to Evelyn our condolence and tell her this. If she would wish to return to the home of her virginity, she will be most welcome. But I can by no means allow her to bring this bastard child into the clan or my house. He is an Englishman, conceived in lust, and of your Norman nobility if he has any name at all, not the Clan McCairn. As his poor mother is my kinswoman and my charge and you are presently lord of the castle that bore him, I say he is yours to do with as you will.*

Perhaps you think me harsh to speak of taking a babe from his mother, or being yourself a bachelor, find it unjust that I should place the responsibility for this child on your shoulders. In either event, I have spoken to the holy father in charge of the Convent of Our Lady in Edinburgh, and for a small consideration (to which I would be happy to contribute), he will take the child or Evelyn or both. If that is your preference, you need but send me word by this messenger where you would wish to meet to discuss the particular details.

Malcolm, Laird McCairn

Aiden was up the next morning at dawn, and the knights commenced their oaths of fealty directly after breakfast. But rather than the grand and solemn ceremony a new lord from London might be expected to require, the matter was settled casually as a kind of formality among friends. If Aiden had learned nothing else at the knee of King Henry, he knew the value of assuming authority over enforcing it. If he acted as if it were a foregone conclusion that he was in charge and these oaths were no more than a trifle, the knights would automatically believe it and never think to question him.

He sat on the dais in the great hall in the dragon-carved chair his father had been kind enough to lend him for just such occasions, and he looked very grand in his best scarlet robe over shining chain mail armor. But rather than glaring down like Solomon, he kept one foot propped on a side stool, the list of knights held in one hand and a cup of wine held in the other. As each man came forward to swear his loyalty, he would ask him a question or make a joke, putting him at ease, until every man felt that life at Glencairn must be on the mend.

Evelyn was helping tremendously with this impression, whether she realized it or not. Commanding a full battalion of housemaids, she had taken him at his word and attacked the gloomy hall with vigor as soon as the breakfast tables were cleared. Now as the oaths were being given, the women of the castle were sweeping the walls and washing the windows and making their own sly jibes about Sir This or young Master That, Esquire, much to the men's delight. Evelyn herself was standing at the top of a ladder, taking down a tattered velvet drape and looking impossibly beautiful, Aiden thought as he heard the stumbling oath of a very young and very nervous squire.

"And I do swear myself inconstant—I mean, most constant," the squire stammered.

"You confuse me, Oliver," Aiden teased him, looking at the boy instead of Evelyn at last. "Let's end the suspense—do you mean to stab me in my sleep?"

"No, my lord!" Oliver cried, appalled, and Evie stifled a laugh behind the back of her hand.

"Then I shall think myself well served," Aiden said as the rest of the knights chuckled and Oliver's knightly master, Sir Brutus, gave him a clap on the back. "I thank you."

In the midst of Oliver's congratulations, the great outer doors swung open, and a man Aiden didn't recognize came in, a Scotsman in the tartan of the Clan McCairn.

"Forgive the intrusion, my lord," he called with perfect courtesy, falling to one knee as everyone turned to look. "I bring ye greetings from the laird of Clan McCairn." He glanced around the room, obviously looking for someone, then stopped when he found Evie coming down her ladder. "May I read his letter?"

"The question is, can you, Ralph?" Evelyn said, making the knights laugh again and covering her own nervousness. She knew this messenger well enough—he had made a fool of himself for one whole spring and summer, begging her to marry him. If Malcolm had sent him to the castle with a message, the news could not be to her good. "When did you learn to read?"

"I am glad to hear from your lord, sir," Aiden said

with a somewhat less mocking smile as he got up from his chair. "But I can read his letter myself."

"Laird Malcolm wants it read aloud," the Scotsman answered, his eyes still fixed on Evelyn. "If ye don't mind, my lord."

"Of course not," Aiden said easily, coming down the steps. "By all means, Ralph, read away."

"Thank ye, my lord." He got up and opened his scroll. " 'Best regards and welcome . . .' "

Evelyn listened as Malcolm's words were read, her blush burning hotter and hotter. She was welcome in her father's house, if she abandoned her child. Or she could go to a convent—he would even split the cost, if the English lord should press him for it. She looked over at Aiden and found him looking back, a strange expression on his face, a sadness and softness that didn't seem to fit. He felt sorry for her . . .

" '. . . send me word by this messenger where you would wish to meet to discuss the particular details,' " Ralph finished, rolling up the scroll. Evelyn had moved closer as he read until now she was standing directly before him, a look of such fury on her face, the man went pale as milk.

"Tell Malcolm I do thank him for his kindness," she said bitterly, her blue eyes flashing fire. "Then tell him he may shove it up his arse." Taking a deep, heady breath, she spat hard in his face. "And take that kiss to my sister." Turning from him, she found Margaret staring at her in horror, Max clasped in her arms. "Go with him," she ordered the old woman. "Help him remember what I said." Avoiding the eyes of the English, all of them gaping in shock, she stormed out of the hall.

Aiden watched her go, a slow smile twisting his mouth. "My lord?" the Scotsman said, wiping his face with all the dignity he could muster. "What is your reply?"

Aiden looked at him with the cold eyes of the dragon. "Deliver Lady Evelyn's message instead." He looked over at one of the kitchen maids—Molly, he thought he'd heard someone call her. The poor child looked ready to cry, and he gave her a lecherous wink. "And tell your laird I will call on him myself to discuss the particular details."

He followed Evie out of the hall, reaching the steps just as she was starting across the courtyard. Four of the kitchen builders were staggering toward her in the other direction, carrying a huge iron cauldron full of mortar on a bracing of thick wooden beams. Evelyn tried to dodge around them, but these chivalrous souls kept trying to step aside, putting themselves directly in her path no matter which way she turned. Aiden started down the steps to help just as she let out a roar like nothing he had ever heard in his life, too throaty to be called a shriek but undeniably feminine. As he watched in shock, the cauldron cracked in two and fell from its braces, spilling mortar in a turgid flood over the feet of the men and onto the cobblestone yard. Gooseflesh prickled on his skin as Evie continued on, barely stopping to look at what she had done, if indeed she had done it. *Faery speak*, Aiden thought, amazed. *That was faery speak.* She disappeared through an archway, and he broke into a run.

Evelyn barely realized the cauldron had broken, her mind was in such a whirl. She pushed her way past the shocked and speechless masons and hurried through the archway, headed for the only place in the castle she had ever been able to be alone for more than a moment. The tiny garden huddled at the foot of the same tower in which she slept, a tiny sanctuary walled in on every side. Collapsing on a mossy bench, she tried to think clearly about what Malcolm had written, to get past her fury long enough to make a plan.

She had never meant to go back home, but she had never once imagined she could not. That was her father's house, damn Malcolm to hell, as much her home as Rebecca's. Malcolm might be laird now, but she was still a highborn member of the clan, and so was her son, no matter how she might have gotten him. But she ought not to curse only Malcolm; that letter had Rebecca's bile all over it. *My wife is very much grieved*, he had written, or words to that effect.

"Bitch!" she shouted, clenching her hands into fists. She wanted to hit something—or better yet, someone—just as hard as she could, over and over until they felt just as bad as she did. "Jealous, bloodless, sanctimonious cow—"

"Well spoken," Aiden interrupted with a grin as he

came through the arch. "But who are we talking about?"

"You?" she demanded, embarrassed now as well as furious. "What do you want?" In truth, she ought to be falling all over herself to be nice to him. Her situation was even more precarious now than it had been before, and he was her only hope. She couldn't go home without Max, whatever Rebecca might think, and she couldn't even imagine herself in a convent. So she ought to be working up some pretty maiden's tears, flinging herself on his mercy or at least his knightly bosom, and agreeing to whatever he might ask in return for his protection. But she couldn't make herself do it, not with Aiden. She couldn't let him think she was a weepy, worthless ninny who answered such an insult with tears and threw away her pride for the sake of her skin. Her pride might be as foolish and misplaced as Margaret said it was, but it was hers, and she wouldn't give it up.

"Nothing," he promised, his hands up in surrender. "I was just concerned." *What did you just do, Evie?* he wanted to ask her. *That cauldron was solid iron—how did you know the word to break it?* But she would probably look at him as if she thought him mad, particularly when she had so many more immediate problems to work out. No doubt the thing was old and rusted through already, needing no more magic than another heavy load to make it break. "I was afraid you might be out here killing someone," he teased her instead.

"I wish I were," she grumbled. "No, I don't, I suppose. I just . . ." She got up from the bench, unable to say just what she meant. A trio of rosebushes languished at her feet, obviously gasping their last, and she looked down on them in despair. She had planted them herself when she had first come to Glencairn, trying to re-create a tiny piece of home. But they were failing, too, just like everything else she touched. "Go ahead, Aiden," she said, kneeling down to look at them more closely. "Laugh at me; I don't care." The bottom leaves were covered in a sickly sheen of moldy-looking white. "I'm hilarious."

"Sometimes," Aiden admitted, leaning on a tree. "But not today."

She looked up, surprised, but he was barely smiling, neither mocking her nor particularly sympathetic. The look of pity that had so horrified her in the hall was gone. "Thanks," she mumbled, turning back to the roses. "By the way, I'm not going back home and abandoning Max to your mercy." One bush was so far gone, it seemed cruel to even try to save it. "Just in case you were wondering," she said grimly, tugging it out of the ground.

"You're damned right you are not," he answered. "What would I do with a baby?" In truth, the laird's letter had shocked him more than he would have cared to admit. The very idea that Evelyn's family could turn her away was more than he could work out. In his own family, sinners were invariably forgiven—he was proof enough of that. Mark was perfect, of course, and Mary's only fault was a tendency to be flighty. But he could be a parent's nightmare, and his older sister, Malinda, had put his exploits to shame, seducing a godless brigand with her magic just to prove she could and plotting treason with Queen Eleanor and nearly getting herself killed. But none of them had ever once considered abandoning her to her fate; they had all moved heaven and earth to save her, even Aiden, then only six years old. But Evelyn's people were apparently ready to write her off as a loss and her son with her.

"What did you do to them, Evie?" he asked, barely aware he had spoken aloud.

"Not them so much," she answered, engrossed in plucking away the damaged leaves from the two remaining bushes. "Just her—my older sister, Rebecca." She sat back on her heels to examine her handiwork, but the roses didn't look much better. The bottom vines looked painfully vulnerable without their leaves, and the single blossom left on one bush was already drooping over though barely out of bud. "She hates me. She always has."

The matter-of-fact way she said it touched him more deeply than any tears could have. She didn't even fight it anymore; she just accepted it as fact. "You must have been a brat," he teased, making his tone sound light.

"I was," she admitted with a wry smile. "And our father loved me better because I was prettier. I told you I was spoiled."

"I could have guessed it even if you hadn't," he said.

"You're a fine one to talk," she retorted, standing up. Once again, she had somehow fallen into talking with him as if it was the most natural thing in the world. "He never made me do anything I didn't want to do, and Rebecca hated it. It was unfair, I suppose." She brushed the dirt from her skirt. "Then when Da died, she said she had to get rid of me to keep peace in the house."

"Oh, dear," he said, raising an eyebrow. "Were you loud as well as lazy?"

"I wouldn't pick a husband," she explained, then caught sight of his expression. "Oh, never mind—you'll just mock me for it if I tell you, and tell me how heartless I am."

"You are heartless," he teased, wiping a smudge of mud from her cheek with the lightest touch of his thumb, unable to resist, and she allowed it, barely frowning. "But I won't mock you, I promise."

"Of course you won't," she said sarcastically, but she smiled a little, too. "I didn't know who would be better—for a husband, I mean." She walked away from him to one of the birch trees, the white moss on its bark similar enough to the roses' blight to cause concern. "Rebecca and Malcolm were already married, and Mother and Da were gone." She picked a piece of white and rubbed it between her fingers—definitely moss. At least her curse hadn't spread to the trees, she thought with a morbid inward sigh. "All these boys kept asking me—Ralph for one example. They kept telling me they loved me, but I didn't believe it. I didn't love them. I didn't even know them, really." She slowly realized she had never said these things aloud before; indeed, she had barely thought them in words. But now they just seemed to come falling out of her mouth. "So I couldn't decide which one I should choose." She looked over at him and smiled. "Rebecca said I was just conceited, that I played them off one another for the sake of my vanity, and I suppose I did, a little."

"How wicked," he teased, joining her.

"It was," she admitted. "But it was fun, watching them all make such fools of themselves, all these big, strong men who ought to have known better. But I didn't mean to hurt any of them or Rebecca and Malcolm, either." She looked up at him from underneath her lashes, flirtatious and shy at the same time. "So do you think I'm horrible?"

"Not a bit," he promised, bracing a hand on the tree trunk. "But I'm no judge." She ducked under his arm, moving away, and he grinned. "So with half the clan proposing, how did you end up betrothed to English Charles?" he asked.

"That was Malcolm's doing," she said. "Rebecca had decided it was time she took matters into her own hands, since I wouldn't choose, and my suitors kept fighting and creating a ruckus in the clan, and Malcolm didn't seem to care." She tried to make it all sound like a joke, something funny that had happened so long ago she could laugh about it. But a hurt and bitter edge still crept into her tone. "She made a contract with a widower from the Lowlands, a cousin of our mother's. He was twice my age with a passel of brats who needed looking after, and Rebecca thought I would be just the lass to do it."

"How kind of her to look after your interests," he said sardonically.

"She's always been thoughtful that way," Evie agreed. "She told me, and I was scared to death. I didn't know what to do. So I went to Malcolm." She leaned against another tree again, her mind returning for the thousandth time to that day and all the other things she might have done, the better choices she might have made. "He told me not to worry," she said softly, gazing off into space. "He and the old Lord Glencairn had been working out a new treaty for months, ever since Da had died, and he offered me as wife to Charles to seal the deal." She realized he had moved closer again, but this time she didn't move. "And so I came to Glencairn," she finished, smiling up into his eyes.

"Was that what you wanted?" Everything about her story made him angry, he realized, but it shouldn't have done. In truth, her situation was hardly unusual; marriages were made for noble maidens without their consent all the time. He didn't really think Katherine was mad with joy to be betrothed to him, did he? But for Evie, it just seemed wrong.

"I didn't mind it," she lied, looking away. The pity

she despised from him had crept back into his eyes; she had already confided too much. "Rebecca was furious, not just because Malcolm broke the contract she had made, but because Charles was English." She looked back at the tower rising over them and smiled. "And I think it made her angry to think of me living in a castle," she admitted. "It was as if I was getting over her again, her little sister forgetting her place. She was married to the laird; I was supposed to marry one of his henchmen, not an English noble."

"Is that why Malcolm won't let you come home with Max?" Aiden asked, his voice turning gentle without his noticing.

"Very like," she nodded. "Malcolm has three sons of his own to think of, and their place in the clan is not so sure that he's wanting competition." She took a step away, her mind racing forward. She had never thought of it before; she had been so busy worrying about Glencairn, but Max had as clear a claim to the title of laird as any of his cousins. Malcolm hadn't been born of their clan; his title came from his marriage to Rebecca and the fact that he was recognized as heir by their father before his death. But succession to his son was far from assured. "And it's no use lying, Aiden," she said, turning back to him. "This English castle is a scary sight to us. Our people still remember King Henry's wrath too well."

"So Max could split the difference," Aiden said. "If Charles had lived, Max could have grown up to be both the English lord and the laird of the clan." She was smart, he suddenly realized with a prickle of shock, smart and sad and strong. He had known she was clever from the first moment they met, a practiced flirt with wit as well as beauty. But underneath the flirt was someone else, a mind and heart as complicated as his own with ambitions much like his. He found himself remembering the cauldron in the courtyard, the oath she had shouted that had sounded so much like faery speak. Could it really have been?

"But Charles did not live," she answered with a weary smile, interrupting his thoughts. "And Malcolm won't even let Max in his house, baby that he is."

"So what then?" he asked, adopting his customary grin. "Do you want to go to the convent? It would be a terrible waste."

"And a sacrilege, too, no doubt," she retorted. "No, Aiden, I do not want to go into a convent. I don't want to go back to the clan." Her eyes met his, a promise as much as a plea. *Give me what I want*, they seemed to say. *I swear you won't regret it.* "If you will allow it, Max and I will stay here."

"Allow it?" He leaned down and kissed her softly on the cheek, a gesture to answer her eyes. "I will have it no other way."

"Mistress Evelyn?" a girlish voice was calling from the courtyard. "My lady?" Molly appeared at the arch, stopping short when she saw Aiden and blushing as red as a berry. "I'm sorry to come in on you so . . . but it's Margaret," she explained. "She's done just what you told her to and gone off with that Scotsman, and now Max is crying, and we don't know what to do." She glanced at Aiden again, still standing far too close to Evie for propriety, and she smiled, shy but obviously fascinated. "But we could figure it out, I suppose," she finished, looking at Evelyn instead.

"Never mind, Molly," Evelyn said sternly, a daunting look in her eye that sobered the girl at once as she moved toward her. "I'll come right now." She stopped and turned back to Aiden. "Thank you, my lord," she said, making a curtsy.

"Not at all, my lady," he answered, bowing to her in return.

8

Aiden still had much to do at his own manor. The knights who had sworn themselves his were still a lazy, insular lot who'd spent their years of glory halfheartedly defending a castle no raider in his right mind would attack in the middle of a Scottish wilderness. But he had a visit to make before he could begin.

The Scottish village was much as Sir Alan had described it, a neat, well-tended settlement like any he might have found in England, perhaps a bit more prosperous than most. As he rode through the gates at a nonthreatening walk, the normal workday activity continued with barely a pause—women hanging out their washing, the blacksmith shoeing a horse, and a group of children chasing a flock of squawking geese across the lane. But all of them stopped for a moment to steal a glance as he passed, their eyes furtive but not unfriendly. But none of them spoke a word or even so much as nodded. They treated him like a ghost passing among them, some sort of Highland ghoul everyone could see and wonder at but no one dared acknowledge for fear it might carry them off.

Malcolm's house was easy enough to find. It was three times the size of any other structure in the village, a single, sprawling story of fieldstone roofed in thatch and set up on a hill. But the freshly swept dooryard was deserted. He trotted his horse through the open gate and waited, but no one came to greet him. "Hello!" he called out, watching the open doorway, his shout startling his mount into a prance. "Who is in the house?"

A woman appeared in the doorway, wiping her hands on a towel. "Who is it that asks?" She was what his mother would have called a handsome woman, smooth-skinned and red-haired like Evelyn. But her jaw and brow were square where Evelyn had a perfect oval, and her expression of suspicion would have given a basilisk a shiver. Two other women huddled behind her, peering out at him over her shoulders.

"Aiden Brinlaw of Glencairn," he answered, standing in the stirrups to make her a bow. "I believe I have come to see your husband. You are Mistress Rebecca, are you not?"

"My husband the laird is not here," she answered. "He got your message." She stepped out into the light, eyeing him up and down as if he might have been a chicken being passed off as a goose. "He said if you really did turn up, I should send you to find him in the fields. He and our boys are hunting rabbits and looking over the crops."

"I thank you, lady," he said, nodding again as he

brought his horse around. "Tell me, what did you think of my lady Evelyn's message?"

Rebecca's face went pale, but her eyes were bright with fury. "My sister is a prideful, silly girl," she answered. "I wish you joy of her."

Aiden grinned. "Then I do thank you again." Nodding one last time to the other women lurking in the doorway, he rode off at a gallop, jumping over the gate and kicking up dust behind him.

He found Laird Malcolm and his sons flying hawks over a field of grain so near to ripe, he could smell the kernels baking in the sun. The laird was not tall, he noticed, slowing to a stop, but he was powerfully built, an impressive figure in his green tartan kilt. As Aiden dismounted to approach them, he was showing little Hamish how to launch his sparrow-hawk, the man bent over the child with obvious affection and patience, his hands on his shoulders as the boy raised his fist and the bird sailed free in the air.

"Well done, Hamish," Aiden called.

"My lord Glencairn," the lord said, coming to meet him. "So you have come after all."

"Forgive me, Laird Malcolm," Aiden answered, clasping his arm in a knightly salute. "I thought I was expected." He looked over at the two older boys as they came to join their father. "Hello, Gerald. Hello, Davey."

"So you remember them," Malcolm laughed. "Then they must beg your pardon—Gerald has his mother's kindly nature, I'm afraid." He nodded to his oldest son.

"Tell Lord Aiden you regret trying to murder him like a bandit on the road."

The boy's eyes met Aiden's for barely a moment before sliding away, a telltale blush creeping into his freckled cheeks. "We are sorry, my lord," he mumbled.

"No need," Aiden answered with an easy smile. "Go and look on my saddle. I have brought back something that belongs to you."

"The claymore." Malcolm nodded as all three boys went to investigate. "He'll be glad to have it back. It belonged to the old laird, his grandfather."

"So did Lady Evelyn," Aiden said, getting to the point while the boys were out of hearing. "I wonder that you don't value her as highly as a sword."

Malcolm smiled. "She is a pretty thing, isn't she?" he said with a sigh. "You mistake me, my lord, if you think she is not valued. We'd be glad to have her back. I know some boys who would likely get up quite a party for her welcome."

"But not her son," Aiden said, smiling back on the outside but cold underneath. He had no real reason to take such offense on Evelyn's behalf. In truth, her affairs had very little to do with him or his interests. But the very idea that such a woman as he had come to believe her to be should be so discounted offended him very much. 'Twas his mother coming out in him, no doubt, getting the better of his good sense the way she always did.

"No," Malcolm said. At least he had the decency to

look a bit uncomfortable. "That child ought never to have been born."

"But he was," Aiden pointed out. "And it wasn't Evelyn's fault."

"You think not?" Malcolm laughed. "Then you do not know her very well, my lord—our Evelyn would not have had a child if she hadn't wanted one." Gerald had found his claymore, and he looked back at Aiden and nodded his thanks. "So what's it to be then, now that the girl has had her say," the laird continued. "Is she going to the convent, or is she coming home?"

"Neither," Aiden answered, waving to the boy. "She and Max will remain at Glencairn under my protection."

"Your protection?" Malcolm echoed. "And what does that mean?" One of the hawks swooped down with a screech, and all three boys went running to the center of the field to see her make her kill. "Do you intend to take Charles's place in this as well as in his castle?" Malcolm asked. "Will you marry her yourself?"

For a single moment of madness, Aiden wanted to say yes, just to see the look on the Scotsman's face when he did it. But as satisfying as it no doubt would have been, he wouldn't tell such a lie, even for a joke. "No," he answered. "I will not be her husband. But I have written to Prince John on her behalf."

Malcolm smiled. "No doubt that will be a great help," he said with acid burning in his tone. The hawk that had made the kill had escaped the boys and was flying toward them, and Malcolm raised his hand, whistling between his teeth.

But Aiden had some experience with hawking himself, his faery grandmother having been a falcon for the last fifteen years of her mortal life. He put up his own hand, barely gloved as it was, and the hawk changed course at once, landing on his fist so gently he barely felt her talons. *"Never mind, my lady,"* he soothed in faery speak, stroking her soft, feathered breast to comfort her for the loss of her kill. *"They're saving the best bits for you."*

"I'm impressed," Malcolm said. His tone was easy, even friendly, but his eyes were cold. "I raised that hawk from a hatchling; she allows no one to touch her but me or one of my sons."

"My mother was born at a place called Falconskeep," Aiden answered with a small smile of his own. "I have it in my blood, I'm afraid."

"Indeed," the Scotsman answered, watching as the hawk nibbled gently at the cuff of Aiden's leather glove. "You should take her, then, since she seems to like you so well."

"No, thank you, my laird." Whispering a final word in faery speak to the bird, he launched her again. "I have no need of a hawk." He clasped Malcolm's hand again. "And I will trouble you no more."

"No trouble at all," Malcolm insisted with a smile, but a wariness had come into his eyes that had not been there before. "My sons told me you were odd, my lord, not like Charles at all," he said as Aiden turned away. "I see now they were right."

Aiden looked back with a smile. "Odd, you say?" he asked, remembering the spell that had made Gerald's claymore look like a dragon. Malcolm hadn't mentioned it, but surely the boys must have told him. "Yea, Malcolm, I probably am."

"Never mind," Malcolm laughed. "We won't hold it against you. You must come and see us again when we're drinking."

Aiden nodded. "And so I will," In truth, he found it hard to dislike this Malcolm. But he didn't trust him, and he could well believe Evie had reason to dislike him very much. "And you must come to Glencairn." He went back to his horse.

"Have a care for the wee folk!" Malcolm called, pointing to the crown of crags at the top of the mountain that stood in the direction Aiden was headed. "You'll want to look sharp, riding back."

Aiden shook his head at the joke. "I will," he promised, waving to the boys as he rode off.

The road took him to the very foot of the mountain's final steep slope, and the standing stones cast long shadows in the dust before him. "The wee folk," he muttered, shaking his head again. He had already heard much about these mythical creatures from the people of Glencairn, enough to know that they were a colloquial designation for the same race from whom he was himself descended and who were by no means "wee." But regardless of their size, they were apparently to blame for every ill that ever happened in Scotland. "Faeries," Sir Alan had explained, rolling his eyes. But now that he considered it in the shadow of their sanctuary, Aiden thought they might be worth a look.

Leaving his horse to wait for him by the road, he climbed the slope. He had noticed the ring on his first approach to Glencairn, a jagged silver crown of rock that rose from the mountain's green brow. He had assumed they were like the standing stones at Glastonbury, another druid's ring. He had stood in such temples often in his travels with King Henry and Prince John, and gazing back through time, he had seen the rituals that had passed there a thousand years ago. But these visions had not touched him, had not felt like anything that had to do with him. He had witnessed their passing the same way he could "see" the past of any modern castle, a fascinating nothing. It was a faery trick; his mother and sister saw such things as well. But as he reached the avenue of these stones, he felt something else entirely. Standing at their ancient gates, he felt as if he belonged.

"*Who are you?*" he asked in faery speech, touching the cold, rough face of a column a half-a-man taller than he was himself. The stone that looked like silver from the glen below was actually mottled black and white, the colors swirled together in a pattern like the lines in the palm of his hand. "*Who has set you in this place?*" He laid both palms flat against the stone, bracing against it as if he were pushing open a heavy door, and his flesh melted into faery until anyone watching would think he had disappeared inside his clothes. "*Answer if you will,*" he called. "*I have come to hear you.*"

A low moan rose from the ground at his feet like the sigh of some great beast. A cold wind swirled around him, and he closed his eyes. Suddenly he saw fire, a great stone hearth blazing with logs so thick he could not have reached around them. Great beams of some dark wood curved high above him like the ribs of Jonah's whale, and men stood all around him, bearded and tall with long, straight spears of polished wood with blades of gleaming rock. But the fire held no heat; its breath was as cold as any winter wind. The hall was a shadow; between the beams, he could see the stars. And the men were ghosts. He reached out to one of them, a giant with thick black hair like his own, and the man turned to him and smiled in recognition; indeed, he looked as if his heart would burst with joy to see him there. But when Aiden tried to clasp his hand, he found himself holding nothing more than empty air. "*Who are you?*" he called as the scene began to fade. "*Why do you wait here in the shadow?*"

"*My lord,*" the man called out, and the others took up the call. "*My king . . . we wait for you. . . .*" Then everything was dark.

Aiden opened his eyes and found the world again, the mountain and the stones. But his heart still ached for the warriors he had seen. When he was a child at

Falconskeep, the ancient spirit there had sometimes shown him such visions, shadows from a world more old and deep than even faery where the figures were creatures like she was herself, the very veins and bones of the earth imbrued with life and pain. As a child, he had wept for their sorrow even though he didn't understand it.

He touched the stone again, and the grains of the rock seemed to dissolve, to melt into the surface of a mirror. *"Forgive me,"* he said sadly. *"I will not awake you."*

He turned away from the stones to look down on the valley below him, his own red-brown castle nestled in the joining of the bright green fields to the crystal blue of the loch. That was where his future lay, not in the ancient past. Whatever these spirits might want of him, he couldn't give it. Leaving them behind him, he went back to his horse and Glencairn.

Evelyn, my love, you have finally lost your mind, she thought to herself as she rode down the English village's single muddy street. Certainly the soldier who had given her directions had thought as much. "Mistress, are you certain?" he had asked her, shocked and dismayed. She had assured him that she was, and he had told her what she wanted with barely more than a stammer. He had even offered to come along with her. "For protection," he had said. But this was one quest she felt she ought to make alone.

She stopped where the new soldiers' barracks was being built against the wooden palisade wall, then doubled back along an alley that ran behind the communal stables, just as the soldier had directed. A few men passed her on foot on the way and gaped at her, obviously shocked, but none of them said any more than a hastily muttered, "Well met, my lady," before hurrying away. No doubt they were no more glad for her to be seeing them than they thought she would be that they saw her, though in truth she didn't care.

She found the collection of mud-spattered tents where a clear-running stream passed beneath the wall. Women in strange costumes of peasant garb with bits of finer frippery scattered here and there milled about between them, tending cooking fires and stringing up lines of washing to dry in the afternoon sun. As Evelyn approached, they stopped to stare at her with eyes full of contempt, some half a dozen harlots in all.

"Good morrow," she called as she climbed down from her horse.

"Lose something, *cherie?*" one of them asked her as she approached, her skirt trailing in the mud. "Or did you lose someone?" Her French accent was so thick, Evelyn could barely understand her, but all of the other women laughed.

"Who among you has a child?" Evelyn asked, neither imperious nor cowed. These women had no more chosen their lot in life than she had chosen her own.

"Why do you ask, my lady?" another one asked with

mocking emphasis on the title, making a mincing curtsy in the bargain. "Don't you have one of your own?" This one was English and so thin she must surely have been ill, but her grin was bright with loathing. "What do you need with another?"

"Aye, *lassie*, we know who you are," a third declared, mimicking Evelyn's own lilt. "What are you doing down here? Checking the lay of the land for when the Dragon puts you out?"

"I need a woman with experience with children," Evelyn said, refusing to be rattled. In truth, she was shocked to think they recognized her, but she supposed it was only natural. Aiden's men would visit them; that's why they were here, and the soldiers must surely gossip about their lord—the Dragon, as they called him. Still, it was rather disconcerting to think they would talk about her, and the devil forbid she should ever hear exactly what they said. "I need a nursemaid for my son."

"*Mon Dieu*, she is mad!" the first whore who had spoken cried, and the others laughed again. "Show us your purse, *mam'selle*; let us see what you can pay."

"Aye," the skinny English one agreed as she moved closer. "Let us see your purse." All of them were moving closer, a greedy light in their eyes.

"Leave her alone," a stern voice ordered from behind them, and they froze. Another woman emerged from the closest tent, carrying a baby in her arms. "What will Brinlaw do if she is harmed, do you think?" she demanded, glaring at her companions. She was tall with golden hair that was probably quite striking when it was properly tended, and her face would have been beautiful but for a livid purple scar that cut across it from the corner of her left eye to the right side of her jaw. Unlike the others, her clothes were clean, for all they were rags, and the babe she carried was swaddled in the same. "Go on," she ordered, giving the French girl a shove. "Leave us be." The others dispersed, casting final glances at Evelyn with varying degrees of malice.

"Is your baby a boy or a girl?" Evelyn asked the blonde.

"A girl, more pity for her," the woman answered. The child let out a fussy wail, and she bounced her gently in her arms, soothing her with obvious affection.

"And who is her father?" Evelyn asked.

The woman met her eyes with her own, neither ashamed nor defiant. "I don't know," she admitted. "And no one you know, either." She looked back at the others who had gone back to their tasks. "Lita is right, my lady—you must be mad," she said. "Why would you come here looking for a nurse?"

"Because I have to have one, and I need her to be loyal to no one but me," Evelyn answered. "The English women in the castle are either idiots or children, or they have husbands of their own, and they wouldn't serve me in any case because I am a Scot. And no woman of my clan will come to help me for fear of my sister, Rebecca." She smiled at the baby girl who was now twisting her tiny head to gaze at her with bright, unfocused eyes. "My son is like my life to me," she said. "I need a woman who will care for him as she would her own child."

"And what would this woman receive in return?" the woman answered, her green eyes interested but the rest of her expression blank.

"A home for herself and her child. Clothes and food enough to feel secure." She turned back the baby's blanket to touch her tiny cheek. No woman who took such tender care of an infant could be bad, no matter what her occupation might be, she thought. The little darling was perfectly plump and clean as a new morning. "My friendship and protection." She looked up at the mother. "What is the little one's name?"

"She is Grace, my lady," she answered, her eyes assessing Evelyn as closely as Evelyn had judged her. "And I am Agnes." She looked around for a moment at the filthy tents and the women who lived inside them, all of them still staring even as they kept their distance. "I am Agnes," she repeated, turning back to give Evelyn a surprisingly graceful curtsy. "And if you will have me, I am yours."

9

When Evelyn came back to the castle, she found the courtyard full of knights and soldiers battling as if their lives depended on it. "Careful, my lady," Sir Alan said, coming to meet her just inside the gates.

"What on earth is going on?" she asked, handing him the reins of her horse. Sir Brutus and another knight were sparring so close, she could smell their sweat, both of them laughing like fiends and chiding one another with oaths to make her blush.

"Drills." Sir Alan grinned as he helped her down. "Lord Aiden thinks we've gotten soft."

"God's teeth," she laughed, swearing an oath of her own. "If this is soft, I should hate to see you fierce." She took the arm he offered and let him lead her around the fray. "Sir Alan, I need your help."

"Anything, my lady," he said with a smile, the irony lost on neither of them. A week before, he had refused to send his men out to find her cow, fond of her as he had been. But now, with her made Aiden's chatelaine, he wouldn't dare refuse her anything, no matter what he might think of her himself.

"I have engaged a nursemaid from the village," she explained, stopping at the top of the steps leading into the castle proper. "Her name is Agnes, and she has a daughter of her own. She will stay here in the castle, so someone must take a wagon and fetch her and her belongings here to me."

He frowned. "I know of no such woman in the village. Who is she?"

"I'm pleased to hear you don't know her," she said with a laugh. "She is a harlot, come to Glencairn following Aiden's camp."

"My lady!" he sputtered, but in truth, she barely heard him. She had finally seen Aiden.

Like the rest of the knights, he was wearing a chainmail shirt over his leather hose, the hood pushed back and his hair tied back in a thong. He was sparring with a man nearly twice his size, and his face, streaming sweat, was distorted with the strain of battle. But he was so beautiful, he made her knees go weak. He had always seemed too handsome to be real, from the very first moment she had seen him, and it was obvious from his physique that he was strong. She had seen him stripped to the waist that very first morning and had been quite favorably impressed. He was clever; he was charming; he seemed to have it in him to be kind. But even knowing his history as Prince John's enforcer, she had never really thought of him as a warrior before. But she would never make that mistake again.

The knight he was fighting lunged for him, and she

gasped, her hand against her mouth—practice or not, if he struck him so, he would surely knock him unconscious. But at the last possible moment, Aiden ducked into a crouch, knocking the other man's knees out from under him with the flat of his sword, sending him tumbling backwards. Of course, the man nearly accomplished with clumsiness what he'd failed to do with skill—Aiden had to roll out of his way to keep from being crushed. But it was a most impressive maneuver just the same.

He said something Evie couldn't hear, laughing as he sat up, and she smiled without knowing she had done it. *He's magnificent*, she thought, a wave of longing like nothing she had ever felt coming over her. *If we were his, we would be safe.*

"My lady," Sir Alan repeated. "You don't really mean to bring a common harlot into the castle to help you care for your child?"

"I do mean to, and I will," she answered, tearing her gaze away from Aiden to face the marshal. "Now go and fetch her, please."

"Who is being fetched?" Robin asked, coming out of the hall. While the rest of the fighting men of the garrison, from Aiden himself to the youngest of the squires, were covered in sweat and grime and panting from exertion, Robin looked fresh as a daisy.

"Max's new nursemaid," Evelyn replied. "But look at you—how did you manage to escape the wars?"

He grinned. "Skill, my lady, naught but skill."

"I will find this creature in the village?" Sir Alan asked, sour but resigned. "What is her name again?"

"Agnes," Evelyn repeated. "She will be waiting for you in the whores' camp behind the stables."

"Agnes?" Robin echoed as the marshal left. "Saxon Agnes?"

"I didn't ask her nationality," Evie answered primly.

"A big, blond wench with a scar on her face?" Robin said helpfully from the sophisticated heights of thirteen years.

"That wench, as you call her, could break you in two like a twig." Evelyn frowned. "A bit of courtesy, young sirrah, if you please."

"Yes, of course; pray pardon, my lady," he hastened to amend. "But, Lady Evelyn, she is a whore."

"Not anymore, she is not," she said firmly. "She is Max's nurse, and I will hear no more about it."

"Yes, my lady," he nodded, the boyish soul of contrition. A horn sounded, and the mock battles began to break up. "Dinnertime," he explained as the squires began to gather up the equipment and the knights to drift toward the steps. "Will you dine with my lord in the solar?"

Evie looked again at Aiden, now engaged in conversation with his opponent and another man. Last night she had been forced to fend off his amorous advances with a sharp tongue and a laugh, and it had taken all the moral fortitude she could muster to make herself do it. After what she had just seen, tonight she would be lost. "I think not," she said aloud. Aiden looked up and saw her and waved, his devilish grin breaking on his face, and she waved back, smiling herself. "Tell my lord I will join him in the hall."

Aiden thought Evie would wait for him, but as he approached the steps, she went inside, laughing at Robin as he made her his most courtly bow. "She thinks you're ridiculous," he teased the boy as he joined him.

"She must not think much more of you," Robin retorted. "She has refused to dine with you tonight."

Aiden just stared at him, genuinely shocked. "You lie."

"God's truth," Robin swore. "On my honor."

"Your honor," Aiden scoffed, letting the subject drop for the moment, still not believing the boy. Why should Evie refuse his company? "Where was your honor when we were running drills?"

"Polishing your helmet." Robin grinned, utterly without remorse. "I thought you might need it."

"Did you, in faith?" Aiden muttered, too occupied with other matters to scold his squire as he deserved. If the little laggard got himself cleaved in two in his first battle, he'd have only himself to blame. "Tell me truly, Robin, no more jests. Where did Evelyn go?"

"Into the hall for dinner, my lord, with everyone else," Robin answered. "God's truth, I swear it. She's just come back from finding a new nurse for the baby—in faith, you'll never guess who it is." Aiden just glared at him. He had never been one for guessing games in the sunniest of moods, and just now he was feeling more stormy by the second. "Saxon Agnes."

Aiden thought he must have misheard, so much so he was momentarily distracted from his more personal griefs. "Saxon Agnes?" The camp follower with the blond locks and the appalling scar was so notorious for her temper, even Aiden himself had heard tell of it. Many of his soldiers had suffered far more grievous wounds in her tent than they had ever found in battle. Indeed, an entire mythology had evolved around her, that she had been the daughter or sister or true love or simple comrade-at-arms of the Saxon bandit king of Nottingham, Robin of the Hood, or some figure like him. Thus her nickname, Saxon Agnes.

"The very same," Robin nodded. "She sent Sir Alan to fetch her and her baby—did you know she had a baby?" He snickered. "You should have seen the man's face."

"I can imagine." How in hell would Evie have met a soldiers' whore in the first place, and having met her, what would possess her to take the creature as a servant? Once again, he couldn't guess. Her motives were beyond him. And now she was refusing to dine with him alone, in spite of everything he had done for her that day. Ungrateful little wretch... "Did she say why?" he demanded of the squire.

"Not to me, she didn't," Robin said, still intent on the subject of Max's new nurse. "I tried to tell her Mistress Agnes was a whore, but she told me in no uncertain terms to keep my peace on the subject. In faith, my lord, she can be as bossy as you are."

"No," Aiden said impatiently. "Did she say why she wouldn't dine in the solar?"

"Oh," Robin nodded, suppressing a smile. "That. No, my lord, she did not. She was standing here on the steps with Sir Alan, watching you fight, and I came up, and she sent him off to fetch Agnes. I said Agnes who? And she . . ." Catching sight of his master's face, he decided to make a long story short while he still had a tongue to do it. "Anyway, while we were talking, the horn was blown for dinner," he continued. "I asked if she would dine with you in the solar, and she said, 'I think not—tell my lord I will join him in the hall.' " Aiden was still glaring at him, obviously expecting more, and he shrugged. "That's all, I swear. She went in, and you walked up." The courtyard was now almost empty. "So will you go in?" he ventured, barely louder than a whisper.

Aiden shook his head, nonplussed and annoyed. Here he had wasted the better part of the afternoon trading pleasantries and insults with some peasant prince in defense of her honor, not to mention the inarguable fact that he was all that stood between her pretty self and baby and a cold, uncaring world, no matter how many nursemaids she might pluck out of the stews, yet she had no desire to see him alone whatsoever. She shouldn't just consent to dine with him; she ought to be eager to do it, her little heart fairly racing with joy at the prospect. Other little hearts had raced for his company with far less cause. But no, Evie preferred to take her dinner in the hall with everybody else.

"My lord?" Robin repeated, now barely audible. "Will you go in?"

"Yes, damnit, yes," he said, handing the squire his sword. "By all means, let us dine."

Looking around the great hall, Evelyn felt quite pleased with her handiwork. The once-bare walls were now hung with rich tapestries, and the number of torches had been doubled to flood even the darkest corners with flickering light. Instead of having the knights line up and be served by the cooks in their dirty aprons, she had set trestle tables on three sides of the fire to hold the food for the squires to serve while their masters sat at their ease. All of the tables were covered with linen cloths, and while the dogs still wandered underneath them far more freely than she would have liked, the rushes on the floor were fresh, and the dog boys had strict instructions to keep them that way by whatever means necessary. Even the dinner itself was much improved over the normal fare after her instructions.

But the changes she had wrought in the hall were nothing compared to the change Aiden's efforts had made in the men who gathered there. For the first time since she had come to Glencairn, they seemed less like a gang of well-dressed brigands and more like noble knights, speaking more softly, drinking less deeply—an hour into dinner, no one had even suggested a brawl yet. And the most obvious object of all this new courtesy was Evelyn herself. The barely civil crowd of ruffians Sir Alan could barely hold in check had become a collection of charmers falling over themselves to pay her compliments and make her feel at ease. They praised the dinner; they lauded the new décor; they marveled at the beauty of her eyes, her hands, her gown.

"You must not think of leaving us, my lady, whatever your kinsman may say," Sir Brutus said, deep in his cups and beaming at her from the far end of the dais where she sat at Aiden's side. "You or little Max either one."

"No," Aiden agreed, watching her over the rim of the cup they shared between them. "You must not." The only knight who didn't seem to be enjoying the new Glencairn was the very man who had made it. Indeed, his temper seemed as ill as she had ever seen it, his usual mocking grin turned to a permanent scowl. Even Robin seemed skittish, spilling gravy and tripping over his own feet every time his master looked at him. "We should be bereft," Aiden finished with barely detectable sarcasm as he set the cup aside.

"As would I, my lord," she answered with a smile, pretending she didn't hear anything but sunshine in his tone. Her own father had been prone to fits of melancholy, but she'd never thought to see Aiden succumb. "May God so will that I should stay." She lifted her cup to take a sip, and the knights all followed suit as if she'd made a toast. "God and your Prince John," she finished, setting it down again.

Aiden smiled but not with happiness. "Amen," he muttered, taking a sip of his own. Robin cleared away the soiled meat trenchers and set fresh ones before them laden with stewed fruit and bread. "I saw your sister today," he remarked just as Evie took a bite.

"You saw whom?" she said, barely sputtering.

"Your sister, Rebecca," he answered. "She is very much as you describe her, charming as a snake." He took a bite of his own, obviously gauging her reaction. "But I rather liked her husband."

"Malcolm?" she said evenly, forcing her tone to stay pleasant. What had she done that he should be baiting her this way? "How did you meet him?"

"I went to your village expressly for that purpose," he answered, taking another long sip and motioning for Robin to refill the cup. He had drunk quite a bit that evening, she noticed. Was that his problem? "I wanted to tell your laird in person that I had decided to keep you," he continued, then stopped as if to correct a mistake. "To write John on your behalf."

The talk among the other knights had all but stopped. Everyone was listening to them. "And was he pleased?" she asked, still eating as if she were barely interested in his answer, merely making conversation.

"I suppose," Aiden said, turning his attention to his

food as well. "In truth, he didn't seem to care much one way or the other." He didn't look to see the effect of this barb on her expression; he didn't have to. After what she had told him this morning, he knew just where that particular chink in her armor lay. So why did he feel compelled to exploit it? He had only been mildly annoyed at her, surely—why should he care more than a little where she chose to have her dinner and with whom? But somehow over the course of the evening, as his knights made a fuss over her as if she might have been Helen of Troy, mild annoyance had shifted dangerously close to a genuine fit of temper.

"Lady Evelyn, you have quite outdone yourself," Sir Alan said, obviously determined to change the subject or be damned in the attempt. "I don't know when I have eaten so well."

"Thank you, sir knight." Evie laughed, as delightfully merry as ever. "Though I fear Lord Aiden has taken a bad pear." Aiden looked at her, and she smiled at him so sweetly, he didn't know whether he should kiss her or wring her little neck. "It has put him quite out of humor."

"Not at all, my lady," Aiden answered, smiling back. "Sir Alan is right; you have worked miracles." She was reaching for their cup, and he caught her hand so quickly she let out a tiny gasp of surprise. "Have you any other talents?" he asked, giving the back of it a swift, soft kiss.

"As a matter of fact . . ." She smiled, refusing to be

rattled. Whatever demon had possessed him, she wouldn't feed its wrath or its satisfaction. "I sing," she said, curling her fingers around his to return his mocking caress.

Aiden's own breath caught in his chest, though he was more skillful in hiding it. "Show us," he urged, the gentle pressure of her hand holding his racing through him like wildfire. "Sing for us."

She smiled, feeling the tremor in his flesh, the power she held over him, woman that she was. She thought for a moment of the warrior she had seen in the courtyard, the savage fighter who lurked beneath the courtier's facade, and a shiver slipped down her spine. "But what shall I sing, my lord?" she asked. "I don't know any English songs."

"So sing a Scottish one," he ordered. "A love song, if you please." His eyes were warm but challenging, blue ice in fire.

"Very well." She nodded, winking at Sir Alan and making him blush, old soldier that he was. "A love song of the Highlands, then." She tried to withdraw her hand, but Aiden wouldn't let go. "I think I know just the one."

Aiden watched her close her eyes, her lashes dark against her skin, her hand still clasped in his, delicate and warm. She was a solid, living, breathing thing, a woman he desired. But as soon as she began to sing, she seemed to be transformed, her luscious flesh dissolving in his perceptions to a creature of pure spirit, a voice without a form. The words she sang were not foreign to him at all, certainly not Gaelic. *Faery speak*, he thought, amazed, as her song went on. *"You have my soul, my heart, my love,"* she sang, a chorus repeating. *"I choose you over immortality."* His grip on her tightened, and she opened her eyes, still singing every word he had ever longed to hear. *"Over ancient lands, I choose you. In you I choose my life. Forsaking all, I choose you, love, even unto death."*

Evie stopped, lost in the sudden storm of Aiden's gaze. He seemed to be accusing her of something, as if something in her song had offended him. But how could he have understood? "That's it," she said in English as the knights broke into applause.

"Well done, my lady," Sir Alan said as Aiden let go of her hand. His smile was the same as always, charming and mocking at once, but his eyes still searched her face, hungry and vulnerable in a way she could never have imagined he could be. "What does it mean?" the marshal asked.

"In truth, I do not know," she said lightly, looking away from those eyes. "It is a song of the ancient queen of the cairn, the founder of my clan." Robin refilled their cup, and she took a grateful sip. "They say she died of love, and that was her love song."

"But you do not know what the words mean?" Aiden demanded with more heat than he'd intended. "How is that possible?"

"My father taught them to me by the sound, just as

his granddam taught him," she answered. "All I know is that she made her fortress in the glen and died for the love of a man." Molly was lurking near the corner of the dais, having ventured ever closer all night, and Evelyn gave her a wink. "The wee folk, don't you know?"

"I think I've heard them mentioned," Aiden said with a tiny smile. "So the standing stones on the mountain belonged to this queen?"

"So they say," she answered. "My father said they were her warriors, waiting for the hour of her return." She looked around at the knights of the hall, all of them still hanging on her every word, and a mischievous smile crept over her face. "He used to say they would drive the English out."

"Then stone may they remain," Aiden declared, joining the general laugh. To her it was all just a story, an ancient folktale of the glories of the past. No matter how sweetly she had sung the words of faery, she didn't understand them in the least.

"For your sake, I hope so," Evelyn answered, standing up. "And now, my lords, I will leave you." She offered Aiden her hand to be kissed again, her smile both tempting and serene. "Good night."

"Don't go," he ordered, standing up himself.

"I must," she said. "I have to see to Max." Withdrawing her hand, she bobbed a curtsy instead and left the hall.

For the sake of his dignity, Aiden knew he should let her go. He could hardly allow his sworn knights to see him chasing after a woman in his own castle, no matter how lovely she might be. But for once, dignity would have to go hang. "Carry on," he muttered to Sir Alan, headed for the stairs.

He caught her at the foot of the spiral stairway that led up to her tower. "Evie, wait."

She stopped and turned back with the same sweet, noncommittal smile. "Yes, my lord?" In truth, her mind was in a whirl, remembering all that had happened that day, all of it wrapped up in him. But she could still keep her feelings hidden behind the mask of her pretty face, a woman's mysterious smile. "What is it, Aiden?"

Aiden tried to think of the words that would make it seem sensible and right that he should have followed her instead of desperate and foolish, the taunt that would incite her temper or the joke that would make her laugh. He wanted her to come to him now the same way he had wanted her to come to the solar, to know she was like all the others, that she wanted him more than he could ever want her. But she didn't, and she wouldn't; he could see it in her smile. She could walk away from him—she had done it already. And for once, with this woman, he couldn't let her go. Without a word he caught her in his arms.

His mouth came down on hers, brutal and tender at once, and his arms were around her, the same arms that swung a sword so skillfully now crushing her hard to his chest. She couldn't breathe, couldn't think, but she felt him, tasted the wine on his tongue, smelled the spice and musk of his skin. "Evelyn," he murmured, kissing a path along her jaw, and her knees went weak with desire, her arms enfolding him without a conscious thought. She could surrender and be happy; he would make it sweet. He raised his head and smiled at her as if he heard her thoughts, his eyes warm with a desire of his own. But how would he look on her tomorrow?

"No." He had bent to kiss her lips again, and she put her hand to his mouth. "Aiden, no." He moved to shift her closer, and she struggled in his arms. "Let me go—"

"I will not." She was pretending; he knew it, foolish modesty playing at virtue. She wanted him; he could taste it on her lips and feel it in her touch. "Why should I—?"

"Because I wish it!" She pushed him with surprising force, breaking free of his arms. "Aiden, I will not." The look in his eyes was familiar, hurt and betrayal and rage mixed with his want. She had seen this look before from other men and laughed, seeing proof of her powers. Now she was more determined to resist it than she had ever been before, but it touched her in a way the others never could have. "You know that I am not a maid," she said, backing a step away. "I have no virtue left to lose, and no modesty, either. But I'm not a stupid girl."

"No one could think that you are," he answered sullenly, not wanting to hear her. "Certainly not me."

"I will never make love with a man who isn't my husband again." She thought of the look of pity in the eyes of the women who attended Max's birth, and the memory steeled her resolve. "I have sworn to God."

"Careful, Evie," he said with a shadow of his wicked smile. "Never is a hard oath to keep."

"But I will keep it, Aiden." Even now she wanted to touch him, to feel his arms around her, making her feel safe and cherished, even for just one night, a perfect dream of love. But dreams were not the truth, she knew, and she could afford them no more. She would have him; she would give herself to him, heart and soul and body if that was what he wanted. But it would be real. He would be her husband. "If you've only let me stay here because you think otherwise, I will leave tonight."

"No." He made himself smile at her, putting on the mask. She was even smarter than he'd realized and even more ambitious. But she was still a woman. She wanted him; he knew that now. He would still win in the end. "Forgive me, lady," he said, taking her hand. "Your beauty overwhelms me, and I forget myself." He kissed it lightly, a courtier's caress, before he let it go. "But I would not have my rudeness drive you from your sanctuary. Of course you must stay."

Evelyn couldn't help but smile. Arrogant he might

be, but no one would ever call him clumsy. "Then I may rely on your chivalry, my lord?" she asked. "Will you promise to make no further base advances?"

"No, Evie." He grinned. "I will not. You'll just have to keep remembering to stop me." Before she could answer, he gave a lock of her auburn hair an insolent tug and went back down the stairs.

10

Evelyn climbed the stairs to her room and found Agnes waiting for her, sitting at the window feeding little Grace. "Well, hello," she said, smiling at the peaceful picture they made in spite of her own chaotic feelings of the moment. Dressed in a clean blouse and kirtle with her hair pinned up in a veil, the other woman looked like a new woman, even with her scar, and Grace looked like a tiny angel, swathed in one of Max's old gowns. Max himself had apparently taken to his new nurse like a duckling to water. Whenever she had left him alone with Molly or even Margaret after dark, she would find him wakeful and sniffling when she returned. But now he was sleeping on Evie's bed, his thumb tucked into his mouth, showing no signs of distress whatsoever. "I didn't think you'd still be awake," she said, sitting down beside him.

"You don't lie with him, then?" Agnes asked. "The Dragon?"

Evie looked up at her, surprised. "No," she admitted at last. She looked back at her sleeping child, trying not to think about how she had felt in Aiden's arms. "Why do you call him that?"

"That's what his soldiers call him." She switched her baby from one breast to the other. "They've all seen the mark he carries," she explained. "They say an evil spirit gave it to him, a succubus who fell in love with him and didn't want to let him go."

"Are you serious?" Evelyn smiled. "How did he start that rumor, do you think?" Such fantastic tales of fierceness and villainy were common enough among the warrior chiefs of the Highlands, but she had never heard tell of an English feudal lord using such a story to keep his men in line.

"I cannot tell, my lady." The corner of the other woman's mouth quirked up in a cryptic smile of her own, the effect made more mysterious by her scar. "I've heard it said his mother is a witch."

He's a witch! Hamish had declared the first time she heard tell of Aiden Brinlaw. *He turned Gerald's sword into a snake!* But that was ridiculous, as silly now as it had been when the child had said it. Aiden had no morals she could discern beyond a haphazard adherence to the code of chivalry, and he had the power to have whatever he wanted, money, strength, and charm in an abundance that to the ignorant might seem supernatural. But he was still just a man with a man's simple desires. That much she knew only too well. "Indeed?" she said aloud as she got up to undress. "Maybe his mother's just mean."

"Maybe so, my lady," Agnes agreed. "I have never seen her myself, nor do I know any other who has." She put Grace down in Max's long-abandoned cradle, turning her back as Evie changed into her shift. "So if you aren't his mistress, what do you want from him?"

"Good lord, Agnes." Evie laughed, combing out her hair. "Are you always this inquisitive?"

"Not usually," Agnes admitted. "But if I'm to help you, I have to know what you want."

Evelyn looked back at her, surprised again, but the other woman's eyes were serious. "Why would you want to help me?"

Agnes almost laughed. "How could you ask?" She looked around at the tower room that to Evelyn seemed cramped as if it might have been the palace of a queen. "You've saved me, my lady. I am yours."

Watching her, Evie believed her completely, good sense and judgment be damned. Agnes might have been a whore, and she might look like a brigand's lost bride, but Evelyn trusted her more than she had any other woman in her life, even her own sister. They had a great deal in common, she and Agnes. They understood each other.

"I want him to marry me," she said aloud. "I have to make Aiden love me enough to want me for his wife."

Agnes's eyes widened for a moment, but she nodded. "You can do it." She spread her pallet on the floor at the foot of Evelyn's bed. "You're smart and pretty enough, and I will help you."

"Thank you, Agnes." Feeling much encouraged, she climbed into bed, pulling Max close in her arms.

* * *

Aiden closed his door and bolted it, abandoning Robin to the hall. He was fond of his squire, but he could live without his company tonight.

He ought to be happy, he thought, tearing out of his clothes and letting them lie where they fell. He had accomplished quite a bit since he got up that morning. His knights were sworn; he had seen them fight. His hall was finally habitable. He had introduced himself to the local laird and served his interests well, he thought. Malcolm knew he was no boy to be dismissed, at least, or ought to.

But he wasn't happy, not one bit. In fact, he was as fiendishly unsatisfied as he had ever been in his life.

Over ancient lands, I choose you, Evelyn had sung to him, her hand clasped tightly in his. He stopped before the mirror, absently touching the frame. *In you I choose my life.* She swore she didn't know the meaning of the words, but he had known it as he knew the shape of his own hand, the mark of the dragon the ancient spirit had drawn there. But of course he couldn't tell her so. Even if he had told her, she wouldn't have believed him; she would have thought he was mocking her, making another jest.

But what if she had not? For one moment he let himself imagine telling her the truth. "I know your words because I feel them in my blood," he might have said. "I have seen your ancient fortress, walked among the warriors of stone and passed through time." Could she have believed him? What would she have thought of him if she had? For that one moment, he let himself believe she wouldn't have been frightened, that she would have smiled and said, "Show me. Teach me what you know."

But that was foolishness.

He touched the mirror's glass, focusing his mind on it with a single murmured word in faery speak, and his reflection faded into silver mist. He had been a squire at the royal court when he had made the mirror, a homesick child conjuring to make himself feel less alone. When it was done, he had used it to spy on the worlds of love and safety he had lost, his parents and Falconskeep with his little sister, Mary, and Mark at Brinlaw, and most especially Malinda, his beautiful sorceress sister. Growing up under the tutelage of the king, he had watched her sail the world with Tarquin, the pirate and brigand who had married her and taken her away. He had seen them build their beautiful villa on an island in the Mediterranean; he had watched as their sons were born there, first one, then another three years later. But the older he grew, the less often he had looked into the mirror's magic. As he became a man, other interests had consumed him, darker magic of his own, and the sight of his sister and her destined love was no longer a comfort to him. The longing he had felt when the mirror was made had turned to jealousy, a dangerous emotion for a wizard.

"Malinda," he said now, still in the faery tongue. "Show me Malinda."

The mist on the mirror cleared away to reveal a brilliant blue sky and bleached white columns rising from a terrace. A woman stood among them, her long blond hair dancing wildly on the wind, and Aiden smiled. Malinda would be forty now or older, but she still looked like a girl. She called and waved to someone as he watched, and a man came bounding up the steps to meet her, a giant with dark red hair who scooped her up in his arms. As they kissed, he passed his hand over the mirror, the image dissolving into mist like a reflection in a pool moved by the wind. "Godspeed," he murmured, turning away.

Tarquin was his sister's destiny. As a sorceress of Falconskeep, she had found her soulmate, the one man in all the world who would love her without question and whom she could not help but love just the same in return. Their mother had been the same, her heart destined for Brinlaw from the very moment they met. As he was a wizard, as close akin to their faery past as they were, it had always stood to reason that he would be the same, that somewhere in the world a woman waited who would be his destined love. But he was a man; he couldn't just follow his fancy, destiny or not. Lady Alista had been very lucky. The man the fates had chosen for her just happened to hold the royal charter on the castle where she lived. Malinda had behaved like an idiot and nearly gotten herself murdered twice to be with Tarquin, a man with no lands, little charm, and a criminal occupation, but ultimately, she could afford it.

Criminal or not, Tarquin could support her. Aiden had seen well enough the kind of life they had built together, the passion they still shared. But Aiden was a man. He didn't have that luxury; there would be no one to build a life for him, and he couldn't do it with magic. He had to make his way with grosser gifts, to find his place and claim it on his own. That meant he must marry the princess.

A hawk flew past the open window, screaming to her prey, and he shivered. His grandmother, the faery Lady Blanche, had been a sorceress as well. Her destined love had been Lord Mark, the man Aiden was so often said to favor in his darkly handsome looks. She had loved him so much she had destroyed her mortal body and nearly damned her soul trying to find out he was safe, then lived fifteen more years in the body of a falcon rather than leave him behind. When he died, she had been trapped—even when she tried to follow, she could not. For twenty years longer, she had neither lived nor died but wandered as a ghost with no company but a little boy who reminded her of him.

"No," he said, facing his reflection again as he remembered that last morning in London when his mother had tried to convince him to wait for love. "Destiny isn't always such a happy thing." He thought of Evelyn, the beautiful enigma now sleeping in his tower. She wanted him as much as he wanted her, but she refused him even so, declaring she would marry before she would give up her charms. Did she believe in destiny? Or was she merely fighting to survive? Either way, he supposed they had something in common.

He picked up the linen shirt he had just taken off, and a gentle whiff of Evie's rose and heather scent drifted up to him, still clinging to the fabric after their kiss. He held it to his face and barely inhaled, his desire rising again as he remembered the softness of her body captured in his arms. She had threatened him, sworn she would leave him. *I will keep it, Aiden,* she had sworn of her chastity vow. *If you've only let me stay here because you think otherwise, I will leave tonight.* He had known she was bluffing, of course. Where could she have gone? But what if he had called her bluff? Would she have given in? Would she be here with him now, distracting him from his painful thoughts with the sweetness of her passion?

He thought of her that morning, spitting in her clansman's face, and he smiled, tossing the shirt away. *Tell him he may shove it up his arse,* she had said of Malcolm's charity, her rage like summer lightning. *And take that kiss to my sister.* No, he had made the right choice. Bluffing or not, she would have stood by her wager. If he had pressed her, she would have packed up and gone because she'd said she would. Her pride wouldn't have let her do otherwise.

He put out the rush light and climbed into bed. Evelyn would not be pushed, he decided. But she could be persuaded. Musing on that pleasant thought, he drifted into sleep.

* * *

In his dream he was a warrior, a chieftain of an ancient race. Marauders were screaming at the gates of his fortress, a great, curved hall with a fireplace shaped like the snarling jaws of a dragon. A young boy handed him a sword of iron, and as he took it, he saw the dragon on his wrist, painted green and blue. But his arm was different, the downy hair that covered it golden, not black, and his fingers were shorter and thicker than he knew them to be. He was not himself.

"No, love, you will not!" a woman's voice called from behind him. *Evelyn*, he thought, recognizing her at once, but when he turned to answer, he found someone else, a beauty with dark hair and eyes like his mother's. She ran to him, a tiny creature whose head barely reached his chest. "You will not leave the gates!" she ordered, grabbing for his sword.

"You will not tell me what I will not do." He knew this woman as his love, but he was angry with her, angry enough to hurt her, and somehow he feared her as well, tiny and fragile as she obviously was. "Leave me be—"

"Leave you to die?" she demanded. "What mortal foolishness is that? Inside the gates you are safe; our children are safe—"

"And will we hide forever?" He put the sword aside to catch her by the shoulders. "Do you not hear them howling? Do you not hear their taunts?"

"What are their taunts to me?" Tears glistened on

her cheeks. "Why should we care for the howling of dogs? We are immortal—"

"You are immortal." His rage was like a kind of madness boiling up inside him, ready to explode. "I am the dragon." She reached for him, her hands slipping over his shoulders, and he wanted to push her away. But he could not make himself do it. "You cannot keep me tame," he protested, growling and pleading at once.

"I want to keep you safe." She raised up on tiptoe to twine her arms around his neck, her cheek pressed to his throat. "If you leave me, you will die," she whispered, her tears stealing her voice. "I have foreseen it."

"You see far," he said coldly, his body responding to her in spite of his fury. "But you do not see all." Another wave of shouting from outside assailed his ears, the barbarians shouting for blood, and a crash rang through the hall. "You hear their battering ram—"

"Their weapons are nothing against me," she insisted. "My hall will stand—"

"Your hall, lady," he cut her off. "Not mine." He pushed her from him, turning away.

"Wait!" she called out, and once again he was seized with the certain knowledge that the voice he heard was Evelyn's. He turned, and she was in his arms, kissing his mouth, and he was lost, consumed by the fervor of her love, his fury turning to passion. He lifted her up to reach her, and she wrapped her legs around his waist, her rough-woven skirt sliding over her powerful little thighs. "Love me," she murmured, husky-voiced with desire, as his hands moved over her hips. "Do not go." He devoured her mouth with his own, unable to help himself, and he tasted strange, wild sweetness on her tongue, the wine of another world. Others watching fell away as he carried her from the hall, his guardsmen still holding spears of iron making way for them to pass. He fell with her to a bed of twisted branches, a mattress softer than goose down where he crushed his love beneath him, the dragon in a snare of spider's silk. Her tiny hands caressed his face, cradled his head to her breast as he pushed her gown from her shoulders. But the shouts of the wild men at the gates continued, refusing to be ignored, and the crash of their battering ram echoed through the fortress. He lifted his head, clasping her wrist in his hand when she reached to draw him down to her again.

"Release me," he begged her, looking down into her pleading eyes. "If you love me, you must let me go."

"Yes," she answered, as the dream began to fade, tears spilling from her eyes. "You are free, my love. . . ."

Evelyn sat up in bed, the killing sadness of the dream still tearing at her heart even as the details faded from her memory. She had been herself, but not herself, and the man was someone she had known, but she couldn't see his face. Whoever he was, she had loved him more than all the world, but she had let him go.

She got up and went to the window, careful not to wake Max. The first streaks of dawn were painted on the horizon, the standing stones like sentinels of black against the purple sky. She shivered, remembering strange oaths and shrieking like an echo in her mind. She remembered golden hair as long as her own falling on her cheek as he bent over her, this dragon of her dream . . . the dragon. She had been thinking of Aiden as she fell asleep, gotten him mixed in with all the dreams that haunted her, his wild tale entwined with her father's. She thought of the phantom of the stones the night before Aiden had come to Glencairn, the tender voice she had heard. He had loved her like this phantom of her dream. For one tantalizing moment she had felt what it was to be loved. But those were only dreams.

She looked over at Agnes, dreaming herself on her pallet, her beauty ruined by some lover's blade. They were alike, both of them ruined by a lie they had taken for love. But they were not phantoms; they were women, strong and smart, and they wouldn't stay ruined forever. *You can do it*, Agnes had promised when she'd said she would marry Aiden. *I will help you.* She smiled, going back to her bed. Whatever dreams might come, she did not need them. She would have the truth.

11

A letter of John, Prince and Protector of England, to Sir Aiden Brinlaw, Heartless Ruffian and Scoundrel

Warmest Greetings, Heartless Fiend—

If I had any character to speak of, I would chastise you most harshly in defense of my poor little sister. As I do not, I can only wish you luck. Is this Scottish wench really so sweet as you have written? God's blood, but you are gifted. You could find a quim of honey on the moon.

Speaking as I must of Katherine, I have been forced to move her. With Richard safely tucked away in Germany and me struggling daily with the task of raising his ransom, our cousin in France has begun to make bold with our duchies of Aquitaine and Anjou. While my lady mother whom you do love so well refuses to leave her home even to flee the French, she has agreed that Baby Kate is far too rich a prize to leave so unprotected.

Therefore, I have sent your brother, Mark, to fetch her back to the custody of your father at his hold of

Falconskeep—if he cannot keep her safe there, she is marked for misfortune, and there's naught that I can do. I would have recalled you from your duties there to fulfill this quest yourself, but I knew that you were otherwise engaged. Besides, it seems as though you have your office in Scotland well in hand, and I would not disturb you. You and I alone know how deeply your Glencairn may come to figure in our plans. If things progress as you have foreseen, I will bring you back to London in the spring, well pleased with your efforts and generous to a fault.

All love and friendship,
John

"Holy Christ," Aiden swore, leaning back in his chair in the solar as Robin finished reading John's letter aloud. "Papa is going to kill me, and Mark will spit on my grave."

The summer had slowly wended its way to a close. The castle and village at Glencairn had been much improved, and the harvest was nearly all in. That very morning the traveling peddlers who stopped there every autumn had set up their market on the village green, attracting English and Scotsmen alike to view their wares. As soon as he finished his correspondence, Aiden meant to have a look himself—his supply of decent wine was running low, and he was desperate for something new to read.

"I wouldn't worry about them, if I were you," Robin

agreed, handing him the scroll. "Lady Alista will have turned you into a frog long before they get at you."

"Holy Christ," Aiden repeated, trying to imagine his mother playing hostess to a princess. "John must have lost his mind."

"It wouldn't be the first time," the boy said sullenly, not at all his usual merry self, Aiden suddenly noticed. "At least he said you could have Lady Evelyn."

"True," Aiden said with a wry smile. "For all the good his permission will do me."

Ever since the night Evelyn had told him of her vow, she had taken great pains never to be alone with him again. She was in his presence all the time, of course, charming him at every turn. If he heard a peasant dispute in the hall, she took up her spinning by the fire and offered her advice. If he and his knights went hunting in the hills, she agreed to ride along, a rosy-lipped Diana on her little mare. The day the sheaves of wheat and oats were cut, she had stayed close by his side, organizing the women who gleaned behind the reapers and making sure everyone was fed. Even now she was waiting in the hall with Agnes and Max for him to escort them to the fair. But if he so much as suggested she should ride out with him alone or take a solitary walk with him in the garden, she adamantly refused. "You cannot be trusted, my lord," she would say when pressed for a reason. "In faith, I may not trust myself."

"I wouldn't worry, my lord," Robin said now, gathering up the papers from the table. "You'll win her in the end." He shot his master an unmistakably ill-tempered glance. "You always do."

"I don't think I like your tone," Aiden said with an indulgent smile. "What ails you, Rob?"

"Nothing," Robin insisted. "Will you reply to the prince before we go?"

"No, I will not," Aiden answered. "Now tell me what I've done to offend you."

"I'm not offended," the squire insisted, sitting down on the hearth. As a child, he had thought of Aiden like an older brother, much closer to him in age and temperament than either of his actual brothers, Phillipe and Paul. When he'd come to London to stay as Aiden's squire, he had tried to change his attitude accordingly and be properly respectful. But old habits sometimes died hard. "It's just . . . Aiden, it's that damned Lady Penelope all over again!"

"I beg your pardon?" Aiden laughed, confused but not offended. Penelope was the little idiot who had spoiled her wedding by declaring her passion for him over the groom.

"You and Lady Evelyn," Robin answered. "Everything is going just the way you want it here, and you know in the spring you're going home to marry the princess. But all you seem to care about is having Lady Evelyn just to prove you can."

"Rob, Evie is nothing like Pen," Aiden promised. "I only tupped Penelope because her stupid prig of a fiancé accused me of cheating when I trounced him in the lists."

"I know that!" Robin exploded. "I knew that then, and I was only twelve years old. But Lady Pen didn't know it. She thought you cared for her." He looked away, blushing red. "She loved you."

"So you think I should have married Pen?" Aiden said, losing a bit of his good humor. No man was a hero to his squire, but his seemed to think he was a pig.

"No," the boy said, shaking his head. "But at least you could have, if you'd wanted to. She was a proper English lady with a dowry, and you weren't engaged to someone else. Now you're after Lady Evelyn, knowing bloody well you're going to marry the princess. You even told Prince John about her like it's some big joke. But I don't think she's going to think it's funny."

Aiden smiled in spite of himself. Robin had always been far more resistant to feminine charms than most boys his age, but apparently he had finally been smitten. "You like her, then?"

"Yes, my lord, I do," the squire answered without the slightest trace of boyish embarrassment. "And I don't understand why you do not."

"Robin, I do like her very much," Aiden protested. "I think she's adorable. I think her stupid Charles treated her horribly. But he's dead, through no fault of mine, and there's nothing I can do about it. But I promise, if he were here, I would punch him in the face on her behalf."

"But you mean to treat her far more cruelly than he did," Robin pointed out. "Who's going to punch you?"

"You, from the sound of it," Aiden retorted, his mood turning darker by the moment.

"You don't know; I just might," the boy said bravely, then he shook his head. "No, I won't," he admitted, looking away.

"Rob, listen to me." He sat down beside him on the hearth. "As sweet as Evie is, and as wicked as my intentions may be, I'm not quite the villain that you seem to think I am." The boy looked up at him with suspicion in his eyes. "I swear." He grinned. "For one thing, Evelyn is not some innocent virgin, and she's not an idiot like Pen. She knows full well that I will never marry her."

"Does she know about the princess?" Robin asked.

"No," Aiden admitted. "But like I said, she's not a fool." A most uncomfortable pang of some feeling he had no wish to examine drove him up from the hearth. "For the other thing, I have no intention of abandoning her to her fate," he said, appalled to hear himself sounding so defensive. "Whether or not I ever see her in my bed, I do intend to help her, to make sure she's taken care of. That's more than Charles did or her kinsmen, either."

"I suppose," Robin agreed, getting up as well.

"You suppose?" Aiden echoed sarcastically. "Good God, Rob—remind me when you're seventeen; I want to discuss this again and see if you still feel the same." He ruffled the boy's hair, resisting the urge to box his ears instead. "Now come, let's go to the fair."

Evelyn was waiting in the hall as promised, beautiful as ever in a pale pink gown embroidered at the sleeves and bodice with deep red rosebuds—for a common chieftain's daughter from the back of beyond, she certainly dressed to perfection. "Finally," she teased with a smile as they came down the stairs. "We were about to go on with Sir Alan."

"Alas for Sir Alan, I have come," Aiden answered, smiling back. He did like her; he would help her. If she were hurt, it wouldn't be the first time or the worst. He scooped up Max from Agnes's arms and swung him onto his shoulder, making him shriek with delight. "Come on; let's go."

The fair was by far the grandest Evelyn had ever seen. Word of the new lord's wealth had apparently spread, attracting tradesmen from all over Britain and beyond—one rug merchant even had a tiny monkey tethered to his wrist. The English village was full to bursting with Scots, many of whom were strangers to her but most of whom came from her clan. "Malcolm's village must be empty today," she said to Aiden as they stopped at a booth selling wine. "Most of the clan must be here."

"Imagine that," he teased with a grin, charmed and amused by the look of wonder on her face. "I'd say most of the Highlands is here."

"Oh, I don't know about that," she demurred. "There may be more of us than you realize." Max was still perched on Aiden's shoulders, obviously thrilled and astonished by the chaos of activity around him. "Max, don't pull Aiden's hair," she scolded, reaching up to untangle his grip. "Here, I'll take him."

"He's fine where he is," Aiden promised. "My father used to carry me this way whenever we went to London to keep me from being stolen."

"Stolen?" Evie echoed, instantly alarmed. Every stranger's face in the crowd suddenly looked suspicious, the face of a slaver trolling for new stock.

"Don't worry," Aiden said, smiling again. "I've got him."

"Aunt Evie!" Hamish came running toward them through the crowd, splashing mud from the street on every poor soul in his path.

"Amish!" Max shouted back, elated.

"Hamish, be careful," Evie scolded as he reached her, but she smiled. "Watch where you're going," she ordered, catching his chin in her hand.

"I will," he promised, glancing over at Aiden. "Hello."

"Hello, Hamish." Aiden smiled. "Where are your brothers?"

"Somewhere." He shrugged. "I don't know."

"You're not here by yourself?" Evie asked him, Aiden's joke about abductors not quite worn off yet.

"Da is with me," he said, looking behind him. "Here he comes."

Malcolm was coming toward them, a striking figure

in his tartan cloak and kilt with the brooch that marked his office on his shoulder. The Scots in the crowd parted before him in respect, and even the English gave him a second curious glance. "My lord Aiden," he said, clasping Aiden's hand in greeting. "What a fine helmet you have."

"Thanks," Aiden said pleasantly, reaching up to steady Max. "I'm rather fond of it myself."

"And Evelyn." Malcolm smiled. "Don't you look pretty today?"

"Do I?" she asked coolly, and Hamish reached for her hand.

"You always do," the laird of the clan decided. "Your son quite favors you, though he has his father's coloring."

"Do you think so?" she said, barely aware of Agnes moving up closer behind her. "I think he looks like his grandfather, the laird."

The Amazon queen and her bodyguard, Aiden thought as he watched her face Malcolm with Agnes at her back. "What about you, Hamish?" he asked the other child, trying to lighten the mood just a bit. He didn't much care for Malcolm either, but he saw no point in antagonizing the man. "Who do you look like?"

"Just me, I think," Hamish answered shyly, almost smiling back. "My mammy a little bit."

"He has her hair, that's certain," Malcolm laughed. "And her redheaded temper to match it." He pretended to be suddenly fascinated by a nearby display of armor. "But come, Hamish—here is just what we need." He nodded to Evelyn. "Well met, my lord."

"And you," Aiden agreed as Hamish joined his father. They turned away, and he found Evelyn glaring at him. "What is it?" he protested with a laugh.

"Nothing," she said airily. "Come, Agnes, I need to find some cloth."

"Evelyn!" he called, mystified by her reaction. But she was gone with Agnes in her wake. "So much for you, King Max," he said, nonplussed. He watched as the women stopped at a rich display of silks and velvets, brilliant in the midday sun. As he drew closer, Evelyn held up a particularly fine length of deep blue silk, and he smiled. The color suited her perfectly; the gown would be exquisite.

"Look, Agnes," Evelyn said, fingering the silk with the yearning touch of the true-born slave to fashion. "Have you ever seen anything so gorgeous?"

"It is beautiful," Agnes agreed as the cloth merchant approached them, grinning from ear to ear. "But it will be expensive."

"Oh, yes," Evelyn agreed. "I couldn't possibly buy it." She set the bolt regretfully aside and turned to face the merchant. "Show me what wool you have in that color."

"Wool in that color?" He laughed. "Nay, my lady, there is no such thing. Rough fabrics will not hold such blue as that." He looked her up and down, measuring her frame with his eyes. "You should buy the silk. You wouldn't require much, and your beauty demands it."

"My beauty may say what she likes," Evie said wryly. "My purse prefers the wool. Show me the blue that you have." Aiden reached them as the merchant pulled another bolt from underneath the table, a perfectly serviceable fine-woven wool. "How much is this?" she asked, testing the thickness between her thumb and forefinger and frowning in the time-honored fashion of bargain-seeking women everywhere.

"What happened to the silk?" Aiden asked, lifting Max down and handing him to Agnes.

"Nothing happened to it," Evelyn answered, still annoyed with him for being so friendly to Malcolm. A woman she knew from the clan, a particular friend of Rebecca's, was browsing at the other end of the booth. "I've chosen this instead."

Aiden laughed. "You're joking."

"Your lady is a rare blessing, my lord," the merchant said, smiling again. "She means to save you the extra expense."

"I'm not saving him anything; I am the one buying cloth," Evelyn said, trying not to grit her teeth. "Unless he needs another fancy doublet." Her clanswoman was about to tip a table over, she was leaning in so far to listen to every word they said.

"Show me the silk," Aiden ordered, taking the wool away from her and setting it aside.

"I don't think it's your color," Evelyn said lightly as the merchant whisked the bolt of silk back out like a conjurer's trick.

"Oh, I don't know." Aiden grinned. "I think it would suit me rather well." He lifted a corner of the fabric to her cheek. "Particularly on you." Before she could answer, he had turned back to the merchant. "Bring the whole bolt to the castle, and the steward will pay you," he ordered. "And that pale green there as well."

"Very good, my lord," the merchant said, his eyes fairly gleaming with joy.

"You are too kind, my lord," Evelyn began, trying not to lose her temper in front of all the world. "But I couldn't possibly—"

"Consider it a favor to me," Aiden cut her off, merrily oblivious. "I'm the one who has to look at you." At that, Rebecca's friend did tip over the table, spilling a fortune's worth of velvet into the street.

"You bastard," Evelyn hissed under the cover of the uproar that ensued. "How dare you?"

"What are you talking about?" he protested, genuinely shocked. But again, she was already gone, shoving her way through the crowd with Agnes right behind her.

"Ay-ben!" Max called, reaching for him over Agnes's shoulder, but he apparently had no more influence over the women than Aiden did himself.

"Evie!" Aiden shouted, furious and not giving a tinker's damn what the crowd might think of him shouting in the street. What in the name of God was wrong with the woman?

"My lord?" the merchant asked timidly as his assistants rushed to save their stock. "Will you still have the cloth?"

"Yes," Aiden answered impatiently as Evie disappeared. He was buying her a present, something she obviously wanted. Why should she be angry? "No..." Every McCairn within hearing was staring at him, he suddenly noticed, most of the women glaring disapproval while most of the men just smiled. Even Malcolm had stopped looking at armor to watch him in obvious amusement. "Yes," he said firmly to the merchant. "Bring it to the castle exactly as I said."

"Very good, my lord," the merchant said with a bow. "And good luck," he added more softly as Aiden headed for the castle.

Agnes and Max were in the hall, but Evelyn was nowhere to be seen. "Where is your mistress?" he asked the nurse.

Agnes looked up from lacing Max's little shoe, obviously unimpressed with Aiden's position as her lord. "I don't think she wants to talk to you."

"I didn't ask what she wanted," Aiden said, holding his temper in check with Herculean will. "I asked where she could be found."

To his further shock, the woman smiled. "I think she's in the new kitchen," she said, looking down with a dry little cough.

"Many thanks," he said sarcastically.

"Me doe," Max suggested, holding up his arms.

"Not this time," Aiden answered, making himself smile at the child. Poor little monster—his papa was dead, and his mama was insane.

The kitchen still wasn't quite complete. The stone and mortar walls were up, and the fireplaces at either end were functional. But the timbers of the roof were still bare and open to the sky, waiting for their thatch. A small crew of servants had stayed behind from the fair to work here in this open space, preparing stores of food for the winter. Herbs were being tied up in bunches and hung along the rafters, and apples and pears were being cored and sliced, the slices then strung in long garlands to be hung up to dry as well. Evelyn was with this group, slicing apples in her pretty pink gown and looking like a gerfalcon lady visiting a henhouse.

Aiden stopped in the doorway. "What are you doing?" he demanded, oblivious to everyone else. "What is the matter with you?"

Evie looked up from the other side of the room, her little silver knife poised in mid-slice. "With me?!" For half a breathless moment, he was sure she meant to fling the knife at him, but she threw the apple instead, missing him by inches only because he ducked. "Leave me alone," she advised, dropping the knife on the table and storming out the other door.

"Evelyn!" He pushed his way through the snickering

cooks to chase her into the courtyard, feeling like a perfect fool and becoming more furious by the moment. "For Christ's sake, stop!"

She turned halfway across the courtyard, her own rage shining blue flame in her eyes. "Christ doesn't want me to stop," she informed him, coming back to meet him. "Christ knows if I stop and look at you for more than half a minute, I may stab you where you stand."

"But why?" he demanded. "What terrible offense have I committed?"

"You know damned well what you did," she cut him off, her voice rising close to a shriek. "You tried to buy me a fortune's worth of silk in front of all the world."

"Yes!" he exploded. "I thought it would please you—"

"Please me?" she cried, aghast. "I am supposed to be pleased? Why did you not march me to the village cross and make a general announcement? 'Behold, O Scotland, my whore!' Robin could have rung a bell before me, just to get everyone's attention." Some of the women from the kitchen had been bold and curious enough to venture out to listen, but one glare from Evelyn was enough to send them scurrying back inside. "Grant me one favor, Aiden," she finished sarcastically. "Don't try to please me anymore."

"Don't worry," he retorted. She started to walk away, but he stepped into her path. "Nay, lady. I will have my say, too." She crossed her arms, shifting her weight to one hip and arching one delicate brow. "I did not mean to make any statement beyond 'Here, have some silk,' " he began, refusing to be quelled. As if he should be called to task by a snip of a girl with a lunatic's grasp of morality—the nerve of the wench was enough to knock him breathless. "You wanted the damned stuff, so I bought it for you, the same way I put a roof over your pretty little head and food in your pretty little mouth. If you want it, and I can afford it, and I am willing to buy it, what in hell is the harm?"

"Do you not hear yourself?" she demanded. "Did you not see their faces? That woman who knocked over the table is in my sister's house right now, telling her with thrilling details just how low her poor, pitiful slut of a sister has sunk, letting her Sassenach lover buy her clothes in front of God and all the world without showing the least bit of shame."

"Why should you be ashamed?" He laughed. "You've done nothing wrong—*that* I will cry from the village cross and cite my sleepless nights for proof."

"And who will believe you?" she scoffed.

"Not a soul, but why should we care?" She really was upset, he suddenly realized, not just angry. "Evie, darling—"

"Don't you dare call me that!" she ordered. "I never once said you could call me that." She turned away, unable to face him anymore. When she'd first walked away from him at the fair, she had been blind and deaf with fury, her thoughts a babbling whirl of righteous indignation. Once inside, she had turned her attention at once to the nearest work at hand, her mind focused on her grievance with an arrow point's precision while her hands kept busy cutting fruit. *Bastard*, she had chanted in her head. *Thoughtless, bloody bastard.*

But now with the bastard before her, she couldn't seem to hold her bearings; her rage kept getting mixed up with fear and hurt and the very real shame that made her sick to her stomach every time she thought about it. He hadn't purposely meant to hurt her; he really had meant to make her happy with his gift. But he hadn't been stupid, either; he had known exactly what everyone would think, what everyone thought already. *I put a roof over your pretty little head and food in your pretty little mouth.* He knew what everyone thought she was, and he didn't care.

"Forgive me," he said now, his tone turning cold. "I didn't realize my endearments would be offensive, too."

"It's all very well for you to say 'Who cares?' " she said, scornful and blushing at once as she turned back to him. "You're a rich English lord with a rich, English lord for a father who can buy you out of trouble, assuming anyone ever dared to cause you trouble in the first place."

"And you're a woman with a baby and no husband," he shot back, wounded far more deeply by her words than he would ever have dared to let her see. "If you haven't learned to be shameless yet, I'd say you need the practice."

She slapped him harder than she had ever imagined striking anyone in her life, trembling all over from the impact. "Bastard," she breathed, unable to say anything else.

"Nay, lady." He smiled, rubbing his stinging cheek. "My parents had been lawfully wed a full fifteen years when I was made." In truth, the hurt in her eyes made him feel a twinge of regret for what he'd said, but he wouldn't confess it for the world. She turned away again, and he caught her gently by the arm. "Evelyn, really," he said, his tone softening as well. "You're being ridiculous."

"How so, my lord?" she asked with acid sweetness. "By fretting for my good name when I have none left?"

"For caring what a lot of barbarian peasants say about you in a village hut," he answered. "They're going to say it no matter what you do, so why bother trying to appease them?" This philosophy had served him well for more than a decade in London, soothing the sting of the gossip against him until he barely felt it at all.

"Those barbarian peasants are my clan," she pointed out. "I am one of them. And that hut, as you call it, was my father's house. It was my home, far more than this cold, empty castle ever could be, no matter how many tapestries I hang up on the walls or candles I light in the windows." His hand was still resting on her arm, and she pointedly brushed it away. "I thank you for the roof and the food you so kindly provide us, my lord," she said with deadly courtesy. "I don't ask you for anything else."

"My gifts are mine to choose, Evie," he answered, stung but smiling. "You can only choose not to accept them. And really, why bother?"

"Because, as you say, it's the only real choice I have left." She wanted to run from the courtyard and from him, but she made herself stand fast. "Are you done having your say?"

He put a hand over his eyes, resisting the urge to throttle her, self-righteous little lunatic that she was. Was there no reasonable woman to be found in all the world? Did they really all have to be crazy? "Yes, Lady Evelyn," he said when he trusted his voice again. "I am quite done wasting my breath."

"Fine." Bobbing a curtsy, she turned and walked at a dignified pace back to the castle, through the hall, and up the first flight of stairs, ignoring the curious looks of everyone she passed. *Just a few steps more*, she kept promising herself, her blush burning hotter and hotter. As soon as she reached the second floor, she broke into a run, bounding up the spiral stairway to her room and slamming the door shut behind her.

12

Robin trudged back down the stairs to the hall with obvious dread in every step. "She isn't coming," he announced to the knights gathered for dinner, including Aiden, sitting on the dais.

"Yes, she is," Aiden said firmly, color rising in his cheeks. "Go back and inform her that I didn't mean my last word for an invitation but an order, and my dinner is getting cold." This was met with a murmur of approval from the knights—that should put the wench's mind to rights.

Robin, however, looked at his master as if he thought he'd lost his mind. "Yes, my lord," he said gamely even so. "Just as you say."

He trudged back up the stairs and knocked again on Lady Evelyn's door. Agnes opened it and glared at him, looking no more friendly now than she had ten minutes before. "What do you want now?" she demanded.

"I have another message." She stepped aside and let him into the room where Evie was playing with Max, rolling a ball back and forth on the floor to his apparently infinite amusement. "My lord says you must come down to dinner," the squire began.

"I heard you the first time, Robin," Evie answered, smiling at her son. "I'm not hungry."

"He said it wasn't an invitation," Robin said, bracing for an explosion. "It was an order, and his dinner's getting cold."

She turned her pretty smile on him, and he heard Agnes snort once behind him in amusement. "He should eat it, then." Max tossed the ball in the air and miraculously caught it, producing a look of such surprise on his face, she and Agnes both laughed. "Aren't you the clever boy," she applauded, and Max dropped the ball to laugh and clap as well.

"My lady, please," Robin begged, too miserable to be amused. "If I go back down without you, Lord Aiden is just going to come roaring up here himself and carry you down by force."

"Or so he might believe," Agnes said darkly, her scar adding an extra note of sinister credibility to the threat.

"Aiden must do as he chooses in this as in everything else," Evelyn said as Max toddled to her and dropped the ball in her lap. "I choose to stay here."

He looked at her as if she might have been crazy, too. "Yes, my lady," he said with a sigh as he turned to trudge back out.

Downstairs, the squire stopped directly in front of Aiden, but he didn't say a word.

"Well?" his master finally prompted with a frown. "Where is she?"

"In her room." The boy heaved a sigh so heavy it was comic. "She says if your dinner is getting cold, you had better eat it." A few nervous snickers peppered the general mumble of righteous disapproval. "She says she won't come down."

Aiden felt like sighing himself and swearing a bit for good measure. The woman was baiting him, no question, trying to make him lose his temper, though why she should want to do so only another madwoman could guess. The point was, she was very nearly succeeding. If he weren't careful, he'd be making a spectacle of himself again like he had that day at the village fair, chasing after a Scottish commoner like she might be queen of the May, only this time they would be performing in front of his entire household instead of a lot of strangers. Every knight and maid and squire was waiting for it with bated breath, expecting him to go stomping up the stairs to drag her down by her hair.

"Fine," he said, standing up, and a gasp swept over the hall. *Here it comes*, he could almost hear them all thinking. "Robin, prepare a tray for Lady Evelyn and her servant—Molly will help you carry it up." The little kitchen maid looked ready to faint from the stress of being mentioned by name by the great and terrible lord of the manor, and he smiled, feeling better already. "And tell the lady that if she wishes to lock herself in her tower like a penitent, I have no wish to disturb her."

"Thank you, my lord," Robin mumbled, obviously relieved.

"She is hardly the only female to be found in the Highlands, after all," Aiden continued, heading for the door to outside. "The fair is in town. I'm sure I can find more amiable company if I try."

"Well spoken, my lord!" Sir Brutus laughed, and his comrades seemed to agree. Several of them rose to join him as he put on his mantle and gloves, and they followed him into the night.

"He did what?" Evelyn demanded.

"He went out," Robin repeated. "He said if you wouldn't dine with him, he'd find some wench who would." He perched on the end of her bed and filched a roll from her tray. "He will, too," he asserted around a mouthful of bread. "Prince John swears he could find . . . a lady's favor on the moon."

"Kindly spare me, sirrah," Evelyn said with a frown. "I have no interest in hearing the details of Aiden Brinlaw's debauchery."

"Is he really so bad as they say?" Molly asked, wide-eyed with interest of her own.

"Worse." The squire laughed. "He knows the name and face of every bawd in Cheapside."

"A magnificent accomplishment," Evelyn muttered to Agnes, who only smiled.

"But it's the noble ladies who always turn out the worst," Robin continued, sampling Evie's roasted chicken as well. "Either they're widows who end up wanting him to marry them, or they have living husbands he has to fight in the lists."

"Charming," Evelyn muttered, catching Max before he dragged the cloth off the table.

"Does he kill them?" Molly asked breathlessly. "The husbands, I mean?"

"No, silly," Robin scoffed. "First he'll try to pay them for their trouble, give them enough gold to make them forget they've been cuckolded. If that doesn't work, he will fight and make them look silly. He knocked one knight off his horse four times before the poor sot would yield."

"And what does his father say?" Evelyn couldn't stop herself from asking.

"What can he say?" Robin shrugged. "He doesn't approve, nor Lady Alista, either, but there's not much they can do with them at Falconskeep and him in London with the prince and a man full-grown besides." He suddenly seemed to realize he'd eaten most of her dinner, and he jumped down from the bed with a start. "But I should go. . . ."

"Not so fast," Evie ordered. "Sit down and finish that—I've already eaten an hour or more ago. That's why I wasn't hungry."

He gave her an admiring grin before he hurried to obey. "Thanks, my lady."

"Tell me more about your master," she said, glancing at Agnes. "Are he and the prince really such great friends?"

"Yes, indeed." He nodded, attacking the food with new vigor. "Prince John loves him better than his own brothers, I think, and many in London say the same."

"Thick as thieves," Agnes muttered, going to pick up Grace.

"So what is he doing in Scotland?" Evie asked.

The boy looked up at her, suddenly wary. "Securing Glencairn Castle," he answered, choosing his words with care. "King Richard sent word back to the prince that Lord Charles was dead, and Prince John wanted to be certain the manor would hold." There was obviously something more the boy wasn't saying, but she was already fairly certain she knew what it was. No one in Scotland really trusted the English peace. When Richard returned from his holy adventures, he would want the country back under his rule. An English castle in the Highlands would be of excellent use.

"Poor Aiden must be bored out of his mind," she said aloud. "If he's half the scoundrel you describe, he must find very little at Glencairn to amuse him."

"Well, there's you." Robin grinned. "And he's quite serious about the castle." He chewed philosophically on the last chicken leg. "But yea, lady, I must admit, I've been surprised at how well he's behaved since we've come here."

"The strain must be exhausting for him," she said sarcastically, suddenly picking up her spindle from its basket and starting to spin new thread like the souls of the innocent depended on it. "No wonder he's had to cut himself loose for the night."

"No wonder," Robin agreed, mumbling over his plate with a secret, worried smile.

Sometime after midnight Aiden half-strode, half-stumbled into the last of the brightly colored tents set up outside the village wall, a half-empty bottle in one hand and an utterly inebriated Sir Brutus leaning on his shoulder. "Bring me a woman with teeth!" he demanded of the procurer as the little man rushed forward to greet the castle lord with proper enthusiasm. "Lots and lots of teeth! Teeth all the way across the top and at least four on the bottom!" Smiling and nodding, the man hurried off to obey.

"Well met, my lord," a pleasant voice said from somewhere west of his elbow. Turning, he found Malcolm at one of the tables with his elder son, Gerald, Sir Ralph the Messenger, and three or four other Scotsmen Aiden had never seen. "What brings you here?" the laird asked with a grin. "Has the changeling put you out of your castle at last?"

"You . . ." Aiden began, then shook his head, waving the Scotsman off and dropping Sir Brutus in the rushes like a sack of mud in the process. "I don't want to talk to you," he decided, turning away.

"Wait, Lord Aiden." Malcolm laughed, standing up. "Come, sit down with us." He glanced down at Sir Brutus, who was snoring. "Pour that swill you carry over the dead man for luck and come have some fine Scotch whiskey."

"Scotch what?" Aiden said as he was ushered to a stool. "Does this have anything to do with the stomach of a sheep?"

"Nae, my lord, I promise," Malcolm grinned, handing him a cup.

Aiden took a healthy swallow and felt every drop of blood in his body burst into flame at once. "Holy Christ!" he sputtered, glaring at the laird. "Do you mean to kill me?"

"It wouldn't do me any good," Malcolm answered, his grin turning wry as the rest of the Scotsmen laughed. "Another one would just turn up to replace you." He refilled Aiden's cup from a mossy-looking bottle. "Give it another try."

Against even what little judgment he had left, Aiden obeyed, sipping gingerly this time. A warm glow spread through him, the friendly embers left behind by the shocking explosion of before. The pleasant dizziness he had felt when he came into the tent deepened into a kind of drunken clarity. Everything suddenly seemed brighter, and he felt perfectly lucid, even though it seemed he was losing the use of his extremities for the moment. "Changeling," he mumbled, shocked to hear himself slur. In his mind, he was clear as a bell. He took another sip. "You said changeling just now, that the changeling had put me out. What did you mean?"

"Your lady, Evelyn," Malcolm said, taking a sip of his

own. "Her mother always swore she was a changeling child, left by the wee folk in place of her proper babe. Rebecca still believes it."

"Bollocks," Aiden scoffed. No faery in her right mind would trade a babe of her own for some squalling Scottish brat, he privately believed. "No such thing."

"I wouldn't be so sure, lad," Malcolm said, shaking his head. "There's something not quite of the world about the lass, if you see my meaning, and I don't just mean her pretty face." Ralph let out a hearty snort of what sounded like agreement as he took a snort of whiskey. "Here, poor Ralph could tell you."

"The woman is bewitched," Ralph insisted. "Or a witch herself; I cannot tell witch—which." He leaned across the table to stare Aiden straight in the eye. "All I know is she put a spell on me. So long as I was away from her, I was a reasonable man, the right pleasant sort of laddie you see now with naught ill to say to any man alive. But let me clap eyes on Evelyn once or God forbid hear her speaking, and the next thing you know, I'm brawling like a fiend, ready to slit the throat of my dearest friend in the world, just to win her favor." He took another long draw from his cup. "Why, just the other day in your own hall, with the lassie spitting in my very face, I was ready to run you through," he confessed. "Now, why should I quarrel with you, as bonny a Sassenach bastard as any I've ever seen?"

"She's not a witch, Ralph," Aiden said, refilling the Scotsman's cup in sympathy. "She's crazy. Self-love has driven her mad." He drained the dregs of his own cup, the whiskey's fire now no more than a comforting warmth, a blanket for the soul. "You say she is my lady, Malcolm," he said through a cough as the laird refilled his cup. " 'Tis not so, I swear it on my eyes." Gerald, he noticed, was watching him with unmistakable dislike, giving him a momentary chill. But another sip of his father's excellent whiskey banished that quickly enough. "This is important," he asserted. "You should know this, Malcolm—Evie would want you to know it. She cares that your wife thinks she's a slut, though why I can't imagine."

The procurer reappeared with a raven-haired near-beauty who smiled hugely at Aiden to show him her excellent teeth, sending every man but Gerald into helpless gales of laughter. "Come here, sweetheart," Aiden said, drawing her into his lap. "How much must I pay him to keep you for the night?"

"Seven silver pennies," she answered. "To be given before, not after."

"Seven silver pennies." He reached into his purse and counted them out in her little palm. "Behold, gentlemen, seven silver pennies, given before, not after," he said as the girl passed them over to her master. "This girl is now mine for the rest of the night, to do with what I will, this excellent girl with many fine teeth who smells only a little bit worse than my horse."

"Congratulations," Gerald muttered.

"And well you might say so, Gerald," Aiden agreed.

"For I've given your auntie a full tower in my castle, full charge over my household, all the food and drink she cares to have for herself, her child, and her servant, not to mention my most charming affection and, as of today, two fine bolts of silk, yet she has yet to give me more than a kiss for it in return, and that I have to beg for."

"Aye, laddie." Ralph nodded, clapping him on the shoulder with such friendly vigor, he nearly knocked him off his stool. "That is Evelyn."

"I believe you, lad," Malcolm said with a smile. "And I will tell Rebecca, though I'm thinking she will not." His pale brown eyes turned serious. "But what are you going to do? Why do you keep her there?"

Aiden made a face, impatient, but no glib reply would come. Suddenly the stench of the little whore's perfume was making him sick; the softness of her body pressed against him was like the spongy rot of a corpse. "Because that is my choice," he said at last, drinking deeply from his cup.

"What, ho?" Sir Brutus mumbled blearily, making an attempt to sit up. He almost made it, arms flailing the air like a windmill for a moment, then he crumbled again, falling back on the rushes with a juicy-sounding belch.

"Someone better have a care for him," Malcolm said sagely. "He'll drown in his own vomit."

"Landlord!" Aiden called, standing up so fast the girl on his lap nearly landed on Sir Brutus. "Have him dragged into a room and put him on a pallet on his side." He hooked Brutus's purse from the fallen man's belt and took another handful of silver from it to give to the girl. "My true love here can watch him." He touched her chin, turning her face up to his. "Do not let him drown."

"I won't," she promised, making a miserable face. "But are you coming back?"

"No," Aiden answered, meeting Malcolm's eyes with his own. "I've purchased better company at home." Gerald was glaring at him again, and he smiled. "Gerald, you should meet my squire," he suggested, ruffling the boy's hair and making him flinch. "The two of you could be great friends, I think." Making a bow to Malcolm and his men, he turned to leave.

"Be careful, laddie!" he heard Ralph warn from behind him as the flap of the tent fell shut.

Evelyn had been lying awake for hours, listening to the drunken shouts from the courtyard, knights and soldiers staggering back from the fair. "Agnes?" she said at last. "Are you sleeping?"

"No, my lady." She heard a rustle in the dark. "Who can sleep?"

Evie rolled over on her side. "Do you think I'm being stupid, locking myself up here?"

"I don't know," Agnes answered, her tone quite serious. "Why did you do it?"

"I don't know." She rolled her pillow into a fatter shape. "I suppose I needed time to think."

"And what have you decided?"

"I don't know." *You're a woman with a baby and no husband,* Aiden had said. No one had ever dared to speak to her so brutally before, not even Rebecca. *If you haven't learned to be shameless yet, I'd say you need the practice.* "I think that I was stupid," she said aloud. "I thought that he was on my side. I thought he understood me."

"You weren't stupid, my lady," Agnes answered, a disembodied voice in the dark. "You wanted to believe it, so you did." Another rustle sounded as she shifted on her pallet. "I loved a man once, and I believed he loved me, even when he swore to me he didn't. I thought he just wanted to protect me." She took a deep, rattling breath, and Evie waited, breathless herself. "Even when he hurt me, I wouldn't believe he didn't care," the Englishwoman said at last. "When your Aiden finally killed him, I cried like a newborn babe."

"Aiden killed him?" Evie said, aghast.

"It was a mercy to him," Agnes answered. "Prince John wanted him drawn and quartered with his guts taken out alive. But before the prince could get there, the Dragon cut off his head. He did it himself with his own sword so the prince couldn't blame the executioner."

The Dragon, Evelyn thought, a shiver running up and down her spine. *The royal assassin whose mercy was murder done quickly.* "Was he the father of your babe?" she asked. "This man whom Aiden killed?"

"No, my lady," Agnes said, her smile clear in her voice. "He was dead long before I got Grace. But I like to fancy sometimes that he was." After a pause she continued. "And I'll tell you something else. As badly as it all turned out, I wouldn't change a moment of the time I knew he loved me, not for all the world. So no, my lady, I don't think you're stupid."

"But I don't love Aiden," Evelyn pointed out. "I don't even know him." *And now he's off with someone else,* she thought. *He'll have found a whore he can manage.* Why should she have ever believed she could win him? What did she have to offer him in return for his name and his castle that a thousand others wouldn't give him for far less?

"He wants you," Agnes said as if answering her thoughts more than her words. "You need not give up on him yet."

Aiden stood at the bolted door, his hand over the latch. The spell was not an easy one, particularly when he was drunk, but he was determined. It would work. Murmuring softly, he felt the wood turn hot, smelled it burn as the metal of the bolt on the other side turned molten and melted away.

He climbed the spiral stairway, silent as a cat, his eyes adjusting easily to the dark. The door at the top stood open, leading to Evelyn's room.

Saxon Agnes was sleeping on a pallet near the door with her baby in a cradle at her feet. He slipped around them, still silent, and approached the bed, a tall cabinet carved in the same style as his own downstairs, but smaller. His heart beat faster as he saw Evelyn's sleeping face, impossibly beautiful in the pale blue light of the moon. Poor Ralph was sure she had bewitched him. Looking at her now, he could almost believe it was true. Her lips were slightly parted, dewy pink like the petals of a rose, and her auburn hair was spread across the pillow, glowing bright as copper in the tender light. He lifted a lock of it between his fingers, soft and sleek as silk. She was his, bought and paid for, a treasure he had never thought to find. But now that he had found her, he would not give her up, even to herself. He would claim her or be damned, or both at the same time.

He sat down on the edge of the bed and traced the shape of her mouth, more silk warm with her breath. She stirred slightly, her brow drawn in a frown, and he waited for her eyes to open, for her to find him there. But her face relaxed after a single sigh, slipping back into repose. "What do you want from me, Evie?" he murmured, caressing her pure, white brow. "What gift do you want me to give?" He could kiss her, overpower her easily, make her his at last—the thought of it made him drunker than Malcolm's Scotch whiskey ever could. Or he could cast a spell on her to make her willing, carry her down to his own bed, a yielding, languid thing entranced first by magic, then by the pleasure he could make her body feel.

But that would not be Evie. And if he forced her,

raped her with her child asleep by her side, he would not be himself. Bending closer, he pressed a kiss to her mouth, too delicate to wake her.

Agnes watched as the Dragon left the bed, clutching the dagger tightly in her fist. He went back out the way he had come, a nearly silent shadow, and slowly she relaxed, her heartbeat falling to its normal rhythm. *You needn't worry, my lady*, she thought. *You will have him yet.*

Aiden went out the door from the solar that led into the courtyard and down the steps to Evie's little garden. Looking up, he saw a tower window with firelight barely glowing around the edges of the shutters—the window to her room.

Moving slowly to the foot of the tower, still gazing up, he stopped before her pitiful little rosebushes, more stunted and weak-looking than ever after the autumn frosts. He knelt down and plucked the single, wilted bloom, its petals falling as he lifted it up. He kissed the faded blossom as he had kissed her lips, so delicately the petals barely shuddered. Then he gripped the stem of the rosebush tightly in his fist, letting the thorns pierce his flesh until his blood flowed over the vine. Singing an ancient conjure, he sank his bleeding hand into the dirt, mingling his blood around the rose's roots. He gathered up the petals from the single blossom and crushed those as well, still singing under his breath. Looking up at Evie's window one last time, he smiled and went to bed.

13

Evelyn woke up smelling roses. Max was still sleeping peacefully beside her, but when she rolled over, she found Agnes already up, nursing little Grace. "Do you smell that?"

Agnes nodded. "Open the shutters and see."

Wan morning light had just begun to creep through the cracks around the window, lighting her way. She tried to open the shutters, but they wouldn't budge, and the rose scent was suddenly so intense, she could have swooned. She tugged harder, and suddenly the lash gave way. The shutters opened, and a swirling rain of scarlet petals showered over her. "God's mercy," she whispered, pinning back the wooden latch.

Thick green vines were twined and twisted all around the window frame, and every vine was heavy with blossoms clustered so thickly she could barely see daylight. "Agnes, look," she murmured, still not certain she wasn't dreaming. How could roses bloom so thickly in September, even if such vines as these somehow could be real? She touched one of the blooms, half-expecting it to melt away to mist. "Do you see this?"

"I see it," Agnes said, coming to stand behind her with Grace still in her arms. Some of the flowers were barely budding, and a few were fully blown. But most of them were just beginning to open, the petals soft with dew and barely parted, a secret waiting eagerly to be revealed.

"So beautiful," Evie said softly, still barely daring to speak for fear the vision might disappear. "But where did they come from?" She brushed the vines aside to look down at the ground—her own pitiful little garden. "My roses were all but dead."

"They say he is a wizard," Agnes reminded her. "Perhaps this is your proof."

"Aiden?" she said, still touching the blossoms, unable to stop. "But, Agnes, that's insane." Wizards and warlocks were supposed to be nasty old men with dirty beards and crooked backs who smelled of brimstone and stole babies from their cradles to pop them into soup. Aiden was wicked, no question, with no morals she could easily discern, but he was hardly a monster. He was beautiful.

"Oo," Max said, crawling down from the bed with shocking agility. "Pitty."

"Yes," Evie agreed. "Very pretty." She touched another stem, and a thorn tore into her thumb. "And very sharp," she added with a wince.

"Let me see," Agnes ordered.

"No, it's all right." A single drop of blood the same deep scarlet as the rose petals welled up from her flesh, and a strange weakness welled up inside her, making her feel faint. "I'm not usually so squeamish," she said, sitting down. *My love*, a voice whispered inside her head, a memory of a dream. *You have to let me go.*

Suddenly there were footsteps stomping and skittering up the stairs and someone pounding on the door. "I thought the door downstairs was bolted," Evie said, putting her wounded thumb in her mouth for a moment as she got up and Max and Grace both began to cry. "Have you been out already?"

"No, my lady," Agnes answered, comforting the children.

"Who is it?" Evelyn called, throwing a sleeveless robe over her shift.

"Sir Alan, Lady Evelyn," the marshal's voice answered. "And a little friend." Opening the door, she found the knight holding her middle nephew by the collar as he might have held a puppy by the scruff of the neck.

"Davey!" She took the boy from him with a frown. "What has happened?"

"His brother was caught with two other young Scotsmen climbing over the wall, armed with torches and flint," Sir Alan answered. "They've already been taken to Lord Aiden. But I found this one hiding in the gatehouse."

"Oh, for pity's sake," she scolded. "Davey, what possessed you? You'll be flogged for this, and your da will probably give you a beating as well."

"It's a bit more serious than that, my lady," Sir Alan said as tears began to roll down the little boy's cheeks. "Lord Aiden has decreed that any Scotsman caught breaching the walls in secret must be hanged, no matter how young he might be."

"He wouldn't dare!" Evie cried, horrified. "They're children—"

"I'm afraid he might," Sir Alan said, his plain face drawn with genuine concern. "He is known throughout the realm for taking this sort of thing very seriously."

"Gerald didn't want to do it!" Davey suddenly burst out. "The others pushed him into it. They said he wouldn't because you were the Sassenach's doxy, and he was afraid. They said Da would sell the clan to the English the same way he sold you." He looked up at Evelyn, pleading with his eyes. "He didn't want to, Aunt Evie, I swear. But he couldn't just let them say that."

"It's all right," she promised, hugging him. "No one is going to hang." Indeed, she couldn't begin to imagine the Aiden she knew sending boys to the gallows, no matter what he might have decreed or how angry he might be. But then she looked at Agnes and saw her scar and remembered what she'd said about the Dragon's justice. "Where are they now?" she asked Sir Alan. "Where is Aiden?"

"Questioning the prisoners in the solar," Sir Alan said. "Or was, the last I heard."

"Stay with Sir Alan and behave yourself," she ordered Davey, holding his hot little face in her hand for a moment before she kissed his cheek. "I will be right back."

Aiden sat at the table, holding his aching head. Scotch whiskey, indeed—Malcolm had lied. He had meant to kill him, just a little at a time. And now, somehow, he was supposed to look fierce enough to scare some sense into a pack of baby barbarians, one of whom was Malcolm's own son. "Diabolical Scottish bastard," he muttered with a snort of bitter laughter, cursing the laird as he deserved. "All right. Bring them in."

Sir Brutus, looking like death warmed over himself, opened the solar door, and the kilted trio of would-be marauders was led in, not a one of them a day older than sixteen. Two were strangers, a gangly youth with lank, reddish-brown hair and a bloody nose and a stocky, golden-haired cherub who looked scared out of his wits. The skinny one had to be dragged in by three guardsmen, he was flailing and fighting so, shouting Gaelic oaths with every breath—it was easy to see how his nose had been bloodied. The pudgy one was quiet, staring at the floor.

Gerald was quiet, too, but he held his head high, a captured prince in his shackles. "I thought you said they were brigands, Sir Brutus," Aiden said, meeting the boy's gaze with the thinnest shadow of a smile. "These little girls need a nurse."

"Sassenach dog," the skinny one snarled. "Why don't ye lick my arse?"

Aiden stood up quickly and carelessly, with no deliberation, drawing his sword as he went. Giving the blond one just long enough to gasp a swallowed scream of horror, he raised it hilt-first and slammed it into the side of the skinny one's head, dropping him to his knees. "Shut up," he said mildly as the boy spit more blood onto Evelyn's rug. "You." His eyes slid past Gerald to the blond. "Who are you?"

"I . . ." The boy was trembling so savagely, he could barely stand, but he raised his eyes to Aiden's. "I will not tell," he managed, his fair face going green. "Though you eat my heart with me living."

Aiden let his smile widen just a hair. "A Scottish delicacy, no doubt," he said, glancing over at Sir Brutus. "Closely kin to haggis."

"No doubt, my lord," Sir Brutus agreed with an exaggerated shudder.

Aiden turned back to the table and the warrant he had already written out. "You have trespassed on the sovereign soil of England," he began.

"Sovereign soil of England?" Gerald exploded, the first sound he had made. "Nay, you must be joking."

"The items you carried show an evil intent," Aiden went on, meeting the boy's eyes with his own as the only sign he had heard. "Therefore, as required by decree, your lives are forfeit." Twin spots of livid color appeared on Gerald's freckled cheeks, and the blond boy let out a moan. The skinny, rude one was openly weeping. "You will be hanged at noon." In truth, he had no intention of hanging anyone at any time of day, but he hadn't decided yet how he would avoid it. He sat back down in his chair. "Will you not give me your names so your kin can be informed?"

"You know my name already," Gerald answered, his voice surprisingly calm.

"Aye, Gerald, I do," Aiden answered, letting the slightest edge of brotherly warmth creep into his tone. "And I cannot believe your father, wise laird of his clan that he is, could countenance such an attack."

"What do you know about my father?" the boy shot back, suddenly fearless in fury. "He is laird in this glen; these lands are his, not yours, and I don't give an ox's arse for your king or your lordship, either."

The door burst open before Aiden could answer, and Evelyn rushed in. "Aiden, stop," she ordered, ignoring the stares of the others. She was still undressed, wearing nothing but a shift beneath her sleeveless robe, but she barely seemed to notice. "Stop this nonsense at once."

"Good morning, my lady," Aiden said, barely touching her arm, giving Sir Brutus a quelling frown. In truth, every man in the room but one was openly gaping at her, and he could hardly blame them. The two unknown prisoners were staring as if she might have been an angel sent from heaven to deliver them from death. But Gerald took one look at her and turned away, blushing bright red. "Take the prisoners to the dungeon," Aiden ordered. "I will speak to Lady Evelyn alone."

Evie watched as the boys were taken away, touching Gerald's arm as he passed. "It will be all right." He nodded, trying to smile. Angus McGraylin, Molly's sweetheart, had a bloody nose and bleeding mouth, and little Terry Pike was obviously sick with fear. *It serves you right, you little rodents,* she thought, remembering what Davey had said. She could just hear them, taunting Gerald; she could just imagine the pretty names they had found for her. Yet now they were looking at her with the moist eyes of a pair of newborn lambs begging her to save them from slaughter.

"You look lovely, Evie," Aiden said when they were gone, shuffling his papers. "I think of all the gowns I've seen you wear, that one may be my favorite."

"You can't really be serious," she said, sitting in the other chair.

"No, I am," he insisted. "The cut is a bit revealing, but the color suits you excellently well."

"Stop it," she scolded. "Tell me you don't really mean to put those boys to death."

"And why should I not?" he asked. "They meant to burn my new kitchen, of which I happen to be quite proud, not to mention the fact that I have already sworn I would." She really did look beautiful with her hair all mussed and no shoes on. *How did you like your roses, Evie?* he wanted to ask. "I don't see where I have much of a choice in the matter."

"Lamb's dung, Aiden," she scoffed. "Whatever nonsense you might have decreed when you got here, you can always change your mind. You are lord here, are you not?"

"Nonsense, lady?" he echoed. "How is protecting my castle from foreign invaders nonsense?"

"Foreign invaders my . . . foot," she said, amending her oath at the last moment before propriety gasped its last. "You Sassenach are the foreigners here, not us. And if your stronghold is so weak it can't withstand an assault from the likes of those three, you'd better pack up and go home."

"Words of treason spoken under my very roof, from the lips of my chatelaine," Aiden said, trying not to smile. "Who knows where it will end?"

"Aiden, they are children," she insisted, catching his arm.

"They were plenty old enough to scale the walls—"

"And young enough to get caught with half your guard carousing in the village and the other half drunk at their posts," she pointed out. "Gerald didn't even want to come; the others goaded him into it."

"And how do you know that?" For a single, horrifying moment, the thought that Evie might be directly connected to this barbarous stupidity made his head ache even worse. She had been furious with him last night, certainly, but surely she wouldn't have recruited her nephew and his friends to vandalize his castle.

"Davey told me," she answered, not liking the look

that had just come into his eyes. "He's upstairs in my room with Agnes and Sir Alan, frightened half out of his wits."

"So Davey was part of it, too?" Aiden asked, smiling in relief.

"Aye, Aiden, he was the one who planned it. You ought to hang him first," she said sarcastically, encouraged by his smile. "Of course, he's only ten years old and weighs less than one of your legs, so you'll have to tie rocks to his feet."

"A most practical suggestion," Aiden retorted. "I'll take it under advisement." He was beginning to see a way out of his dilemma that might profit them both, though Evie probably wouldn't see it that way. "Of course I won't hang the little one," he said aloud. "What kind of monster do you think I am?"

A wizard, she almost said without thinking. *Tell me about the roses.* "I don't know," she said instead, focusing her mind back on the matter at hand. "Not when you keep insisting that you mean to hang the others." She still couldn't believe he really meant to do it, no matter what Sir Alan or Agnes or even he might say. He was a fierce warrior, a servant of the English crown, a scoundrel, a bit of a drunkard, and possibly even a wizard. But he wasn't a murderer. "Aiden, please—"

"And what will happen if I don't?" he cut her off, voicing the argument he'd been having with himself inside his own head ever since the guards had woke him up with the news. "I made it plain to the people who live beneath my rule that I would protect them, that if any Scot should dare to breach our walls for any reason but friendship or trade, he would be hanged before the day of his capture was done. What will happen if I go back on that promise now? The English of Glencairn will never feel safe, and why should they? The Clan McCairn will have their proof that they may treat us however they please because I won't strike back."

"Aiden," she began again. She could see some sense in what he said, but the whole discussion still seemed ludicrous. What was a promise to the manor and the appearance of strength compared to the lives of three children? "You can't honestly see Gerald and his friends as a serious threat to you or your castle, and neither do your English, I'm certain. If a patrol of grown Scotsmen armed with swords instead of torches should come clamoring over the gates with murder in their eyes, I could see your being committed to making them an example. Hang them; I will pull the lever myself. But three boys who only meant to annoy you?" She took his hand in hers and was gratified to see him smile. "Mercy is not weakness."

His smile broadened into a grin. "You sound just like my mother."

"Then your mother is very wise," she said, smiling back. "Spare their lives for her sake, and for mine."

"For yours?" He laughed, letting her go. "Why should I want to do anything for you?"

"I beg your pardon?" she asked, taken aback.

"You won't even leave your tower to dine with me," he pointed out as he got up from his chair. "You make me a laughingstock before my own garrison."

"Fine," she said primly. "If you will spare these boys, I will never fail to dine with you again."

"Not good enough," he retorted. "Yesterday you railed at me like a drunken fishwife for trying to buy you the makings of a single gown in front of your relations. What do you think they'll say if I give you three half-grown Scotsmen?"

"You really are the devil," she said, clenching her teeth and her fists to stop herself from screaming and boxing his ears. "You never had any intention of hanging those boys—"

"I said I would, didn't I?" he cut her off, pure triumph gleaming in his dark blue eyes. "Are you willing to take that chance?"

She turned in her chair to face him. "What do you want?"

He grinned. "You know very well what I want," he said, leaning back against the table.

"Nay, sir, by no means," she said, crossing her arms and turning away.

"You would let your kinsmen hang to save your precious virtue?" he said, the furious set of her sweet little jaw making him positively ache to kiss her. "That's rather selfish, Evie."

"You should hang yourself," she retorted. "By your toes over a cauldron of vipers."

"What a lovely image." He smiled. "If you find that fine Scottish husband you're so determined to have, perhaps he'll make it happen."

"I'll pray for it every night." He was so close to her, she could feel the warmth of him against her cheek, and she stood up, moving away. "What are your terms exactly, my lord?"

"Nothing horrific, I promise." His perfect jaw was shadowed with prickly stubble; his hair was falling in his eyes; his linen shirt was half-unlaced, and he wasn't even wearing a tunic. With the look in his eyes and the grin on his face, he looked like pure sin made a man. "For one, you help me stage this hanging as a pageant, play your part and say exactly what I tell you to say."

"I can do that," she said. "If you promise me the pageant ends with the boys going home to their mothers." *Oh, glory, Rebecca,* she thought with a sinking heart. *What would Rebecca say?*

"I swear it on my life, if we can agree on the other condition," he answered.

"So what is it?" she said, steeling herself for the worst. "Tell me exactly."

"Just this." He took her hand in both of his, caressing her delicate fingers. "You must swear to pass a single night in my room." He laced his fingers with hers. "In my bed."

"A single night?" She looked down as if she were embarrassed, but in truth, a sudden inspiration was threatening to make her smile.

"Yes." He lifted her hand to his lips. *One night is all I will need, sweeting,* he thought but didn't say. *You will never want to hide from me again.*

"One night," she repeated slowly, looking up to meet his eyes. "In your chamber. In your bed. And you will spare the boys?"

"Yes." He nodded. "I promise."

She took a deep breath and let it out in a sigh of pure surrender. "Very well. I promise, too." She drew her hand from his with an appropriate maidenly shiver. "Now teach me what to say."

At noon Aiden stepped out into a brilliant autumn day, the sky bright blue and the air thick and sweet with the fragrance of roses. The spell he had worked had run riot. The tower where Evie slept was completely covered in blossoming vines, and the cobblestones of the courtyard were strewn with fallen red petals.

"Lord Aiden, we are ready," Sir Alan said gravely, joining him on the steps. A freshly built gallows with three traps stood just opposite the roses, its new wood gleaming white and cruel. A small crowd of Scots and his own English peasants had gathered at the foot of the platform to mourn or watch the show, and the garrison was assembled, both in the courtyard and all around the walls. He glanced over at the door of the chapel, built against the castle wall halfway between where he stood and the gallows, and he saw it stood ajar.

"All right." He nodded. "Fetch the prisoners."

Sir Alan turned to the guardsmen waiting at the door that led to the dungeons and nodded. "The prisoners come!"

The three young Scots were led into the courtyard. The smallest one was staring at the ground and did not look up, even when a woman with his same coloring and build screamed out and tried to rush the guards to reach him. The tall, skinny one who had called Aiden a Sassenach dog was sobbing openly, and when Molly, the kitchen maid, saw him, she screamed out, "Angus!" and slumped to the ground in a faint.

Gerald walked out last, his head held high as ever. But when he saw the gallows, he stopped, his face draining all its color in a single moment. He looked toward the crowd as if looking for someone specific, and Aiden almost smiled. *Don't worry, Gerald,* he thought. *She's coming.*

Then the boy seemed to collect himself. Raising his chin again, he walked past the others, leading the way up the steps to the platform. *He would do it,* Aiden realized, rather awestruck by the simple courage of this Scottish child. *If he had to, he would die well.*

"Hear the royal warrant," Sir Alan called as the accused were put into place. "The Scottish Gerald of the Clan McCairn and two companions unknown are hereby sentenced to their deaths for crimes against the sovereign rule of England at the Castle of Glencairn." A smattering of applause broke out among the English peasants, and shouts of defiance were heard from the Scots, though they kept a wary eye on the guards all the while. "Decreed and signed this twelfth day of September, the year 1193," Sir Alan finished, "by William Aiden Brinlaw, servant of the Crown." He turned and looked at Aiden.

Aiden resisted the urge to look toward the chapel again. "Hangman," he called out, his voice carrying easily over the spellbound crowd. "You may commence."

"Wait, my lord!" The whole courtyard turned as one as Evelyn emerged, a perfect angel of mercy in a pale yellow gown with her auburn hair flowing freely down her back. In her hands, she carried a bouquet of blood-red roses.

The crowd parted before her, opening a path to the gallows until she stood directly between Aiden and the prisoners. "Terry Pike!" she said, her voice sweet and clear on the wind. "Do you repent your crimes?"

The round, blond boy blinked as if waking from a trance. "Aye," he stammered, his voice thick with emotion. "Aye . . . my lady. I do."

She looked back at Aiden. "Angus McGraylin," she said. "Do you regret what you've done?"

"Aye, Lady Evelyn," the skinny one croaked, the title coming to him as easily as a baby's gurgle. "May God strike me dead if I do ever pain His Lordship anymore."

She walked to the very foot of the gallows. "Gerald, son of Malcolm," she said, pleading with the boy with her eyes. Gerald didn't know this was all a performance; his answer could ruin everything. "You are my kinsman, and I love you well. For my sake, will you ask Lord Aiden for pardon?"

The boy's face worked frantically, his stoic mask threatening to melt. "Aye, Aunt Evie," he said at last, looking straight at Aiden. "For her sake, my lord, I most humbly beg your pardon."

Evelyn walked to the steps and laid her roses at Aiden's feet, a touching gesture of her own design. "These boys have confessed and repented," she said, one corner of her mouth barely curling up with a smile for Aiden alone. "Will they be absolved?"

Aiden's part had come, but for a moment he could barely remember what he was meant to say. He had known Evie's plea would touch the hearts of everyone in the courtyard, Scot and Englishman alike. But he had never expected to be so affected by her himself. "Why should you ask for this, my lady?" he asked, going down the steps. "What have your kinsmen done for you, that you should plead mercy for their sons?"

Evelyn lifted her chin much as Gerald had done. "My clan has given me life," she answered, her words her own, not Aiden's. "For their sake, I give that life to you."

A murmur of shocked admiration swept through the crowd, and Aiden felt his own heart beat faster. How would it feel to hear her say such a thing to him for real? "Your life is precious to me," he said aloud, picking up the roses. "For your sake, they will be spared." He pressed the bouquet into her hands as the crowd exploded in cheers.

"Well done," he murmured under the cover of the chaos, leaning close to her ear.

"You, too." She looked up at him with the wickedly flirtatious smile that always drove him mad. "I will see you tonight." Then she was being swept up in the thankful embrace of Terry Pike's mother, swept away from him and swallowed up by the Scottish crowd.

14

Aiden sat in the solar and watched the fire die, listening to his knights carousing in the hall. They were happy tonight, celebrating their lord's great, merciful victory over the Scots. The son of the laird had been humbled, forced to yield his pledge of faith. And Evelyn, the Scottish beauty who held them all in such thrall, had been brought to heel as well, forced to swear a far more personal oath of her own. In the world at large and in his own hall, the Dragon had carried the day. But the more he thought about it, the more he realized he wasn't particularly pleased.

In his mind he kept seeing Evie's face as she made her promise. *My clan has given me life*, she had told him, abandoning the script he had given her to make a deeper, sweeter vow. *For their sake, I give that life to you.* No one in the courtyard could have mistaken her meaning. All her pretenses of virtue were to be abandoned. She would be his possession, his mistress, to save her nephew's life. *One night*, she had promised him privately in this very room. *In your chamber. In your bed.* When she'd said it, he had been happy, as giddy with triumph as the knights drinking to his health and pleasure in the hall. But now he wasn't so sure.

For their sake, I give that life to you. He drained his cup, the wine rich and slightly bitter in his throat. In spite of all her ambitions, all her oaths of chastity, Evelyn was his, but not because of him. He had trapped her with her own misplaced loyalty to the family that had abandoned her. She loved her clan, not him. Not that he loved her, either; he didn't. But it was the principle of the thing. He hadn't won her; he had bought her, the same way he had bought the little gypsy the night before; only the price had changed. Instead of seven silver pennies given to a procurer, three boys' lives had been given back to their laird. "Given before, not after," he said, dashing the dregs of his cup on the embers in the fireplace, making them hiss and spark.

"My lord?" Robin mumbled, dozing on a stool near the open door.

"Come on, Rob," Aiden said, getting up. "We are going to bed."

Evelyn heard a roar rise up from the hall downstairs, laughter and cheers of encouragement, shouts in praise of the Dragon. "Aiden must be on his way up," she said to Agnes, trying not to shiver.

The nursemaid went on braiding Evelyn's hair for bed. "That would be my guess."

"God help us," Molly murmured, flopping back on her pallet.

The master bedroom at Glencairn had probably never been so crowded. Grace's cradle was set at the foot of Agnes's pallet, which was spread before the hearth. Molly was bedded down in the alcove of the deep bay window, and Angus McGraylin's little sisters, Katie and Marlene, were already snoring, wrapped in blankets on either side of her. Max was sleeping, too, piled on up the pillows of Aiden's own bed like a tiny Roman emperor. Evie sat on the edge of the bed beside him, and Agnes stood behind her. "Hush," the Saxon woman said to Molly now.

"It's all right, Molly," Evie promised. "I hope."

"We won't leave you, my lady," Agnes said, tying off the end of Evie's braid with a ribbon. "If the Dragon tries to bed you, he'll have to do it in front of all of us."

"Funny," Evie mused with a shaky little laugh. "Somehow that doesn't make me feel any better." In truth, she wasn't nearly as worried about Aiden's bedding her as she was that he might wring her neck for wriggling out of their bargain.

The door opened, and Aiden came in. But as soon as he saw Agnes and the others, he froze in mid-step, so abruptly Robin crashed into the back of him. "Evie?" he said, raising an eyebrow. "What is this?"

"Not so loud, my lord," she said, climbing into bed. "You'll wake the babies." He crossed his arms on his chest and waited, obviously not amused. "You said you wished for me to sleep in here with you," she pointed out, propping a pillow behind her.

"Yes," Aiden agreed. Robin was looking around at the flock of females with his mouth hanging open in dismay, and he almost smiled in spite of himself. "But I don't recall inviting everyone else." In truth, he didn't know whether to feel furious or relieved.

"Perhaps not in so many words," Evie allowed. "But you might as well have done." Saxon Agnes was watching him with a strange little smile of triumph on her ruined face, a warrior woman of the ancient world armed and ready for battle.

"Do tell?" he asked Evelyn, returning the other woman's gaze with a dry little smile of his own.

"Max has never spent a night away from me," Evie pointed out. "I couldn't just abandon him. And if I have Max, I need Agnes, particularly if . . ." Her voice faltered for barely a moment. ". . . I'm meant to be occupied entertaining you," she continued. "Agnes couldn't leave Grace; she still needs to nurse at least once in the middle of the night." Aiden's eyebrow quirked up even higher, but she pressed on. "Molly has had an extremely traumatic day, what with your meaning to hang her heart's beloved. Plus her mother is quite put out with her, now that she knows about Angus and that he is a Scot. And of course, Katie and . . ." She paused, racking her brain.

"Marlene," Agnes prompted.

"Marlene are particular friends of Molly," Evie finished. In truth, Molly had begged the girls' mother to let them come at Evelyn's request, and after the day's events, Dame McGraylin had felt she could hardly refuse. "They knew how upset she was, so they would not leave her."

"I see," Aiden nodded, pulling a solemn face. In all his years as a patron of liars and fools, he had never heard such a load of hogswaggle as this, and Evelyn obviously knew it. Her eyes barely touched his once in all this recitation. He was the victim of a conspiracy, plain and simple. "So where am I meant to sleep, my lady?"

He was not believing a word that came out of her mouth, but at least he wasn't shouting. "I assumed you would sleep in your usual place, my lord," she said, looking away again to settle the blanket more warmly over Max's shoulders. "That was our original agreement. But if you would prefer to go to another room or send us back to the tower, I can certainly understand."

"Oh, no," he said, pulling off his shirt. Molly gasped; Agnes took a firmer stance, and even the little strangers in the corner sat up on their pallets to glare at him, rubbing their sleepy eyes. "I wouldn't dream of it." He sat down on the bed and unlaced his boots, and Robin spread his own pallet in front of the door, shaking his head all the while. "My brother has always said I ought to have a harem," Aiden finished, swinging his legs into the bed and claiming his own share of the covers. He leaned across Max to take Evelyn's startled but indescribably pretty face in his hand. "Good night, sweeting." He kissed her solidly on the lips. "Pleasant dreams."

Evelyn's heart was beating so fast, she felt dizzy, but Aiden lay back on his pillow and closed his eyes, his arms crossed on his chest. She looked at Agnes, who shrugged but smiled, going off to her own pallet. "Good night," Evie answered, putting out the rush light.

She dreamed of torches on the mountain, a procession that stretched as far as she could see in both directions under a black, starless sky. At first it seemed that she was only a torch bearer, one of the many pale-skinned women and men dressed in dark green robes. But then she seemed to rise above the others, to be floating between parallel lines of flickering light. She was kneeling on a litter carried by three on either side, and beside her lay a man, her heart's beloved, hovering near death.

Aiden! she cried out in her mind, but the body that possessed her was saying something else, singing her love song in the ancient tongue of faery, the same song Evelyn had sung in the hall, the song she had sung since childhood without understanding the words. *"You have my soul, my heart, my love,"* she sang, and this time, she understood. *"I choose you over immortality."* She lifted her lover's cooling hand to her cheek, kissed the mark of the dragon that was painted on his wrist. A mighty battle had been fought upon the mountainside. She could see the bodies of the dead on either side of the procession, the barbarian horde that had fallen like wheat beneath the Dragon's sword. But a spear of stone had found its mark. The Dragon had fallen as well.

"*Over ancient lands, I choose you,*" she sang as tears streamed down her cheeks, stroking his golden hair. At the crest of the mountain stood the Dragon's men, the mortals of the North who had sailed with him to this ancient realm of faery. They waited in a ring of honor, bearing torches of their own. "*In you, I choose my life,*" she sang, facing their stony grief. Their pyre was built already, waiting for fire and the corpse of her beloved. But she would not let him die. "*Forsaking all, I choose you, love, even unto death.*"

"Give him to us, lady," the leader of the sentries begged, kneeling on the rocky ground before the litter. "Let us follow our prince to the halls of our fathers. Allow us to join him in death."

"No," she answered, falling on her lover's chest, his blood staining her cheek, and again, for a moment, Evelyn was not the queen but only one of the procession, one of the many daughters of the faery and her mortal love. "We will not die," the queen insisted in her ancient tongue, and once again, Evelyn was her, facing them drenched in the Dragon's blood. But the man who was dying was not Aiden at all; his hair and beard were blond. When he opened his eyes to look at her, silently pleading, they were the blue of ice, not midnight.

She took a dagger from her belt, and a great moan of grief rose up from the procession, the children of the Cairn. "My blood will hold us both immortal as the sinews of this mountain," she said, holding the blade over her heart. "Our hall will sink beneath the earth to

WICKED CHARMS

hide itself in grief." She turned to her children, their faces stained with tears that glistened in the torchlight. "Go from this place into the glen and prosper in the light," she told them. "These few will serve us well enough, as they have served their master long."

"So be it, lady," the leader of the northmen said, rising from his knees to put his hands on the hilt of the knife. "As you have ensnared our prince with love, let us be captured as well." She touched her lover's mouth as blood rose to his lips, and the dagger plunged into her heart.

"No!" Evie screamed, or thought she had—she sat straight up in bed. But everyone else was still sleeping; no one else had so much as stirred, even Max, snuggled close beside her. Aiden had rolled onto his side to face her, his head resting on his arm. For a moment she thought she would have to wake him just to see his dark blue eyes, hear him speak, and know that they were alive, that this was real and the other was nothing but a dream. But what would she say if she did? She had tricked him out of his prize already tonight, and even though he had taken it quite well, she knew he must be angry. If she woke him, what would he think?

"Not real," she whispered, touching his stubbled cheek as she lay back down again. "It was only a dream."

Aiden had thought he would never fall asleep, that he would spend the whole night listening to Evie breathe and cursing himself for a fool, and for a long time that was just what he did. *I'll have to leave Scotland,* he thought with bitter humor. *My reputation as a man and a soldier will never recover from this.* His knights had cheered him up the stairs to claim his prize; what would they say when they heard he had left it untouched? But what else could he have done?

Idiot, he muttered inside his own head, rolling onto his side. He could have swept Evelyn's accomplices out of his room in half a moment by brute force if necessary and sent the children with them; that was what else he could have done. Max let out a little hiccup in his sleep, and he stroked the baby's brow, barely aware he was doing it.

Evelyn obviously thought herself quite clever. He ought to have known that morning she was giving up far too easily—in faith, she was to be congratulated for not laughing in his face. All her pretty speeches to the contrary, she had never had the slightest intention of surrendering anything, least of all herself. She had no more meant to let him tup her without a messy, brutish scene than he had meant to hang Gerald and his friends for climbing over the walls. They were a pretty pair of liars, both of them.

For their sake, I give that life to you, she had told him in the courtyard, laying the roses he had conjured for her at his feet, and for half a moment he had let himself believe it. In fact, he had spent the rest of the afternoon and half the evening fretting over it. *Bollocks,* he thought, sinking into the pillow and drifting off to sleep.

In his dream a man was lost, wandering for miles untold through trackless wilderness. Sometimes he was the man himself, dying of thirst with barely enough strength to lift the sword he carried in his hand to cut a path through the brush. Other times he seemed to walk beside him, a silent, invisible ghost. Others had fallen behind him, too weak to follow any further without water, but he was their leader, the Dragon. He had brought them to these mountains in search of a land route home. He must find a way out.

His feet slipped out from under him, and he fell, the hillside giving way. Aiden felt the first jolt as his shoulder struck the spongy ground then seemed to drift away again to watch him tumble down the slope, a giant with long, blond hair. The trees gave way to open land at the bottom of the hill, and when the Dragon staggered to his feet, he saw the loch spread out before him like a crystal mirror. *Glencairn,* Aiden thought in wonder as he staggered to the water's edge. *He has found Glencairn.* The man fell to his knees to drink, too thirsty to care if the water might be poison, and Aiden drank with him, the blessed cool of it healing his throat.

He gazed down at his own reflection, sickened by the haggard fear he saw in his own eyes. He had been so certain he was right to follow his vision, so sure that he would win glory. Even when his ship had been broken into kindling, he had not been afraid. The spirits of his ancestors were with him; his destiny was here. A seer as well as a warrior, he had never doubted his course, and his men had trusted him and followed, as fearless as he was himself. But now his men were dying, and the halls of their people were lost somewhere beyond these mountains, beyond a sea he could no longer sail.

The face reflected in the water changed, desperate man into innocent woman. *It's her,* Aiden thought, but the Dragon didn't know her; he fell back from the water, afraid. It was the tiny faery Aiden had dreamed of before, the creature he had mistaken for Evie. She smiled as she rose from the water, her face unlined and open as a child's, her skin so pale it seemed to be the same blue-white as the water. She was naked, but her jet black hair enrobed her, falling over her shoulders like a silken mantle to her knees. "You are new," she said in faery speak, coming near the Dragon where he sprawled half-prone on the shore. "You should not be here."

"Who are you, lady?" Aiden asked her in the Dragon's voice. "Where is your house? Who are your kin?"

"I have no kin." She bent down to touch his mouth, her brow drawn in concentration, and for a moment she was Evelyn; the expression and gesture were strangely familiar to him. "I am alone." He caught her gently by the wrist, and she frowned. "You must let me go."

"I cannot." His men were forgotten and the halls of the north; all he cared about was here, this faery in his grasp. Even Aiden seemed to be forgetting he was dreaming, losing himself in this vision of the past.

"Yes, you can." She smiled, the same wicked smile that Evie had used to bewitch him the first time they met. "I will release you if you wish." Her smile faded to sadness as her free hand brushed his cheek. "But I do not wish it."

"No," the Dragon answered, standing up to take her in his arms. "I do not wish it, either." Aiden closed his eyes as his kiss fell on her lips, cold and sweet as the water of the loch. Suddenly the vision faded and changed; the cold streamed into him, freezing his blood, and he was falling backward, a burning pain in his chest.

He opened his eyes on a starless midnight sky, the smoke and stench of torches thick in the air. The faery knelt over him, clothed now in a robe of black, a golden circlet set with jewels on her brow. She held a dagger to her breast, and he tried to reach for her to stop her, but his limbs had turned to stone. Another hand closed over hers, and the blade plunged into her heart, her forehead drawn in concentration as her fingers touched his mouth.

He opened his eyes in reality on cold, gray dawn, his heart pounding like thunder. Evie was sleeping beside him, one arm curled protectively around her sleeping child, and for a moment he meant to wake her to tell her his vision, explain the cold, gray fear that was closing over his heart.

But he couldn't. If he told her his dream, she would probably agree that it was upsetting, but she wouldn't understand why it was important, and he could never explain. To make her understand, he would have to tell her the truth about his faery heritage, confess that he was a wizard, and that would frighten her more than any vision ever could.

He got up slowly from the bed, careful not to wake her or the others, and reached for his shirt and boots.

The grooms were barely awake when he went into the stable, and he saddled his horse himself. "Take care, my lord," one of them cautioned through a yawn as he rode off toward the loch.

He skirted the edge of the water at a walk, trying to remember the spot from his dream, but it was pretty well hopeless. Everything about the terrain had changed, even the shape of the loch itself. But even as he rode through the bracing morning rain, his memory of the vision didn't fade, and he was still just as certain it was real as he had been when he first opened his eyes. This Dragon and his faery had left unfinished business in the Highlands, business that was somehow reaching out for him and probably for Evelyn, too. *You will be the Dragon*, the spirit of Falconskeep had told him, touching him with freezing fire to burn her mark on his wrist. Was this what she had meant?

"She can see far through time but not through distance," his mother had explained to him when he was just a child, trying to warn him away from the caves of Falconskeep and the spirit that lived within them. "She is jealous of our lives, our abilities to move and feel, to live and grow and die. Through your eyes, she will seek the places you will go someday and the man you will become, and even if she loves you, she will only speak in riddles that can bring you far more harm than good." This was how his grammy, Blanche, had fallen to her doom, questing for secret knowledge through communion with the wraith. When he had put his hand into the pool and received the dragon mark and the knowledge of a thousand magicks untold, had he done the same?

He stopped halfway around the loch and looked back at the castle. Evelyn was part of this, too—a changeling, Malcolm had called her, a faery child. "My clan was born on the mountain," she had said herself after she sang her song. "The clan has given me life," she had told him when she asked that Gerald be spared.

The pealing of a bell rang out across the water from the Scottish village—an alarm, from the frantic sound of it. Lights were just appearing in the windows of the cottages along the cliffs, and he thought he could see torches being carried up the hill to the house of the laird. "What has happened, Malcolm?" he murmured, barely aware he had spoken. "What trouble is coming for you?"

He looked back at the slope rising behind him, and

suddenly it was familiar. This was where the Dragon had fallen through the brush. He got down from his horse and moved to the edge of the water, falling to one knee among the rocks. His reflection was as clear as it had been in the dream, except this time it truly was himself. Then the rain started again, distorting the surface, making his face seem to melt.

"*Show me,*" he ordered in faery speech, putting a hand into the water as his body melted into the mist. "*If you want me to see, let me see.*"

He saw the ancient warrior drinking beside him. He smelled the rankness of the skins he wore and saw bright sunlight gleaming on his golden hair. He saw the faery rise from the loch to ensnare him, blameless and unknowing as the ocean where a man might drown. "Real," he said softly as they kissed, his heart moved and despairing at once. "The vision was real." He turned his face away, coming back to the present. If their meeting had been as he had seen it in his dream, their doom must have been the same as well.

He took his hand out of the water, his fingers numb with cold, and started to stand up. But suddenly his boots slipped on the rocks and the sandy bank gave way, plunging him into the loch. Before he could even cry out, he had disappeared under the surface into the icy depths.

15

Evelyn rolled over, still half-dozing, as Agnes picked up Max. "Go back to sleep, my lady," the nursemaid said as the child draped his arms around her neck. "The boy, Robin, has gone downstairs to breakfast, and he said his master was gone when he woke up."

"No." Evelyn yawned, rubbing her eyes. "I'm getting up, too." But the bed was so cozy and warm, and she could finally stretch out. "In just a moment," she mumbled, wrapping her arms around an extra pillow.

When she opened her eyes again, the sun was well up, and she was alone. She sat up, brushing her braid back from across her face. All of the pallets had been stowed away, and a clean gown was laid out over a chest for her with her shoes set out before it. A plate of bread and cheese was set on the ornate little table Aiden used as a desk, along with a flagon of wine.

"Agnes, you are a treasure," she sighed, having a lovely stretch. When was the last time she had slept until she woke up on her own? She couldn't even remember—sometime before Max was born. But where had Aiden gone?

She used the privy quickly, then rinsed her mouth with water, rubbing her teeth with a towel. She poured herself a cup of wine and took a sip as she tugged the ribbon from her hair. Turning, she found herself facing Aiden's mirror, face to face with her own reflection. "There you are," she said softly, touching the cold glass. "Look at me, Da. I'm rich." When she was a child, she had boasted that someday she would have a mirror that could show her how pretty she was from the top of her head to her toes. Of course, this mirror was Aiden's. But then again, so was she.

She loosened the waves of her braid, draping her hair on her shoulders. What were they saying about her downstairs this morning? Everyone would know she had spent the night in Aiden's bed; there would be no denying it. Agnes and Molly might say all they had done was sleep, but none of the knights would believe them nor the other women, either. She might as well face it. For all intents and purposes, she was a fallen woman. She ought to have been horrified, and in her heart she was.

But the beauty in the mirror smiled. She combed her hair smooth with her fingers, making a tiny kiss at her reflection. The girl in the mirror knew the truth. She knew just how deeply Aiden's kisses made this pretty body shiver, the wicked little secret that threatened to undo her. For all her protests of virtue and desperate games of hide-and-seek, she wanted Aiden every bit as much as he had ever wanted her. "Someday," she promised the mirror-Evie, pulling a lock of hair across the swell of her breast, studying the effect of the gleaming auburn glowing bright against her alabaster skin. "Someday we shall have him." But why should she have to wait?

She unlaced the bodice of her shift and let it fall to the floor, entranced by her own beauty. This was what had ruined her, this shell of creamy flesh. This was what had made her unbearable to her sister, what had made the men of the clan fight like dogs to have her. This was who she was; she couldn't help it. Why should she be punished for it? Why should she have to wait?

Aiden stood in the doorway, bewitched, loathe to even breathe for fear of disturbing the tableau before him. He had been forced to swim a quarter of the way around the loch before he'd found sufficient footing to climb out, and he was soaked to the bone and freezing. But watching Evie watch herself in the mirror, he forgot everything else—the cold, the wet, even the disturbing visions that had driven him out to the loch in the first place. He crossed his arms across his chest, dizzy with desire. One step to the right, and the mirror would capture his reflection, too. But he wasn't quite ready to be seen.

Her hair fell down her back like a shimmering veil to barely brush the rounded cleft of her behind as she turned her head, her flesh pink with warm, vibrant life. How could he confuse her with a chilly, blue-white faery? She gathered up the gleaming auburn curtain and piled it on top of her head, admiring her own perfection, her lips pursed in a pout. He smiled, delighted in her vanity, the naughty angel she became when she thought she was alone. He could almost keep his peace forever just to watch her in secret. Almost, but not quite.

"Good morning, Evie."

She whirled around, her heart stopping short, then leaping into her throat. "Aiden!" He was watching her, standing in the doorway with his familiar, fallen angel smile, but it was different now. He watched her preen before the mirror and smiled as if he knew her vanity and cherished it, knew her body and soul as no one else ever had and was glad to know it. He might mock her, tease her, but he didn't judge her, even now, and seeing that, she could not judge him, could not turn away, not this time. A proper, godly lass would scream and run from him, pretend she was offended even if she were not. But what would be the point?

"Good morning to you," she answered, her voice holding barely a quaver as she faced him. She had crossed her arms to shield her breasts as soon as he had spoken, instinctively ashamed. But now she let them fall again, not quite posing, but not hiding from him either, letting him look at her for a long moment before she reached for her gown.

"No." He crossed the room in three long strides and stopped her, catching her wrist. "Leave it, darling, please."

She braced her hand on his chest to hold him back, her face flushed hot and pink. "I can't—"

"You can." He smiled. "I promise." He kissed her sweetly, wet but soft, and slowly drew her closer. She tried again to hold him off, but her hands slipped over his shoulders instead, felt him as a solid thing, warm beneath his cold, wet shirt, and she smelled him, the clean scent of fresh-cut herbs and water over the spicy musk of his skin.

"Good God, man, you're soaking," she protested with a shaky laugh, tilting her head to one side, her hands clenched into fists between them as his kiss moved to her throat. "Did you swim the loch?"

"Only part of it." He touched the hollow notch at the base of her throat, pale violet now with her blush. "Do you like my mirror?"

"I . . . I cannot tell." Her knees felt weak, and her face was burning with shame, but she felt exhilarated, too, drunk with the feel of him against her, warm and wet and alive. Surrender felt like dying, flying, freedom from the earth. "Why do you have it?"

"The mirror, love? I made it." He bent his head and kissed her mouth again, his arm around her waist, and she allowed it willingly enough, her sweet shape formed to his. But she made no move to hold him, and he could feel her heart was racing. When he let his mouth leave hers at last, she dipped her head to his shoulder, hiding her face against his throat. "It's magic," he said softly, caressing her jaw.

"A magic mirror?" She smiled, her heart racing faster. *They say he is a wizard.*

"Yes." He took her hands in both of his and kissed them one by one. "I use it to ensnare fair maidens with their own vanity." He smiled down on her wickedly. "You see how well it works."

"Yes." He laid her hands against his waist, inviting her to touch him, and she savored it, her touch sliding slowly upward over the hard, curved planes of his chest, exploring like she never had before. But when she saw his face, she stopped, embarrassed. "Aiden, I can't," she protested, trying to back away. "I have to go find Max—"

"Max is fine," he cut her off, his voice an animal's growl as his arms encircled her, cutting off her escape. He bent and kissed her mouth again, holding her close, and her hands slipped over his shoulders, surrendering again for good and all.

He let his hand trail slowly down her spine, savoring the satin of her skin. This was what he'd hungered for, what he'd desperately wanted for weeks, longer than he had ever waited for such pleasure in his life, but she was worth it, her last traces of shyness only underscoring the sweetness of her surrender. Her head fell forward as his kiss strayed to her shoulder, her eyes half-lidded with desire in the mirror's reflection, and his knees felt weak to see her. "Look, Evie," he murmured, turning her around. "Look at how lovely you are." He reached around to cup her breast, soft and sweetly heavy in his hand.

"No," she whispered, breathless, putting her hand over his as if to push him away. But she made no move to do it, enchanted by his touch.

"Nothing else could be so beautiful." He felt her nipple harden in his palm, and he pressed a kiss to her throat. "You are everything I could wish." He slipped a hand between her legs, hot velvet drenched in dew.

"Stop," she ordered, gasping through her teeth, but she didn't mean it. She was lost, insane, bewitched by ecstasy like dying in his arms. He held her close, and she could feel him, hard and throbbing against her even through his clothes. Yet he touched her gently, languidly, as if all he cared about was pleasing her. His hand slid lower on her sex, and she cried out, unable to stop herself, her eyes falling closed.

"It's all right," he whispered, cuddling her close with his free arm. "Open your eyes, Evie. Let me show you what I see."

She opened her eyes slowly, certain she must die of shame. But Aiden's eyes were looking back at her, meeting her gaze in their reflection, and suddenly she felt no shame at all. His touch slid deeper inside her, and she welcomed it, bracing against the mirror to move against his hand. "Angel," he murmured, shifting her closer, and she smiled and saw him smile back. Then suddenly the world was dissolving, burning up from a fire inside her, and she screamed, her head thrown back against his shoulder.

"Faery," he murmured, as lost in her climax as he might have been in his own, so lost he slipped into the faery tongue. *"Look into the mirror, pretty darling. Let me show you your dream."*

"What?" She still felt weak, her body lost in pleasure, but Aiden was speaking, words she couldn't understand. "Aiden, what did you say?"

"Look into the mirror," he repeated in English, holding her hand to the glass, his sudden inspiration too thrilling to give up, even though his mind knew better. "Let me show you your dream." The spell would be nothing to her; all she would see would be him, her tender lover, all that she could wish. But he would see that she saw him and be sure of her forever after, certain she was his; his doubts, the demons that plagued him more sorely than anything else in the world, would be put to rest. *"Spirits of my blood's command, hear me and obey,"* he sang in faery song. *"Feel this woman, my body's one desire; look into her heart. Reach out into time and show us what will be."*

"I don't understand." She reached back and touched his face, his mouth as he was singing, a low, hypnotic murmur in her ear that seemed to dull her mind even as her senses came alive. "Aiden, what is it?" The reflection in the mirror had gone cloudy as if from a sudden chill, but the air around them was hot. *I should be afraid,* she thought, thinking of the roses that covered her tower, their sweet, intoxicating scent. *But I am not.*

"Reach into this woman's heart," Aiden murmured as he kissed her shoulder, the magic made more potent with his desire for her. *"Show us her deepest desire."*

"I don't understand you," she protested, trying to turn to face him, then the words stopped in her throat. The mirror's glass had cleared again, but it no longer showed their reflection. Instead she saw a knight with wide, blue eyes and long, straight hair of gleaming strawberry blonde. His armor glowed in the sunlight, and his smile was dazzling, as if it held all the joy in the world. "Max," she whispered, voiceless with shock, reaching out with both hands to touch the glass.

Aiden didn't hear her, didn't hear anything. He could barely think. He saw the man reflected in the mirror, and jealousy like madness overwhelmed him, worse than any doubt could ever be. *Charles*, a bitter, mocking voice laughed lunatic in his head. *That is Charles of Glencairn.* Aiden might touch her, kiss her, teach her to feel pleasure like nothing she had ever known—it was his special gift, his most practiced and practical enchantment. But when he looked into her heart, he saw the father of her child. She might desire Aiden, but her soul still mourned for Charles.

"Enough," he said aloud, letting her go as the image shattered, shards exploding into mist.

"No!" Evie said, reaching out for the mirror. "Aiden, what was that?" She turned to him, demanding, desperate. "What just happened?" He wouldn't even look at her; all hint of passion had vanished like the image in the glass. "What did we just see?" She caught him by the arm. "Aiden!"

"Nothing!" he answered, his eyes flashing real fury, making her take a step back. She had seen him vexed before, annoyed, put out by her tricks, wearied by his knights' occasional bouts of stupidity. But she had never seen him genuinely angry, and it frightened her, more than any sorcery she had seen. "Nothing," he repeated, his voice and his eyes going dull, the rage fading away. "Forget about it, Evie."

"I can't," she protested, meaning his touch as much as the mirror's strange and wonderful vision. She felt bereft to lose them both, frightened and confused by all that he had made her feel and see, and she wanted to reach out to him, to make him hold her and explain. But she couldn't make herself do it; her feelings were still too new and confusing, too tangled up in fear. "Aiden, please—"

"I promise you; it was nothing." She had seen a vision of her dead beloved—how was he supposed to explain that? How could he, her seducer, be expected to comfort her for her loss?

Horns sounded from the battlements—someone was approaching. "I have to go downstairs." He barely touched her arm, and for a moment he was captured all over again by the sheer exquisite beauty of her, naked and too overwrought with feeling to remember to be ashamed. But she wasn't his any more than any other pretty nothing he had ever had before. Robin was right; as hard as she had fought against capture, she was still Lady Pen all over again. "I'm sorry, Evie."

"Aiden, wait," she ordered as he went out the door, but he didn't listen, and she couldn't follow, naked as she was. Cursing an oath under her breath, she turned to grab up her gown.

Robin met Aiden at the foot of the stairs. "My lord, there's something you should see—"

"Who is coming?" Aiden asked, trying to work the wet lacings on his shirt.

"Those Scots, I think," the squire answered. "The guards say half a dozen with boys—it looks like a hunting party." He touched Aiden's arm. "Why are you wet?"

"I went swimming," Aiden answered sarcastically.

"You should change before you catch a chill," the boy said sagely, jogging to keep up as Aiden strode across the hall to the dais. "But a letter has come with your father's seal."

"I'll read it later," Aiden decided, sitting in his dragon chair. The last thing he needed just now was a page of complaints about his royal fiancée peppered liberally with advice he couldn't use. Robin nodded, settling on the steps at his feet as the outer doors were opened. "Laird Malcolm!" Aiden called. "Welcome to Glencairn."

"Long has Clan McCairn been welcome in this house," Malcolm answered with brusque courtesy, his expression grim as he came to the foot of the dais.

"And long may such welcome continue," Aiden answered. Gerald was standing behind his father with both his little brothers and four other grown men, including Aiden's old friend, Ralph. "I hope you haven't come all this way to thank me for sparing Gerald's life."

"Why should I thank you for saving your own soul from eternal damnation?" Malcolm answered. "Better you should thank God." He turned slightly as Evie came down the steps, dressed now quite properly with her hair under a veil. "Or Evelyn," the Scotsman added, giving her a warm smile.

"So why have you come, my dear laird?" Aiden asked with an ill-concealed frown. He had meant for the Scots to be grateful to Evie for her part in the boys' pardon; he had specifically devised the scene to that purpose. But just now the sight of her kinsman smiling on her did nothing for his mood.

"We need your help," Malcolm replied. He motioned to one of his men, and the man dropped a bundle on the floor, the canvas falling open to reveal the mutilated corpse of a sheep.

"Malcolm, good God," Evie said, turning away in disgust.

"What is this?" Aiden asked. "What does it have to do with me?"

"It will have much to do with all of us, I fear," Malcolm answered. "Our village enclosure is full of such horrors, my lord, a full three dozen sheep slaughtered with their throats ripped out."

"My sympathies," Aiden said, coming down to look at the sheep. "It looks as though we have a wolf."

"A whole pack, my sentries tell me," Malcolm agreed. "They saw nothing until they heard the cries of the shepherds, and by the time they reached the enclosure, the damage was done. They fired arrows at the wolves, but it was dark, and the beasts were too quick for them, escaping over the wall." He glanced at Evelyn before his eyes met Aiden's. "One of the shepherd boys was badly mauled himself."

"Will he be all right?" Evelyn asked.

"No one can tell yet, lass," Ralph answered. "He's badly frightened, as are they all. They all swear the leader of the pack made all the kills himself, one after another without feeding, while the others watched."

"Why would a wolf kill without feeding?" Aiden scoffed.

"A fair question, my lord," Malcolm answered with a sardonic smile. "But whether the boys be mad with fright or speaking the honest truth, we mean to put an end to this wolf and his pack." Something in Malcolm's words and the look in his eyes as he faced Aiden made Evie's spine tingle with apprehension, though she couldn't say just why. "Will you join us?"

No! she wanted to shout, foolish as it was. If a wolf pack had attacked the Scottish flock inside the village wall, it was only a matter of time before the English were attacked as well, and such brazen predators weren't likely to stop with sheep. It was only right and natural that Aiden, as lord of the manor, should join the hunt; it was part of his sworn duty as protector of his holding. But she didn't want him to do it; she feared for him if he did. Or maybe she just wanted him to stay, wanted to pin him down and make him explain what had passed between them.

"Of course." Aiden nodded. "Sir Alan, choose your men; five or six should be enough. We will ride out with our friends as soon as I change my clothes."

"Thank you, my lord," Malcolm said with a nod of his own.

"Aiden," Evelyn began, but he was already gone, headed up the stairs with Robin as the knights in the hall quarreled like little boys over who would be allowed to join the hunt.

"Evelyn," Malcolm said, catching her arm. She turned, and he hugged her suddenly, crushing her in an embrace. "Thank you, lass," he murmured. "We all of us thank you more than we could say."

"You're welcome," she managed, dumbfounded with shock.

"Pack your things," he ordered before she could say more. "And Max's." He cupped her cheek in his hand and smiled. "As soon as we come back from the hunt, you're both of you coming home."

She stared at him for a moment, unable to speak. She didn't want to go home; she was home, and so was Max. "Malcolm, I can't—"

"You need not worry anymore about Rebecca," he

promised. "After what you've done for my son, I'll hear no word against you, even from her. You should be welcome in your father's house for as long as you care to stay there, and your son will be welcome as well, as welcome as one of my own." He pressed her hand between his. "You have my solemn word."

"Pardon me, my lady," Agnes said, giving Malcolm a suspicious nod. "I think you'd better come upstairs with me."

Wait! Evelyn wanted to scream. She wanted to go stop Aiden, to make him explain the vision in the mirror and the roses and the dreams, and most of all, why he was so angry with her he didn't want her anymore. But Malcolm was changing his mind, changing everything, and now Agnes, who never asked for anything, was asking her to come. "What is it?" she asked her aloud.

"It's nothing, I hope," Agnes answered. "But I think you should see."

She saw a flash of worry in the other woman's eyes that chilled her to the bone. "All right." She nodded. "Thank you, Malcolm," she said, kissing his cheek as a sister. "We'll talk when you return." She followed Agnes up the stairs, meeting Aiden at the top. "Aiden—"

"Good-bye, Evie," he answered, putting his sword in its scabbard. "We should be back soon."

"Aiden, wait." She caught him halfway down the stairs and kissed him, her arms around his neck, with her kin and all the garrison watching. "Be careful."

He smiled at her slowly, his dark blue eyes going wide with unfeigned shock. "I will," he promised as she broke the kiss. She smiled back shyly, at least a little reassured, and he drew her close and kissed her again more deeply, his tongue slipping into her mouth.

"Wait." She put one hand against his chest to push him back but took his hand in the other. Glancing down the stairs over his shoulder, she met Malcolm's eyes with her own for barely more than a moment, but the expression on his face was enough to make her blush. "Come," she said softly to Aiden, drawing him back up the stairs and around the corner away from prying eyes. "Kiss me better now."

He smiled again as he drew her close, a shadow of the wicked grin she loved, and the haunted look of pain she had seen in his eyes when he left her at the mirror was all but gone. He lifted her to tiptoe in his arms, and she wrapped her arms around his neck again. His mouth came down on hers with almost brutal passion, and for once she didn't hold back; she let herself surrender, let him feel her wanting him as desperately as he had ever wanted her. He shivered as his face drew back, and she touched his mouth. "Aiden, I'm scared," she confessed, barely louder than a whisper. "I don't want you to go."

Aiden felt as if the earth was turning soft under his feet again as he looked into her eyes. Again, she was a mystery, her heart a hidden treasure, a book written in a tongue he'd never heard, open but impossible to read.

She was afraid—of what? Of him? He thought again of the image in the mirror and the fearful hope he had seen in her eyes as she had seen it. But she was saying she wanted him to stay. He wanted to stay, to kiss her and talk to her, tell her all his secret thoughts and make her tell him hers. But Malcolm and his men were waiting.

"I have to go," he said, making himself smile as he caressed her cheek. "But you don't have to be scared." Robin had come around the corner, carrying his highly polished helmet. "I will be right back." Pressing a final, more chaste kiss to her forehead, he let her go to join the hunt.

16

Evelyn followed Agnes to their tower room and found Molly sitting on the bed with Max. "Mamee," he whimpered as soon as he saw her, holding out his arms.

"What is it, precious?" she said, picking him up. "What's wrong?" She kissed his brow as he clung to her and felt it was burning hot with fever.

"I sick," he told her tearfully, scrubbing his face on her shoulder. "Mamee, make it stop."

"I will, lambie, I promise," she said, sitting down to cradle him in her lap and trying not to panic. *Would you see him in an infant's grave?* Margaret had asked her in this very room, keening like a crow. "Does your head hurt?" she asked him.

"Yes," he sniffled, laying his head on her breast.

"He first complained when I gave him his breakfast, saying he was hot," Agnes said. "Then his breakfast came back up."

"Oh, dear." Evie sighed, making herself smile for the baby's benefit. "Poor Agnes." She stroked his brow, trying to think what to do. Whenever he had fallen ill before, Margaret had been there to take care of him, skilled and efficient in spite of all her prophecies of doom. "We should keep Grace away from him, just in case whatever he has is catching," she decided. "And we have to get him fed. Molly, go downstairs and have one of the cooks draw him some broth."

"Yes, my lady," Molly nodded, obviously relieved to have a task. "I don't need them; I can do it." She ran out.

"Agnes, I have a rosary in that chest," Evie said. "Would you see if you can find it?"

Agnes frowned. "It won't come to that, my lady, surely."

"No, of course not," she said lightly, her child's fever burning her own skin through the fabric of her gown. "But a prayer can't hurt." She looked down at Max. "Will you drink some water for me?"

"Yes." He nodded. "I thirsty."

"I know you are." Agnes left off looking through the chest to bring a cup. "Here, lambie," Evie soothed, helping him hold it. "Sip it slowly." He tried, but suddenly a loud, hacking cough racked through him, bringing up every drop he had swallowed. "It's all right," she promised, trying to comfort him even though she wanted to cry herself.

"We'll try some more in a minute," Agnes said, wiping his face with a towel.

"Agnes, get Grace out," Evie told her, catching her arm.

The other woman's eyes met hers, and she nodded.

"I will leave Molly to watch her," she promised, getting up. "Then I will be right back."

Max coughed again as they left, his whole body shaken as if by some evil spirit. "Ayben come," he whimpered when it was done. "I want him."

"Me, too, lambie," Evie admitted, hugging him close, remembering her awful dream and the premonition she had felt with Aiden and Malcolm in the hall. *'Tis you who've brought this on him*, a hag's voice croaked inside her head. *Consorting with a wizard.* She looked out the open window at the roses nodding in the breeze, as fresh as ever in spite of the autumn chill. "It's all right," she insisted, rocking him back and forth. "Aiden will be home soon."

The hunting party tracked the wolf pack high into the hills over rocky slopes and through thick patches of woods. Several times Aiden thought surely he would have to use magic to recapture the trail, but Malcolm's dogs never faltered. "Your pack is extraordinary," Aiden told him as the dogs found the scent of the wolves again at the bottom of a watery ravine and crashed back up the other side.

"I thank you." Malcolm smiled, riding beside him. "But I cannot take the credit." He pointed to a grizzled-looking black hound with a silver muzzle. "The old Gaffer there was trained by my father-in-law, and it's him that trains the others."

Aiden opened his mouth to call him on the jest—no

dog that old could be of more than sentimental use in the field. He could barely keep up with the pack. Then he saw him nip the flanks of a younger dog to bring him back to the right, and the whole pack turned with him. "Amazing," Aiden marveled, shaking his head. "How can I part you from one of the Gaffer's pups?"

"Grandpups, more like," Malcolm laughed. "I'll make you a gift of one as soon as we get home."

"I saw the wolves," Hamish said suddenly. He had trotted his pony up close beside Aiden's charger. "I heard the sheep all screaming, and I looked out the window," he said, his eyes wide and bright. "The big one looked straight at me." He looked at Aiden. "He had yellow eyes."

Gerald smiled. "I think you were dreaming."

"No, in faith," the little boy insisted. "I was not."

Aiden believed him. "My mother killed a wolf once," he remarked.

"Nay," Davey scoffed, riding up to join them. "She never did."

"Aye, she did, I swear, when she was barely older than you are," Aiden insisted. "The pelt still hangs in the solar at my father's castle at Brinlaw."

"How many castles does your father have?" Davey asked.

"Two of his own," Aiden answered. "One in England and another in Anjou. And my mother has another."

"Tell us how she killed the wolf," Hamish ordered. "Did she put a spell on it?"

"Hamish," Malcolm scolded, giving the boy a warning look.

"No," Aiden answered easily. "Of course not. She killed it with her dagger."

"Sheep's balls," Davey swore, making them all laugh. "No girl could kill a wolf by herself, surely not with just a dagger."

"She was saving her father," Aiden explained. "The wolf had attacked him without warning, and he would have died. So Mama, barely bigger than our Hamish here, jumped off her horse and stabbed the wolf in the gullet." All three boys were listening, enthralled, even Gerald, and Aiden and Malcolm shared a smile. "When he snapped his head around to bite her, she took her silver dagger and slit his wicked throat."

"Truly?" Hamish said, his eyes wide now with hope.

"Upon my life," Aiden swore. "She always says you never know what you can do until you have to do it."

"And so she is right," Malcolm said. "But we are losing the light."

They made camp in a clearing with bare oaks all around. "We'll set sentries through the night," Malcolm said as Davey helped Ralph start a fire. "Come, Lord Aiden, let's have a last look at the trail to see how fresh it might be. I'd rather not be mauled in my sleep if the pack is close."

"All right," Aiden said, getting up. He noticed Gerald looking away at anything but him, and Ralph was doing the same. He put the sword he had laid aside back in its sheath. "I will follow you."

They stopped some quarter mile away from the camp on the muddy bank of a stream. "Look here, Malcolm," Aiden said, his faery eyes still keen in spite of the fading light. "Look at these tracks." The wolves had drunk at the stream sometime within the last hour; the tracks were still wet. "We should not camp," he decided, looking up, then he froze.

The tiny clearing was full of Scotsmen, twice as many as had ridden with them on the hunt. All of them had their swords drawn and wore the expression of executioners. " 'Tis nothing personal, laddie," Malcolm said. "I like you, wizard or not." He drew his own sword. "But the clan can't risk letting you live."

Aiden had been half-expecting some sort of ambush all day, but nothing so elaborate as this. "You mean to murder me?" he asked with a smile, as if he didn't believe it. "What's the point? You said yourself: If I should die, John will just send another Englishman to replace me."

"Aye, he will." Malcolm nodded. "But maybe the next one won't be a conjurer, too." He took a step toward him, and Aiden drew his sword. "Fight if you will; raise the alarm," Malcolm said, stopping again. "Your men admire you; they will come to your aid. But we will have to kill them, too."

"Malcolm, this is madness," Aiden warned, his blood beginning to tingle. "No matter why you lured me out here; there is a wolf pack in these woods—"

"Aye, and who's to say you didn't conjure the beasts yourself to murder us all?" the laird cut him off, the first sign of anger he had shown. "You mean to wipe us off the mountain, Aiden Brinlaw, like your father would have done before you. Only you mean to use your mother's enchantments to do it."

"That's a lie," Aiden insisted, losing a bit of his temper himself.

"Then why did you mean to hang my son like a common thief?"

"Why did your son mean to burn my castle?"

"Because you turned his aunt into a harlot!" the Scotsman retorted. "You have sisters, do you not? How would you feel in his place?"

Remembering the less-than-tender feelings he had harbored for Malinda's husband, Tarquin, over the years, Aiden had to admit he had him there. "Why do you call me a wizard?" he began again, trying another tack.

"Please, man, do you think I'm a fool?" Malcolm scoffed. "My son tells me you changed his sword into a serpent, and I think he was just frightened, that his fancy got the better of him. I hear your castle tower is covered in summer roses in the middle of September, and I think we've been having an unusually warm fall, but it gives me pause. But when I see Evelyn, the most prideful, ill-tempered, arrogant little baggage who ever drew breath, refuse the right and safety of her father's hearth to follow your steps like a spaniel and kiss you

WICKED CHARMS

full on the lips before God and the assembly, I know there's witchery going on somewhere."

"Enough of this," one of the others scoffed—one of Evie's many former suitors, no doubt. He charged Aiden, sword raised, but his feet slipped on the muddy bank, and Aiden avoided the blow, kicking him squarely in the rump as he lunged past and sending him head first into the stream.

But the battle was on. The next Scot was more careful, landing a blow to Aiden's armored shoulder before he could turn around. *"Rise fire!"* Aiden shouted in faery, and the man's sword turned as molten hot as it had been when it was made, and the Scotsman dropped it with an oath. But he could only cast so many spells at a time. Another man came at him at a run, an ax raised high over his head, and Aiden charged him like a bull, butting him hard in the chest to send him sprawling backward, then rolling to the side to avoid the slicing blow the man tried to make as he fell. His own boots skidding in the leafy mud, he raised his sword to parry another attacker.

"Da!" Davey screamed, running into the clearing. "Da, come quick! The wolves!"

The Scotsman fighting Aiden struck again, but Aiden knocked his blade away, smashing an elbow into his face as he moved to recover and knocking him unconscious. "Come on, man!" Malcolm shouted to Aiden, running for the camp, and his own men took the hint and followed, leaving Aiden alone. Barely pausing to catch his breath and spit out a mouthful of blood from the split he'd put in his lip charging the ax-wielder, Aiden went after them.

The camp was chaos—Aiden had never seen so many wolves in his life, and they were huge, black and sleek and fat with autumn plenty. The first man he recognized was Gerald, who was being attacked from either side by two of the beasts. Aiden flung his dagger at one of them, stabbing it neatly through the gullet, and Gerald dispatched the other with his sword. Then Aiden heard Hamish.

"No," the child was saying softly, a haunting murmur under the battle's din. "No, you won't." The child was standing at the edge of the clearing, his little sword held out before him to hold off what had to be the ruler of the pack, a wolf twice the size of any of the others.

"Hamish, don't move!" Aiden shouted, looking around frantically for a crossbow.

"He says he means to eat me," Hamish answered, his face pale with shock but his eyes determined. "But I won't let him." Aiden found the weapon he sought in another man's pack and armed it, creeping closer as quietly as he could in hopes the wolf would not be startled into charging Hamish. "I'm going to kill him, Aiden, just like your mama did."

"I believe you, Hamish." At the sound of his voice so close, the wolf swung its head around, and Aiden saw its eyes, yellow, just as Hamish had said, and its black lips drawn back over fangs as long as his dagger. He fired the crossbow at one of the eyes, but his aim was slightly off, and the beast shook its head and knocked the steel bolt aside like it might have been a feather.

"Stop!" Aiden roared in faery, his eyes locked to the wolf's. *"This boy is not for you!"*

"Holy Christ," Malcolm mumbled from behind him as the wolf howled in rage and many others of the pack fell writhing and whining to the ground.

"Believe in your sword, Hamish," Aiden ordered, letting his own blade fall, his mind casting about desperately for the best enchantment. The wolf lord was no ordinary beast, but a creature of the ancient world in the form of a wolf, he was almost certain. No dumb creature could have looked at the wizard with such malice. But Hamish was an innocent and brave. His power would be greater than he knew. "Believe that it can cut his throat."

"I do," the boy said, tightening his grip. "I believe it."

He looked so small, Aiden felt his heart clench in his chest, but he couldn't let himself doubt the child's power, either, or not even what little magic he could do to help would work. *"Leave him,"* he ordered the wolf. *"Bring your quarrel to me."*

The wolf let out another roar, knocking the child flat on his back and planting a massive paw in the center of his little chest. "No!" Davey cried out, trying to run forward, but Gerald caught him and held him back.

"It's all right," Aiden promised. "Hamish still has his sword." He took a step toward them, his eyes still locked to the wolf's. "Do it, Hamish. Cut his throat." He closed his eyes, focusing all his will and power into the boy's tiny blade.

"I will," Hamish said, tearful but resolved. "I'm going to do it." The wolf raised his head to clamp down on the boy's tender throat, his fangs gleaming in the light of the moon, and the boy thrust the blade upward with all his strength, piercing the tough, black hide and releasing a torrent of blood. The wolf shrieked in shock and agony, and Aiden lunged for it, grabbing the blade and ripping it from side to side until the beast collapsed.

"I did it," Hamish sobbed. "Aiden, I did it."

"Yes, you did," Aiden said, pushing the carcass away to hug the boy. "You were perfect." Malcolm was still standing frozen, staring at them, as the remaining wolves were killed or fled into the woods. "Go to your father," Aiden murmured, giving Hamish a final squeeze before he set him on his feet. "Go on."

"Hamish!" Davey cried, running forward to scoop his little brother up himself. Gerald came to join him, and Aiden clapped him on the shoulder before he turned away.

"My lord!" Malcolm called from behind him. "Aiden!" Aiden stopped and looked back, one eyebrow raised in question. He didn't want to talk to Malcolm; he didn't want to talk to anyone. He just wanted to go home.

The Scotsman came to him, barely ruffling Hamish's

hair as he passed his sons, though it was obvious from the expression on his face how frightened he had been for the child. "Thank you," he said as he reached Aiden. "Whatever it was that you did just now . . . I don't pretend to understand it." His skin was pale as paint, and his eyes were overbright. "But I am in your debt."

"Are you, in faith?" Aiden muttered. "How nice for both of us." Half an hour ago this idiot savage had been ready to murder him in cold blood for practicing sorcery; now he was thanking him for it? If he could have found the energy, he would have laughed. Every muscle in his body ached; his head was throbbing; and he suddenly realized he was bleeding, too—something warm and wet was trickling into his eye. "Can I take that to mean you've decided not to kill me?" he asked with sardonic humor as he wiped his brow with his sleeve.

"I don't see how I can," Malcolm admitted, matching his humorous tone, but his eyes were still as serious as ever. "You saved my son—"

"Hamish saved himself," Aiden cut him off. "No one should forget that, especially Hamish." He remembered far too well how it felt to be the baby brother who always had to be protected. He looked back at the boys and smiled in spite of his own wretched condition. Hamish was already regaling his brothers with the details of his triumph like they hadn't been there to see it for themselves.

"So he did, I suppose," Malcolm admitted slowly. "Though I still say I don't know how." Aiden started to walk away again, and Malcolm caught his arm. "So what now, my lord?" he asked. "What are your plans for the clan?"

The clan? Aiden echoed in his mind, aghast and amused. As if he cared a tinker's damn about the clan just now. All he cared about, all he wanted, was to go home to Glencairn, have a bath and a rest and see Evelyn again, continue the progression of events that had begun when she kissed him good-bye. But Malcolm cared about the clan; he had cared enough to kill a man he purported to like to save it. He wasn't likely to give up without an answer.

"My plans for the clan?" he said aloud, his tone dripping with sarcasm. "You already guessed it, Malcolm. I'm going to turn you into peasants or wipe you off the mountain. Wouldn't you do the same?" Without looking back to see if the laird knew he was joking, he walked off to join his own men. "Come, Sir Alan," he called. "I think I need a bandage, then we are going home."

Ralph joined his laird as the Englishman walked away. "I think we're well and done with the wolves, my laird," he said. "But what about our bonny friend, the wizard?"

"What about him?" Malcolm answered, his face set like stone with blank resolve. He looked over at his three fine sons, the heirs of his line. They didn't remember the wrath of King Henry, the days when Scotland had been England's possession, her people no better than slaves. But Malcolm remembered too well. "Come on, Ralph," he said aloud. "He's right. It is time to go home."

Aiden walked back into his own hall sometime near dawn the next morning. "Sweet saints," Robin said, coming to meet him. "Look at you."

"Aye," Aiden said, opening the flagon of wine on the table and drinking without bothering with a cup. "Look at me." His mantle was caked with blood, and he had discarded his chain mail shirt halfway home because he was just too tired to bother trying to carry it anymore, leaving only the padded tunic he wore underneath it, stained with blood as well. A wound on his upper arm had been clumsily dressed by Sir Alan, but a more shallow gash in his forehead had been left to scab over on its own.

"Did you kill the wolves?" Robin asked.

"Yes, Rob, we killed the wolves." He set the empty flagon down. "And now I am going to bed."

"Of course." His squire nodded. "Except you still haven't read Lord Brinlaw's letter."

"My lord!" Agnes came running down the steps, her usually-stony face drawn with worry. "Thank God you have come."

"Aiden," Robin began again, taking the scroll from his pocket.

"My lady needs you," Agnes cut him off. "Her little boy is sick."

"Max is sick?" Robin echoed, obviously surprised. "Why didn't you tell someone before now?"

"You can help him, I know," the woman pressed on, clutching Aiden's sleeve. "I know your soldiers. You are a healer." Her grip tightened. "He is dying."

"No, he's not," Aiden promised, running for the stairs.

Evelyn wrapped the rosary around her fingers, holding Max's trembling little body in her arms. "Holy Mother, full of grace," she prayed aloud, trying to remember the words. She had never been very attentive in church; that was the sort of thing her mother and Rebecca liked, not her. But she didn't know what else to do. "Be with us . . . be with my child." The priests used better, more penitent words, but she couldn't remember them, and besides, it didn't matter. She wasn't righteous enough to pray and be heard like a priest. Her only hope was that the mother of mercy still remembered how it felt to love a son. "Help him, holy Mary, please," she prayed, closing her eyes, her lips pressed to the baby's burning brow. "He's such a little thing."

Coming in and seeing them, Aiden forgot to be tired. "Hush now, love," he said, going to them and putting his arms around them both. "It's all right."

"No," she insisted, shaking her head. "He's going to

die, and it's my fault." She ought to fight him off, she knew. He was wicked, and he made her wicked, too, worse than her already-tainted natural inclination. But his arms just now felt so strong, and his voice was so soothing, she couldn't bear to push him away, wicked or not. "Margaret tried to tell me, but I wouldn't listen. She told me if I were a harlot, God would take him from me, but I told her she was a fool."

"She is a fool," Aiden scoffed, pressing a kiss to her cheek. "You are not a harlot. Trust me, sweeting, I'm an expert on harlots." Giving her a final squeeze, he took Max from her, and the child immediately started to cry. But he looked up at Aiden with such pleading in his eyes, it broke his heart. "Hush now," he soothed, holding him in the crook of his arm. Max's face was red and puffy, but that could have been from the crying. More alarming was the heat rising off of him in waves. Touching his tiny face was like putting a hand to the fire. Evelyn was watching him intently, her rosary tangled in her fist, and he tried to manage a smile, but he was worried. Agnes was right; this child was very ill.

"Quiet yourself, little warrior," he murmured in the faery tongue, holding the babe against his heart and smoothing his sweat-soaked hair. Once the squalling faded to an occasional whimper, he laid him on the bed and opened his swaddling blanket.

Evelyn watched them, hardly daring to breathe. Max seemed calmer as soon as Aiden touched him, but his brow was still drawn up in pain, and his eyes were squeezed tightly shut. Aiden lifted up the baby's gown, and she held her breath indeed, bracing for the sight of the pustules she knew he must surely find, the harbingers of a pox she had been dreading to see all day. But Max's flesh still seemed clear, even his back when Aiden turned him over.

"I've been trying to give him water and broth, but he can't keep anything down," Evelyn said. "And we've been bathing him with cool cloths, trying to bring down the fever, but it doesn't help, and I've been afraid he'll take a chill. He cries and says he's cold every time we do it." The tears she had been fighting all night broke free, and she covered her face with her hands to hide them.

"You've done right, darling, I promise," Aiden said, her tears more than he could bear. He wanted to hold her and comfort her, but she needed far more for him to save her child. "Don't cry." He used his thumb to gently open Max's mouth to examine his throat and tongue, and the child allowed it, but he reached for his mother.

"It's all right," Evelyn promised, smiling through her tears. She took Max's hand as Aiden gently probed the swollen flesh around his jaw. "Aiden is going to make you feel better." Let him conjure any spell he wanted; let him call up demons from hell if it would save her child.

"Ay-ben," Max whispered.

"Your mama's right," Aiden promised. The child let out a pitiful cough, and he lifted him to his shoulder again, patting his back as he rocked him back and forth. He had never even tried to heal a child this young before, but the motion came naturally, his faery senses feeling out a way to fight the fever. "Evie, listen to me," he said. "That business about God punishing you by taking your child away, that's just madness." Max hiccuped again, and he patted him harder, an image forming in his mind of tiny lungs fighting for breath against a greenish shadow. "God doesn't work that way."

"How would you know?" she said, barely managing a smile.

"Because my mother says He doesn't, and she's in a position to know." He lifted the baby toward his face to smell his breath. To anyone else, it would likely have seemed fresh, but his faery sense detected something toxic lodged deep in his chest. "She was brought up by a monk, and she's very pious." He spared a smile for Evie. "Not that you'd know it by me."

"I've heard she is a witch." Her eyes searched his for the truth.

"She is that, too, I suppose," he admitted. "Evie, do you trust me?"

She touched his cheek and smiled. "Yes." She nodded. "I do."

He bent and pressed a kiss to her forehead, then put Max back into her arms, kneeling on the floor before them with his face close to the child's. Lacing his fingers with Evie's where they lay across the little chest, he spoke softly in the faery tongue, calling to the shadow lurking inside. *"You will not have him,"* he murmured. *"This child belongs to God and to his mother. She has bought him with her heart."* Max sputtered, gasping through a sob, and Aiden pressed down harder, feeling the baby's heartbeat in his chest and Evie's pulse in her wrist, concentrating on the rhythms until both fell in sync with his own heart. *"He will not die,"* he insisted. *"I will not allow it."*

Evie felt a pulse race through her, a pounding that overwhelmed her heart. Suddenly Max was coughing, fighting for breath through a horrible, racking cough that sounded like Death itself had a grip upon his throat. "Aiden!"

Aiden grabbed the child up by his ankles and struck him hard on the back. A nasty gob of viscous green pus flew out of the baby's mouth and landed thickly on the floor, and Agnes, silent since she'd brought Aiden back, let out a little moan. He hit the baby again, and more of the shadow emerged, still choking the child but weaker—some of Max's sobs were starting to get through. Without thinking, Aiden scooped the baby into the crook of his arm and reached into his mouth, scooping out the green fluid, repeating his spell as he pulled. A double handful of the stuff came out, soaking his sleeve to the elbow. Suddenly Max was free. He let out a lusty yowl of indignation, and Evelyn took him back. "There," Aiden muttered, trying not to feel sick himself as he dropped the poisonous goo into the rushes. Give him a nice, clean battlefield any day of the week.

Evelyn barely noticed. Max still felt too warm, but his skin wasn't burning red or wet with sweat anymore, and his breathing was easier, even through his tears. She wiped the greenish spittle from his mouth and chin, crooning comfort as he fussed. "It's all right, precious angel," she murmured. "You're going to be all right." His gown was stained, and she stripped him out of it, cuddling him closer in his blanket as she fished a clean one from the chest at the foot of the bed, and Agnes came to help. His fingers tangled in her hair, his favorite comfort all his life, and he scrubbed his little face against her shoulder. "Mama's here," she whispered, sitting on the edge of the bed with both arms wrapped around him.

"He isn't completely out of danger," Aiden said. Agnes set a basin of water strewn with herbs beside him and started helping him out of his filthy shirt, and after a moment's surprise, he allowed it, too tired suddenly to argue. "But I think the worst is over."

"Thank you," Evie said, looking up from changing Max. "Aiden, my God, what happened?" His arm was tied up in a bloodstained bandage, and his face was cut, she suddenly realized, and his chest and torso were covered in blue-black bruises.

"It doesn't matter." Pulling free of Agnes's surprisingly gentle ministrations, he went and helped Evie, pulling Max's arms through the sleeves of his fresh gown.

She laid a hand against his cheek and turned his face to hers. "Thank you," she repeated. Slipping her hand to the back of his neck, she drew him to her, raising up to kiss his mouth.

He wrapped his arms around her, savoring her warmth and softness and pushing every other thought away. "You're welcome." He put Max into her arms and pulled the heavy fur coverlet over all three of them, sinking exhausted into the bed, mother and child both cradled close in his arms as Agnes gathered up the dirty rushes from the floor and left the room.

"Night," Max mumbled, snuggled in the double circle of their arms, and Evie smiled. She had never felt so happy, so safe, so relieved; she wanted to savor it. But her eyelids were too heavy. Before she could even think of it, she had fallen asleep.

17

When Aiden opened his eyes again, the sun was setting. Evie and Max were sleeping beside him just as they had been when he fell asleep himself, both of them so beautiful his heart ached at the sight. But Evie had been awake at some point; she was wearing different clothes. He smiled as he eased her gently from his half-numbed arm, careful not to wake her or the child. The heavens might split open and spill stars to the earth, but Evie would still change her gown and put her hair to rights. He put a hand to Max's forehead and found it cool. The fever had passed. Looking down on them, he wanted to lie back down beside them, to pretend that they were his a little longer. But he would only be pretending, and things had become too complicated for that.

He went back to his own room, a thousand different shards of memory whirling in his mind: Charles in the mirror; Malcolm saying he would have to be murdered, just for the sake of the clan; Hamish under the jaws of the wolf; the terrible fever falling out of Max. But over and over his thoughts returned to a single picture, Evelyn turning to him naked and shameless as Eve before the fall. On the long, dark ride back to Glencairn from the hunt, Sir Alan had told him he had overheard Malcolm telling Evie to pack her things, that she and Max were to be welcomed back into the clan for what she'd done, saving Gerald. Would she try to go? Would he try to stop her?

Someone had left a jug of water on the hearth—Robin, no doubt. He filled the marble basin and washed, stripping out of what he still wore of his clothes. Looking in the mirror to examine the gash in his forehead, he lost himself again, remembering Evie, the way she had looked and felt in his arms, the sweetness of her kiss. Her body was a wonder to him, but her heart was the true mystery. That morning she had turned to him for help, and he had given it freely, used his magic without thinking of the cost to save the child she loved. But yesterday his spell had shown another man to be her heart's true desire, and the jealousy had been more than he could bear. Even now, he felt sick, just remembering it, he, Aiden Brinlaw, the rogue who never cared for any lover well enough to fight for her. What right did he have to feel jealous of Evie's affections? In truth, what was she to him? A toy, a way to pass the time in exile—his consolation, he had styled her in his letters to Prince John. What was different now?

"Aiden?" Evie said, standing in the door. She had awakened when he closed the door to her room and come after him as soon as Agnes returned to be with Max. "I have to talk to you." He was staring at her as if she might have been a ghost, but he was the one who seemed unreal, a naked angel fallen to the earth. "Aiden?"

"You were sleeping," he explained, recovering his voice. For a moment he had thought she was a phantom conjured up by his thoughts. "I didn't want to wake you."

"I had already been awake." She came in and shut the door behind her, sliding the bolt into place. "Gerald was here," she said, turning back to Aiden. "He told me what happened to Hamish." She came and took the cloth he'd been using to wash and rinsed it in the basin. "That must have been some wolf," she smiled, dabbing the gash on his forehead far more gently than he had himself.

"It was," he admitted, the light, clean scent of her hair making him feel dizzy. "How is Hamish?" He supposed he ought to put some hose on, just to be polite, though in truth, she didn't seem to mind or even notice he was naked. Was that a compliment or an insult? he wondered with a wry, inward smile. "No ill effects, I hope."

"Quite the opposite, I'm afraid," Evie said smiling, rinsing the cloth again. "Gerald said he's wearing everyone's ears ragged, telling how he killed the wolf all by himself." Her expression sobered a bit. "But he didn't, did he?"

"Didn't he?" Aiden said. She probed the bruise on his side, and he flinched, gasping in pain. "I think one of the ribs may be broken."

"A broken rib from a bite?" she said, appalled. "It's a wonder the beast didn't rip you in half."

"That's not a bite," he said, pushing her hand gently away. "Malcolm and his men lured me off into the wild alone and ambushed me." The look of horror on her face was so extreme and so obviously sincere, he couldn't help but smile. "Didn't Gerald tell you that as well?"

"No," she said angrily, tearing at the bandage on his arm to get a look underneath, furious with Malcolm and with herself for not noticing how badly hurt he was before. "He did not." The wound she had taken for a scratch was in fact a deep slash from a claymore. "Holy Christ . . . Aiden, this needs to be stitched—"

"No, sweet, it's all right," he promised.

"No," she said, shaking her head. "It is not." Malcolm could have killed him; he could be dead. She touched the bruise on his shoulder, her knees going weak. She could have lost him. "They could easily have murdered you," she said, trying to keep her composure.

"Not so easily," he protested, trying to make it a joke.

"Why would Malcolm do that?" She was suddenly, intensely aware of his nakedness, the warmth and smell of his skin, and she turned away to sink in to a chair. "Did he give you any sort of reason?"

"Yes," he admitted, watching her. He could not,

would not say more. He was home now, with her; Malcolm and his reasons weren't important. "It doesn't matter—"

"How can you say that?" she demanded. "I knew it—I knew when Malcolm just showed up here, asking you to join them on the hunt, that something wasn't right. That's why I didn't want you to go."

"You couldn't have known," he protested, trying to soothe her.

"But I did," she insisted. "But it seemed silly to tell you so, particularly when you'd just seemed to be getting over being angry with me."

"Angry?" he said. "Who said I was angry?"

"You didn't have to say it," she said. "You pushed me away, after—" She broke off, her cheeks turning pink. "Let's just say I was very surprised when you left me in here naked by myself."

He couldn't help but smile. "That doesn't seem much like me, does it?"

"No," she said, smiling back. "It doesn't. Or at least, I don't think it does. Aiden, there's so much about you I don't understand, so much you keep hidden from me—"

"I keep hidden?" he said, genuinely amazed. "You're accusing me of hiding myself, lady? You're the one who keeps locking herself in the tower, refusing to even talk to me. I, on the other hand, have made my desires quite plain."

"Your desires, yes," she cut him off, getting up. "But

your desires where I'm concerned are not yourself, not unique at all. They're no different from any other man's I've ever met."

"Evelyn, you really are the most conceited woman the world has known since Jezebel passed on," he teased. "Queen Eleanor is modest next to you."

"As well she might be, being old as Moses," she retorted. "I know you want me in your bed, Aiden, but do you want me in your castle? Do you even like me?"

"Most of the time," he said with a grin. "When you aren't screaming at me like a heathen."

"Stop it!" she said, coming dangerously close to a heathenish scream. "That's just the sort of thing I mean. One moment you're saving Max's life; the next you're mocking me. Can't you for once be serious? Can't you just tell me the truth?"

"And when have I seen your true self, Evie?" he demanded. "One moment you flirt with me outrageously; the next you threaten to slit my throat for daring to buy you a present."

"Is that why you were angry yesterday, because I finally gave in?" she asked. "Do you like me better when I push you away? Or did you mean to push me first?"

"Evie, as God be my judge, I was never angry with you," he insisted.

"Then what?" She turned away from him, trying to think of a better, clever way to charm him into saying what she needed to hear, but it was no use. "Malcolm has said I can come home," she said, deciding on the truth. "I don't want to go; I want to stay here with you."

Why? he wanted to ask her, but he couldn't make himself say it for fear of her reply. "You know you're welcome to stay," he said instead. "I've already told you as much."

"Yes," she nodded. "You have." She sat back down in the chair, folding her hands in her lap. "Malcolm wanted to kill you because he thinks you can do sorcery," she said, looking down at them. "I know you made the roses grow for me. I know you made me see Max in the mirror."

"Max?" He bent down to see her face, light-headed with sudden relief. "The knight in the mirror was Max?"

"Yes, of course." She looked up at him. "You told the mirror to show me my deepest desire, and it did; it showed me Max, grown up and strong, just as I have always dreamed he'd be." She frowned. "Who did you think it was?"

He smiled, taking her hand. "I thought it was Charles."

"Charles?" she echoed, laughing. "God's wounds, Aiden, no."

"I thought you grieved for him," he admitted. "That's why I left you, why you thought I was angry."

"Aiden, no." She touched his cheek. "I do grieve for Charles a little, but I never really cared for him, not that way. How could I, when he thought of me as nothing better than a toy? If we had married and he hadn't left me, things might have been different, but I doubt it." His smile had faded, and a darker, more ironic light had come into his eyes. "What is it? Do you think I'm horrible?"

"No," he promised, kissing her hand. *I am*, he thought but didn't say.

"I didn't love Charles, but I do love Max more than my own life," she said. "Last night, when you were gone and I thought he would die, all I could think about was the image you had shown me in the mirror. I thought some demon had been playing tricks on me, that your spell or whatever it was had turned on me. I thought God was punishing me for . . . for consorting with a wizard."

For a long moment Aiden couldn't answer, though it was obvious she was waiting for him to speak. This was the conversation he had always dreaded; these were the questions he had hidden from all his life. Fear of them had turned him into the empty rogue he pretended to be for the world, had made him abandon any hope of true love in favor of a royal marriage and whatever pretty mistress would have his body without his heart. Now Evelyn, the mistress he wanted more than any other, was asking him for the truth he couldn't give, and he had no one but himself to blame. "And what do you think now?"

"I don't know." She couldn't tell if he was hurt or angry or just didn't care; his beautiful face had gone completely blank. Even his eyes, usually so alive with feeling or merriment, had closed off into empty blue. "I saw you save Max. I saw you call the sickness out of him like calling out a demon, and I know that isn't natural, that somehow you are different, not of the world I've always known. By all rights, I should think you are a wizard, and I should be afraid of you and want to run away." She framed his face in her hands and looked into his eyes. "But how can I do that? How could I condemn you for saving my child, even if I wanted to? I just want to understand."

"Evie, stop." He took her hands and held them, holding on to her and holding her off in a single gesture. "You cannot ask me this," he said, his voice as tender as she had ever heard it. "I cannot make you understand; I can't tell you about the roses or the mirror or how I helped you cure Max of his fever." She didn't seem frightened or angry, just confused, and a terrible, aching need for her rose up in his chest, an almost unbearable desire to tell her the truth. But he couldn't do it; he had kept the secret too close to him for too long. He couldn't stop protecting it now, even from her. "But please, try to believe me," he said, caressing her cheek. "Nothing about me is evil or of the devil, no matter what you've seen or may have always known." He cradled her jaw in his hand, marveling again at the depth of feeling and intelligence that glowed in her wide blue eyes, the wild spirit that lived within her beauty. "Can you believe me?"

To his shock, she smiled, the same flirtatious invitation that had first drawn him to her, deepened by the trusting hope in her eyes. "Yes," she answered, turning her head to press a kiss to his palm. "If that is what you want."

"Darling . . ." He fell completely to his knees before her and kissed her, and she allowed it, reveled in the joy she felt in his touch. Nothing was different, really; nothing had been explained. She was still frightened and confused; she still couldn't be sure of her decision to stay with him and not return to the clan or certain she would ever be more to him than whatever she was right now. But he wanted her; when she had said she could believe him, his face had come alive again with elation. He had reached for her again; his mouth was kissing hers. She couldn't leave him; she couldn't give him up.

She braced her hand against his chest and turned her face away from him to catch her breath and make him stop for a moment, not because she didn't want to kiss him but to see his eyes again. "No, Evie," he protested almost angrily, turning her face back to his. "Don't try to send me away again." He pressed kisses to her forehead, her eyelids, her cheek, a kind of fevered worship or blessing of desire. "Please . . ."

"No," she promised, kissing him the same way, his beautiful angel's face. "I won't, I promise." His kiss fell on her mouth again, and she reached for him, wrapping her arms around his neck as he leaned her back in her chair. His hands slid down her sides to her waist to shift her forward as his tongue pushed into her mouth, tender but insistent, claiming her breath. She sighed once in surrender, letting herself trust him in this as in the other, without thinking, abandoning all her designs. He pushed her gown up over her thighs, and she shivered, his confidence exhilarating, his absolute belief in her desire. "Tell me what to do," she murmured, nuzzling his cheek.

"Kiss me." She closed her eyes and pressed her open mouth to his, rising up to hold him with her hands entangled in his hair when he moved to back away. She felt him smile and his arms fold more tightly around her, and she deepened the kiss, slipping her tongue over his, tasting the luscious strangeness of his mouth.

"Like that?" she said as she drew back, wiping the corner of her mouth, and he wanted to devour her, he wanted her so much, his prideful, arrogant baggage.

"Yes, sweeting," he said teasingly, shifting her closer. "Just like that." He slid a hand up over her thigh, a powerful caress. "Wrap your legs around me."

"Yes, my lord." She smiled, framing his face in her hands, drunk on the drowsy passion burning in his eyes. She locked her legs around his waist, trying not to shiver, trying to be bold, and he smiled, the seductive, half-mocking, half-adoring twist of his mouth that always made her knees feel weak. She kissed him of her own accord, unable to resist him, and he picked her up, his powerful, warrior's arms lifting her out of the chair and over his head, her legs still wrapped around his waist, her arms around his neck, her mouth still feeding on his.

He lay her back on the bed, bending over her, one knee between her thighs. "Let me touch you," he said softly, running his hands over her arms, raising them over her head as he kissed her again. She drew his lower lip between her teeth, a brazen, eager gesture that made him shiver as he burned. This was Evelyn, the self-adoring beauty who had sworn she would never be his mistress, who swore she had no love for love. "Let me see you," he said softly in her ear, barely pleading as he stood up.

"As you wish." She nodded as he drew away, propping on her elbows with a wicked smile as he unlaced her gown, her lower lip barely trembling to give her shyness away. "Do you need help?" He smiled for his answer, his fingers so efficient it was shocking. His hands slid into her bodice, and her head fell back, warm pleasure lapping through her as he caressed her breasts, gentle but possessive. He slid her gown down over her shoulders, kissing the curve at the base of her neck as he unlaced her sleeves.

"So beautiful," he murmured as he pulled them from her arms, leaving the tissue-thin shift. He barely brushed her mouth with his before he moved to her sweet breast, nuzzling the shift aside to suckle the nipple, making it go hard against his lips, a dainty version of the ache he felt himself.

"Aiden . . ." She let herself fall back on the bed, weak but restless, one hand entangled in his soft, black hair as he suckled her breast, her hips rising of their own accord. His hand slid down her stomach to her pelvic bone, pushing her gown away to press her to the bed and hold her still.

"Wait," he said softly, moving to her other breast. "Just wait—"

"No," she ordered, clutching at his hair. His touch moved slowly to her sex, and a deeper pulse of pleasure shook her, building but still incomplete. "I don't want to wait."

"Darling . . ." He kissed her mouth, enraptured, and she reached for him, her hands sliding over his back, seeming just as desperate as he was himself.

She felt him hard between them, a foreign thing that sprang to life as she pushed the hose over his hips, and for a moment she was frightened. She slid her hand down over his stomach to touch him, trace his shape with her fingers, and he bent his head to her shoulder, shaking as from fever, his hands braced on her back to hold her without pulling her closer. "Is this all right?"

"Yes," he promised, barely managing a whisper, nuzzling her throat. Her hand closed over him, and he kissed her, pressing her back to the bed. Her heart clutched once in panic as he moved between her thighs, but his kiss was so tender, so perfect, she felt herself open like the petals of a rose. She felt his hand close over hers, helping her guide him inside.

She opened her mouth to cry out not in pain but in a blissful kind of shock, her flesh enfolding him easily, this other, this tender invader, out of her control. "Evie?" she heard him say tenderly, caressing her brow, and she opened her eyes to find him looking down on her, hardly separate at all. "Are you well?" he smiled.

"Yes," she answered, the word itself a sigh of ecstasy. "I think I am quite well." He kissed her deeply, biting her lip, then slowly moved inside her, deliberately tender. The gentle waves she'd felt before rose higher, engulfing her in pleasure like nothing she had ever felt, tremors from a part of her she had never known existed. She let her eyes fall closed again, all her senses focused on this center where the two of them were joined. Her arms closed around him, her body finding his rhythm, moving naturally without her conscious will. Before when he had touched her at the mirror, she had felt as if she were flying, dying, but now she felt herself coming alive, free but safely grounded in the shelter of his arms, as if she had finally come home. She felt the pleasure building up inside her like a fever, her body melting into his, moving faster to urge him on.

He moved faster, thrusting deeper, and she arched beneath him, her perfect flesh flushed pink with desire too beautiful to bear. He felt his climax building, and he tried to hold it off, to wait for her to be ready. He gathered her up in his arms and sat up, heaving her into his lap, and she cried out, kneeling over him, her head bent to his shoulder.

She was full of him, wrapped up in him, but still it wasn't enough. Her hips moved faster, desperate, her hot skin bathed in sweat, and he held her, helped her, urged her on. She braced her hands on his shoulders, her body finding perfect friction, grinding on one perfect spot, and suddenly the world exploded into blazing light. "Aiden!" she called out, falling into bliss, and he was there, still holding her, his own bliss erupting inside her, their bodies melted into one.

He kissed her as he picked her up, felt her trembling still as he fell from her and lifted her into his arms. He laid her back against the pillows, pressing kisses all over her face, and she smiled, contented as a kitten, her eyes already closed. He kissed her stomach, and she sighed, preening under his touch as his hands slid over her hips. Smiling, he nuzzled her sex, and she gasped, another climax ripping through her as he'd known it would. He bathed her mercilessly with his tongue, holding her still as her hands clutched at the coverlet, her legs locked over his shoulders.

Tremor after tremor shook her to the bottom of her soul, each one so hard upon the one before it she could not judge them apart. She couldn't think, couldn't see, even when she opened her eyes, and all she could hear was the pounding of her blood and a desperate, haunted wail that she slowly came to know as her own voice. The waves at last subsided, and her cry melted into a sob, tears for every pain she'd ever felt, every loss and grief.

"Evie, no . . ." Aiden gathered her into his arms, holding her on his lap, and she wrapped her arms around his neck and sobbed against his shoulder. "Sweeting, stop," he begged her, stroking her hair. "What hurts you?"

"Nothing," she swore, trying to do as he asked, but she couldn't stop crying; she had held it back too long. "Aiden, please don't leave me." His arms closed more tightly around her, and she laughed through her tears, comforted and afraid, her cheek pressed to his heart. "Please don't go away."

"Never," he promised, a hard knot of grief rising in his own throat, grief for all the pain she felt and for his emptiness without her. "I will never go," he swore to her, turning her face up to his, and it was true. Now that he had found her, he would never give her up. Wherever he should go, she would go with him, whatever her kin or his princess might think. Whatever he became, she would be his.

Evie smiled at him, touching his mouth. Tears were still falling on her cheeks, but she was no longer afraid. The hard, determined look on his face was greater comfort to her heart than any lover's vow. "You swear?"

"I swear." He kissed her lips again, and she sank into the bliss of his embrace, exhausted but content. Her virtue might be shattered, but her hopes were not lost. She would still be with him, and she would still make him her husband.

18

Aiden woke as Evelyn was fussing with her gown. "Look at this," she demanded, shaking it at him as he sat up. "I'll never get the creases out again."

"I'll buy you a new one just like it," he promised, smiling at her like a fool.

"That's all very well, my rich and handsome lord," she said, trying hard not to smile back. "But what am I supposed to put on now?" In truth, she had almost hoped to be dressed and gone before he awoke, not because she didn't want to talk to him but because she just wasn't sure what to say. But now that he was awake, she was glad she hadn't done it. "The whole castle is probably lurking in the hallway, waiting to see what I look like now that my virtue is lost."

"Once again, your belief in your own importance staggers the imagination," he teased, getting up to kiss her cheek. "I'm sure everyone is going about their own business hardly thinking of you or me at all."

"You don't honestly believe that," she scoffed, kissing him back.

"Of course I do." He pulled on his hose and shoes

and found a shirt in the chest. "The only one who's likely to have thought the first thing about either of us is Robin, who's supposed to have been in here long ere this to wake me and give me my breakfast."

"I may very well be proud," she said, lacing her shift. "But you, my lord, are lazy—a grown man having his breakfast in bed? You ought to be ashamed."

"Don't scorn it till you've tried it, love," he teased, kissing her mouth. "In fact, you ought to wait here." He pulled on his shirt. "I will send Robin for a tray for two and have a look at Max."

"Max!" She started to put on her wrinkled gown, headed for the door.

"Wait, Evie; it's all right," he promised, catching her. "I will bring him back to you."

"Poor lamb," she sighed. "Abandoned by his mother when he's been so sick."

"Shocking, isn't it?" he teased. He touched her chin and turned her face up to his. "I will be right back."

Max was fine, as expected, and already having his breakfast. "Ay-ben!" he called out from Agnes's lap as Aiden came in. "Where my ma-mee is?"

"Your mummy is waiting for you," Aiden promised, taking him and ignoring the look Agnes was trying to pierce him through with. "Are you feeling better?"

"Better," the little boy nodded, laying a hand on his cheek.

Shouts and horses could suddenly be heard in the courtyard below, and the guardsmen on the battlements sounded their horns. Looking out the window, Aiden saw knights and grooms running about like madmen, scrambling to open the gates, and a long caravan of horses and wagons turning onto the land bridge from the main road, bearing the banners of Brinlaw. "Holy Christ," he mumbled, barely believing his eyes. A fine, high-sided carriage with doors embossed in gold rolled at the very center of the train, and at the front rode his father, unmistakably splendid in shining chain-mail armor. A groom rode beside him and led a riderless brown stallion with a creamy blaze across his nose—Lady Alista's horse. "She must be in the carriage."

"My lord?" Agnes said. "Who comes?"

"My mother," he answered. "My parents—go and help Evie get dressed." Still carrying Max, he ran down the stairs of the tower. "Robin! Come quickly! My father has come!"

He made it out into the courtyard just as they were riding through the gates. "Papa!" he called, rushing forward to greet him. Brinlaw got down from his warhorse as gracefully as Aiden could have done himself and returned his warm embrace in kind. "What are you doing in Scotland?"

"Why do you have to ask?" his father countered with a laugh. "Did you not receive my letter?"

"No," Aiden admitted. "Or rather, I suppose I did, but I haven't read it yet. Things have been rather chaotic—"

"Aiden!" His younger sister, Mary, who at twenty ought to have been more sedate, came scrambling out of the carriage to fling her arms around his neck. "You lunatic—do you realize you live on the far side of purgatory?"

"Mary," their father scolded mildly.

"It's true," she insisted. "We've been stuck in that carriage forever." She drew back and stared at him strangely, but he didn't have time to wonder why. His mother was emerging from the carriage.

"My lady," he said, going to meet her.

"My lord," she teased with a curtsy before she accepted his kiss. "We were worried about you, but you seem to be settling in." She laughed as he drew back, mischief dancing in her eyes. "Indeed, you look quite shockingly domestic."

"What?" Then he realized, he was still carrying Max. "Oh . . . this is Max."

"Hello," Max said quite clearly, waving for good measure.

"He was here at Glencairn when I got here," Aiden explained, still too addled with happy surprise to be artful in his explanation. "But he's been ill; I ought not to have him outside."

"I'll take him," Evelyn said, coming up behind him.

Agnes had come to fetch her on the run, and she had managed to comb her hair and change her gown before she came outside. But there was nothing she could have done to make herself ready for such company as this. Aiden's father was as tall as he was and every bit as handsome; indeed, if she hadn't known the man was old enough to have a full-grown son, she would never have believed it. A girl of about her own age with the same black curls as Aiden and a similar wicked smile was standing beside him, and standing beside her was another woman Evie supposed must be Aiden's mother. But it hardly seemed possible. Her face was as smooth as finest porcelain, utterly unlined—even her hands looked young. Max reached out to her as Evelyn took him from Aiden, and the lady laughed. "Hello, Max," she said, taking the baby's outstretched hand. "I'm sorry to hear you've been ill."

"He's much better now," Evelyn answered shyly.

"Lady Evelyn is Max's mother," Aiden explained.

"Yes," Lady Alista answered. "So I gathered."

"You should read your correspondence, Willie," his father warned, glancing back at the carriage. "You miss things you need to know."

"Willie?" Evelyn couldn't help but ask, turning to Aiden with a wicked smile.

"Yes . . . I mean, no," he protested, charmingly flustered in a way she had never seen and found extremely endearing. "Willie was my nickname when I was a little child." He stopped, staring at the carriage, and Evie turned around to see what he had seen.

Another young woman was emerging. This one was blond and quite thin, an effect accentuated by the full folds of her skirt. Her gown was finer than anything

Evelyn had ever seen, cloth of gold encrusted with tiny pearls, and jeweled rings adorned every finger on her hands. On her head she wore a tiny crown. But she looked frightened half to death.

"Aiden, who is that?" she turned to ask, but he was already walking away. As she watched in stunned silence, he knelt at this stranger's feet. "Majesty," he said, kissing her hand. "Welcome to Glencairn Castle."

"Thank you, my lord," the apparent princess answered with a tiny smile, blushing brightly enough they all could see it. "But you needn't be so formal. We are betrothed, after all."

"Katherine, then." Aiden rose back to his feet, his smile held firmly in place. This was a disaster, no question, but he would put it right. "We truly meet at last." So this was his future bride. 'Twas no great wonder King Richard held her in such high esteem; she looked and spoke just like him. Her nose turned up quite sharply on the end, and she looked shy as a rabbit. Next to Evelyn's vibrant beauty, she looked like an overdecorated doll. Evelyn . . . He turned to find his Scottish angel staring at him, pale but for the two high spots of scarlet on her cheeks.

"Forgive me," Evelyn stammered, surprised she could speak at all. She bobbed a curtsy to Aiden's parents, her knees buckling beneath her. "My son is ill; I have to take him inside." Turning her back on Aiden and his princess, she fled up the steps into the hall.

She made it to the top of the first set of stairs inside

with Max in her arms before Aiden caught her. "Evie, wait," he ordered, grabbing her as she tried to turn the corner to her tower.

"Wait for what?" she demanded, turning on him instead. "She said she was betrothed to you; you said she was a princess." Max began to cry, and she jerked free of Aiden to comfort him.

"She is a princess," Aiden said as she cuddled the child to her shoulder, pretending to ignore him. "But it doesn't matter—"

"Doesn't matter?" she echoed, incredulous with fury. Agnes had come up the stairs with Robin, and Max reached out to her. "Take him upstairs and start packing, Agnes," Evie said, handing him over. "We are going home."

"No," Aiden said stubbornly. "Evelyn, shut up and listen to me—"

"My lord, please," Robin interrupted, the look on the Scotswoman's face turning his own guts to water, and she barely even noticed he was there. "Lord and Lady Brinlaw are going to the solar with the princess. Do you mean to—?" The glare Aiden gave him was no friendlier, and he started again. "I mean to say . . . what shall I do with them?"

Aiden felt like a man whose house was collapsing in an earthquake, unable to brace up one catastrophe for being crushed under another. "Give them some breakfast, tell them a story, and I will be there presently," he ordered.

"You can go right now," Evelyn suggested, her hands clenched into fists. She wanted to hit him hard enough to knock him down the stairs, then scream loud enough to bring the castle down around him. "I am leaving—"

"I said no," Aiden cut her off.

"I didn't bloody ask you!"

Sir Alan had come to the top of the stairs, but when he heard this, he turned on his heel and went back down again with Robin close behind him. "Agnes, go ahead," Evie ordered, and the nurse obeyed, but when Evie tried to follow her, Aiden scooped her off her feet and carried her off the other way. "Put me down, you bastard!"

"Stop making such a scene." He carried her into his bedroom fighting like a demon all the way and kicked the door shut behind them. "Just look at yourself—"

"Look at myself? Look at you." An hour ago she had been watching him wake up—not even an hour. His clothes were still rumpled; his face was still shadowed with stubble. But everything had changed; the whole world was falling apart. "What do you call that display in the courtyard, kissing the hand of that . . . that princess?" she demanded. "And me just standing there watching with Max and your mother and father." Tears of humiliation tried to rise in her eyes, but she fought them down again. She would die and be damned before she cried in front of him again. "What do you suppose they thought, Aiden? What was I supposed to think?"

"That was not supposed to happen." He refused to lose his temper this time, no matter how she railed at him; he couldn't risk it. Things were bad enough already—he had run out of the courtyard after her and left the princess standing with his parents. They all no doubt believed he had lost his mind. "Katherine was never meant to come here—"

"But you mean to marry her," she cut him off. "Or you did. Do you still?" A tiny flame of hope flickered inside her as she looked into his eyes.

"I have to." She tried to turn away from him, but he caught her by the shoulders. "Evelyn, listen to me." He touched her cheek to make her look at him. "I am a second son; I have no title of my own, no lands—"

"You have Glencairn," she pointed out, thinking he meant that a Scottish castle didn't count.

"No, love, I do not," he admitted. "Katherine does. This castle is part of her dowry. I'm meant to secure it for England before we can be married. That's why I am here."

"You're marrying her for a castle?" She laughed, the irony of it almost more than she could bear.

"Yes," he said, encouraged. "I don't care for her, darling, I promise you. Until just now, I had barely clapped eyes on her before." He moved to kiss her forehead, and she shoved him violently away. "Evie, she means nothing—"

"And what do I mean?" she demanded. "If you have to marry Princess Whatever-Her-Silly-Name-Might-Be—"

"Katherine," he interrupted.

"Do you think that I don't know that?" The hurt in her eyes was unbearable, he thought; he would rather she had stabbed him with a knife. "Do you think her name's not branded on my memory, that I will ever for a single moment's time forget how I felt when you said it, kneeling at her feet? You made me think you cared for me—"

"I do," he insisted. "Evie—"

"But it doesn't matter," she cut him off before he could say more, another lie or truth to tear a fresh wound in her heart. "What did you think would happen? You said you never meant for her to come here; what did you mean for me to do?"

"I meant to explain my situation." She was being unreasonable, a woman to the lunatic extreme as always, but surely he could make her understand. "I knew you would be angry, but I thought that I could make you care for me enough to understand."

"You thought that I would be your mistress," she translated, feeling sick. "Even after everything I've said to you, everything you know about my feelings." She thought about the night before, his refusing to explain how supernatural events kept happening around him and how she had let him keep his secret. "You never for one moment meant for me to be your wife."

"No," he admitted, wanting desperately to say something different, some lie that would erase the pain from her eyes, bring back the joy and hope he'd seen the night before. But he could not. "I knew that couldn't be." She turned her face away from him, and he reached out for her arm.

"Don't touch me!" she ordered, rage choking her like bile. "Don't you dare." She wanted to hurt him the way he was hurting her, to peel the cover from his pride and see it torn and raw. "I've spent enough time as a whore already, for all the good it's done." She looked up and made herself smile, grabbing for her bag of tricks, her store of feminine wiles. "I should ask you to give me some lessons."

"I thought that I already had," he answered, forcing himself to sound cold. She was wounded; he had hurt her, but he wouldn't let her hurt him back. Somehow he would make her understand.

"And so you did." She smiled. "Katherine should like you very well." She caught sight of her own face in the mirror, as beautiful as ever, and suddenly she longed to rip it to shreds, to tear her beauty from her skull and be done with it forever. *Show me my destiny now,* she longed to tell the mirror. *Show me Aiden.* But she wasn't a wizard. She couldn't make it work.

"I doubt Katherine will care much for me one way or the other," Aiden said. "I suspect we will live far apart."

"Then I am sorry for you," she retorted. "I plan to live with my husband and love him, too, if I can." He smiled, shaking his head. "You don't believe me?"

"I believe I've heard this game before," he answered.

She was baiting him again, invoking the name of her phantom, future husband just to make him jealous.

"You know what is rather funny?" she said, feigning unconcern with all the skills her years of practice could give her. "Funny, not strange. You're marrying this princess—this Katherine," she corrected with a nod, "so that you can have this castle. And that is just the reason that I meant to marry you." The mask slipped a little as she looked into his eyes. "The difference is I would have loved you." The hunger in his face was almost more than she could bear; her resolve was threatening to weaken. "At least I would have tried."

She tried to walk past him, and he caught her. "Stop it, Evie; enough," he ordered, holding her hard by the arms as if he meant to shake her. "I understand your being furious; I know that you are hurt—"

"Let go of me," she ordered.

"But I cannot play this game with you, not now," he went on, barely hearing her. "My future depends on that skinny little rabbit in a crown, and I've already kept her waiting far too long. I don't even known what they're doing here, but whatever it is, they can't intend to stay in Scotland long. Once Katherine is gone, you can punish me however you wish, however long you like, and I will bear it patiently, I promise."

"I said let go." She couldn't believe what she was hearing, that he had heard nothing of what she had said. He still thought she would be his mistress, that she was still his to control.

"Evie, please," he said in a tone far more commanding than pleading. "I'm sorry the world is as it is; I'm sorry Charles abandoned you; I'm sorry I lied to you or didn't tell you the truth, that I can't be what you wanted." Her eyes narrowed in fury, and he pressed a kiss to her brow. "But I do care for you and for Max. I swear I will take care of you," he promised, folding her close in his arms. "You will just have to believe me."

"Believe you?" she echoed, stiff as iron as he kissed her cheek. His kiss strayed to the nape of her neck, nuzzled sweetly under her hair, and for one brief moment she considered the terms of surrender. She could be his mistress, knowing that was all she would ever be, knowing he was married to another. At least she would have him, his beauty and his kiss, his arms to hold her in the dark. But for how long? How long before her beauty faded and another caught his eye? Long enough for Max to lay claim to his charity, the portion of his wealth he deemed enough for the child of his whore? "No," she said, struggling to free herself from his grasp. "I am going home."

He held her more tightly, shifting her closer, willfully refusing to hear. She couldn't really want to leave him; she was his. He had felt it last night when he held her in his arms, tasted it in her kiss. "You are home, darling," he promised. "It will be all right."

"I said no!" She brought her knee up hard and fast, a trick the boys at home had made her learn only too well, and he doubled over in pain. But when she tried to run away, he still had hold of her arm and wouldn't let go, his eyes burning with rage.

"Stop it," he rasped, trying to draw her closer.

"No . . ." Without thinking, she grabbed the flagon of wine from the table and shattered it over the back of his neck, expecting it to make him let go, but he crumpled to the carpet, unconscious, her wrist still in his grip. "Oh, my God," she whispered, falling to her knees. "Aiden!" He let out a moan, and she wriggled her hand free. "I'm sorry, love," she promised, backing away.

She ran out into the hallway and found Agnes waiting with their belongings, but someone else was there as well—Lady Alista, sitting on a windowsill with Max on her lap. "Forgive me, my lady," Evelyn said, unsure how better to begin. "I think I may have killed your son."

"Oh, I doubt it," Aiden's mother said blithely as Agnes went to look. "What did you do to him?"

"I . . . I kicked him," she confessed, trying not to gape like an addlepated fool. The woman in the window had taken off her veil and wimple to reveal a long braid of ebony hair as thick and lush as Evelyn's own and barely shot with silver, and though she must surely have been nearly sixty years old, her movements as she played with Max were as lithe as a girl's. "And I hit him in the back of the neck with a flagon of wine."

"Smartly done." Lady Alista smiled. "You probably knocked him unconscious."

"I'd say so," Agnes agreed with a nod as she came out.

"You must love him very much," Her Ladyship continued, tickling Max's nose.

"Love him?" Evie echoed, confused. "Because I—?"

"Yes, of course." She looked up at Evie and smiled. "When I first fell in love with Aiden's father, I sliced his face open with a dagger."

"Oh," Evie answered, uncertain what she ought to say to such a remarkable confession, but Agnes laughed aloud as if she understood completely. Lady Alista Brinlaw might be a witch or she might not, but she was certainly the oddest and most lovely woman Evie had ever met. Max seemed to already adore her.

"Where are you going, my lady?" she asked Evelyn now.

"Home," she answered. "My father's home—my sister's home now with her husband. My father is dead."

"I thought he must be." Her Ladyship sighed. "My son is still alive." She put Max into Evie's arms and kissed them each on the cheek. "I wish I could tell you what to do, sweeting, but I don't know."

"I don't know, either," Evie admitted, wishing suddenly she had the time to know this woman, to pour out all her heart to her and hear what she would say. But Aiden, if he wasn't really dying, would be awake soon, and she had to be gone. "But thank you." She started toward the stairs, then suddenly stopped, realization washing over her like an icy wave. "I do love him," she said softly, barely louder than a whisper, as if she were afraid even to hear the words herself. "I don't love anyone but Max; I never have before, just Max and my father, and my father is dead." She looked back at Lady Alista. "But I love Aiden."

"Of course you do," the older woman smiled.

"But I can't stay with him." She looked back at Aiden's door as if she expected to see him come raging through it after her. "If he really means to marry someone else, I can't stay here and be his whore."

Lady Alista came closer and caressed Evie's hair in the sort of gesture her own mother would have sooner suffered the fires of hell than make toward her. "Of course you can't."

"Besides," Evie said, fighting back the tears that only tenderness could draw from her, never pain, "Aiden doesn't love me."

"Are you so certain?" his mother asked gently. "I think he must—"

"No," Evie insisted, shaking her head. "He wants me like he wants Glencairn, as a possession. But he doesn't love me." The other woman was smiling as if she knew better, and Evie wanted desperately to believe her. But Lady Alista lived in a magical, faery-touched world where everyone was cherished and troubles always turned out for the best. Anyone could see it just by looking at her, even a baby like Max. But Evie had learned long ago that her own world was very different. The only person who had ever cherished her was her dear, dream-addled father, and he was dead and gone.

And her troubles had a way of going from bad to worse. "Or if he does, he loves the castle more."

"If that's true, he's not my son or Brinlaw's, either," Lady Alista promised. "And I can assure you he is."

Smiling again and making a curtsy, Evelyn ran down the stairs and out of the castle with her son in her arms and Agnes close behind.

"Now then, Willie Aiden," Alista frowned when they had gone. "Let's see what's become of you."

19

Halfway to the Scottish village, Evie drew her horse up to a stop. The mountaintop loomed over them, the standing stones casting their noonday shadow over the dusty road. *Go and prosper in the glen,* the voice of the ancient queen echoed inside her head, a memory of a dream. *These will be enough to serve us here.*

"My lady?" Agnes said, stopping beside her. Evie had worried that the Englishwoman might be frightened of horses, but in fact she seemed to be a far more expert rider than Evelyn was herself. "Do you want to turn back?"

"Yes, of course." Max was dozing in the crook of her arm, and he stirred at the sound of her voice. "But I'm not going to." She looked up at the stones again, remembering the hours she had spent among them as a child, her fantasies of glory. Now their mysteries seemed dull to her, a weary tale grown long. Even her dreams of the past seemed to have lost their power when she held them up to the reality of her present.

"Who is this coming here?" Agnes said, interrupting her thoughts. Gerald was coming toward them, riding hard around the bend. His horse shied when it saw them, rearing in a cloud of dust, and Evie's mare skidded to one side, threatening to stumble over the edge of the slope.

"Where are you going?" Evie asked the boy when their mounts were back under control.

"I was on my way to the castle," Gerald explained. "I was coming for you." He nodded at Agnes, barely staring for a moment at her scar. "Da sent me to fetch you."

"Your da didn't know I was coming," she answered, confused. "I only just found out myself."

"He didn't know you were meaning to come on your own," he agreed. "But I'd better let him explain it."

They rode on to the village, and at first it seemed almost exactly as Evelyn remembered. People were standing in their dooryards and passing the news on the green, and they all smiled and waved to her and Gerald, many calling out greetings as well. But something was different, wrong somehow, and as they passed the green and started up the hill, she realized what it was. No one was working. It was harvest time; the streets and yards should have been bustling with work, every villager from the laird to the smallest toddling babe out in the world doing something useful to get ready for the winter to come. But all of the people they saw seemed to be just standing around, making a show of their presence. Looking more closely at the houses as they passed, she could see that fully half of them were empty, the doors and windows bolted.

"Where is everybody?" she asked Gerald, waving to a little girl who was leaning on a gate. The wagons and hayricks were missing as well, every sign of the harvest.

"Da will explain." He led the way to the laird's front gate as Davey ran out to greet them.

"Hello, Aunt Evie." The younger boy smiled, holding the gate open for them as they rode through. "Hello, Max."

"Davey!" Max called, perking up at once.

Agnes took both babies as soon as she'd dismounted, Grace in a sling over her shoulder and Max perched on her hip. "Gerald, help her," Evie said as she climbed down herself.

"Come here, Cousin," Gerald complied with a grin, swinging Max over his head and making him crow with glee.

"Be careful!" Evie scolded, trying to laugh and not be horrified. Max's world was about to become far more exciting with his cousins so close at hand. "He's been sick."

"We'll be careful," Davey promised, going to join them.

"That was quick," Rebecca said, appearing in the open doorway. "You must have been waiting at the gate."

"We were already on our way here," Evie answered. "We met Gerald on the road." She hadn't spoken directly with her sister since the day she had left to be betrothed. She had kissed her cheek on this very patch of ground, refusing as always to cry for fear of marring her face or her pride, and Rebecca hadn't shed a tear, either. "Malcolm said we could come home."

"Aye, he did," Rebecca answered. "Though I never for a moment thought you would." She eyed Agnes and her Grace. "You've brought your servant, too, I see. How do you mean to pay her?"

"My lady pays me well enough," Agnes answered for herself, more than a match for Rebecca.

Malcolm came around the corner of the house. "You're here already?" he said, hugging Evie. "Good." He nodded to Agnes. "Well met, mistress." He shot Rebecca a warning look. "Come, let's go inside."

The shutters in the front room were still open, but the furniture was all gone, down to the spit from the hearth. "What has happened?" Evie asked, turning to Malcolm in shock.

"We're leaving," he answered. "Most of the women and children are gone already, packed off at dawn as soon as the Brinlaw banners were sighted."

"Leaving?" Evie echoed. "Leaving to go where? The Clan McCairn has lived in this glen for a thousand years—"

"Or so the legends say," Malcolm agreed. "But no law says we have to stay." Other Highland clans lived like nomads, moving from place to place to follow the crops or the weather, and none thought ill of them for it. Malcolm himself had been born to such a clan. But the Clan McCairn had always kept to its same village, farmed in its same fields, lived in the shadow of the mountain. *Prosper in the glen,* the memory whispered again. "Brinlaw means to take our lands, Little Sister," Malcolm finished. "Whether it be of his own will or his prince's, I cannot say, but I won't wait here and make him kill us to do it."

"His father didn't come here for war," Evie insisted. "He came to bring Aiden's fiancée to him, one of King Richard's sisters. He has his wife and daughter with him, Aiden's mother and sister."

"Fiancée?" Rebecca repeated. "The Sassenach is meant to marry a princess?"

"He will marry her," Evie answered, facing her with calm. "He told me so himself."

"Did he, in faith?" Her sister laughed. "And what did you tell him?"

"Becca, hold your tongue," Malcolm ordered. "Whoever may be with the young lord's father, his reason for coming to the Highlands can't be peace. And even if it were, I wouldn't risk it. Aiden Brinlaw is a conjurer—"

"You don't know that," Evie protested.

"Aye, lass, I do," he answered. "His hand has fallen on this glen, and he means to hold it. For love of you, he has spared Gerald, and Hamish was saved by his sorcery, I have no doubt. So I will not do him harm." His face turned grim. "But neither will I stay and wait for him to wipe us off the mountain."

Evie thought of Aiden's face when he told her he

must marry Katherine, the dark resolve in his eyes. He had laid claim to her, though promised to another, and she had been forced to knock him senseless to escape, so powerful was his will. *He takes such things quite seriously*, Sir Alan had said to her on the morning the boys were sentenced to hang. *His squire said he hanged a hundred Saxon bandits in a single day*, Molly had reported his very first day at Glencairn. *He killed him*, Agnes had said of her lover. *It was a mercy to him.* But he had held her and made love to her so tenderly, had comforted her as she cried....

"I cannot believe he would do it," she answered aloud. "But you are laird, not me."

"How kind of you to notice, my lady," Rebecca scoffed, mocking her with the title she had never held the right to claim. "Tell us more about the kindness of your lover. When his princess turned up this morning, did he help you pack your bags before he tossed you out on that twitching little tail of yours?"

A year ago Evelyn would have literally run away from such a question, too furious to answer without tears. But that was a year ago. "What would you know about it, you cow?" she demanded. "Unless a thing happens in the church or in this house, you never know the truth of it, and even what you do hear you haven't got the wit to understand." Her sister's face had gone bone white, and she couldn't resist a final jab. "And by the way, Becca, you could use a good twitch."

"I hear enough to know the truth of you, harlot,"

her sister answered, their cold, self-righteous mother reborn down to the soles of her shoes. "Just how many English bastards do you mean to raise?"

"Enough!" Malcolm roared, his fury aimed squarely at his wife. "Have you forgotten why our son still lives?" he demanded.

"No," Rebecca answered, her eyes still locked to Evie's. "I have not forgotten our sons." Casting a final glance at Agnes, she turned and left the room.

"I will speak to her," Malcolm promised, clapping Evie on the shoulder. "Once you've been back with us for a while, she will remember how dearly she loves you."

Once you see that I'm not pregnant? she wanted to ask. *How will she remember what was never true?* "When are we going?" she asked aloud instead.

"Another group will leave at dusk," he said. "We don't want to raise their suspicions, just in case they do have mischief planned. Our household will be among the last, sometime in the night."

Aiden woke up sometime after nightfall, far too long a time to be unconscious for a simple knock on the head. His mother was sitting at his bedside, calmly reading a book. "What did you do?" he demanded, sitting up, his tongue thick in his mouth and his skull feeling ready to split.

"No worse than you've done to yourself a thousand times in London," Lady Alista answered resignedly, setting her book aside. "You came around too quickly; I thought you could use a bit of rest." She examined the cut on his forehead with a critical eye. "You look horrible, by the way," she added, probing it gently. "I know Lady Evelyn hit you with a flagon, but she didn't do all this."

"I was ambushed by her clan two nights ago," he said, pushing her hand away to get up from the bed. "Where is Evie now?" Whatever potion she had given him, he must have had a double dose; his legs felt numb as stone.

"She's gone home," Lady Alista answered. "You shouldn't try to walk before the morning."

"Lovely," he muttered, trying anyway and having fair success, though he felt like death warmed over. "What did I ever do to you?"

"Not me, my darling Willie," she retorted. "What are you playing at?"

"What is it about women that makes you bond together on sight against every man in the world, including your own son?" he complained. "I'm assuming you're angry with me on Evelyn's behalf?"

"Not all women," she demurred. He looked at himself in the mirror and had to admit she was right; he did look terrible. "And yes, I am quite put out with you. How dare you treat that girl as you have? You ought to die of shame—I am ashamed for you."

"Really, Mama?" he sighed, splashing cold water on his face. "And what else is new?"

"All we've heard from everyone in this castle is what a fine, kind, lovely woman Lady Evelyn is," she continued. "Yet you treat her like a common doxy, lying to her—"

"I never lied to her," he cut her off, a spark of anger flaring for a moment.

"You told her about Katherine, then?" she retorted. "Funny, she seemed quite surprised."

"Where is Katherine now?" he asked blandly, refusing to rise to the bait.

"Somewhere with Mary," she answered. "Thank heavens they seem to get on well, or I'd have lost my reason long ere this. You hurt her feelings, by the way, abandoning her to chase after your mistress. I wanted to tell her the truth and be done, but your father insisted on telling her you were taken ill."

"Thank God for Papa," he muttered. He was starting to feel a bit less like he'd risen from the tomb; his head was beginning to clear. "What kind of truth would you have told?"

"That you are in love with Lady Evelyn," she said. "That Katherine couldn't see it for herself is a testament to her royal stupidity, I'm sad to say. When Brinlaw told her you were sick, she forgot the other girl even existed, or at least she pretended to forget it." Aiden finished washing, refusing to answer, and pulled on a clean shirt. "So what do you mean to do?"

"Nothing much tonight, as I have been drugged," he said with a twisted half-smile. "Pay my respects to the princess." He put on a fresh tunic. "In the morning I am going to fetch Evelyn home."

"Aiden, are you mad?" She caught his face and looked into his eyes, her own bright with worry. "You are—"

"No, Mama, I am not," he said, pushing her gently away.

"Yes, you are," she insisted. "Or still drunk, at least. Can you not hear yourself? Evelyn thought she had killed you." He went to get his boots, and she followed him. "As dearly as she loves you, she bashed you in the head to get away because she will not stay with you and watch you marry another woman. How do you think you will change her mind tomorrow? How will you convince her to come back?"

"I don't mean to convince her of anything," he answered, lacing his boots. "I will just bring her back."

"Aiden, you can't do that," she protested. "She's not a toy you can pick up or drop as it pleases you; she is a woman."

"I know she is a woman, Mama," he answered, getting up. "I have seen her naked."

"I don't doubt it for a moment," she said bitterly. "But that does not mean she belongs to you. She is not yours—"

"Yes, she is," he cut her off, the dangerous fury returning to his eyes.

"Darling, please," she said, touching his cheek. "You are my son; more than anything in the world, I want you to be happy." She smiled tenderly. "But you can't keep a princess for a wife and your heart's true love your prisoner."

"Of course I can, Mama, if I have to," he said, smiling back. "I am a wizard, remember?"

The hall was full when he walked in, Sir Alan and the rest of the knights gathered around his father and Mary and Katherine playing chess at a table by the hearth. "There you are, thank God," his sister said, coming to meet him. "Are you all right?"

"Fine," he promised, accepting her embrace. "Good evening, Highness." He made his best courtier's bow. "I fear I must beg your forgiveness."

"Not at all, my lord," she answered, her gracious nod perfect but her cheeks flushed pink with shyness. "Your father told me you had fallen ill. With this horrid weather, I think it's a miracle anyone in Scotland survives."

"The princess misses Aquitaine," Mary explained. "Phillipe has promised to come and fetch us to Belleforte in the spring, French or no French." Phillipe was their sometime-cousin, Robin's older half-brother, and a close, dear friend of King Richard. Belleforte was his magnificent manor in Aquitaine, a true palace by the sea.

"That sounds lovely." Aiden smiled, taking Katherine's hand and kissing it. "Perhaps we can be married there." Had Evie ever seen the ocean? he wondered. She and Max would adore it; perhaps he could even build her a house of her own in Aquitaine or even Anjou, near his father's estates.

"Perhaps." Katherine nodded, blushing brighter. She was actually rather sweet, in a childish, baby-rabbit way. "My lord, do you think you might be catching?"

"No," Aiden promised as Mary bent her head to hide a smile. "I am almost positive I'm not."

All through this exchange, Lady Alista had stood at her husband's shoulder, murmuring urgently into his ear. Now Lord Brinlaw stood up. "Pardon the interruption, Aiden, but I must speak with you." His expression was pleasant enough, but his eyes were stern. "Alone."

"Of course." Pausing just long enough to kiss Katherine's hand once more and make her giggle, Aiden led his father to the solar. "Don't tell me; let me guess," he said as soon as the door was closed. "Mama has ordered you to make me see reason."

"Yes, she has, but I told her I'd be wasting my breath," Brinlaw answered. "Whether you believe it or not, I have been where you are, afflicted by the same madness, and I know you are past all cure." Suddenly Aiden realized he wasn't just disappointed or annoyed; he was genuinely furious. "But I never in my life thought once to behave so dishonorably as you seem to mean to now."

"How so, Papa?" Aiden asked evenly, collapsing into a chair with all the insolence he could muster, his headache getting worse.

"It may be understandable for a man like Henry was to take a mistress, though I do doubt it," Brinlaw answered. "His moral character was never the best, and when Eleanor stopped stroking his ego day and night and started disagreeing with him in front of his privy council, it was probably inevitable that he would seek better comfort elsewhere. At least he dearly loved his wife in the beginning and meant to keep his wedding vows when he made them. But you . . ." His face had gone red enough with temper to bring out the ghostly scar his own beloved's dagger had left on his cheek some forty years before. "You say without the slightest trace of shame or remorse that you will make vows to one woman while bedding another. Your mother insists that you love her; frankly, I don't care."

"My mother should mind her own business," Aiden said under his breath.

"You're twice a fool to say so," Brinlaw shot back. "I cannot believe your knightly vows could mean so little to you."

"Can you not?" Aiden asked with a bitter smile.

"No, sirrah, I cannot," his father answered. "You do not have a weak moral character, and you were not brought up to abandon your honor and destroy a lady's as well, no matter what you feelings for her might be."

"How would you know how I was brought up?" Aiden demanded, his own rage breaking free at last. "You had no part in it." Brinlaw's face went white, his blue eyes flashing fire, but Aiden didn't care and couldn't stop, even if he'd wanted to. "As for King Henry, I hate to dispel your illusions, Papa, but he was tupping whores two nights after his wedding just 'to cleanse his palate,' as he expressed it to me. That's who you sent me to grow up with. I am what you sent me to become."

"I sent you to learn politics and warfare from Henry," Brinlaw said. "Not to become him."

"And so I have not," Aiden retorted. "Henry died a bitter, sick old drunk with no one to love him but a son with the warmth of a snake and a squire who reminded him just enough of the friend of his youth to comfort him in his illness. That will not be me."

"And why do you think not?" Brinlaw asked, his voice terse and cold but his eyes warm with what looked suspiciously, maddeningly like pity.

"Because I am not Henry," Aiden answered. "I am not a king, but I have powers he couldn't even have dreamed of, powers you can't begin to understand." He stopped, feeling dizzy for a moment, an aftereffect of his mother's potion, no doubt. "What do you want from me, Papa?" he said wearily, not really expecting an answer as he headed for the door.

"Some sign of remorse would be a start," Brinlaw said from behind him, stopping him at the threshold. "Some word or token that you can still feel shame for what you've done, even if you still believe you must do it."

Aiden turned on him, rage like madness boiling up

inside of him. But his voice was cold. "I've never had to learn how to be ashamed of myself, Papa," he answered. "You've always done it for me." Before his father could reply, he walked out to the gallery. "Sir Alan! Muster the troops—we ride on the Clan McCairn at dawn."

"No," Brinlaw said urgently but softly for Aiden's ears alone. "This is pure stupidity—you're not ready for war with the Scots, even if you had cause."

"I don't recall asking for advice," Aiden said, trying to turn away, but his father caught him by the arm with surprising force.

"Stop this now," he ordered. "I forbid it—"

"You forbid?" He made no effort to pull free of Brinlaw's grasp, but the threat of violence in his tone was unmistakable, and the skin on his face burned hot with angry blood. "This castle belongs to me, my lord. You cannot forbid me anything."

His father slowly let him go. "Belongs to you for how long?" he countered. "Would you challenge me?"

Only a few months before, Aiden had bluffed his way through a similar confrontation in John's audience chamber, declaring he would sign his betrothal with or without Brinlaw's permission. But both of them had known it was a bluff. Now neither of them could be sure.

"Yes," Aiden answered. "If you mean to take authority at Glencairn, you will have to force me out." He looked down at his assembled knights and his father's men scattered among them, all of them watching in shock as the contest of wills was played out on the gallery above them. "Me and all my knights." Mary and the princess had apparently retired, but his mother was watching as well, her dark eyes wide in a face as pale as milk.

"No," Brinlaw said, sounding tired as he ended the suspense. "Of course I will not." He put a hand on Aiden's shoulder, and Aiden flinched, his resolve wavering for barely half a moment when he felt his father's touch. "I have no need of Glencairn." Aiden wouldn't look at him; he didn't dare. Finally he let him go to walk down the gallery stairs, and Lady Alista met him at the bottom. Together they left the hall.

"We will be ready, my lord," Sir Alan said, breaking the silence. "We will ride out at dawn."

"Aye, my lord!" Sir Brutus said, rising to his feet with his ale cup raised in salute. "We'll have Scotsmen for breakfast!" Others took up the toast as well, and Aiden made himself smile. Right or wrong, he would still be lord at Glencairn, and Evie would still be his.

Sometime after midnight under a full orange moon, the last of the Clan McCairn rode out of the glen and into the Highland hills. Evelyn had given up her horse to join Max, Grace, and Hamish in the back of one of the wagons, but Agnes rode beside them, her skirts tied up so she could ride astride. "Just to be safe," she had explained when Evie asked, refusing to elaborate. She had never hesitated for a moment when Evie said she would go with the clan, never once suggested that she would not accompany her. But she made it no great secret that she didn't trust Evie's kin any further than she might have flung them, particularly Malcolm. "He sold you once to save their skins," she had pointed out that evening as they packed. "Why wouldn't he do it again?"

"Look, Aunt Evie," Hamish said, pointing back the way that they had come. The standing stones were behind them now, glowing faintly orange in the light of the harvest moon. "They make me sad."

"Me, too," Evie admitted, hugging him close to her side.

"Mamee, where we go?" Max asked sleepily, rubbing his eye with his fist.

"Someplace new, lambie," she said, taking him into her lap.

"Why?" He looked around. "Where Ay-ben?"

"Aiden is at his castle," she answered, kissing the top of his head. "He has to stay at home."

"Don't worry yourself, Max," Hamish said, squeezing his cousin's foot but looking at his aunt. "I'm thinking we'll see him again."

20

After their argument Aiden had hardly expected Brinlaw to join him on his quest to the Scottish village. But when he came down to the courtyard with Robin, he found his father waiting for him, already in the saddle. "Well met, Papa," he said in a peacemaking tone. "What are you doing here?"

"What does it look like?" Brinlaw answered, raising his visor on an expression stern as rock. "I'm going with you to help you kidnap your mistress."

Aiden shook his head and smiled. "That really isn't necessary." He mounted his own horse.

"Oh, but it is."

Robin handed Aiden his sword.

"All your wild misconceptions to the contrary, I love you."

Aiden looked up from putting the sword in its sheath.

"I want you to have what you want," his father finished.

"Indeed?" Aiden answered sardonically, but inside he felt much better. "Even when you think me a dishonorable cad for even wanting it?"

"Even then," his father answered with a ghost of a grin of his own. "Besides, like I tried to say last night before we both went mad, I know just how you feel."

"Forgive me, Papa," Aiden said, nodding to Sir Alan, who shouted the order to mount to the other knights and soldiers in turn. "I doubt that very much."

"Do you, in faith?" Brinlaw smiled. He followed Aiden through the gates then trotted his horse alongside him as soon as they'd crossed the bridge. "When your mother tried to leave me, I threatened to clap a monk in molten irons and string him up by his thumbs to make him tell me where to find her." The look of shock on Aiden's face must have been spectacular because it made his father laugh. "How's that for deviltry?"

"Impressive," Aiden had to admit. Robin's mother, Lady Druscilla, had been Lady Alista's dearest friend for years before either of them were married, and she had often hinted that the early days of his parents' romance had been rather stormy. But he had never suspected anything like this. "She left you?" he said, still incredulous. "But still, she was your wife. If she did abandon you, you had every right to bring her home by whatever means necessary."

"My rights as a husband didn't matter to me worth a bean," Brinlaw scoffed. "I loved her, and I was furious to think she didn't feel the same for me." He glanced at Aiden's face and smiled. "Just as you are furious with Lady Evelyn now."

"I'm not furious with Evie," Aiden insisted. "And I don't love her."

"Really?" His father laughed. "Then what are we doing now?"

Aiden stopped and looked back at the line of troops that extended fully half a mile behind them, a force sufficient to level the village of McCairn without breaking a sweat. If any of his men thought they were on a fool's errand, none of them were willing to say so. Sir Alan rode just behind him and his father, his sword ready in its sheath and a torch appropriate for the firing of thatch unlit but lashed to his saddle. With any luck, Malcolm would be as willing to give up Evie now as he had always been in the past. But if the Scots put up a fight, they would be ready.

"I want her," he said to his father, turning his horse to ride on. "That is reason enough."

But when they reached the village, the gates were still shut. "No one seems to be awake yet, my lord," Sir Alan said. Brinlaw looked at Aiden, a warning in his eyes.

"Ho there," Aiden called, riding to the gate. "Open up!" But no one answered, and no face appeared at the lookout. A small patrol of foot soldiers ran up at his motion with axes to break it down. But as soon as they struck the first blow, it swung open.

Aiden drew his sword, braced for an ambush, but the gatehouse was apparently abandoned. "Has Malcolm lost his mind?" Sir Alan said, riding up beside him. "Leaving his village unguarded?"

But apparently there was nothing left to guard. The village was deserted, every cottage, business, and barn. "This isn't possible," Sir Alan insisted. "I was just here yesterday, having my horse shod."

"Our English blacksmith is not good enough for you, Sir Knight?" Aiden said mildly in spite of the fury that was growing inside him with every empty house.

"I wanted to look in on Lady Evelyn," the marshal answered staunchly. "I saw her, too, hanging out washing with one of her sister's housemaids."

"So where is she now?" Aiden asked testily, kicking his horse into a gallop.

The laird's house was completely stripped; even the shutters were gone. Leaving his horse abandoned in the dooryard, Aiden clattered through every room, his spurs ringing out on the bare, wooden floors. In a tiny room barely bigger than a closet, he found the empty wooden frame of a cabinet bed, and nailed to one of the posts was a folded packet with his name *Aiden* written on the outside in an unfamiliar hand.

Aiden,
Agnes is writing this for me because I don't know all the words yet that I need to write. I'm so sorry that I hit you. It broke my heart to do it. (I pray it did not break your head.) But I was very angry, and you wouldn't let me go. You were not hearing me, Aiden, and I doubt you will hear me now.
I know you think I am a silly woman to care so

much that you won't—or can't—marry me. But I have more than just myself to think of. I have Max, and I am all he has in the world. There is no one else to protect him or look after his interests but me. I cannot abandon my hopes for him even to be with you. And to be truthful, I cannot abandon myself. Maybe I am a silly woman. Maybe I am too proud. Maybe I really am no better than a harlot or not good enough to be any man's wife, much less the wife of a lord. But I was not brought up to think of myself that way. Foolish as he may have been, my father taught me I was better than that, and I still have to believe him.

But leaving you is almost more than I can bear. If I were alone, I would very likely be your mistress, just to be with you as long as you might let me. I love you, Aiden, wizard or not. I would never have given over so much of myself if I did not.

Evelyn

The signature was in Evie's own hand, the first word he had taught her.

Sir Alan and his father were conferring in the yard when he came out. "Aiden has already been ambushed by these people once," Brinlaw was pointing out. "There's no telling how many Scotsmen could be waiting for us in those hills."

"I agree," Sir Alan nodded, looking quizzically at Aiden, who was walking like a man in a dream with the letter clutched in his fist.

"Son, what is it?" Brinlaw said, alarmed.

Aiden looked at him like he was waking up. "Nothing. No one has to go into the hills." He looked down at the crumpled parchment, grief and fury burning in his eyes. "She loves me, Papa," he said softly, a dry rasp in his throat. "She loves me, and I let her go."

For the first time since he and Alista had come to Scotland, Will felt as if he was with his son, the passionate, open-hearted child he had loved so fiercely now grown into a man. "At least she told you," he said gently, poor comfort but the best he could muster. "At least you know."

"But she's gone." He looked up, rage like madness in his eyes. "I love her, and she's gone." Glancing at Sir Alan, who was just standing there, poor faithful soul, stunned speechless, he headed for his horse.

"Aiden, wait," Will called, going after him. "What will you do?"

Aiden swung into the saddle. "I will find her." Without waiting for an answer, he brought his mount around and galloped toward the castle.

The Scottish caravan stopped just after noon at another clan's summer encampment, a dozen or so round huts built on the bank of a river. "They don't mean to stay here?" Agnes said, bringing her horse alongside the wagon where Evelyn was riding with the children.

"No," Evie answered, standing up to stretch. "This isn't nearly far enough from Glencairn for Malcolm to feel safe." They were speaking English, and the driver of the wagon gave them a quizzical look. But when they both just stared back at him, he shrugged and walked away. "Rebecca's sore behind is probably the only reason we're stopping," Evie finished with a smile. As much as her sister hated riding, she had still adamantly refused to join Evie in the wagon.

"You don't really think the Dragon means your people any harm?" Agnes said, as abrupt and probing in her conversation as ever.

"I don't know," Evie admitted. "I don't think so. I can't imagine it." Max was trying to climb over the side of the wagon, imperiling his life with his usual abandon. "But Malcolm insists Aiden said he would turn the clan into English peasants or murder them in the attempt." She caught the baby and set him over the side before starting to climb out herself.

"Aunt Evie," Gerald called, running to help her down. "Da says I should help you and Mistress Agnes make camp."

"We're spending the night here?" Evie asked.

"That's what he says," the boy shrugged with a mischievous grin. "We'll make up the time tomorrow after the little ones are better rested."

"The little ones, eh?" She grinned. "Aye, Gerald, we'll be glad for the help."

Aiden stalked through the great hall, barely hearing the questions of the knights who had been left behind to guard the castle or seeing their faces. Mary and Katherine were playing chess again; his mother was reading a book. But they all looked like ghosts to him, creatures of another time conjured by his fevered brain, no more real than the ancients he had glimpsed through the portal in the stones. *I love you, Aiden,* Evie had written, *wizard or not.* But Evelyn was gone.

"Aiden?" his mother said, or so he assumed—her lips made the shape of his name. But he couldn't hear her. "Aiden, what is it? What happened?" She stood up, but he walked past her, never even slowing down.

He slammed his chamber door against the wall as he went in, the wood cracking like thunder. The surface of the mirror was already boiling with mist, the carved wooden eyes of the dragon glowing red as his own pounding blood.

"*Come to me!*" he shouted in the faery tongue, a thousand echoes rolling through the mist. He threw his sword aside and yanked his chain mail over his head like it might have been a linen shirt. "*You have made me to command your will, so come!*"

Images spilled across the glass, glimmers in the mist. He saw the sea at Falconskeep, waves crashing on the cliffs then melting into a desert soaked with blood, then darkness split by scarlet light. A snow-white falcon flew and fell among the stars, fell to earth amidst a battle, armies clashing on a field of grass, splashes of blood amidst the green, all brilliant in the sun.

"Show me myself," he ordered, unimpressed. He

took the letter he had dropped while taking off his knightly trappings and held it up before the glass, and the parchment caught fire from the fury in his mind. It burned in his fist as the smell of crystal water soaked into the air, the tapestries of his bedroom dissolving into stone that shone like ice, a mirror that enclosed him like a mottled crystal ball, reflecting the flame that he held. His boy-self stood inside the dragon frame, his blue eyes dark with rage. "Show me as I am," he snarled, and the boy snarled, too. "Show me the greatness you promised."

A keening wail rose all around him, and wind whipped through his hair. "Show me!" He plunged the flame of Evie's love into the glass as into a pool of water, the pool of Falconskeep, and the boy dissolved into blinding, white light. "Come to me!" he roared, and the light exploded outward, tossing him back like a broken doll as the mirror shattered. Glass fell like a crystal rain as the room seemed to shatter as well. Shielding his face against the flying shards, he tried to look at the light, but all he could see was the shape of the stones of the Cairn, a black crown edged in fire. The wind sucked back into the light with a terrible roar, and the light went out.

"That's always the problem with magic." His mother came into the room, her little slippers crunching on the broken glass. She stopped where he was lying sprawled on the floor. "It works until you really need it."

He looked up at the ruin of his room. The mirror's

glass was shattered into pieces barely bigger than the grains of sand where it had begun, and its frame was twisted so the dragon seemed to be springing forward, frozen in mid-pounce. The shutters were ripped back and hanging from their hinges, and the windows were broken as well, every tiny pane ground into powder. The chamber door was hanging loose, the solid oak cracked in two.

"She's gone, Mama." He looked down at the letter, its parchment still crumpled in his fist unscathed by the magical flame. "I don't know where she went." He looked up at her, the helpless tears of a child on his handsome wizard's face. "And I don't know the charm to bring her back."

Lady Alista bent down beside him and laid a hand on his cheek. "You are the charm, my darling," she promised, smiling through tears of her own. "If you are meant to love her, that will have to be enough."

21

Evelyn had made a token effort to be sociable, joining her family and the other adults around the communal fire after the tents were up and dinner was done. But when she heard Max crying from her tent, she knew it was time to make her escape. "If he once gets started, Agnes will never get him to sleep," she explained, getting up.

"He'll sleep when he's tired enough," Rebecca advised. "You should let him cry it out a night or two, or you'll make a coward of him."

"My son is not a coward," Evie answered. "Good night."

By the time she made it to the tent, Max had worked himself up into a full-scale tantrum. "Here, now, what is this?" she scolded, picking him up from where he thrashed among the blankets. "Aren't you ashamed, treating poor Agnes this way?"

"No," he sobbed, struggling against her neck and shoulder. "No seep here! Go home!"

"Hush," she scolded, holding him more tightly. "Hush yourself." She carried him to the tent flap, gazing out at the stars as she rocked him back and forth. "We'll be home soon," she said when he fell quiet. "A new home with Hamish and Davy and Gerald. You'll like it."

"No!" he cried, still pitiable but with somewhat less conviction. "Ay-ben come."

"Aiden cannot come." She kissed his cheek, her own single tear mingling with his. "Aiden must stay in his castle." His arms crept up around her neck, and she settled him more comfortably against her shoulder, crooning a lullaby....

At Glencairn, Aiden stood on the bank of the loch with the castle rising behind him, listening to the wind. Inside in his rich, well-lighted hall, a princess was waiting for him. His family was warm at his hearth, sheltered in his fortress, just as he had always wanted them to be. His best, most practical hopes had all come true, all the things he had promised himself standing in front of his mirror on the day he was betrothed. But the magical mirror was shattered, and he still wasn't himself. The lord who would marry Katherine and claim Glencairn was a pretender, an ordinary scoundrel come to greatness by guile, not magic, a practical rogue with barely any heart to speak of. But now, as much as he might try, Aiden could no longer be that man. He was a wizard, and he had a heart that ruled him now far more than his clever head. And all his heart wanted was Evie.

He bent and put a hand into the icy water, remembering his vision of the past. The ancient Dragon had reached into the water and drawn out his heart's beloved, the faery who would claim his soul. "Let me be so cursed," he said aloud, a half-unconscious spell that made his heart beat faster. He heard an echo on the water, a Gaelic lullaby, and he knew that it was Evie, calling him from wherever she had gone. "Take me to my love. . . ."

Evelyn felt Max go limp and heavy in her arms, surrendering to sleep. "There you are," she whispered, kissing his cheek. She tucked him into his pallet again, touching his face one more time, his skin as fine and soft as a rose's petals. Smiling once at Agnes, she slipped back out into the night.

She considered going back to the fire but quickly decided against it. There was nothing she wanted there. She headed toward the river instead, disappearing among the long-deserted huts to emerge at the water's edge.

The moon was up, a waning orb of red that burned above the mountains. Looking up at it, she felt an almost irresistible urge to simply flee into the night. Agnes was watching over Max; he would be fine. Even if she never came back . . . but no. She still belonged among the living, tired as she was.

"Aiden," she said aloud, for that was what she really wanted, to forget her responsibility for Max's future and his promise to the princess and just be with him. "Aiden." She stared into the darkness over the rippling river, willing her desire to appear like a child might wish on the moon. "Come to me." The wind whispered around her, caressing her face and her hair, and she smiled. "Come," she said, opening her arms. . . .

Aiden felt himself fading into mist, as when he turned invisible, but the feeling was more intense, an icy power in his blood as he felt himself dissolve into the loch. For barely a moment he seemed to be moving through the water more quickly than thought, the power of the magic coursing through him. Then suddenly he was rising, emerging on a distant shore, a thing of flesh again.

Evie saw a shape appear, the outline of a dragon in the black with the moonlight glowing green along its scaly shoulders as it reared up from the water. Then suddenly, it was Aiden. "Lady, I am here," he said, coming closer. "Command me as you will." For a moment she felt dizzy, almost faint. Then he reached her, and she touched him, felt his cold but solid flesh, and she smelled him, the clean scent of fresh-cut herbs over spicy musk, like no other man in the world.

"You are real," she whispered, running her hand over the muscles of his arm. "You are here."

"Yes." Her hair was loose on her shoulders, so beautiful she stole his breath away, and her eyes were wide, but not with fear. She was his destined love, and his magic had brought him here to say good-bye. "You called me." He kissed her, and she kissed him back in desperation, returning his passion in kind.

For one brief moment she thought of all the reasons she should turn away, all her fears and questions. How had he come to be here? What would happen tomorrow? What, if anything, had changed? But this was what she'd asked for, what she'd conjured on the moon, this kiss, this love, this single night. She would not give him up. She buried her hands in his thick, soft hair to hold his mouth to hers, meeting his tongue with her own. He wrapped his arms around her waist, and she pressed herself against him, felt him cold as the water of the river, as if his blood held no heat at all. "Aiden . . ." Suddenly she thought of all the ancient tales, dead warriors returning to give their best beloved one last kiss, and she was afraid. Then he was kissing her again, and all her fears were forgotten.

"It's all right," he promised, kissing her throat. He nuzzled underneath her hair, and she circled his neck with her arms, the soft flesh of her breast and thighs burning soft and thrilling against him. "We made the spell together."

"You make no sense," she protested as he scooped her off her feet. "You never make any sense." He kissed her mouth again, cutting off her protests, and she clasped her legs around him, devouring his kisses as he carried her into one of the huts. "We have to be quiet," she warned him, her last clear shred of logic. If the others should discover them together, hell alone could tell what they might do. "No one must hear."

"I'll try," he said, smiling, trailing tiny kisses down her jaw. "But I can't promise." He lay her on the cozy little bed, bending over her even so, drunk on her embrace. He buried his face in the curve of her shoulder, learning the graceful curve of flesh and bone by feel against his lips. The hollow at the base of her throat was moist with salty sweetness, and he lapped it with his tongue, curved over her on his hands and knees.

Her hands slid up his arms again, and she tore at his shirt, catching the collar in her fists and tearing with all of her strength before she pulled her own gown over her head. She wanted to see him, to feel his naked skin on hers—she was starving for him, she who had never felt such hunger for any other man. She was trapped between his muscled thighs, and his mouth fed on her throat, but she was not afraid. She welcomed it, delighted in his power. His lips found hers again, his tongue an aggressor in her mouth, but only for a moment, and she sighed, bereft and pleading, as he broke the kiss. But he was relentless, moving lower over her, tearing at her shift the way she had torn at his shirt but with far better success. His mouth pulled at her breast, a wolfish mockery of a nursing babe, and a bolt of pure pleasure shot through her, making her feel faint. "Holy saints," she whispered, struggling for breath, and still his mouth drew harder, his tongue both rough and slick against her nipple.

He picked her up to reach her, sitting back to lift her to his mouth. Her head fell back as he lifted his to watch her, a perfect arc of creamy throat exposed to his kisses. He moved to the other breast, ravenous but tender, and her body jerked beneath him, the little saddle of her sex, still covered by her shift, pressed to his erection for one sweet, torturous moment. He was already so hard for her he ached, but it was agony he savored, reveling in her surrender. He lowered her back down to the bed, her waist encircled by his hands, and he kissed her stomach, nuzzling its softness.

She stroked his hair, petting him like some wicked beast she had somehow managed to tame, lost in the wondrous-strange sensations of his touch. He tugged at her shift again, and she lifted her hips from the mattress, turning her face to the pillow, too lost in her desire to even feel ashamed. His tongue slipped into her navel, and another violent jolt of pleasure pierced her through, this one racing to the very center of her want, making her feel weak. He stroked her hips and thighs, kissing his way back to her breast, and she cradled him against her, her palms molding his back. He was beautiful and cruel; he broke her heart and held her soul in his fist. But she could not give him up. She touched his cheek and smiled as he raised his head to kiss her. He was her fallen angel.

"Aiden," she whispered, tracing the shape of his mouth, her smile more beautiful than heaven. "Come to me." He fell into her kiss, and she enfolded him, rising up to meet him as he pushed himself inside.

She felt like she was falling, swooning, dying, the brutal heat of his desire setting her aflame. He kissed her as he moved inside her, his tongue a softer counterpoint to the harder invasion below. His movements were as slow as they were urgent; like the first time he had kissed her, he seemed to be entreating her to dance. When she opened her eyes, his eyes were open as well, focused on her face, not glazed and blind with lust but warm with love. She touched his face, her breath coming in gasps, and her hips seemed to move of their own accord, quickening the pace.

He let her move with him, holding back the full force of his need to let her find her own. He wouldn't hurt her for the world, or frighten her, or use her. If this would be the last time he could touch her, he would make her know she was loved, even if he couldn't say the words. But when her rhythm quickened, his heart leapt up in relief. She bit her lip, and he kissed her, his soul mingled with hers.

The muscles in her thighs felt weak as if melting in a fire, and she seemed to be opening up, her very core inviting him deeper. His hands shifted beneath her, lifting her up, and the flames inside exploded, the pleasure she had felt before no more than a chill next to this. She called his name, a cry to wake the dead, and his mouth came down on hers, muffling the sound by taking it into himself, and still the flames burned higher until every thought was lost.

She wrapped her arms and legs around him as if she

were jealous even of the air, and he thrust inside with all his strength, lost in his release. He felt her tremble as he came, a shiver of new pleasure, and he nuzzled her throat and cheek, drunk on her delight.

She heard him moan against her cheek, the world slowly returning as the waves of pleasure fell back. He kissed her brow, her nose, her lips, and she smiled, lying back to let him, her eyes still closed. But suddenly his weight seemed to fall back from her, not gone as if he'd left her but fading, as if he were dissolving into air. She opened her eyes and still saw him, but she could barely feel him anymore. "Aiden?" She reached for him to wrap her arms around him, but it was like reaching for a ghost.

"Evie . . ." One moment he could see her, her lips forming his name; the next he was blind again, a spirit racing back through space. He found himself on the shores of the loch again alone, the castle rising behind him. "No," he said, his voice thick in his throat as life flowed back into his limbs. He wasn't ready; there was still so much to say. "No!" he repeated, roaring at the moon.

Evie rose from the tiny, straw-stuffed bed, holding the tatters of her shift around her. Aiden was gone as if he had never been there, as if it had all been a dream. "No," she said softly as she left the hut. "He was here." She looked down at the muddy ground and saw two sets of footprints by the light of the moon. "He was here," she repeated, a sob caught in her throat. "But he's gone." Going back into the hut, she picked up her gown, and his scent washed over her like an embrace, bringing fresh tears to her eyes. "I will not cry," she insisted, pushing them back as she put on the gown. Her wizard was gone, lost forever. But at least he had kissed her good-bye.

Sometime in the next afternoon Evelyn dozed off in the back of one of the wagons, Max sleeping on a bundle of linens beside her and Grace cradled sleeping in her lap. But suddenly she woke up with a start, crying, "Stop!"

"What for?" the man driving the wagon complained, startled half out of his skin.

"Not you," she answered, flustered, in a panic. "Yes, you—stop the wagon. Pull to the side."

"The laird won't like it," he warned. "He wants to catch up to the others before night."

"I don't give a tinker's damn what he wants," she ordered. "That horse is mine, and I say stop."

"Aye, mistress," he surrendered, turning the horse out of the procession. "Whatever you say."

"What is it, my lady?" Agnes asked, riding up beside them. "What's wrong?"

"I need to borrow your horse," Evie explained. "I have to go back."

"All right, but I want to come with you," her friend protested.

"No," Evie said, shaking her head. "I need you to stay with the clan to look after Max. He could get sick again or scared." The very thought of leaving her child alone at Rebecca's mercy was more than she cared to imagine. "I know it sounds stupid, but I had a dream, a terrible dream." Images flashed through her mind of Aiden bleeding, dying, and no one could save him but her. And he had come to her in the night, a magical visit that should not have been possible. "I think I may have really hurt Aiden when I hit him."

"What is this, Little Sister?" Malcolm said, riding up with Rebecca riding pillion behind him. "Why have you stopped?"

"I have to go back," she said brusquely. "I can't explain it—"

"Can't you, now?" Rebecca scoffed. "I can. You miss your lover and mean to abandon your bastard to us. Well, I, for one, won't have it—"

Before anyone could have imagined what was about to happen, Agnes had grabbed her by the front of her gown and flung her to the ground, leaping from her horse to crouch over her with a dagger to her throat. "I've heard all I mean to hear from you," she told her, cool and calm as a loch in February. "One more word, just one, and that viper's tongue of yours is coming out."

"Agnes," Evelyn said, as shocked as anyone else. Several of the Scotsmen had put hands on their sword hilts, but none of them had drawn. No one seemed to know quite what to do. "You don't have to do that."

"Believe me, my lady, it's a pleasure," Agnes answered, straightening up. Several men did draw then, but Malcolm shook his head, waving them off as he bent down to help his wife up. "Take the horse." The Englishwoman smiled, handing Evie her reins. "I will watch after our Max."

Aiden sat in his place in the great hall and tried to focus on what Sir Alan was saying and not on the ache in his heart. "If the Scots have truly gone for good, I say it is a pity," the marshal insisted, stabbing a piece of meat for emphasis.

"The lasses will be missed, that's certain," Sir Brutus agreed, then glanced at his liege lord and blushed. "Sorry, my lord."

"But surely they mean to come back," Mary said, giving the flustered knight a sympathetic smile that dazzled him right out of his embarrassment. "Papa, didn't you say some of the clans live in one place in the summer and move someplace else in the fall?"

"Yes," Brinlaw agreed. He and Lady Alista shared another worried look, the same as they had been doing all night. Indeed, everyone in the hall seemed anxious and unhappy tonight. Aiden's little magical tantrum had gone unnoticed by no one, though no one was quite daring to talk about it yet. And little Molly sitting sobbing in the corner just added to the gloom. "But I believe those are mostly cattle farmers; the Clan McCairn keeps fields."

"No, the McCairn has never left the glen that I have heard of," Sir Alan said, glancing sadly at his lord.

But Aiden didn't hear him. He was listening to something else, the music of a bell. "The church in the Scottish village," he said suddenly. "Do they have a bell?"

"No, my lord," Sir Alan answered, confused. "They barely have a church. The priests rarely come this far into the Highlands." He frowned. "Why do you ask?"

"Can't you hear it?" The ringing was much louder now, high and sweet and slow as a heartbeat dying on the autumn wind. He went to the double doors and pushed them open, expecting to find the bell-ringer waiting in the courtyard. But other than the usual guardsmen, the cobblestone yard was deserted.

"Aiden, what is it?" Lady Alista said, coming to touch his arm as everyone else just stared. "What do you hear?"

"Nothing," Aiden answered. "It's gone now." The bell had stopped. But looking up toward the mountain, he saw a double line of lights twining like a dragon over the hills. "There," he said, pointing, as the procession climbed higher. "Do you see that?"

"No," she admitted, fear mixed with the worry in her eyes. "What is it?"

"Lights," he answered. "Some sort of a procession." He could smell the torches, the burning stench of pitch, and his hand went unconsciously to his chest as if it pained him. For a moment in his mind he saw the faery queen, kneeling over him in her jeweled crown, her dagger at her heart. "I have to go."

"Aiden, no." Her touch on his arm tightened into a grip. "Leave it be—"

"I can't—"

"You must!" Her face was pale with fear. "There is ancient magic here, not evil, but godless and unfeeling. Even Mary has felt it."

"I know," he said impatiently. "That's why I have to go—"

"Aiden, no," she insisted. "Whatever you see, it has nothing to do with you." She paused, then plunged ahead. "Or Evelyn, either."

"But Mama, it does," he promised. "Somehow it does." Part of him wanted to just push her away, he was so desperate to go, but he loved her, the first idol of his heart, and he had to try to explain. "Maybe this is it. Maybe this is the spell." He took her hand from his arm and pressed it to his lips. "I have to go find out."

Evelyn stopped at the foot of the mountain slope as the sun was disappearing into the loch of Glencairn. She had ridden for hours like the devil's dogs were at her horse's heels, but now that she was almost at her destination, she didn't have a clue what she should do.

In her nightmare Aiden had been dying, and somehow she had known that only she could save him. But now, looking down at the castle as lights began to glow from its windows, she had to admit that made no sense whatsoever. She had assumed, in her panic, that the blow she had dealt him in her desperate escape must be threatening his life and that was the reason she'd been seized by premonition, but that was silly, too. Aiden was a warrior, strong as an ox, his beauty notwithstanding. One flagon to the head could hardly be enough to kill him. And even if it were somehow, what could she do to save him? His mother was the witch, not her. Rebecca was right, as awful as she seemed. Evie just wanted her lover.

"I am not abandoning Max," she said stubbornly, her mount prancing to the side, startled by her voice. "And I am not a fool." Something had called her back here, something more compelling than desire. She just didn't know what it was.

A bell was ringing from above her, she suddenly realized—was Ella the cow loose on the mountain again? she thought with an inward smile. But this was no clanging brass cow's bell; this was beautiful, high and clear but sad, a funeral bell. For just a moment she seemed to see a double line of flickering torches snaking its way down the road before her, twisting toward the loch, and a fortress twice the size of Glencairn Castle rising on the banks. "The dream," she whispered, her voice caught in her throat, and the vision faded away. But the music of the bell continued, and suddenly she was afraid. *My blood will hold us immortal as the sinews of this mountain,* the faery queen had spoken in her dream, a dagger at her heart as her lover, the Dragon, lay dying in her lap. *Our hall will sink beneath the earth to hide itself in grief.*

"Not real," Evelyn insisted, climbing down from her horse. "That wasn't Aiden. That was just a dream." But still she couldn't stop herself from climbing up the slope.

22

Evelyn had half-expected to find her dream had come to life, the ancients gathered in a ring around their pyre. But the stones were the same as they had always been, stark and glowing in the cold, clear light of the moon. "What do you want from me?" she called to them, turning in a circle. "Why do I feel like I belong with you?"

"Because you do." For a moment Aiden had thought he must be dreaming, conjuring his wishes into life. But she was real, her beauty poorly disguised beneath a peasant's rough-spun jumper. The shadow of the funeral had faded, leaving nothing but the present and his love. "You do belong with me."

She whirled around, hardly daring to believe what she had heard. "Aiden . . ." She could almost think he was a dream, he looked so much as she loved to remember him, his linen shirt half-laced and uncovered by any tunic or mantle and his dark hair falling into his eyes. "I thought I had hurt you," she explained as he came closer. "I had to come back."

"You did hurt me." He stopped before her at the center of the aisle of stones. "When I read your letter, I thought I was going to die." He dragged the kerchief from her head, freeing her long auburn hair. "So I'm very glad you came back."

"I'm so sorry." Nothing had changed. He no more belonged to her here in this moment than he had when she knocked him unconscious; she was no more certain of his love. But she couldn't fight him anymore. "I never wanted to go."

"I know." He kissed her, holding her hands, and a breath of wind swept through the stones like a lonely lover's sigh. "I never gave you any choice." He pressed her closer for a moment, kissing her hair, and she wrapped her arms around his waist, holding him closer as well. "I'm sorry, too." He took her gently by the hand and led her to the fallen slab to sit. "You asked me to be truthful, and I told you I could not. Do you remember?"

"Of course." He knelt on the ground at her feet like a knight in a painting on a shield. "I asked you if you were a wizard."

"Yes." He smiled, kissing her hand. "But you already knew that I was."

"I didn't know for certain," she insisted. "Aiden, you don't have to tell me—"

"Yes, I do." He held her hand in both of his, delicate as a rose. "You said you'd heard my mother was a witch. She is a faery, or half a one, at least. She is descended from an ancient faery who chose mortality for the love of a mortal man. In every generation since, a sorceress has been born, a woman with magical powers. In my generation, my sister, Malinda, is the Falconskeep faery." He massaged the web of flesh between her thumb and fingers as a kind of nervous distraction, a way not to think before he spoke the words he had kept hidden so long. "But somehow, I have magic, too," he said, meeting her eyes. "The ancient spirit of my mother's castle who has known every sorceress ever born to the line said I was the first man born to faery gifts in a thousand generations. I did make your roses grow to make you forgive me for being such a cad, and I did make Gerald's sword look like a serpent so he would drop it before I had to fight him. I made the image that you saw in the mirror appear because I thought you would see me." He smiled, embarrassed. "I wanted to be certain that you wanted me."

"But was it real?" she asked. "The image that I saw of Max—will it really come to pass?"

"Yes, I think it will," he answered. "The spell is meant to show you what will be, what dreams of your heart can come true." He smiled. "It's one of my best spells."

"Yes, it's very clever," she agreed, smiling back. "I think I need to look again." She touched his face, tracing the arch of his cheek. "I might see something else."

"Do you believe me, then?" he asked, a hungry plea in his eyes. "Can you still want me, now that you know the truth?"

"Of course." She smiled, shocked by the question.

His hand tightened around hers, and his smile was like watching the dawn, but his eyes were still in doubt. "Aren't you afraid?"

"Of you?" She wrapped her hands around his and pressed them to her lips. "I'm afraid of your ambitions," she said softly, telling her own secret truth. "I am afraid that you will leave me, particularly if you marry this Katherine. I am afraid that you might not love me or that even if you do, that you might stop." She raised her eyes to his. "But no, my fallen angel. I am not afraid of you."

"Evie . . ." He wanted to kiss her, to crush her in his arms and never let her go, but there was more he had to tell her first. "I do love you, and I swear that I will never stop." He did kiss her, and she clung to him, as desperate as he felt. "I could never leave you." She kissed his cheek, his eyelids, and he laughed, and she laughed with him. "You are my destined love."

"I love you." She leaned over him, her hands lost in his hair. "I love you."

"I love you." She kissed him, and he took her in his arms, tumbling her to the grass. He kissed her desperately, brushing the silk of her hair back from her face, and she held him to her, feeding on his mouth. He pushed her rough-spun skirt over her thighs, and her hand closed gently over his wrist as if to hold him back. "Please," he murmured, brushing her mouth with his. "Evie, please—"

"Yes," she interrupted, deepening the kiss. She laced

her fingers over his as his hand moved up her thigh, holding him to her as he touched the secret center of her want. "Don't stop."

"Never," he promised, kissing her brow. "I will never stop." He felt her open up to him, her leg curled almost shyly around him as if to urge him on, and he could wait no longer. He pushed himself inside her, and she laughed, a gasp of perfect joy. "I love you," he said, rearing over her, lost in her sweetest embrace.

"I love you." She reached up for him, her hands caressing his shoulders, and her hips arched up to meet him, her soul and body mended and complete. His pace was quicker than before, almost desperate, and she welcomed it, feeling the same. He bent over her to nuzzle her breast, first one then the other, and his breath felt hot through the fabric of her clothes, another layer of pleasure. She felt the first deep tremors of her climax building, and she called his name, "Aiden . . . now . . ." He caught her closer in his arms, crushing her to him, and she let her arms go weak and fall as the waves crashed through her, falling off and rising again as she felt him rise as well, spilling inside her before he collapsed in her arms.

"Evie," he murmured, almost a groan, as he kissed her cheek. "My love . . ." She kissed him back as he rolled off of her and drew her close to his chest.

"My love," she promised, snuggling down to his shoulder, sheltered in his arms. Nothing practical had been decided; no contract had been signed. But she knew for certain he was hers, that they would always be together. She rubbed her palm over his stomach, drowsy and intoxicated by the hard warmth of his flesh.

But something was wrong. Her hand felt wet, soaked in something hot and sticky. Lifting it, she found it thick with blood. "Aiden!" she cried, sitting up. "Aiden, oh, dear God!"

But Aiden was gone. She looked around at the world of her dream. The northmen were gathered around her with her children ranged behind them, and the Dragon lay dying before her, his blood coating her hands. "No," she insisted, the word coming out in the ancient tongue in another woman's voice. "This isn't right." This man wasn't Aiden. He was taller, more massive, his arms and legs thick with solid muscle without Aiden's angel's grace, and his long, thick hair was blond. Only the mark of the dragon on his wrist was the same.

"Give him to us, lady," the man standing at the forefront of the northmen said as he knelt before her. "Let us follow our prince to the halls of our fathers. Allow us to join him in death."

"No!" she insisted. "I am not supposed to be here!" She looked again at the northmen gathered around her, and a cold, cruel fist closed over her heart. These men were the stones that had ever welcomed her, her father's faery child. These were the sentries who had waited here for centuries untold. Could they really have waited for her? "No," she moaned, covering her face with her hands, smearing her cheeks with blood.

Drowsing in the present, Aiden heard her moan. "Evie?" He clasped her hand in his and found it cold. "Darling, what is wrong?"

He sat up with her cradled in his arms, but still she didn't respond. "Evelyn!" Her eyes were closed, and her flesh was freezing, frightening him badly. "Evie, answer me!" he ordered, his heart pounding hard enough to hurt. He leaned close and listened for her breath, and for a moment he could neither hear nor feel it. Then a great sigh shuddered through her, her body shaking as if from a chill.

"Where have you gone?" he demanded. "What has taken you?" A single tear slid down her perfect cheek, and he clutched her closer, rocking her in his arms. "Don't be frightened, darling. I will bring you back."

He laid her gently on the grass and looked around at the stones. "Where have you taken her?" He stood up and approached the nearest column, its surface melting into swirling silver mist. "Show me where she's gone." He saw the torches from his dream, and his heart stopped beating for a moment in dread. The ancient Dragon was dying on his litter, just as he had seen. Only now instead of the faery from the loch, his mate was Evelyn. "No!" he shouted, trying to reach through the mist as he had done before, but the stone closed off like solid glass, refusing to let him inside. "You cannot have her!"

* * *

Trapped inside the ancient world, Evelyn touched the face of the Dragon, and he opened his eyes, silently pleading as he searched her face. "I don't know what to do," she said softly. Could this really be Aiden?

"Release him into death, dread lady," the northman begged. "Release him and return to your own world."

"My own world," she repeated, her mind racing. In her dream, the queen had refused, mingling her faery blood with the mortal blood of her lover to seal them together forever, neither dead nor living, and turning the northmen to stone to stand guard throughout all time. Was that why she was here? She looked back at the people of the cairn, the children of the Dragon and his faery queen. A man looked back at her, weeping, with her father's eyes. As a daughter of the Clan McCairn, was she meant to somehow put this right?

"I will release him," she said, touching the mouth of the Dragon as she drew the dagger from her belt, and she saw him smile. *This cannot be Aiden*, she thought, closing her eyes. *This will take me back.*

"No!" Aiden screamed in the present, banging his fists on the rock until they bled. He couldn't hear what Evelyn was saying, but he saw her draw the dagger from her belt. He had seen the past in his nightmare; he knew she meant to stab herself in the heart. "*Let me in!*" he roared in faery speak. "*You called me; let me in!*" Suddenly the stone dissolved, and he was falling, tumbling into the past.

"I release you!" Evie shouted, raising the dagger over her head to cut the Dragon's throat and let him die. But just as the blade reached the top of its arc, the man who lay dying before her changed, his blond hair turning black. "Wait!" she cried, dropping the dagger before she made the cut as she looked into Aiden's eyes, but it was already too late. The words had been the charm, not the dagger. "Don't go!"

Aiden felt the wound plunge through his chest as his limbs seemed to freeze into stone, and he tried to reach for Evelyn to comfort her. But his spirit still seemed to be falling, flying free of his broken body's reach. "Evie," he gasped as she caught at his hands, trying to hold on. But it was hopeless; he was falling into black.

"Aiden!" she screamed as his eyes fell closed, falling on him and holding on with all her might. "Aiden, please!"

She opened her eyes on the present, the high, full moon and the mountain. Aiden lay sprawled beside her in the grass, his hand outstretched to the first of the stones, and she crawled to him and turned him over, shaking him. "Aiden, wake up!" But even though his shirt and the flesh beneath were whole and untouched by blood or wound, his eyes stayed closed and his body lay still as death. "Aiden, please," she repeated, laying her ear against his chest, trying to hear past the pounding of her own blood. She could barely make out a heartbeat. "Please..."

She stood up and stumbled toward the downward

slope. "Somebody, please help!" This was the dream that had found her on the road, the horror that had brought her back. Aiden was dying; it was her fault; and only she could save him. "Somebody!" She saw a pair of lanterns climbing up the road, two horsemen riding fast. "Hurry!" she shouted, praying they could hear.

Evelyn sat at the window of the tower bedroom that had once been hers, watching as the sun rose through the roses. Aiden was lying on the bed, still as he had been all night, seemingly neither dead nor alive though his body carried no new mark any deeper than a scratch. "How can he be dying?" she asked softly. "The Dragon wasn't him."

Lady Alista looked up from her own vigil at the bed. "I don't know," she answered, exchanging a glance with Aiden's father, who was standing by the door. "I'm not even sure what you mean."

"The Dragon," Evie repeated, anger in her tone. She had barely spoken since they had brought him here. Once Lord Brinlaw and Sir Alan had found them, she had lapsed into a kind of frightened silence, as if by keeping quiet she could make the horror not be true. But now the sight of sunlight falling over Aiden's angel face with it still cold and motionless as death brought the words bubbling out. "The man who was dying on the mountain—he wasn't Aiden at all. He had nothing to do with him." She turned her face away again, unable to look at her beloved anymore or face his mother's eyes. "He was me, and she was me—they were my ancient ancestors, the founders of my clan. Why should Aiden be hurt?"

Lady Alista came and sat across from her at the foot of the bed. "Aiden mentioned a spell," she answered, taking Evie's hand. "I was afraid for him to go to the mountain last night, but he said he had to, that somehow he thought he could bring you back."

"Yes, I know," Evie said angrily, snatching her hand away. "I know it's my fault—"

"No," the older woman shook her head. "That isn't what I meant at all; that isn't true."

"Oh, yes," Evie nodded with a bitter laugh. "It is."

"No," Lady Alista repeated. "Evelyn, listen to me." She waited until Evie turned her head to face her. "You know I am a sorceress," she said, waiting again until Evie nodded. "I have to believe that I can save my son. But you have to help me." She looked back at the bed, her eternally youthful face drawn for a moment in pain. "I can't find any wound on him beyond what he already carried, yet he fights for life like a man already in shadow. You said that this Dragon was dying on the mountain, this man from the past. What was killing him?"

"He was a northman, a Viking," Evie answered, searching the visions of her mind. "Somehow, he and his men came to Glencairn, and he loved a faery here. She begged him not to fight." She could see the dream again, as clearly as the roses at the window. "Barbarians came to the glen, and she begged him to stay in the castle where her magic would always keep him safe. But his pride wouldn't allow it." She went to stand beside the bed, gazing down on Aiden's face. "He would do his own will or run mad."

"That sounds familiar," Lady Alista said, looking again at her husband.

"He was enchanted, you see, for centuries—that's how he lived so long," Evie continued. "She kept him her prisoner with love. But she loved him in return; she couldn't bear to see him so unhappy. So she let him go." She looked down at Aiden's face, struck once again by the injustice of this horror, how different he was from the man in her tale. "He and his men and his sons all went out of the fortress to fight, and the barbarians were slain. He was the Dragon; how could they stand?" In her mind she could see it as from a great height, the fields strewn with the dead. "But just as the battle was over, just as the wild men were defeated, he turned back to look upon the face of his queen, who was watching from the tower, and the barbarian prince with his last bit of strength flung his spear and pierced the Dragon through." A shudder passed through Aiden, and a groan as from great pain rose from his lips. "Can he hear us?" Evelyn asked.

"I don't know," Lady Alista admitted. "Finish your tale."

"The faery queen would not allow her love to die, but

WICKED CHARMS

she could not save him from death," she continued, watching Aiden's face for any sign of life. "She had him carried to the mountain and used her blood to work an evil magic, binding them both to the earth." She looked back at the sorceress, willing her to somehow understand. "That is what I saw last night, like a dream I couldn't escape. I was the faery queen, and the Dragon was dying, and I had the choice. His man begged me to release him and return to my own world, and I thought he meant that I could put it right, that the evil spell would be broken and I could just be myself and be with Aiden. But just as I was saying the words, the Dragon changed into Aiden. He just appeared there in the other man's place, and it was too late to stop. I didn't hurt him any more, but I had already said the words to release his spirit. When I did come back to the present and back to myself, Aiden was there as you see him now."

"He meant to rescue you," Lady Alista said. "Somehow he must have seen you and followed you into the spell."

"You see?" She knelt beside the bed and clasped Aiden's cold hand in hers, remembering the night when he had driven the fever from Max and held them in this very bed. *My fallen angel*, she had promised. *I am not afraid of you.* "It is my fault."

"No," the sorceress promised, laying a hand on her shoulder. "You didn't make this happen, and you've told me much that will help us, I think." She passed a hand over Aiden's brow. "Will, stay here with Lady Evelyn. There is something I need from my trunk." Kissing Evie's cheek, she left.

Brinlaw came and sat down on the other side of the bed. "It will be all right," he promised, though it was obvious from his eyes that he was very worried. "She's healed far worse than this."

"I hope you're right," Evie answered, trying to smile. Malcolm and the others spoke of this man like he might be the devil incarnate—the very sight of his banner coming into the glen was enough to send them scurrying for cover. But to her right now, he just seemed handsome and kind. "I love him very much."

"So do I." He smiled. "He is my third child, and I loved his older sister and brother better than my life from the very first moment I saw them. But Willie—Aiden was the first that felt like mine." He arranged the coverlet more carefully over his son as if he couldn't bear to not do something. "I was away so much when the first two were small, they always seemed more like little extensions of Alista than people in their own right. But I carried Aiden in front of me in the saddle when he was three days old."

She smiled more easily. "No wonder he's so spoiled."

He smiled back and nodded. "I thought he was perfect, and I wanted his life to be perfect as well. Alista would try to tell me that was impossible, and I would pretend to believe her. But secretly, I was sure that if I tried hard enough, I could spare him every pain I had ever felt and give him everything I had ever wanted."

"I know just what you mean." She laid her cheek on Aiden's hand. "I love Max, my son, like my own soul, and I keep doing things that are probably very silly, trying to protect him." It was strange to think of Aiden as a child like Max, riding in his father's saddle. He had always seemed so powerful to her, so strong. "I'm never quite sure what I should do."

Brinlaw nodded. "And that never goes away. When Aiden was six, we discovered he could do magic like his mother and his sister, and suddenly I was lost. I had always taught him everything; I had always been the one to keep him safe. But suddenly I was useless. I couldn't teach him how to work spells; I couldn't protect him from spirits. He had powers I couldn't begin to understand." He laid a hand on Aiden's brow as if he might have still been a child. "Suddenly he wasn't mine anymore, and there was nothing I could do about it, and I hated it. As dearly as I love her, I was so jealous of his mother, I could hardly stand it, because he was like her; she was the only one who could be a help to him. I knew I was wrong, that it was wrong of me to feel that way, so I tried to let him go. I tried to let him become the man—the wizard—he was meant to be, even though it broke my heart to do it." He smiled ruefully, looking down at Aiden's face. "So now the idiot believes I am ashamed of him."

Lady Alista had returned long since and had heard much of what her lord had said. Now she came back into the room completely and laid her hands on his shoulders. "Aiden has forgotten who he is," she said, smiling at Evie. "We must call him back."

Aiden had wandered for hours along a rocky beach, trying to remember where he was or how he had found himself there. At first there had been others with him, a great force of warriors with long hair and beards, carrying spears of iron. They had led him to the beach, allowing him to walk in their midst as if he belonged. But when they reached a dragon boat that waited at the water's edge, he couldn't seem to make himself climb aboard.

"Come, brother," their leader had called to him, a man with long, blond hair. "You have joined us; come and take your place."

"No," he had protested, turning away. "I cannot." He had no place with them. Watching as their sail unfurled, emblazoned with a dragon, he had felt a faint stir of recognition. But he knew he belonged somewhere else.

So he wandered. Sometimes the beach looked familiar—several times he spotted the spires of a castle in the distance, and he broke into a run, knowing it as his home. But it never seemed to get any closer, and eventually it always disappeared.

"Aiden." The voice was familiar, masculine, a voice of both comfort and dread. "William Aiden Brinlaw!" It came from the cliffs overlooking the beach, and he scanned them frantically, searching for the source.

"I am here!" he shouted back. "Papa, I am here!"

"Come home," his father called to him, but he still couldn't see him, and the castle was still lost. "Come home where you belong."

"I can't," he protested, near tears with frustration. "I can't find the way!"

"Aiden!" His mother's voice swept over his head, swooping through the air like a falcon in flight. "Come back to the living, darling. You can still come back."

"I can't," he insisted. He dropped to his knees in the sand. "I am lost."

"I will follow you." A figure walked toward him from the water, rising like a goddess from the surf. "I will not let you go." She held out her hands to him, and he knew her. She was Evelyn, the one who held his heart. "You said I was your destined love." He took her hands, and she smiled, raising him back to his feet. "You must come back to me."

"I will," he promised, pulling her closer. "I must." He bent and kissed her mouth.

He opened his eyes on the tower room at Glencairn, on Evelyn leaned over him, her lips still dewy from his kiss. "My love," he murmured, reaching to kiss her again.

"There you are," his mother said, smiling. "Your father was terribly worried."

"I was," Brinlaw admitted. "Ask Evelyn; she'll tell you."

"I will," Evie agreed, touching his cheek.

"I heard," Aiden answered, pressing her hand to his mouth. "I think I heard."

Suddenly a steady, droning hum rose all around them, louder and louder, and the castle began to shake. "Aiden!" Evie said, reaching for him in alarm. "What is it?"

He got up from the bed, his arm around her shoulders as screams and shouts rose from below. Standing at the window with his parents close beside them, they watched in awe as beams of light rose up from the ground all around the castle, even from the center of the loch. Columns rose inside the beams, but no, not columns but towers, stone and mortar building row upon row until they seemed to touch the sky. A wall rose up between the towers, its battlements nearly level with the window where they stood, and the great stone hall from the dreams they had shared reared up from the loch like the armored belly of a dragon.

"The hall of the Dragon," Evie said, barely audible over the din. "We have released them; their fortress has returned." The earth shifted again with a mighty groan, and she hid her face against Aiden's chest, certain they were lost. But before the thought had formed inside her head, the world had fallen silent.

"Sweet saints," Lady Alista murmured, clinging to her husband. "Look at it."

The hall was surrounded on seven of its eight short sides by the towers, each as tall as the Tower of London, but slender, almost delicate against the bright blue sky.

On the eighth side was a kind of crenellated causeway, the starting point of the wall that branched out in opposite curves to make a crooked oval that completely surrounded the original castle and created a long, grassy courtyard between it and the new hall and towers. A deep channel had opened up in the earth around the outside of the wall, and the loch had flowed into it, creating a moat all around.

"God save us," Aiden agreed, holding Evie tighter to his side.

"Oh, good lord, look at you," his mother fussed, the strange new structure forgotten as she remembered her son. "Are you all right?"

"I'm fine, Mama, I promise," he said, hugging her close. "Thank you. Thank you, Papa." He looked down at Evie and smiled as he kissed her. "I've finally found my way home."

Epilogue

Spring

A letter of Prince John, Protector of England, to Sir Aiden Brinlaw

Dear Aiden—
I am quite put out with you and shocked beyond all words. Have you lost your mind? I think that you must have and replaced it with an organ far less suited to guiding your course. It's all very well to take a pretty mistress, but no doxy, no matter how lovely, is worth such madness as you seem determined to exhibit. Even now, as I reread your latest letter, I must almost believe it is a forgery—in love with Evelyn of the Clan McCairn indeed. Fool, fool, fool a thousand times—I am heartily ashamed of you. When you return to London in the spring, I intend to school you most harshly in the rules of fealty to one's sovereign and the proper place of women in the world. You will be most fortunate if I agree to forgive you at all.

For make no mistake, dear friend and vassal, you

will return to London as soon as you are summoned, and you will marry Katherine as planned with all the pomp my brother's ransom can purchase for the event. Do not attempt to fight me on this, Willie. You know how dear you are to me and how sorely I would grieve if I were forced to fling you in the Tower for the good of your treasonous soul. But don't think for a moment that I won't. You of all people know me too well to think that. Honestly, Aiden, if you were here, I might even strangle you myself.

But enough. If this Scottish girl cares for you so deeply, she can damned well take her proper station and be happy with it. Your heart's beloved she may be, but I am still your prince.

Until the spring,
John

Aiden climbed the mountain that overlooked Glencairn, the heather nodding in the springtime breeze. Above him, he could hear the shouts of battle, and as he reached the top, a brigand in a kilt of green and gold leapt out from behind a rock.

"En garde, Sassenach!" Hamish shouted, brandishing a wooden sword. "Or do ye be a Frenchman?"

"Glencairn!" Max shouted, pouncing on his cousin from the top of another fallen stone which was waist-high on Aiden but a terrifying height for a warrior barely two years old. Hamish dropped his sword at once, mindful of the baby even in the heat of battle, and the two of them went rolling down the short slope to where Evelyn waited, reading a book among the standing stones.

"Careful," she warned, barely looking up.

"Save me, Aiden!" Hamish cried, laughing and wincing as Max grabbed a handful of his hair.

"Oh, so now it's Aiden, is it?" Aiden laughed as he joined them. "Now that you need my help?" He scooped up the wriggling conqueror so Hamish could make his escape. "Let's call this one a draw, shall we?" he teased, giving the little one a kiss before he set him on his feet.

"Stay where we can see you," Evelyn called, still engrossed in her reading as the two children ran off.

The Clan McCairn had been back in the glen since the snows had first begun to melt from winter. Aiden had gone with Evelyn to their new quarters to fetch Max, Agnes, and Grace as soon as his mother could be convinced he was able to make the trip. He and Malcolm had sat down in council to work out a new treaty, but the Scotsman had been suspicious, to say the least. "You mean you will keep to your affairs at the castle and leave us to our own?"

"Not exactly," Aiden had answered, choosing his words with care. "Prince John wants a presence in Scotland, specifically in this glen. You've seen how many knights he's sent here already, and once I'm gone, more may be on the way."

"Gone?" Malcolm had echoed. "You're leaving?"

"Not by choice," Aiden had admitted. "But the only

way I can lay claim to this castle is to marry Princess Katherine." He had smiled, knowing Malcolm would understand. "And now I'm not so certain I can do that."

"No," Malcolm had agreed with a wry grin of his own. "I wouldn't think so."

"Once Prince John hears that I intend to break the engagement, it is likely he will have me removed and send another Englishman in my place." Just saying the words had made him feel sick—after all that had happened, with the connection he and Evie both had to the very rocks and earth of this place, how could they leave it behind? But could he make a loveless marriage to keep it?

"So what are you saying?" Malcolm had asked. "You have no desire to wipe out my clan, but the next wee laddie might?"

"Maybe he will try," Aiden had answered honestly, determined not to even try to deceive him.

Malcolm had smiled back. "Let him try, Lord Aiden," he had declared. "Just let him try." And by Easter the clan had returned.

"And what are you doing, my lady?" Aiden said now, dropping to the grass at Evie's feet.

"Chaperoning Mary and Calvin," she answered, turning a page. Calvin was a member of the Clan McCairn and Mary's latest suitor. Aiden's sister had chosen to stay at Glencairn when their parents had returned to England, and it had soon become obvious why. Like Evelyn had professed to have before her, she had apparently developed a weakness for a fine pair of legs under a well-pleated kilt.

"And where are they, pray tell?" he asked with a grin.

She looked up in earnest, peering around in every direction before turning to him with a smile. "I haven't the faintest idea." She leaned down and kissed him on the lips. "Are you worried?"

"Yes," he answered, tumbling her into his arms. "But not much."

"Aiden!" Hamish shouted, running back from the summit with Max hot on his heels. "Look down at the castle. Who is that who comes?"

Aiden sat up, then stood up to look down at the road. A small train of men and horses was moving slowly toward Glencairn Castle under the royal banner of England. "This is it," he said, his heart like a rock in his chest. "They ride for John."

Evie climbed to her feet. "Why should we care?" she said, putting an arm around his waist. "After all that we have done, why should we fear an English prince?"

He kissed the top of her head. "Hamish, find the others, please," he ordered. "We have to go and greet them."

Evelyn barely had time to change her gown before the royal delegation was riding into the courtyard. "Please, God, not Katherine," she prayed as she ran down the stairs. "Let it be anyone but her." The princess had returned to England with Lord and Lady Brinlaw before the winter snows and hadn't been heard from since. But technically, Glencairn was still her castle, and Aiden was still her intended.

Evie joined Aiden at the top of the steps to the new hall, and together they went out.

A tall knight in the most magnificent armor she had ever seen was just getting down from his horse. He pulled off his helmet and pushed back his hood to reveal close-cropped golden hair, and when he saw Aiden, his handsome face broke out in a dazzling smile. "Monster!" he called out as he came to meet them.

"Phillipe?" Aiden said, looking stunned but happy as he embraced the other man. "You are back?"

"Yes, thank God. The great Crusade is over." He drew back and smiled again. "Richard has returned." He let Aiden go to look at Evelyn. "My lady," he said, kissing her hand.

"This is Evelyn," Aiden explained.

"Yes, so I guessed," the knight answered. "Lady Evelyn, I heard you were exquisite, but the gossip hardly does you justice. Your future in-laws send their love, by the way—and to you, too, Monster."

"Phillipe is my kinsman, sort of," Aiden explained, missing the hint he had dropped. But Evie had heard it and taken it to heart. *Your future in-laws* . . . "He is Robin's older half brother."

"Much, much older," Phillipe joked. "But come, you rotten infant, give an old man a soft place to sit for a change. And please tell me you have a decent bottle of wine."

"Come, my lord," Evie said with a dazzling smile of her own. "We are honored."

Before a quarter hour passed, they were settled in the hall with cushions and wine all around. Robin had finally turned up, and he looked ready to burst with happiness, running back and forth to fetch clean cups and hot towels and anything else he could think of to make his half brother more comfortable. "Civilization at last," Phillipe sighed, taking another sip.

Indeed, the new hall at Glencairn was a great deal more than civilized. It was huge, at least twice the size of the original great hall. Its walls were slightly bowed with beams that seemed to each be a single, solid piece of wood but that curved up from the floor all the way across the ceiling like the ribs of some huge beast. More gigantic tree trunks had been split in two to make tables set on short, curved legs that ranged all along the walls with benches of the same construction set at each. The floor was hard-packed earth but for a round, wooden platform in the center of the room. Twice as broad as Aiden was tall, it was polished smooth as glass and colored with glossy paint, a bright red background with a dragon in brilliant green devouring its own tail to form a circle. At one end of the room stood a fireplace like a yawning mouth of stone complete with long, curved fangs, large enough that two men could have easily both stood inside with plenty of room for attendants. In short, it was as grand a room as any in the kingdom, its pagan wildness only adding to its splendor.

"Phillipe has been with Richard Lionheart," Aiden explained to Evie. "He and the king are..."

"Very great friends," Phillipe finished for him with a twinkle in his eye. "You might also mention I'm a duke if you're trying to impress her."

"Your Grace," Evie said, rather alarmed.

"Sweeting, please," Phillipe cut her off with a laugh. " 'Phillipe' will be just fine."

"Phillipe!" Mary said, running in.

"You see?" he joked, giving her a hug. "Here is Mary, looking gorgeous as always, even with grass in her hair." He looked over at Calvin, coming in behind her, and grinned. "I wondered why you had refused to go home with your mama and papa. Now I see."

"But, Phillipe, why are you here?" Mary asked, taking his teasing in stride.

"King Richard sent me," he answered, going back to his seat. "Princess Katherine wasted no time telling him all that Aiden had done for her in his absence."

"Did she, in faith?" Aiden said, taking Evelyn's hand. "What did she say?"

"That you protected her from John and his scheming, of course." Phillipe grinned. "She said you even pretended to be betrothed to her to stop him marrying her off to some scoundrel. She was quite effusive in her praise of you, actually, and Lady Evelyn as well. She said both of you sacrificed a great deal of your happiness to fulfill your duty as subjects of the Crown. And you know Richard—he positively glowed at that."

"Her Royal Highness is quite gracious," Aiden said slowly, hardly daring to believe his ears. "But what about Glencairn?"

"Glencairn belongs to you, of course," the duke replied. "Good God, boy, you more than doubled the size of the place, did you not? And what does Richard want with a castle in Scotland? He can barely be bothered to visit the one he has in London." He took a scroll from his sleeve and handed it to him. "And I have something for you as well, my lady." He looked around the room. "Where is your little son?"

"I'll get him," Robin offered, running out.

Aiden opened the scroll. "This is a royal charter," he said, speaking like a man in a trance. "This makes me Lord Glencairn."

"Of course it does." Phillipe laughed. Robin came back in, leading Max by the hand, and the duke stopped, his expression softening at once at the sight of the child. "Hello," he said, holding out his hand. "Are you Max?"

"Yes," the little one answered, meeting his gaze with a smile, utterly unafraid. "Who are you?"

"I am Phillipe," he answered, smiling back. "Will you come and sit with me?"

"Yes." To Evelyn's shock, he went to the duke at once and climbed into his lap.

"This is for you, but we'll let your mother hold it,"

Phillipe said, handing her another scroll. "Someday you may find it very useful."

"What is it?" Evie asked, confused.

"A dispensation from the Pope to legitimize his birth—a favor for Richard," Phillipe answered. "His father died in the holy war; the King thought it only fitting."

"That's what Richard thought?" Aiden said, arching an eyebrow.

"I may have given him a nudge," Phillipe admitted. "Heaven knows His Holiness owes me a favor or two as well." He looked down at Max and smiled. "Of course, Richard has already given you the boy's inheritance, Aiden, so that point is moot." Max was fascinated by the jeweled dagger sheath strapped to his belt, and he took it off, relieved it of its weapon, and handed it to the child. "So Richard and I put our heads together and found a little patch of ground in France that should suffice, a place called Belleforte. It isn't much, but he can live off the rents if nothing else."

"Belleforte," Aiden repeated. "Is that not your estate, Your Very Dear Grace?"

"At the moment, yes, but I can hardly live forever, can I?" Phillipe answered briskly. "And you know I have no heirs." He ruffled Robin's hair. "Paul is absolutely determined to stick with this clergyman nonsense, and this one will already end up with half of Brittany from his father."

"But you are still a young man," Evelyn protested.

"How can you be so certain you will have no sons of your own?"

"Trust me, sweet, I'm certain," he smiled. His eyes met Aiden's. "Your father has done so much for me, I could never in a century repay him," he finished. "Please, let me do this for you."

"It isn't up to me," Aiden said, turning to Evie. "My lady, what do you think?"

I can't, she thought. *I can't think. I can't even breathe.* In a single moment with two scraps of paper, this delightful stranger had fulfilled most of the dearest hopes of her heart and hinted she might have the other. He had given her beloved his castle; he had given her son his name. How could she imagine taking any more? She looked at Phillipe, this handsome knight who held her child so comfortably yet would have no sons of his own. Like Aiden, he seemed to see Max as a blessing, not a burden; a miracle, not a sin. "I think His Grace the Duke Phillipe is the kindest creature I have ever heard tell of," she said. "My son will be proud to be his heir."

"Wonderful!" Mary cried, running to give her a hug.

"It is," Aiden agreed, smiling at her as if he read her thoughts. "Quite wonderful indeed." She left Mary's arms to run to his and kiss him, oblivious to all who were watching, even when they started to applaud.

Evelyn found Aiden standing on the wall, gazing down at his castle. "Congratulations," she said, giving him a kiss.

"You, too," he answered, kissing her again. He put his arms around her and kissed her more deeply, his heart aching with love.

"Um, very nice," she murmured, pressing her cheek to his chest and squeezing him. "I think things have turned out rather well."

"Do you, in faith?" he laughed. "Perhaps you're right." In truth, his destiny had turned out to be far sweeter than he could ever have planned. "The castle is nice, anyway."

"Yes, I like it," she agreed. "It looks rather like a dragon; have you noticed?" She pointed toward the new, slender towers. "Those are like the dragon's horns, and the hall is like the head." She turned in his embrace, her face tilted up to his. "The older fortress is the belly with little, fat towers for spines on its back. And this wall is the dragon's tail, twisted all around."

"Dear lord, what does that make the loch?" he teased her. "I think you may be stretching just a bit."

"Scoff if you will," she said airily, pulling away.

"Don't go," he protested.

"I'm not," she promised with a smile, settling closer to his side again.

"You know, love, a thought just occurred to me," he said. "I don't think that I'm betrothed to the princess anymore."

"No," she agreed, not daring to look at him but hearing the grin in his voice. "I got the impression from the duke that you were not."

"Which leaves me free to marry someone else." She was gazing with perfect attention at the loch, and he smiled, not fooled for a moment. "Someone local, perhaps—a Scotswoman, I mean."

"An excellent notion, my lord," she said, looking up at him at last with a frown that scolded him for teasing. "Just who did you have in mind?"

"No one in particular." He smiled. "Though now that you mention it . . . would you perhaps be interested?"

"Well, I don't know," she mused, pretending to consider it. "With Max being made the future Duke of Belleforte, I really don't need a husband so much anymore." She rubbed her chin. "Of course, there will be the new child to consider. He might turn out to be a boy, and there I would be, stuck all over again with a son with no inheritance. A girl I'm pretty certain I can marry off—Englishmen are fairly easy to hook, I've noticed."

"New child?" Aiden echoed, happily in shock. He made her look at him, holding her by the shoulders. "Evie, what are you saying?"

"What does it sound like I'm saying?" she teased. "You can't honestly be surprised, Aiden. It was rather inevitable."

"Yes, but I hadn't thought . . ." He took her hand in his. "Evie, will you marry me?"

"Because I'm pregnant?" she asked, mischief still dancing in her eyes.

"Because you love me," he answered. "Because I love you so much I can't live a single moment without you."

"Yes," she said, smiling, as she touched his cheek. "If those are the reasons, then yes." He kissed her, softly at first, then swinging her up in his arms and spinning her around until she was dizzy. "Aiden, stop!"

"Never," he promised, setting her down to kiss her more deeply again. "I will never stop."

Visit the Simon & Schuster
romance Web site:

www.SimonSaysLove.com

and sign up for our
romance e-mail updates!

Keep up on the latest
new romance releases,
author appearances, news, chats,
special offers, and more!
We'll deliver the information
right to your inbox—if it's new,
you'll know about it.

POCKET BOOKS

"So, Lady Evelyn, what shall I do with you?"

Aiden smiled at Evelyn and leaned back against the table, a casual, cat-like pose that made his legs look even longer, his shoulders even more broad.

"What do you mean, Lord Aiden?" she asked, determined to keep her nerve. He was just a man, and men were born to be managed. But would this man, cruel and proud and beautiful himself, be susceptible to beauty? "Why should you be obliged to do anything with me at all?"

"I am a knight of chivalry, my lady," Aiden pointed out, watching as a thousand different emotions passed over her lovely face. "Say I find you charming. Say your plight has touched my heart. Say I want to help you."

"Say that, then," she answered, a challenge in her eyes. "What would you suggest?"

He smiled, and Evelyn shivered. Many men had looked on her with lust, but none had ever dared to smile at her like this one did or speak to her with such warmth.

"A dangerous question, my lady. . . ."

Praise for Jayel Wylie's
A FALCON'S HEART

"Tender and moving . . . unforgettable."
—Tracy Fobes, author of *My Enchanted Enemy*

Also by Jayel Wylie

A Falcon's Heart
This Dangerous Magic

Available From Pocket Books